TRYING TO SAVE PIGGY SNEED

TRYING TO SAVE PIGGY SNEED

JOHN IRVING

ARCADE PUBLISHING · NEW YORK

FIRST U.S. EDITION

Library of Congress Cataloging-in-Publication Data

Irving, John, 1942–
        Trying to save Piggy Sneed / John Irving.
            p.   cm.
        ISBN 1-55970-323-7
        I. Title.
    PS3559.R8T78   1996
    813'.54—dc20   95-17756

Published in the United States by Arcade Publishing, Inc., New York
Distributed by Little, Brown and Company

10   9   8   7   6   5   4   3   2   1

BP

Designed by API

PRINTED IN THE U.S.A.

IN MEMORY OF

Ted Seabrooke

Cliff Gallagher

Tom Williams

&

Don Hendrie, Jr.

CONTENTS

ACKNOWLEDGMENTS

"Trying to Save Piggy Sneed" first appeared in *The New York Times Book Review* (August 22, 1982).

A portion of "The Imaginary Girlfriend" first appeared in a fall 1995 issue of *The New Yorker.*

"My Dinner at the White House" first appeared in *Saturday Night* (February 1993).

"Interior Space" first appeared in *Fiction* (vol. 6, no. 2, 1980).

"Brennbar's Rant" first appeared in *Playboy* (December 1974).

"The Pension Grillparzer" first appeared in *Antaeus* (Winter 1976).

"Other People's Dreams" first appeared in *Last Night's Stranger: One Night Stands & Other Staples of Modern Life,* edited by Pat Rotter, published by A & W publishers (1982).

"Weary Kingdom" first appeared in *The Boston Review* (Spring–Summer 1968).

"Almost in Iowa" first appeared in *Esquire* (November 1973).

"The King of the Novel" first appeared, in a much shorter form, in *The New York Times Book Review* (November 25, 1979); and in this form, as an Introduction to the Bantam Classic edition of *Great Expectations* (1986).

"An Introduction to *A Christmas Carol*" first appeared, under the title "Their Faithful Friend and Servant" and in a slightly different form, in *The Globe and Mail* (December 24, 1993); and in this form, in the Modern Library edition of *A Christmas Carol* (1995).

"Günter Grass: King of the Toy Merchants" first appeared in *Saturday Review* (March 1982).

MEMOIRS

TRYING TO SAVE PIGGY SNEED

This is a memoir, but please understand that (to any writer with a good imagination) all memoirs are false. A fiction writer's memory is an especially imperfect provider of detail; we can always imagine a better detail than the one we can remember. The correct detail is rarely, exactly, what happened; the most truthful detail is what *could* have happened, or what *should* have. Half my life is an act of revision; more than half the act is performed with small changes. Being a writer is a strenuous marriage between careful observation and just as carefully imagining the truths you haven't had the opportunity to see. The rest is the necessary, strict toiling with the language; for me this means writing and rewriting the sentences until they sound as spontaneous as good conversation.

With that in mind, I think that I have become a writer because of my grandmother's good manners and — more specifically — because of a retarded garbage collector to whom my grandmother was always polite and kind.

My grandmother is the oldest living English Literature major to have graduated from Wellesley. She lives in an old people's home now, and her memory is fading; she doesn't remember the garbage collector who helped me become a writer, but she has retained her good manners and her kindness. When other old people wander into her room, by mistake — looking for their own rooms, or perhaps for their previous residences — my grandmother always says, "Are you lost, dear? Can I help you find where you're *supposed* to be?"

I lived with my grandmother, in her house, until I was almost seven; for this reason, my grandmother has always called me "her boy." In fact, she never had a boy of her own; she has three daughters. Whenever I have to say good-bye to her now, we both know she might not live for another visit, and she always says, "Come back soon, dear. You're *my boy,* you know" — insisting, quite properly, that she is more than a grandmother to me.

Despite her being an English Literature major, she has not read my work with much pleasure; in fact, she read my first novel and stopped (for life) with that. She disapproved of the language and the subject matter, she told me; from what she's read about the others, she's learned that my language and my subject matter utterly degenerate as my work matures. She's made no effort to read the four novels that followed the first (she and I agree this is for the best). She's very proud of me, she says; I've never probed too deeply concerning *what* she's proud of me *for* — for growing up, at all, perhaps, or just for being "her boy" — but she's certainly never made me feel uninteresting or unloved.

I grew up on Front Street in Exeter, New Hampshire. When I was a boy, Front Street was lined with elms; it wasn't Dutch elm disease that killed most of them. The two hurricanes that struck back to back, in the '50s, wiped out the elms and strangely modernized the street. First Carol came and weakened their roots; then Edna came and knocked them down. My grandmother used to tease me by saying that she hoped this would contribute to my respect for women.

When I was a boy, Front Street was a dark, cool
street — even in the summer — and none of the
backyards was fenced; everyone's dog ran free, and
got into trouble. A man named Poggio delivered gro-
ceries to my grandmother's house. A man named
Strout delivered the ice for the icebox (my grandmother resisted refrigerators until the very end). Mr.
Strout was unpopular with the neighborhood dogs —
perhaps because he would go after them with the ice
tongs. We children of Front Street never bothered Mr.
Poggio, because he used to let us hang around his
store — and he was liberal with treats. We never
bothered Mr. Strout either (because of his ice tongs
and his fabulous aggression toward dogs, which we
could easily imagine being turned toward us). But
the garbage collector had nothing for us — no treats,
no aggression — and so we children reserved our capacity for teasing and taunting (and otherwise making trouble) for him.

His name was Piggy Sneed. He smelled worse
than any man I *ever* smelled — with the possible exception of a dead man I caught the scent of, once, in
Istanbul. And you would have to be dead to look
worse than Piggy Sneed looked to us children on
Front Street. There were so many reasons for calling
him "Piggy," I wonder why one of us didn't think of
a more original name. To begin with, he lived on a
pig farm. He raised pigs, he slaughtered pigs; more
importantly, he lived *with* his pigs — it was *just* a pig
farm, there was no farmhouse, there was *only* the
barn. There was a single stovepipe running into one
of the stalls. That stall was heated by a wood stove
for Piggy Sneed's comfort — and, we children imagined, his pigs (in the winter) would crowd around
him for warmth. He certainly smelled that way.

Also he had absorbed, by the uniqueness of his retardation and by his proximity to his animal friends, certain piglike expressions and gestures. His face would jut in front of his body when he approached the garbage cans, as if he were rooting (hungrily) underground; he squinted his small, red eyes; his nose twitched with all the vigor of a snout; there were deep pink wrinkles on the back of his neck — and the pale bristles, which sprouted at random along his jawline, in no way resembled a beard. He was short, heavy, and strong — he *heaved* the garbage cans to his back, he *hurled* their contents into the wooden, slat-sided truck bed. In the truck, ever eager to receive the garbage, there were always a few pigs. Perhaps he took different pigs with him on different days; perhaps it was a treat for them — they didn't have to wait to eat the garbage until Piggy Sneed drove it home. He took *only* garbage — no paper, plastic, or metal trash — and it was *all* for his pigs. This was all he did; he had a very exclusive line of work. He was paid to pick up garbage, which he fed to his pigs. When *he* got hungry (we imagined), he ate a pig. "A whole pig, at once," we used to say on Front Street. But the *piggiest* thing about him was that he couldn't talk. His retardation either had deprived him of his human speech or had deprived him, earlier, of the ability to learn human speech. Piggy Sneed didn't talk. He grunted. He squealed. He *oinked* — that was his language; he learned it from his friends, as we learn ours.

We children, on Front Street, would sneak up on him when he was raining the garbage down on his pigs — we'd surprise him: from behind hedges, from under porches, from behind parked cars, from out of garages and cellar bulkheads. We'd leap out at him

(we never got too close) and we'd squeal at him:
"Piggy! Piggy! Piggy! Piggy! OINK! WEEEE!" And, like
a pig — panicked, lurching at random, mindlessly
startled (*every time* he was startled, as if he had no
memory) — Piggy Sneed would squeal back at us as
if we'd stuck him with the slaughtering knife; he'd
bellow OINK! out at us as if he'd caught us trying to
bleed him in his sleep.

I can't imitate his sound; it was awful, it made all
us Front Street children scream and run and hide.
When the terror passed, we couldn't wait for him to
come again. He came twice a week. What a luxury!
And every week or so my grandmother would pay
him. She'd come out to the back where his truck
was — where we'd often just startled him and left
him snorting — and she'd say, "Good day, Mr.
Sneed!"

Piggy Sneed would become instantly childlike —
falsely busy, painfully shy, excruciatingly awkward.
Once he hid his face in his hands, but his hands were
covered with coffee grounds; once he crossed his
legs so suddenly, while he tried to turn his face away
from Grandmother, that he fell down at her feet.

"It's nice to see you, Mr. Sneed," Grandmother
would say — not flinching, not in the slightest, from
his stench. "I hope the children aren't being rude to
you," she'd say. "You don't have to tolerate any rude-
ness from them, you know," she would add. And
then she'd pay him his money and peer through the
wooden slats of the truck bed, where his pigs were
savagely attacking the new garbage — and, occasionally, each other — and she'd say, "What beautiful
pigs these are! Are these your *own* pigs, Mr. Sneed?
Are they *new* pigs? Are these the same pigs as the
other week?" But despite her enthusiasm for his pigs,

she could never entice Piggy Sneed to answer her. He would stumble, and trip, and twist his way around her, barely able to contain his pleasure: that my grandmother clearly approved of his pigs, that she even appeared to approve (wholeheartedly!) of *him*. He would grunt softly to her.

When she'd go back in the house, of course — when Piggy Sneed would begin to back his ripe truck out of the driveway — we Front Street children would surprise him again, popping up on both sides of the truck, making both Piggy and his pigs squeal in alarm, and snort with protective rage.

"Piggy! Piggy! Piggy! Piggy! OINK! WEEEE!"

He lived in Stratham — on a road out of our town that ran to the ocean, about eight miles away. I moved (with my father and mother) out of Grandmother's house (before I was seven, as I told you). Because my father was a teacher, we moved into academy housing — Exeter was an all-boys school, then — and so our garbage (together with our non-organic trash) was picked up by the school.

Now I would like to say that I grew older and realized (with regret) the cruelty of children, and that I joined some civic organization dedicated to caring for people like Piggy Sneed. I can't claim that. The code of small towns is simple but encompassing: if many forms of craziness are allowed, many forms of cruelty are ignored. Piggy Sneed was tolerated; he went on being himself, living like a pig. He was tolerated as a harmless animal is tolerated — by children, he was indulged; he was even encouraged to be a pig.

Of course, growing older, we Front Street children knew that he was retarded — and gradually we learned that he drank a bit. The slat-sided truck, reeking of pig, of waste, or *worse* than waste, careered through town all the years I was growing up. It was permitted, it was given room to spill over — en route to Stratham. Now there was a town, Stratham! In small-town life is there anything more provincial than the tendency to sneer at *smaller* towns? Stratham was not Exeter (not that Exeter was much).

In Robertson Davies's novel *Fifth Business,* he writes about the townspeople of Deptford: "We were serious people, missing nothing in our community and feeling ourselves in no way inferior to larger places. We did, however, look with pitying amusement on Bowles Corners, four miles distant and with a population of one hundred and fifty. To live in Bowles Corners, we felt, was to be rustic beyond redemption."

Stratham was Bowles Corners to us Front Street children — it was "rustic beyond redemption." When I was 15, and began my association with the academy — where there were students from abroad, from New York, even from California — I felt so superior to Stratham that it surprises me, now, that I joined the Stratham Volunteer Fire Department; I don't remember *how* I joined. I think I remember that there was no Exeter Volunteer Fire Department; Exeter had the other kind of fire department, I guess. There were several Exeter residents — apparently in need of something to volunteer *for?* — who joined the Stratham Volunteers. Perhaps our contempt for the people of Stratham was so vast that we believed they could not even be relied upon to properly put out their own fires.

There was also an undeniable thrill, midst the

routine rigors of prep-school life, to be a part of something that could call upon one's services without the slightest warning: that burglar alarm in the heart, which is the late-night ringing telephone — that call to danger, like a doctor's beeper shocking the orderly solitude and safety of the squash court. It made us Front Street children important; and, as we grew only slightly older, it gave us a status that only disasters can create for the young.

In my years as a firefighter, I never rescued anyone — I never even rescued anyone's pet. I never inhaled smoke, I never suffered a burn, I never saw a soul fall beyond the reach of the safety bag. Forest fires are the worst and I was only in one, and only on the periphery. My only injury — "in action" — was caused by a fellow firefighter throwing his Indian pump into a storage room where I was trying to locate my baseball cap. The pump hit me in the face and I had a bloody nose for about three minutes.

There were occasional fires of some magnitude at Hampton Beach (one night an unemployed saxophone player, reportedly wearing a pink tuxedo, tried to burn down the casino), but we were always called to the big fires as the last measure. When there was an eight- or ten-alarm fire, Stratham seemed to be called last; it was more an invitation to the spectacle than a call to arms. And the local fires in Stratham were either mistakes or lost causes. One night Mr. Skully, the meter reader, set his station wagon on fire by pouring vodka in the carburetor — because, he said, the car wouldn't start. One night Grant's dairy barn was ablaze, but all the cows — and even most of the hay — had been rescued before we arrived. There was nothing to do but let the barn burn, and hose it down so that cinders from it wouldn't catch the adjacent farmhouse on fire.

But the boots, the heavy hard hat (with your own number), the glossy black slicker — *your own ax!* — these were pleasures because they represented a kind of adult responsibility in a world where we were considered (still) too young to drink. And one night, when I was 16, I rode a hook-and-ladder truck out the coast road, chasing down a fire in a summer house near the beach (which turned out to be the result of children detonating a lawn mower with barbecue fluid), and there — weaving on the road in his stinking pickup, blocking our importance, as independent of civic responsibility (or any other kind) as any pig — was a drunk-driving Piggy Sneed, heading home with his garbage for his big-eating friends.

We gave him the lights, we gave him the siren — I wonder, now, what he thought was behind him. God, the red-eyed screaming monster over Piggy Sneed's shoulder — the great robot pig of the universe and outer space! Poor Piggy Sneed, near home, so drunk and foul as to be barely human, veered off the road to let us pass, and as we overtook him — we Front Street children — I distinctly heard us calling, "Piggy! Piggy! Piggy! Piggy! OINK! WEEEE!" I suppose I heard my voice, too.

We clung to the hook-and-ladder, our heads thrown back so that the trees above the narrow road appeared to veil the stars with a black, moving lace; the pig smell faded to the raw, fuel-burning stink of the sabotaged lawn mower, which faded finally to the clean salt wind off the sea.

In the dark, driving back past the pig barn, we noted the surprisingly warm glow from the kerosene lamp in Piggy Sneed's stall. He had gotten safely home. And was he up, reading? we wondered. And once again I heard our grunts, our squeals, our oinks — our strictly animal communication with him.

The night his pig barn burned, we were so surprised.

The Stratham Volunteers were used to thinking of Piggy Sneed's place as a necessary, reeking ruin on the road between Exeter and the beach — a foul-smelling landmark on warm summer evenings; passing it always engendered the obligatory groans. In winter, the smoke from the wood stove pumped regularly from the pipe above Piggy's stall, and from the outdoor pens, stamping routinely in a wallow of beshitted snow, his pigs breathed in little puffs as if they were furnaces of flesh. A blast from the siren could scatter them. At night, coming home, when whatever fire there was was out, we couldn't resist hitting the siren as we passed by Piggy Sneed's place. It was too exciting to imagine the damage done by that sound: the panic among the pigs, Piggy himself in a panic, all of them hipping up to each other with their wheezy squeals, seeking the protection of the herd.

That night Piggy Sneed's place burned, we Front Street children were imagining a larkish, if somewhat retarded, spectacle. Out the coast road, lights up full and flashing, siren up high — driving all those pigs crazy — we were in high spirits, telling lots of pig jokes: about how we imagined the fire was started, how they'd been having a drinking party, Piggy *and* his pigs, and Piggy was cooking one (on a spit) and dancing with another one, and some pig backed into the wood stove and burned his tail, knocked over the bar, and the pig that Piggy danced with *most*

nights was ill-humored because Piggy *wasn't* dancing with *her* . . . but then we arrived, and we saw that
this fire wasn't a party; it wasn't even the tail end of a
bad party. It was the biggest fire that we Front Street
children, and even the veterans among the Stratham
Volunteers, had ever seen.

The low, adjoining sheds of the pig barn appeared to have burst, or melted their tin roofs. There
was nothing in the barn that wouldn't burn — there
was wood for the wood stove, there was hay, there
were 18 pigs and Piggy Sneed. There was all that
kerosene. Most of the stalls in the pig barn were a
couple of feet deep in manure, too. As one of the
veterans of the Stratham Volunteers told me, "You get
it hot enough, even shit will burn."

It was hot enough. We had to move the fire
trucks down the road; we were afraid the new paint,
or the new tires, would blister in the heat. "No point
in wasting the water," our captain told us. We
sprayed the trees across the road; we sprayed the
woods beyond the pig barn. It was a windless, bitter
cold night, the snow as dry and fine as talcum pow-
der. The trees drooped with icicles and cracked as
soon as we sprayed them. The captain decided to let
the fire burn itself out; there would be less of a mess
that way. It might be dramatic to say that we heard
squeals, to say that we heard the pigs' intestines
swelling and exploding — or before that, their
hooves hammering on the stall doors. But by the
time we arrived, those sounds were over; they were
history; we could only imagine them.

This is a writer's lesson: to learn that the sounds
we imagine can be the clearest, loudest sounds of all.
By the time we arrived, even the tires on Piggy's
truck had burst, the gas tank had exploded, the

windshield had caved in. Since we hadn't been present for those events, we could only guess at the order in which they had taken place.

If you stood too close to the pig barn, the heat curled your eyelashes — the fluid under your eyelids felt searing hot. If you stood too far back, the chill of the winter night air, drawn toward the flames, would cut through you. The coast road iced over, because of spillage from our hoses, and (about midnight) a man with a Texaco emblem on his cap and parka skidded off the road and needed assistance. He was drunk and was with a woman who looked much too young for him — or perhaps it was his daughter. "Piggy!" the Texaco man hollered. "Piggy!" he called into the blaze. "If you're in there, Piggy — you *moron* — you better get the hell out!"

The only other sound, until about 2:00 in the morning, was the occasional *twang* from the tin roof contorting — as it writhed free of the barn. About 2:00 the roof fell in; it made a whispering noise. By 3:00 there were no walls standing. The surrounding melted snow had formed a lake that seemed to be rising on all sides of the fire, almost reaching the level of heaped coals. As more snow melted, the fire was being extinguished from underneath itself.

And what did we smell? That cooked-barnyard smell of midsummer, the conflicting rankness of ashes in snow, the determined baking of manure — the imagination of bacon, or roast pork. Since there was no wind, and we weren't trying to put the fire out, we suffered no smoke abuse. The men (that is to say, the veterans) left us boys to watch after things for an hour before dawn. That is what men do when they share work with boys: they do what they want to do; they have the boys tend to what they don't want to tend to. The men went out for coffee, they said, but they came back smelling of beer. By then the fire was low enough to be doused down. The men initiated this procedure; when they tired of it, they turned it over to us boys. The men went off again, at first light — for breakfast, they said. In the light I could recognize a few of my comrades, the Front Street children.

With the men away, one of the Front Street children started it — at first, very softly. It may have been me. "Piggy, Piggy," one of us called. One reason I'm a writer is that I sympathized with our need to do this; I have never been interested in what nonwriters call good and bad "taste."

"Piggy! Piggy! Piggy! Piggy! OINK! WEEE!" we called. That was when I understood that comedy was just another form of condolence. And then I started it; I began my first story.

"Shit," I said — because everyone in the Stratham Volunteers began every sentence with the word "shit."

"Shit," I said. "Piggy Sneed isn't in there. He's crazy," I added, "but nobody's that stupid."

"His truck's there," said one of the least imaginative of the Front Street children.

"He just got sick of pigs," I said. "He left town, I know it. He was sick of the whole thing. He probably planned this — for weeks."

Miraculously, I had their attention. Admittedly, it had been a long night. *Anyone* with almost *anything* to say might have easily captured the attention of the Stratham Volunteers. But I felt the thrill of a rescue coming — my first.

"I bet there's not a pig in there, either," I said. "I bet he ate half of them — in just a few days. You know, he stuffed himself! And then he sold the rest. He's been putting some money away, for precisely this occasion."

"For *what* occasion?" some skeptic asked me. "If Piggy isn't in there, where is he?"

"If he's been out all night," another said, "then he's *frozen* to death."

"He's in Florida," I said. "He's retired." I said it just that simply — I said it as if it were a *fact*. "Look around you!" I shouted to them. "What's he been spending his money on? He's saved a bundle. He set fire to his own place," I said, "just to give us a hard time. Think of the hard time we gave *him*," I said, and I could see everyone thinking about that; that was, at least, the truth. A little truth never hurt a story. "Well," I concluded. "He's paid us back — that's clear. He's kept us standing around all night."

This made us Front Street children thoughtful, and in that thoughtful moment I started my first act of revision; I tried to make the story better, and more believable. It was essential to rescue Piggy Sneed, of course, but what would a man who couldn't talk do in *Florida?* I imagined they had tougher zoning laws than we had in New Hampshire — especially regarding pigs.

"You know," I said, "I bet he *could* talk — all the time. He's probably *European*," I decided. "I mean, what kind of name is *Sneed?* And he first appeared here around the war, didn't he? Whatever his native language is, anyway, I bet he speaks it pretty well. He just never learned *ours*. Somehow, pigs were easier. Maybe *friendlier*," I added, thinking of us all. "And now he's saved up enough to go home. That's where he is!" I said. "Not Florida — he's gone back to *Europe!*"

"Atta boy, Piggy," someone cheered.

"Look out, Europe," someone said, facetiously.

Enviously, we imagined how Piggy Sneed had gotten "out" — how he'd escaped the harrowing small-town loneliness (and fantasies) that threatened us all. But when the men came back, I was confronted with the general public's dubious regard for fiction.

"Irving thinks Piggy Sneed is in Europe," one of the Front Street boys told the captain.

"He first appeared here around the war, didn't he, sir?" I asked the captain, who was staring at me as if I were the first *body* to be recovered from this fire.

"Piggy Sneed was *born* here, Irving," the captain told me. "His mother was a half-wit; she got hit by a car going the wrong way around the bandstand. Piggy was born on Water Street," the captain told us. Water Street, I knew perfectly well, ran into Front Street — quite close to home.

So, I thought, Piggy was in Florida, after all. In stories, you must make the best thing that *can* happen happen (or the worst, if that is your aim), but it still has to ring true.

When the coals were cool enough to walk on, the men started looking for him; discovery was a job for the men — it being more interesting than waiting, which was boys' work.

After a while, the captain called me over to him. "Irving," he said. "Since you think Piggy Sneed is in Europe, then you won't mind taking whatever *this* is out of here."

It required little effort, the removal of this shrunken cinder of a man; I doused down a tarp and dragged the body, which was extraordinarily light, onto the tarp with first the long and then the short gaff. We found all 18 of his pigs, too. But even today I can imagine him more vividly in Florida than I can imagine him existing in that impossibly small shape of charcoal I extricated from the ashes.

Of course I told my grandmother the *plain* truth, just the boring facts. "Piggy Sneed died in that fire last night, Nana," I told her.

"Poor Mr. Sneed," she said. With great wonder, and sympathy, she added: "What awful circumstances forced him to live such a savage life!"

What I would realize, later, is that the writer's business is *both* to imagine the possible rescue of Piggy Sneed *and* to set the fire that will trap him. It was *much* later — but before my grandmother was moved to the old people's home, when she still remembered who Piggy Sneed was — when Grandmother asked me, "Why, in heaven's name, have you become a *writer?*"

I was "her boy," as I've told you, and she was sincerely worried about me. Perhaps being an English Literature major had convinced her that being a writer was a lawless and destructive thing to be. And so I told her everything about the night of the fire, about how I imagined that if I could have invented well enough — if I could have made up something truthful enough — I could have (in some sense) saved Piggy Sneed. At least saved him for another fire — of my own making.

Well, my grandmother is a Yankee — *and* Wellesley's oldest living English Literature major. Fancy answers, especially of an aesthetic nature, are not for her. Her late husband — my grandfather — was in the shoe business; he made things people really needed: practical protection for their feet. Even so, I insisted to Grandmother that her kindness to Piggy

Sneed had not been overlooked by me — and that this, in combination with the helplessness of Piggy Sneed's special human condition, *and* the night of the fire, which had introduced me to the possible power of my own imagination . . . and so forth. My grandmother cut me off.

With more pity than vexation, she patted my hand, she shook her head. "Johnny, *dear,*" she said. "You surely could have saved yourself a lot of *bother,* if you'd only treated Mr. Sneed with a little human decency when he was alive."

Failing that, I realize that a writer's business is setting fire to Piggy Sneed — *and* trying to save him — again and again; forever.

Trying to Save Piggy Sneed (1982)

AUTHOR'S NOTES

My grandmother, Helen Bates Winslow, died in Exeter, New Hampshire, only a few days short of her 100th birthday and not long after this memoir was originally published in *The New York Times Book Review* (August 22, 1982). As you may know, the *Today* show routinely wishes Happy Birthday to every 100-year-old in the United States — provided that the *Today* show knows about it. At my mother's request, I had alerted the *Today* show; they knew that my grandmother's 100th birthday was pending, when — quietly, and almost purposefully before the great event — my grandmother died. I suspect that she had been dreading such a public announcement; she probably believed that her 100th birthday was nobody's business but her own.

Later, in my novel *A Prayer for Owen Meany* (1989), I gave these particulars to a fictional grandmother, Harriet Wheelwright; in that story, Mrs. Wheelwright would have been 100 years old on Halloween. In several interviews I have admitted that Harriet Wheelwright is the most autobiographical character in any of my fiction, and that the details of Mrs. Wheelwright's death are as close as I could come to imagining the death of my grandmother, Mrs. Winslow. I see now that "Trying to Save Piggy Sneed" was the beginning of *A Prayer for Owen Meany,* and that the description of Harriet Wheelwright's death in that novel is an alternative ending to the memoir about my grandmother. Therefore, it seems only fitting that I should attach the description here.

My grandmother *hated* Halloween; it was one of her few quarrels with God — that He had allowed her to be born on this day. It was a day, in her view, that had been invented to create mayhem among the lower classes, a day when they were invited to abuse people of property ... my grandmother's house was always abused on Halloween. Eighty Front Street was feathered with toilet paper, the garage windows were dutifully soaped, the driveway lampposts were spray-painted (orange), and once someone inserted the greater half of a lamprey eel in Grandmother's letter slot. Owen had always suspected Mr. Morrison, the cowardly mailman.

Upon her arrival in the old-age home, Grandmother considered that the remote-control device for switching television channels was a true child of Satan; it was television's final triumph, she said, that it could render you brain-dead without even allowing you to leave your chair. It was Dan who discovered Grandmother to be dead, when he visited her one evening in the Gravesend Retreat for the Elderly. He visited her every evening, and he brought her a Sunday newspaper and read it aloud to her on Sunday mornings, too.

The night she died, Dan found her propped up in her hospital bed; she appeared to have fallen asleep with the TV on and with the remote-control device held in her hand in such a way that the channels kept changing. But she was dead, not asleep, and her cold thumb had simply attached itself to the button that restlessly roamed the channels — looking for something good.

THE
IMAGINARY
GIRLFRIEND

Faculty Brat

In my prep-school days, at Exeter, Creative Writing wasn't taught — the essay was all-important there — but in my years at the academy I nevertheless wrote more short stories than anything else; I showed them (out of class) to George Bennett, my best friend's father. The late Mr. Bennett was then Chairman of the English Department; he was my first critic and encourager — I needed his help. Because I failed both Latin and math, I was required to remain at the academy for an unprecedented fifth year; yet I qualified for a course called English 4W — the "W" stood for Writing of the kind I wanted to do — and in this selective gathering I was urged to be Creative, which I rarely managed to be.

In my memory, which is subject to doubt, the star author and most outspoken critic in English 4W was my wrestling teammate Chuck Krulak, who was also known as "Brute" and who would become General Charles C. Krulak — the Commandant of the Marine Corps and a member of the Joint Chiefs of Staff. No less a presence, and as sarcastic a critic as the future General Krulak, was my classmate in English 5, the future writer G. W. S. Trow; he was just plain George then, but he was as sharp as a ferret — I feared his bite. It was only recently, when I was speaking with George, that he surprised me by saying he'd been deeply unhappy at Exeter; George had always struck me as being too confident to be unhappy — whereas my own state of mind at the time was one of perpetual embarrassment.

I could never have qualified for Exeter through normal admissions procedures; I was a weak student — as it turned out, I was dyslexic, but no one knew this at the time. Nevertheless, I was automatically admitted to the academy in the category of faculty child. My father taught in the History Department; he'd majored in Slavic Languages and Literature at Harvard — he was the first to teach Russian History at Exeter. I initiated a heightened level of intrafamily awkwardness by enrolling in his Russian History course. Dad rewarded me with a C+.

To say that Exeter was hard for me is an understatement. I was the only student in my Genetics class who failed to control his fruit-fly experiment. The red eyes and the white eyes were interbreeding so rapidly that I lost track of the generations; I attempted to dispose of the evidence in the drinking fountain outside the lab — not knowing that fruit flies could live (and breed) for days in the water pipes. When the unusable drinking fountain was declared "contaminated" — it was literally crawling with wet fruit flies — I crawled forth and made my confession.

I was forgiven by Mr. Mayo-Smith, the biologist who taught Genetics, because I was the only townie (a resident of Exeter) in any of his classes who owned a gun; the biologist needed me — more specifically, he needed my gun. Boarding students, quite understandably, were not allowed firearms. But as a New Hampshire native — "Live Free or Die," as the license plates say — I had an arsenal of weapons at my disposal; the biologist used me as the marksman who provided his Introductory Biology class with pigeons. I used to shoot them off the roof of the biologist's barn. Fortunately, Mr. Mayo-Smith lived some distance from town.

Yet even in my capacity as Mr. Mayo-Smith's marksman, I was a failure. He wanted the pigeons killed immediately after they'd eaten; that way the students who dissected them could examine the food contained in their crops. And so I allowed the pigeons to feed in the biologist's cornfield. When I flushed them from the field, they were so stupid: they always flew to the roof of his barn. It was a slate roof; when I picked them off — I used a 4X scope and a .22 long-rifle bullet, being careful not to shoot them in their crops — they slid down one side of the roof or the other. One day, I shot a hole in the roof; after that, Mr. Mayo-Smith never let me forget how his barn leaked. The fruit flies in the drinking fountain were the school's problem, but I had shot the biologist's very own barn — "Personal property, and all that that entails," as my father was fond of saying in Russian History.

Shooting a hole in Mr. Mayo-Smith's barn was less humiliating than the years I spent in Language Therapy. At Exeter, poor spelling was unknown — I mean that little was known about it. It was my dyslexia, of course, but — because that diagnosis wasn't available in the late 1950s and early '60s — bad spelling like mine was considered a psychological problem by the language therapist who evaluated my mysterious case. (The handicap of a language disability did not make my struggles at the academy any easier.) When the repeated courses of Language Therapy were judged to have had no discernible influence on my ability to recognize the difference between "allegory" and "allergy," I was turned over to the school psychiatrist.

Did I hate the school?

"No." (I had grown up at the school!)

Why did I refer to my stepfather as my "father"?

"Because I love him and he's the only 'father' I've ever known."

But why was I "defensive" on the subject of other people calling my father my stepfather?

"Because I love him and he's the only 'father' I've ever known — why shouldn't I be 'defensive'?"

Why was I angry?

"Because I can't spell."

But why *couldn't* I spell?

"Search me."

Was it "difficult" having my stepfather — that is, my father — as a teacher?

"I had my father as a teacher for one year. I've been at the school, and a bad speller, for five years."

But why was I angry?

"Because I can't spell — and I have to see *you*."

"We certainly *are* angry, aren't we?" the psychiatrist said.

"I certainly *are*," I said. (I was trying to bring the conversation back to the subject of my *language* disability.)

An Underdog

There was one place at Exeter where I was never angry; I never lost my temper in the wrestling room — possibly because I wasn't embarrassed to be there. It is surprising that I felt so comfortable with wrestling. My athletic skills had never been significant. I had loathed Little League baseball. (By association, I hate all sports with balls.) I more mildly disliked skiing and skating. (I have a limited tolerance for cold weather.) I did have an inexplicable taste for physical contact, for the adrenal stimulation of bumping into people, but I was too small to play football; also, there was a ball involved.

When you love something, you have the capacity to bore everyone about *why* — it doesn't matter why. Wrestling, like boxing, is a weight-class sport; you get to bump into people your own size. You can bump into them very hard, but where you land is reasonably soft. And there are civilized aspects to the sport's combativeness: I've always admired the rule that holds you responsible, *if* you lift your opponent off the mat, for your opponent's "safe return." But the best answer to why I love wrestling is that it was the first thing I was any good at. And what limited success I had in the sport I owe completely to my first coach, Ted Seabrooke.

Coach Seabrooke had been a Big 10 Champion and a two-time All-American at Illinois; he was *way* overqualified for the job of coaching wrestling at Exeter — his teams dominated New England prep-school and high-school wrestling for years. An NCAA runner-up at 155 pounds, Ted Seabrooke was a handsome man; he weighed upward of 200 pounds in my time at the academy. He would sit on the mat with his legs spread in front of him; his arms were bent at the elbow but reaching out to you from the level of his chest. Even in such a vulnerable position, he could completely defend himself; I never saw anyone manage to get behind him. On his rump, he could scuttle like a crab — his feet tripping you, his legs scissoring you, his hands tying up your hands or snapping your head down. He could control you by holding you in his lap (a crab ride) or by taking possession of your near leg and your far arm (a cross-body ride); he was always gentle with you, and he never seemed to expend much energy in the process of frustrating you. (Coach Seabrooke would first get diabetes and then die of cancer. At his memorial service, I couldn't speak half the eulogy I'd written for him, because I knew by heart the parts that would make me cry if I tried to say them aloud.)

Not only did Ted Seabrooke teach me how to wrestle; more important, he forewarned me that I would never be better than "halfway decent" as a wrestler — because of my limitations as an athlete. He also impressed upon me how I could compensate for my shortcomings: I had to be especially dedicated — a thorough student of the sport — if I wished to overcome my lack of any observable ability. "Talent is overrated," Ted told me. "That you're not very talented needn't be the end of it."

A high-school wrestling match is six minutes long, divided into three two-minute periods — with no rest between the periods. In the first period, both wrestlers start on their feet — a neutral position, with neither wrestler having an advantage. In the second period, in those days, one wrestler had the choice of taking the top or the bottom position; in the third period, the choice of positions was reversed. (Nowadays, the options of choice have been expanded to include the neutral position, and the wrestler given the choice in the second period may defer his choice until the third.)

What Coach Seabrooke taught me was that I

should keep the score close through two periods — close enough so that one takedown or a reversal in the third period could win the match. And I needed to avoid "mix-ups" — free-for-all situations that were not in either wrestler's control. (The outcome of such a scramble favors the better athlete.) Controlling the pace of the match — a combination of technique, correct position, and physical conditioning — was my objective. I know it sounds boring — I was a boring wrestler. The pace that worked for me was slow. I liked a low-scoring match.

I rarely won by a fall; in five years of wrestling at Exeter, I probably pinned no more than a half-dozen opponents. I was almost never pinned — only twice, in fact.

I won 5–2 when I dominated an opponent; I won 2–1 or 3–2 when I was lucky, and lost 3–2 or 4–3 when I was less lucky. If I got the first takedown, I could usually win; if I lost the first takedown, I was hard-pressed to recover — I was not a come-from-behind man. I was, as Coach Seabrooke said, "halfway decent" as a counter-wrestler, too. But if my opponent was a superior athlete, I couldn't afford to rely on my counter-moves to his first shots; my counters weren't quick enough — my *reflexes* weren't quick enough. Against a superior athlete, I would take the first shot; against a superior *wrestler,* I would try to counter his first move.

"Or vice versa, if it's not working," Coach Seabrooke used to say. He had a sense of humor. "Where the head goes, the body must follow — usually," Ted would add. And: "An underdog is in a position to take a healthy bite."

This was a concept of myself that I'd been lacking. I was an underdog; therefore, I had to control the pace — of *everything*. This was more than I learned in English 4W, but the concept was applicable to my Creative Writing — and to all my schoolwork, too. If my classmates could read our history assignment in an hour, I allowed myself two or three. If I couldn't learn to spell, I would keep a list of my most frequently misspelled words — and I kept the list with me; I had it handy even for unannounced quizzes. Most of all, I rewrote everything; first drafts were like the first time you tried a new takedown — you needed to drill it, over and over again, before you even dreamed of trying it in a match. I began to take my lack of talent seriously.

An imperious Spanish teacher was fond of abusing those of us who lacked perfection with the insensitive (not to mention elitist) remark that we would all end up at Wichita State. I didn't know that Wichita was in Kansas; I knew only that this was a slur — if we weren't *talented* enough for Harvard, then Wichita State would be our just reward. Fuck you, I thought: my objective would then be to do well at Wichita State. Ted Seabrooke had gone to Illinois. I didn't suppose that this Spanish teacher thought too highly of Illinois either.

I remember telling Ted that I'd had two likable Spanish teachers, and one unlikable one. "I wouldn't complain about those odds," he said.

The Half-Pound Piece of Toast

My time at the academy was marked by two important transitions in Exeter wrestling under Coach Seabrooke. First, the wrestling room was moved from the basement of the old gymnasium to the upper reaches of the indoor track, which was called "the cage." The new room, high in the rafters, was exceedingly warm; from the hard-packed dirt of the track below us, and from the wooden track that circumscribed the upper level, came the steady pounding of the runners. Once our wrestling practice was underway, we wrestlers never heard the runners. The wrestling room was closed off from the wooden track by a heavy sliding door. Before and after practice, the door was open; during practice, the door was closed.

The other wrestling-related change that marked my time at Exeter was the mats themselves. I began wrestling on horsehair mats, which were covered with a filmy, flexible plastic; as a preventive measure against mat burns, this plastic sheeting was modestly effective, but — like the sheet on a bed — it loosened with activity. The loose folds were a cause of ankle injuries; also, the shock-absorbing abilities of those old horsehair mats were nonexistent in comparison to the comfort of the *new* mats that arrived at Exeter in time to be installed in the new wrestling room.

The new mats were smooth on the surface, with no cover. When the mats were warm, you could drop an egg from knee height and the egg wouldn't break. (Whenever someone tried this and the egg broke, we said that the mat wasn't warm enough.) On a cold gym floor, the texture of the mat would radically change. Later, I kept a wrestling mat in my unheated Vermont barn; in midwinter the mat was as hard as a floor.

Most of our dual-meet matches were also held in the cage, but not in the wrestling room where we practiced. An L-shaped wooden parapet extended like an arm off the wooden track. From this advantage — and from a loop of the wooden track itself — as many as 200 or 300 spectators could look down upon a less-than-regulation-size basketball court, where we rolled out the mats. There was barely enough floor space left over for a dozen or more rows of bleacher seats; most of our fans were above us, on the wooden track and parapet. It was like wrestling at the bottom of a teacup; the surrounding crowd peered over the rim of the cup.

Where we wrestled was appropriately called "the pit." The smell of dirt from the nearby track was strangely remindful of summer, although wrestling is a winter sport. What with the constant opening of the outside door, the pit was never a warm place; the mats, which were so warm and soft in the wrestling room, were cold and hard for the competition. And, when our wrestling meets coincided with track meets in the cage, the sound of the starting gun reverberated in the pit. I always wondered what the visiting wrestlers thought of the gunfire.

My first match in the pit was a learning experience. First-year wrestlers, or even second-year wrestlers, are not often starters on prep-school or high-school wrestling teams of any competitive quality. In New Hampshire, in the 1950s, wrestling — unlike baseball or basketball or hockey or skiing — was not something every kid grew up doing. There are certain illogical things to learn about any sport; wrestling, especially, does not come naturally. A double-leg takedown is *not* like a head-on tackle in football. Wrestling is not about knocking a man down — it's about controlling him. To take a man

down by his legs, you have to do more than knock
his legs out from under him: you have to get your
hips under your opponent, so that you can lift
him off the mat before you put him down — this is
only one example. Suffice it to say that a first-year
wrestler is at a considerable disadvantage when
wrestling anyone with experience — regardless of
how physically strong or well-conditioned the first-
year wrestler is.

I forget the exact combination of illness or injury
or deaths-in-a-family (or all three) that led to my first
match in the pit; as a first-year wrestler, I was quite
content to practice wrestling with other first-year or
second-year wrestlers. There was a "ladder" posted
in the wrestling room, by weight class; in my first
year, I would have been as low as fourth or fifth on
the ladder at 133 pounds. But the varsity man was
sick or hurt, and the junior-varsity man failed to
make weight — and possibly the boy who was next-
in-line had gone home for the weekend because his
parents were divorcing. Who knows? For whatever
reason, I was the best available body in the 133-
pound class.

I was informed of this unwelcome news in the
dining hall where I worked as a waiter at a faculty
table; fortunately, I had not yet eaten my breakfast —
I would have had to vomit it up. As it was, I was four
pounds over the weight class and I ran for almost an
hour on the wooden track of the indoor cage; I ran
in a ski parka and other winter clothing. Then I
skipped rope in the wrestling room for half an hour,
wearing a rubber suit with a hooded sweatshirt
over it. I was an eighth of a pound under 133 at
the weigh-ins, where I had my first look at my

opponent — Vincent Buonomano, a defending New England Champion from Mount Pleasant High School in Providence, Rhode Island.

Had we forfeited the weight class, we could not have done worse: a forfeit counts the same as a pin — six points. It was Coach Seabrooke's hope that I wouldn't be pinned. In those days, a loss by decision was only a three-point loss for the team, regardless of how lopsided the score of the individual match. My goal, in other words, was to take a beating and lose the team only three points instead of six.

For the first 15 or 20 seconds, this goal seemed feasible; then I was taken down, to my back, and I spent the remainder of the period in a neck bridge — I had a strong neck. The choice was mine in the second period: on Coach Seabrooke's advice, I chose the top position. (Ted knew that I was barely surviving on the bottom.) But Buonomano reversed me immediately, and so I spent the better part of the second period fighting off my back, too. My only points were for escapes — unearned, because Buonomano let me go; he was guessing it might be easier to pin me directly following a takedown. One such takedown dropped me on my nose — both my hands were trapped, so that I couldn't break my fall. (It's true what they say about "seeing stars.")

When they stop a wrestling match to stop bleeding, there's no clock counting the injury time; this is because you can't fake bleeding. For other injuries, a wrestler is allowed no more than 90 seconds of injury time — accumulated in the course of the match. In this case, they weren't timing my nose bleed; when the trainer finished stuffing enough cotton up my nostrils to stanch the flow of blood, my dizziness had abated and I looked at the time remaining on the

match clock — only 15 seconds! I had every confidence that I could stay off my back for another 15
seconds, and I told Ted Seabrooke so.

"It's only the second period," Seabrooke said.

I survived the 15 seconds but was pinned about
midway into the third period — "With less than a
minute to go," my mother lamentably told me.

The worst thing about being pinned in the pit
was the lasting image of all those faces peering down
at you. When you were winning, the fans were loud;
when you were on your back, they were quiet, and
their expressions were strangely incurious — as if
they were already distancing themselves from your
defeat.

I was never pinned in the pit again; the only
other loss I remember there was by injury default — I
broke my hand. When the trainer offered me the slop
bucket — I needed to spit — I saw the orange rinds
and a bloody towel in the bottom of the bucket, and
I promptly fainted. Aside from that misfortune, and
my first-ever match — with Mount Pleasant's Vincent
Buonomano — I associated the pit with winning; my
best matches were there. It was in the pit that I
wrestled New England Champion Anthony Pieranunzi of East Providence High School to a 1–1 draw.
I was not so lucky with Pieranunzi in the New England Championship tournament, where he beat me
two years in a row; despite two undefeated dual-
meet seasons, I never won a New England title.

My years at Exeter were the final years when the
winner of the New England tournament won a truly
All–New England title; 1961 was the last year that
high schools and prep schools competed together in
a year-end tournament — I was captain of the Exeter
team that year. After that, there were separate

private-school and public-school tournaments — a pity, I think, since high-school and prep-school wrestlers have much to learn from each other. But, by '61, the New England Interscholastic tournament, as it used to be called, had already grown too large.

I remember my last bus ride with the Exeter team, to East Providence — to the home mats of my nemesis, Anthony Pieranunzi. We'd checked our weight on the scales in the academy gym at about 5:00 in the morning; we were all under our respective weight classes — in some cases, barely. The bus left Exeter in darkness, which near Boston gave way to a dense winter fog; the snow, the sky, the trees, the road — all were shades of gray.

Our 121-pounder, Larry Palmer, was worried about his weight. He'd been only a quarter of a pound under at Exeter — the official weigh-ins were at East Providence. What if the scales were different? (They weren't supposed to be.) I'd been a half-pound under my 133-pound class; my mouth was dry, but I didn't dare drink any water — I was spitting in a paper cup. Larry was spitting in a cup, too. "Just don't eat," Coach Seabrooke told us. "Don't eat and don't drink — you're not going to gain weight on the bus."

Somewhere south of Boston, we stopped at a Howard Johnson's; this is what Larry Palmer remembers — I don't remember the Howard Johnson's because I didn't get off the bus. A few of our wrestlers were safely enough under their weight classes so that they could risk eating something; most of them at least got off the bus — to pee. I'd had nothing to eat or drink for about 36 hours; I knew I didn't dare to eat or drink anything — I knew I *couldn't* pee. Larry Palmer remembers eating "that fatal piece of toast."

Just the other day, we were remembering it together. "It was plain toast," Larry said. "No butter, no jam — I didn't even finish it."

"And nothing to drink?" I asked him.

"Not a drop," Larry said.

(Lately, we're in the habit of getting together at least once a year. Larry Palmer is Professor of Law at Cornell Law School; one of his kids has just started wrestling.)

On the scales at East Providence, Palmer was a quarter-pound over 121. He'd been a sure bet to get as far as the semifinals, and maybe farther; his disqualification cost us valuable team points — as did my loss to East Providence's Pieranunzi, who was tougher at home than he was in the pit. In two years, Pieranunzi and I had wrestled four matches. I beat him once, we tied once, he beat me twice — both times in the tournament, where it counted most. All our matches were close, but that last time (in East Providence) Pieranunzi pinned me. Thus, the two times I was pinned at Exeter — my first match and my last — I was pinned by a New England Champion from Rhode Island. (Exeter failed to defend its New England team title in '61 — our '60 team was arguably the best in Exeter history.)

Larry Palmer was stunned. He *couldn't* have eaten a half-pound piece of toast!

Coach Seabrooke was, as always, philosophic. "Don't blame yourself — you're probably just growing," Ted told him. Indeed, this proved to be the case. Larry Palmer was the Exeter team captain the following year, 1962, when he won the New England Class A title at 147 pounds. More significant than his 26-pound jump from his former 121-pound class, Palmer had also grown six inches.

It's clear to me now that Larry Palmer's famous piece of toast at Howard Johnson's didn't weigh half a pound. Larry's growth spurt doubtless began on the bus. We were so sorry for him when he didn't make weight that none of us looked closely enough at him; in addition to gaining a half-pound, Larry was probably two inches taller by the time he got to East Providence — we might have seen the difference, had we looked.

The Books I Read

In schools — even in good schools, like Exeter — they tend to teach the shorter books by the great authors; at least they begin with those. Thus it was *Billy Budd, Sailor* that introduced me to Melville, which led me to the library, where I discovered *Moby Dick* on my own. It was *Great Expectations* and *A Christmas Carol* that introduced me to Dickens, and (also in English classes) I read *Oliver Twist* and *Hard Times* and *A Tale of Two Cities,* which led me (out of class) to read *Dombey and Son* and *Bleak House* and *Nicholas Nickleby* and *David Copperfield* and *Martin Chuzzlewit* and *Little Dorrit* and *The Pickwick Papers.* I couldn't get enough of Dickens, although he presented a challenge to my dyslexia — to the degree that my schoolwork certainly suffered. It was usually the shorter books by the authors I loved that drew me to their longer books, which I loved more. Loving long novels plays havoc with going to school.

In an Exeter English class, I was "started" on George Eliot with *Silas Marner,* but it was *Middlemarch* that would keep me from finishing my math and Latin assignments. My father, the Russian scholar, wisely started me on Dostoyevsky with *The Gambler,* but it was *The Brothers Karamazov* that I read and reread with an all-consuming excitement. (My father started me on Tolstoy and Turgenev, too.)

George Bennett was the first person in my life to introduce me to contemporary literature; in addition to his duties as Chairman of the Exeter English Department, George was simply a great reader — he read everything. I was still at Exeter — this was about 10 years before my fellow Americans would "discover" Robertson Davies upon the publication of *Fifth Business* — when George Bennett urged me to read *Leaven of Malice* and *A Mixture of Frailties.* (*Tempest-Tost,* the first novel of *The Salterton Trilogy,* I wouldn't read until much later.) And, not surprisingly, it was reading Robertson Davies that led me to Trollope. (With all there was to read of Trollope, this doubtless caused further injury to my schoolwork.) It has been said many times that Robertson Davies is Canada's Trollope, but I think he is also Canada's Dickens.

Twenty years later, Professor Davies reviewed *The Hotel New Hampshire* (1981) for *The Washington Post.* It was such a likable and mischievous review — and by then I'd read everything of his — that I eventually journeyed to Toronto for the sole purpose of having lunch with him. I'd broken a big toe (wrestling), and the toe was so swollen that none of my shoes would fit. My son Colin already had bigger feet than mine (by the time he was 16); yet it was only a pair of Colin's *wrestling shoes* that permitted me to walk without hobbling. It was either wear the wrestling shoes or meet Robertson Davies in my bare feet.

Professor Davies took me to the York Club in Toronto for a rather formal lunch; he was exceedingly polite and kind to me, but when his glance fell upon the wrestling shoes, his glance was stern. Now my wife, Janet, is his literary agent. Janet and I live part time in Toronto, where we dine frequently with Rob and Brenda Davies. Footwear is never a topic of conversation between us, yet I don't doubt that Professor Davies's memory of our first meeting remains somewhat critical.

When Janet and I were married in Toronto, my two sons from my first marriage, Colin and Brendan, were my best men, and Robertson Davies read from the Bible. Rob brought his own Bible to the wedding service, not trusting the Bishop Strachan Chapel to have the correct translation. (Professor Davies is a great defender of the King James Version in these treacherous modern times.)

Colin and Brendan had not met Rob before the wedding, and Brendan — he was 17 at the time — didn't see Professor Davies, in his magnificent white beard, approach the pulpit. Brendan looked up and, suddenly, there was this big man with a big beard and a bigger voice. Colin, who was 22 at the time, told me that Brendan looked as if he'd seen a ghost. But Brendan, who was not overly familiar with churches of any kind, had had a different thought. Brendan was quite certain that Professor Davies was God.

In addition to providing me with my first opportunity to read Robertson Davies — at a time when I was about the age Brendan was at my second wedding — George Bennett encouraged me to go beyond my initial experience with Faulkner. I don't remember *which* Faulkner novel I was introduced to (in an Exeter English class), but I struggled with it; I was either too young or my dyslexia rebelled at the length of those sentences, or both. I would never love Faulkner, or Joyce, but I grew to like them. And it was George who talked me through my earliest difficulties with Hawthorne and Hardy, too; I would grow to love Hardy, and Hawthorne — more than Melville — remains my favorite American writer. (I was never a Hemingway or Fitzgerald fan, and Vonnegut and Heller mean much more to me than Twain.)

It was also George Bennett who forewarned me that in all probability I would be "cursed to read like a writer," by which he meant that I would suffer from inexplicably strong and inexpressibly personal opinions; I think George really meant that I was doomed, like most of the writers I know, to have indefensible taste, but George was too generous to tell me that.

I can't read Proust, or Henry James; reading Conrad almost kills me. *The Rover* is okay, but most suitable for young males (under 18). *Heart of Darkness* is simply the longest short novel I know. I agree with one of Conrad's unkind reviewers that Marlow is "a garrulous intermediary" — I would call Marlow a tedious narrative device — and the same reviewer points out why I prefer (to *all* the rest) *The Rover,* which is generally looked down upon as Conrad's only children's book. "As nowhere else in Conrad," says the unkind reviewer, "disquisitions on ethics and psychology and metaphysics are conspicuously absent."

Not all "disquisitions" on such subjects are unbearable to me. It was *Death in Venice* that led me to the rest of Thomas Mann — particularly to *The Magic Mountain,* which I have read too many times to count. The literature of the German language wouldn't attract me with full force until I was in university, where I first read Goethe and Rilke and Schnitzler and Musil; they would lead me to Heinrich Böll and Günter Grass. Grass, García Márquez, and Robertson Davies are my three favorite living authors; when you consider that they are all comic novelists, for whom the 19th-century tradition of storytelling — of narrative momentum and developed characters — remains the model of the form, I suppose you could say that I haven't ventured very far from Dickens.

With one exception: Graham Greene. Greene was the first contemporary novelist I was assigned to read at Exeter; it would probably have provoked him to know that I read him not in an English class but in the Reverend Frederick Buechner's extremely popular course on Religion and Literature. I took every course Fred Buechner taught at Exeter, not because he was the school minister but because he was the academy's only published novelist — and a good one. (I wouldn't realize *how* good until, long after Exeter, I read Buechner's quartet of Bebb novels — *Lion Country, Open Heart, Love Feast,* and *Treasure Hunt.*)

We were a negative lot of students at Exeter, when it came to religion. We were more cynical than young people today; we were even more cynical than most of us have since become — that is to say that my generation strikes me as *less* cynical today than we were. (Is that possible?) Anyway, we didn't like Freddy Buechner for his sermons in Phillips Church or in our morning chapel, although his sermons were better than anyone else's sermons I've ever heard or read — before or since. It was his elo-

quence about *literature* that moved us; and his enthusiasm for Graham Greene's *The Power and the
Glory,* which engendered my enthusiasm for all (or
almost all) of Greene, was unstoppable.

I feel that I know Greene's people better than I
know most of the people I have known in my life,
and they are not even people I wanted (or would
ever want) to know: it is that simple. I cannot sit in
the dentist's chair without envisioning the terrible Mr.
Tench, the expatriate dentist who witnesses the exe-
cution of the whiskey priest. It is not Emma Bovary
who epitomizes adultery to me: it is poor Scobie in
The Heart of the Matter, and poor Scobie's awful
wife, Louise; it is Helen, the 19-year-old widow with
whom Scobie has an affair, and the morally empty intelligence agent, Wilson, who is a little bit in love
with Louise. And then there is the ghastly sleaziness
of *Brighton Rock:* the utterly corrupted 17-year-old
Pinkie, and the innocent 16-year-old Rose . . . the
murder of Hale, and Ida drinking stout. They have
become what an "underworld" means to me, just as
The End of the Affair is the most chilling antilove
story I know. Poor Maurice Bendrix! Poor Sarah and
poor Henry, too! They are like people you would shy
away from if you encountered them on the street,
knowing what you know.

"Hatred seems to operate the same glands as
love: it even produces the same actions," Greene
wrote. I used to have that typed on a yellowing piece
of paper, taped to my desk lamp, long before I understood how true it was. Something I understood
sooner — as soon as I began to write — is this
cutting I also made from *The End of the Affair:* "So
much of a novelist's writing . . . takes place in the

unconscious: in those depths the last word is written before the first word appears on paper. We remember the details of our story, we do not invent them."

The End of the Affair is the first novel that shocked me. I read it at a time when most of my contemporaries (those who read at all) were being shocked by *The Catcher in the Rye,* which I thought was as perfunctory as masturbation. Salinger's familiar creation, that troubled boy, knew nothing that could compare to Bendrix's frightening knowledge that "there is no safety anywhere: a humpback, a cripple — they all have the trigger that sets love off."

Later, to think of Greene making the disclaimers he made — or describing some of his work, as he did, as mere "entertainments" — was confounding to me. Greene's manipulations of popular though "lesser" forms (the thriller, the detective story) obviously cost him the critical appreciation that is withdrawn from writers with too many readers.

I am reminded of Maurice Bendrix thinking of one of his critics. "Patronizingly in the end he would place me: probably a little above Maugham because Maugham is popular and I have not yet committed that crime, not yet; but although I retain a little of the exclusiveness of unsuccess, the little reviews, like wise detectives, can scent it on its way." Greene wrote this about Bendrix in 1951; Greene himself was already becoming popular — he would soon commit "that crime" — and the "wise detectives" would sniff at his success and bestow their praise on far less perfect craftsmen than Greene.

If, in the beginning — when I first read him in prep school — Graham Greene showed me that exquisitely developed characters and heartbreaking stories were the obligations of any novel worth re-

membering, it was also Greene, later, who taught me
to loathe literary criticism; to see how the critics
would dismiss him made me hate critics. Until his
death, in 1991, Graham Greene was the most accomplished living novelist in the English language; in any
language, he was the most meticulous.

As Greene was always keen to observe: coincidence is everywhere. Greene's niece, Louise Dennys,
is my Canadian publisher. The man who introduced
me to Greene, the Reverend Frederick Buechner —
no longer the school minister at Exeter — is my old
friend and neighbor in Vermont. (Small world.) And
it is only mildly astonishing to me that by the time I
left Exeter I had already read most of the writers who
would matter to me in my life as a writer; it is also
true that the hours I spent reading them contributed
(in combination with my dyslexia) to the necessity of
my spending a fifth year at a four-year school.

It hardly matters now. And it's a good lesson for
a novelist: keep going, move forward — but slowly.
Why be in a hurry to finish school, *or* a book?

A Backup

While the intelligentsia of my Exeter classmates
moved on to various Ivy League colleges, or to their
elite equivalents — George Trow moved slightly
south to Harvard, where Larry Palmer would go the
following year, and Chuck Krulak was accepted at
the Naval Academy (Krulak had left Exeter for Annapolis the previous year) — I attended the University of Pittsburgh because I wanted to wrestle with
the best.

I would have been happier at Wisconsin, where I was wait-listed for admission because I wasn't in the top quarter of my graduating class. (It's questionable that, if I'd gone to Exeter High School instead of the academy, I *would* have been, although this was my feeling at the time.) Rather than wait for Wisconsin to accept me, I chose Pitt. Why? Because Pittsburgh didn't make me wait.

I made a mistake. I liked George Martin, the Wisconsin wrestling coach, and he liked me; his son Steve, a future 157-pounder for Wisconsin, had been a teammate of mine (and a close friend) at Exeter. When I visited Madison, I loved the place — I loved the Badger wrestling room, too. Had I attended the University of Wisconsin, I might never have been a place winner in the Big 10 tournament — or even a starter on the Wisconsin team — but I know that I would have kept wrestling, and I would have stayed four years (maybe longer) in Madison; there's no question that I would have graduated. But I was 19 — Pittsburgh had accepted me, and Wisconsin had told me to wait and see. When you're 19, you don't want to "wait and see."

Coach Seabrooke warned me that I might be getting in over my head at Pitt; I should go to a smaller school, I should try a less competitive wrestling program — these were Ted's recommendations. But when he couldn't persuade me, he wrote to Rex Peery, the coach at Pittsburgh, giving Rex his evaluation of me. Knowing Ted, I presume he didn't exaggerate my potential. Coach Peery was prepared for me to be no better than "halfway decent"; as it turned out, I was worse than that.

Rex Peery was an Oklahoma boy and a former three-time national champion — even his *sons* had been three-time NCAA champions — and Pittsburgh was loaded with future All-Americans the year I arrived. Dick Martin, the 123-pounder, would be an All-American; Darrel Kelvington (147) and Timothy Gay (157) and Jim Harrison (167) and Kenneth Barr (177) would also be All-Americans. (Harrison was a future national champion; he would win an NCAA title in 1963.) Then there were Zolikoff at 137 and Jeffries at 191 and Ware at Unlimited — I once could recite that lineup in my sleep.

Sherman Moyer, the Pitt 130-pounder and my most frequent workout partner, was married and had completed his military service. Sherm was reputed to smoke one cigarette a week — usually in a toilet stall before his match (at least this was the only place I ever *saw* him smoke) — and he was devastating in the top position. Sherman Moyer was simply impossible to get away from; he could ride me, and did, all afternoon. At the time, it was small consolation to me that Moyer's abilities as a "rider" led him to defeat Syracuse All-American Sonny Greenhalgh twice in that season. (Sonny and I still talk about Moyer.) Nor was it greatly consoling that Moyer was a gentleman; he was always decent and good-humored to me — ever friendly — while grinding me into the mat.

As for my fellow freshmen at Pitt, they were a tough lot, too — especially in and around my weight class. Tom Heniff was from Illinois and Mike Johnson was from Pennsylvania; they were often my workout partners — and Moyer's. Heniff and I were 130-pounders — I had dropped three pounds from my Exeter weight class — and Johnson, who wrestled at 123 and at 130, could take apart anyone in the wrestling room up to about 140 or 150 pounds. In the next year, Mike Johnson would be an All-

American; he was an NCAA runner-up in '63. (Johnson is a high-school wrestling coach in Du Bois, Pennsylvania, today.)

I also worked out with a couple of freshman 137-pounders: a redhead named Carswell or Caswell, who was pound for pound the strongest person I ever wrestled — I remember him as about five feet five with a 60-inch chest — and a smiling guy named Warnick who had an arm-drag that left you looking for your arm. The freshman recruit at 147 pounds was (I believe) a guy named Frank O'Korn; I don't remember him well — I must have wrestled him only occasionally. At 157 pounds, John Carr had won a New England Interscholastic title as a PG at Cheshire. (Carr would transfer from Pitt to Wilkes; until recently, he was a high-school coach in the Wilkes-Barre area of Pennsylvania.) And topping off that freshman class was a highly recruited 177-pounder named Lee Hall.

I knew they would be good — I had gone there because they were the best. But in the Pittsburgh wrestling room, in the '62 season, there was not one wrestler I could beat — not *one*.

My technique was not the problem; I had been well coached at Exeter. The problem in Pittsburgh was that my limited athletic ability placed me at a considerable distance from the top rank of college wrestlers around the nation. Because of Ted Seabrooke, I wasn't a bad wrestler; I also wasn't a good athlete, as Ted had told me. I took a pounding at Pitt. "Halfway decent" didn't cut it there.

I won't presume to define that essential ability which makes a "good athlete" for all sports, but for wrestling good balance is as important as quickness; it is also as uncoachable. And by balance I mean both kinds: the ability to keep your balance — to a small degree this can be taught, by maintaining good position — and how quickly you can recover your balance when you lose it. The latter ability is unteachable. The speed with which I can recover my balance when I lose it is mournfully slow; this is my weakness as an athlete. (It is a sizable limitation for a wrestler.)

In '62, freshmen were ineligible for varsity competition; yet I'd anticipated a challenging schedule of dual-meet matches and tournaments for the Pittsburgh freshman team — we would have been a winning team. But Johnson and Heniff and Warnick and O'Korn and Carr were either academically ineligible or nursing injuries, or both; what there was for a freshman wrestling schedule was canceled. The *only* competition I would see, until the year-end tournament — the Freshman Eastern Intercollegiates at West Point — was the considerable competition in the Pitt wrestling room. And I could easily predict my future, if I stayed at Pittsburgh. I would be a backup to Johnson or Heniff or Warnick (or to all three); later, I would be a backup to whatever talented freshmen would enter *next* year's wrestling room with the new freshman class. I would *always* be a backup. When one of the starters was sick, when he was hurt or couldn't make weight, I would sneak into the lineup; and there was little doubt what my role would be then — it wouldn't be to win but to not get pinned. It would be, at best, a career spent facing Vincent Buonomano — like my first time in the pit.

It was what success I had met with in the pit — *after* the beating by Buonomano — that made the backup role hard for me to bear. At Exeter, I had been a three-year starter. Years later, as a coach, I had the highest respect for the backup wrestlers on good wrestling teams; they were what made the teams good — *as teams*. They were the necessary workout partners who could have been starters at a smaller school, in a less competitive program. But once I'd been part of a program like Pittsburgh's, I couldn't have been satisfied with anything less; nor was I wise enough to recognize the distinction of backing up a wrestler of Mike Johnson's quality. Instead, I was disappointed in myself — in my limitations. I wanted to leave Pittsburgh, but there was nowhere else I wanted to go.

For once I was not struggling academically; yet, for the first time, I was lazy (academically), too. I worked hard in the wrestling room, but — without any outside competition — I couldn't see my own improvement as a wrestler. I could only see that I wasn't improving against Moyer or Johnson or Heniff or Warnick, or Carswell or Caswell — whatever the strong redhead's name was. And I was bored with everything *but* the wrestling; to simply *see* more of it — since I couldn't compete — I asked Coach Peery to take me on varsity road trips as the team manager. Rex took me; he knew I was discouraged, and he was being kind to me — I was an easily distracted manager. (Daydreamers have pathetic managerial skills.)

Rex Peery was always kind to me, except once when he cut my hair. We were traveling — we were in the training room at either Navy or Maryland — and he'd warned me earlier to get a haircut. I wasn't being in the slightest rebellious; I'd just forgotten to do it — I would have done anything to please Rex.

Coach Peery put a surgical basin on my head —

it was a bowl, but not a round one — and he cut my hair with a pair of snub-nosed shears, of the kind used for removing adhesive tape from injured ankles and knees and shoulders and wrists and fingers . . . and whatever else could be taped. (By the end of a wrestling season, almost everything was taped.) All things considered, it wasn't a bad haircut — Rex would never try to make anyone look foolish. Besides, emblematic of my experience at Pitt, I had brought the haircut on myself.

The Hundred-Dollar Taxi Ride

It was about that time when I started smoking — just a little bit, although a little more than Sherman Moyer. Maybe Moyer had inspired me; if I couldn't get out from under him on the mat, at least I could outsmoke him. It was a stupid way to try to say good-bye to wrestling, which I wouldn't say good-bye to until I was 47 — whereas I would quit smoking almost as soon as I started. Most self-destructive behavior is simply ridiculous — never mind how complexly compelled by personal demons. Given my limited talent, I could ill afford to undermine one of my few advantages as a wrestler — before I started smoking, I was in fanatically good shape.

A pack would last me at least a week, often two weeks; and the more I smoked, the *harder* I trained. What was the point of it? So little smoking hardly constitutes an unbreakable habit — I'd never had the habit. In Pittsburgh, I could have used a school psychiatrist — and not for my spelling. In the back of my mind, even as I smoked, I imagined that I could

redeem myself at the Freshman Eastern Intercollegiates; the three Pitt freshmen who were uninjured
and eligible — I was one of them — would get to go.

It was probably because of my brief managerial
experience that I was trusted with the bus tickets and
pocket money for the trip to West Point; Coach Peery
put me in charge. The varsity team was staying in
Pittsburgh, preparing for the nationals; no coach
would accompany Lee Hall and me, and Carswell or
Caswell — I'm going to call him Caswell — to the
tournament at Army. It seemed simple enough. I had
bus tickets from Pittsburgh to the Port Authority in
New York City, together with something called
"transfer passes" from New York to West Point. I was
told to get the three of us to Manhattan and take the
first available bus up the Hudson. What could have
been easier? But the bus from Pittsburgh was de-
layed; by the time we reached the Port Authority, it
was midnight. The next available bus to West Point
was at 8:00 in the morning; from filling out the regis-
tration forms from Army, I remembered that the
weigh-ins were at 7:00 A.M.

"We can't miss the weigh-ins and still wrestle,"
Caswell said.

"What do we do?" Lee Hall asked me.

Inevitably, I recalled the surgical basin on my
head — at either Navy or Maryland — and I wondered what Rex Peery would have wanted us to do.
The whole year the three of us had been wrestling
only our teammates in the wrestling room; it
wouldn't have been like missing one tournament —
it would have meant missing our *only* tournament. I
counted the pocket money that Coach Peery had
given me: $100. I had our return "transfer passes"
from West Point to the Port Authority, and our return

tickets from New York to Pittsburgh. All we had to do was get ourselves up the Hudson to West Point before 7:00 in the morning. What did we need the $100 for? (We had to make weight — we couldn't eat anything, anyway.)

Once outside the Port Authority — now it was well after midnight — I was glad to be in the company of our highly recruited 177-pounder, Lee Hall, and with Caswell, the pound-for-pound strongest person in the world. (Caswell would be wrestling at Army at 137 pounds. I was listed to weigh in at 130.) It took me a dozen cabs, or more, before I found a taxi driver who would take us to West Point for $100.

"West Point? A hundred bucks? Sure, man," the driver said. "Where's West Point?"

Caswell said he couldn't read a map in a moving car without throwing up, and Lee Hall couldn't comfortably fit in the front seat; the meter crowded him (Lee had to cut a lot of weight to weigh 177 pounds). Therefore, I was our navigator — I sat up front with the driver.

"You just go up the Hudson," I told him.

"Sure, man," he said. "Up the *what?*"

I have flown nonstop from New York to Tokyo; I have driven nonstop from Iowa City to Exeter, New Hampshire. But that trip up the Hudson was the longest of my life. Didn't the Dutch explore the Hudson in boats? Not even in a boat could we have made worse time.

In the first place, the only map was a map of Manhattan and Brooklyn and Queens and the Bronx. In the second place, as soon as the city lights were gone, our driver informed us that he was afraid of the dark.

"I never drove in the dark before," he whimpered. "Not *dis* dark!"

We inched along. It began to sleet. It seemed that only back roads led to West Point — at least they were the only roads we found.

"I never seen so many trees," our driver said. "Not *dis* many!"

If our taxi driver was terrified of the dark, and of the unusual number of trees, the soldiers who were dressed to kill — and who guarded the formidable entrance to the United States Military Academy at West Point (I presume they were M.P.s) — were his undoing. The Military Police were not expecting the predawn arrival of three wrestlers from Pittsburgh; the other wrestlers had long ago arrived — the soldiers presumed they'd gone to bed. However, it was not necessary to open our gym bags in order to verify that we were wrestlers; it was only necessary for the M.P.s to get a look at Lee Hall.

It was then a matter of deciding on the whereabouts of our barracks. Where were all the other wrestlers sleeping? The soldiers at the gate, intimidating though they were, were not brave enough to call the Army wrestling coach and ask him where we were to be sheltered — it was about 4:00 A.M., only three hours to weigh-ins. Lee Hall and Caswell knew what I was thinking when I suggested to the soldiers that we sleep in the gym. I explained that the mats were usually rolled out the night before; that way the mats are lying flat by the time of competition — you don't have to tape the corners to the floor. We could sleep on the mats, I offered — we didn't mind.

Lee Hall and Caswell knew that I was thinking of the *scales,* not the mats — I couldn't have cared less about the mats, or sleeping. We had three hours before weigh-ins and we hadn't been able to check our weight since we left Pittsburgh. If I was a half-pound over, I needed to sweat; I'd been a pound and a half over when we left Pittsburgh. I'd eaten nothing, and I'd had nothing to drink; usually, if I was a pound and a half over in the afternoon before a morning weigh-in, I could drink eight ounces of water and still lose the weight in my sleep. I hadn't slept or had my usual eight ounces of water, but I was dying to get on the scales, to be sure.

The M.P.s didn't think that letting us into the gym was a good idea. There was a barracks somewhere for visiting teams; the soldiers sounded more or less sure of this, although they weren't sure which barracks it was.

Lee Hall confided to me that he thought we should go somewhere warm and "just run." That way we'd at least be losing weight. And how much sleep would we get before weigh-ins, anyway? I agreed with Lee.

Caswell looked remarkably well rested; he'd slept the whole way from Manhattan and was now viewing the austere buildings of the military academy with the eagerness of a child who'd just arrived at an amusement park — apparently Caswell never worried about his weight.

It was then I noticed that our taxi driver was too frightened to leave; he couldn't possibly find his way back to the city — "not in *dis* dark," he said. The M.P.s were doubly unsure which barracks might be available for *him*.

One of the soldiers got up the nerve to make a phone call. I don't know the name or rank of the man who was awakened, but his voice was exceptionally powerful and loud. We were brought to a darkened building in a Jeep — our taxi driver, too; he'd happily left the keys to his cab with the M.P.s at the gate. It was one of those stone dormitories where the stairs were lit with timed lights; on each floor, a single switch turned on the lights for the entire stairwell. At every stair landing, next to the hall door, the light switch was indicated by a small bulb that glowed the dull yellow of a cat's eye. The lights "ticked" for two minutes and then they went out; to turn them on, you had to find the nearest cat's eye again. By this torturous method, a few wrestlers were sprinting or jogging up and down the stairs — sometimes in light, sometimes in darkness, depending on the whim of the timed lights in the stairwell. One of these stair runners directed us to a huge, bad-smelling, overheated room where many wrestlers were lying on cots; they were fully clothed, under mounds of blankets — trying to sweat off the extra weight while they slept. (Most of them were lying in the dark, awake.)

"Man, it stinks in here," our taxi driver said.

At first glance, it seemed there were no empty cots, but this didn't trouble Caswell, who made himself comfortable on top of his gym bag on the floor; I think he was asleep by the time Lee Hall and I had changed into our sweatsuits and were running around the stairwell. The guys who'd been running the stairs ahead of us had worked out a system with the lights: when the lights went out, whoever was nearest a stair landing looked for the dull-yellow bulb. We kept running, whether the lights were on or off. Nobody talked on the stairs. Every so often I would call out "Lee?" and Lee Hall would say "What?"

After 15 or 20 minutes, I was sweating the way I wanted to; I started trotting more slowly, moving just fast enough so the sweat didn't stop. I think I was

asleep when I ran into a wall in the dark. My eyebrow was split open. I could feel that I was bleeding,
but I didn't know how badly I was cut.

"Lee?" I called.

"What?" Lee Hall said.

A Thief

I was 128 pounds at the weigh-ins. The Army trainer
shaved my eyebrow and covered the cut with a butterfly bandage; he advised me to have the cut
stitched up properly when I got back to Pittsburgh. I
knew I'd run too much — my legs felt dead.

We went to the mess hall after weigh-ins, and
there was our taxi driver; it's time I gave him a
name — let's call him Max.

"What are you doing here, Max?" I said. For
starters, Max was eating an enormous breakfast —
steeling his courage for the ride back to Manhattan, I
thought. But Max had decided he'd hang around and
watch the preliminary round of matches.

"If you guys win, maybe I'll stay for the next
round," Max informed us. "Anyway, it's still sleeting."
In the daylight, Max appeared to be almost erudite. It
also seemed he had adopted us. We were trying to
get focused on the tournament — we didn't give the
matter of Max much thought. Lee Hall ate a much
bigger breakfast than I did; my stomach was
shrunk — I felt hungry but, after half a bowl of oatmeal, I felt full. Caswell, with his characteristic air of
contentment, took a nap in the locker room after
consuming a generous number of what looked like
pancakes.

They were posting the brackets for the different weight classes on the walls of the gym, and Lee Hall and I looked over the matchups for 130 and 177 pounds. I wished Caswell hadn't been sleeping, because I wanted to drill some takedowns; Lee Hall and I were the wrong size to drill with each other. Instead, I rolled around on the mats by myself and watched the crowd straggle in. I remember it as an old, oval-shaped gym with a wooden track above, like an elongated version of the pit at Exeter, except that the floor space was vast; there were at least six mats rolled out for the preliminary rounds, and a long line of bleacher seats — extending almost to matside — ran the length of the gym wall.

I kept an eye out for my parents; although they were making a two-day trip of it — they had left New Hampshire yesterday and had spent the night with friends in Massachusetts — it wasn't like them to be late. Depending on the number of entries in your weight class, you might have two or three preliminary matches before the quarterfinal round, later that afternoon; the semifinals were that night. The next day would begin with the wrestle-backs (the consolation rounds), which would lead to the consolation finals; the finals would be tomorrow afternoon. It would be dark by the time we got to New York, I was thinking — and a long night's ride on the bus back to Pittsburgh. We would be hungry then, with no more weigh-ins to make — and no money for food. I was also thinking that it was odd to be at a big tournament without a coach.

With me wrestling 130, and Caswell at 137, we would often be wrestling on different mats at the same time, or at overlapping times; we wouldn't be able to coach each other — Lee Hall would have to choose between coaching me and coaching Caswell. As it turned out, when Lee Hall was wrestling, both Caswell and I were available to coach him. Lee, however, needed little coaching; he would easily maul his way into the finals — his opponents rarely lasted past the second period. Caswell and I would shout out the time remaining on the clock; that was all Lee needed to know — Lee didn't need to be informed of the lopsided score.

John Carr, our ineligible (or injured) 157-pounder, had not made the trip to West Point, but his dad was there; Mr. Carr volunteered to coach Caswell and Lee Hall and me. Mr. Carr loved wrestling; he must have spent many exciting years watching his son — John Carr was a very good wrestler. I remember thinking that Mr. Carr must have been disappointed to be watching *me*. I remember little else about the preliminary rounds. I beat two guys from schools with monosyllabic names (like Pitt). I could guess that they were from Yale and Penn, but they could have been from anywhere; it doesn't matter — in both matches, I got the first takedown so cleanly that I kept repeating it.

You take the guy down, you're up two points; you let the guy go, he gets one point — then you take him down again. After your three takedowns and his three escapes, you're leading 6–3. After that, the guy has to chase you, which makes it easier for you to take him down.

I was working Warnick's arm-drag, which Warnick had worked on me all winter in the Pitt wrestling room; I was working a duck-under, although it wasn't nearly as smooth a duck-under as Mike Johnson used to work on me — about a hundred times a week. Anyway, I advanced to the quarterfinals, realizing that I'd actually learned a little wrestling in the course of taking a pounding at Pitt.

In the quarterfinals, I pinned a guy from R.P.I. — I remember where he was from only because Lee Hall or Caswell asked me what "R.P.I." stood for and I realized that I didn't know how to spell Rensselaer *or* Polytechnic. Suddenly I was in the semifinals.

That hour — maybe it was two or three hours — between the quarterfinals and the semifinals . . . that was the best time of my one season of wrestling at Pittsburgh. That was when I knew I wasn't coming back. Lee Hall was talking to me; he was saying what a great freshman team we had — if only most of them had been able to wrestle. He was saying that Pitt would have walked away with the team title at that tournament — if only Johnson and Heniff and Warnick and O'Korn and Carr had been there. I agreed with Lee. But I knew that if Johnson and Heniff and Warnick and O'Korn and Carr had been there, *I* wouldn't have been wrestling; there was no room for me in that lineup. Caswell would have agreed with me: in such a lineup, there would have been no room for Caswell either.

And so I began to savor just being in the semifinals. It's fatal when you do that; you have to think about winning — not that you feel good to just *be* there. It's fatal to get distracted, too, and I was a little distracted; the thought that I would not come back to Pittsburgh had been in my mind before the Freshman Eastern Intercollegiates, of course — only now I *knew* it. I was also worried about my parents. Where were they?

I called their friends in Massachusetts, where they'd spent the previous night; to my surprise, my mother answered the phone. The sleet that was falling at West Point was snow in New England. My mom and dad had to wait out the storm. Whether I won or lost in the semifinals, I would be wrestling the next day — either in the finals or in the consolation matches that could lead to a third or a fourth-place finish. My parents would see me wrestle at West Point tomorrow, either way. It was a long trip for them, from New Hampshire; they'd never missed a match of mine at Exeter, and I began to feel a little pressure — to win for *them*. That's fatal, too — the wrong kind of pressure is fatal. You have to want to win for *you*.

I *wasn't* distracted by the discovery that Max, our taxi driver, was nowhere to be seen; he might not have been as interested in watching us wrestle as he'd claimed. It was later that evening when I learned that some of my fellow wrestlers had been robbed; they'd left their wallets or their wristwatches in the locker room, either forgetting or neglecting to put that kind of stuff in the team's "valuables box." I immediately suspected Max. In retrospect, I thought he had the perfect combination of instant charm and compulsive deceit that I associate with thieves; yet his terror of the night, and of the multitude of trees, could never have been feigned — not unless I have underestimated his thespian skills.

The Semifinals

As for the semifinals, I was what Coach Seabrooke always said I was — I was "halfway decent" — but the other guy was good. He was a kid from Cornell, and the favorite to win the weight class; he was the number-one seed. In the absence of a coach who knew me — Mr. Carr, given the greater abilities of his own son, generously overestimated my potential — I wrestled the kind of careful match that Ted Seabrooke would have recognized as the only kind of match I could win against a better wrestler. I even got the first takedown. But the Cornell kid escaped immediately — I couldn't manage to hold him long enough to gain any riding-time advantage — and he scored a slick takedown at the edge of the mat, just as time was running out in the first period; I had no time to get an escape of my own. I was trailing 3–2 going into the second period, and the choice of position (a flip of the coin) was mine; I chose down. I finally escaped for a point, but the Cornell kid had ridden me for over a minute. It was 3–3 on the scoreboard but I knew he had a riding-time point, which made it 4–3 in his favor starting the third — unless I could keep him on the bottom long enough to erase his riding-time advantage. He got away from me in less than 15 seconds, which made it 4–3 on the scoreboard — in reality, 5–3 (with riding time). I knew that the two-point difference was a *possible* gap for me to close in the final period.

Then I got lucky: my butterfly bandage was soaked through — my eyebrow was bleeding on the mat. The referee called a time-out to wipe up the blood, and I was given a quick rebandaging. However few cigarettes I'd been smoking, I was tired; it's not unreasonable to blame my tiredness on my lack of sleep, or on a dawn spent running up and down the stairs (into a wall) — but I blame the cigarettes. The mainstay of what had made me "halfway decent" as a wrestler was my physical conditioning; now a time-out for bleeding had given me a much-needed rest. (In those days, a college wrestling match was nine minutes long; in prep school, I had been used to six minutes. A three-minute period feels a *lot* longer than a two-minute period. Nowadays, a college match is only seven minutes overall — divided in periods of three, two, two — and the high-school or prep-school match is what it always was: six minutes, in periods of two, two, two.)

And I got lucky again: the referee hit the Cornell wrestler with a warning for stalling. It was a questionable call. With the score 4–3 on the scoreboard (5–3 with riding time), I knew that a takedown could tie it; a takedown could win it for me, too — if I could stay on top long enough to negate his riding-time advantage. The stalling warning against my opponent would hurt him in a tie; in the rules of that tournament, there was no overtime, no sudden death — a draw would mean a referee's decision. I was sure that my opponent's warning for stalling would give any referee's decision to me — I thought a tie would win it.

I don't remember my takedown — whether it was Warnick's arm-drag or Johnson's duck-under, or whether it was a low, outside single-leg, which was my best takedown from Exeter — but there were less than 20 seconds showing on the clock, and the scoreboard said 5–4 in my favor. The Cornell kid had the riding-time point locked up — I couldn't erase his advantage in less than 20 seconds — and so the match would be a draw, 5–5, *if* I could just hold on.

There was a scramble, a mix-up of the kind that Coach Seabrooke had warned me against; fortunately, for me, we both rolled off the mat. When the referee brought us back to the circle, there were 15 seconds on the clock; I had to ride him for only 15 seconds. This is a drill in every practice session in every wrestling room in America. Sometimes the drill is called "bursts." One of you tries to hang on, the other one tries to get away.

I don't remember how my opponent escaped, but he got free in a hurry. I had less than five seconds to initiate a desperation shot at a takedown; I wasn't close to completing a move when the buzzer sounded — I lost 6–5. I couldn't bear watching the Cornell kid in the finals; I don't know if he won the weight class or not — or, as I say so often, I don't remember. All I know is, that kid would never have gotten away from Sherman Moyer — not even in 15 *minutes*.

Point by point, move by move, you never know how close you are to getting into the finals of a tournament until you *don't* get into the finals. I called my parents in Massachusetts and told them to be at West Point early in the morning; the consolation rounds would start early. If I lost my first consolation match, I'd be eliminated from the tournament — I'd be a spectator for the rest of the day. If I won, I could keep wrestling; I could place as high as third, if I kept winning.

My next opponent was an Army boy — a home-crowd favorite of the West Point fans. I remember all those cadets in gray, leaning over the mats from the wooden track above the gym; I remember them screaming. It was a larger teacup than the pit at Exeter, but it was the same teacup effect — except that these were *his* fans, not mine. I'd wrestled as good a match as I could against the Cornell kid. Possibly it was the effect of the cadets, or maybe I was trying to impress my parents with everything I'd learned at Pitt; for whatever reason, my match against Army was not the kind of match Ted Seabrooke would have recommended for me. It was one mix-up after another; it was all a scramble. I knew from the beginning that I wouldn't win a free-for-all.

To be fair to myself, I not only lost the first take-down but I was thrown to my back and lost three points for a near-fall in addition to the takedown points. When I reversed him, I was still behind 5–2; he immediately reversed me, and I immediately escaped. When I had a second to look at the score, I saw I was losing 7–3 and the first period had just started. You can't slow down the pace when you're losing 7–3, and so that was the kind of match I was in — a free-for-all. I kept scoring, but he kept scoring back; whenever I checked the score, I was always no more than 5 but no fewer than 3 points behind. The cadets were screaming, not only because their West Point boy was winning; it was the kind of match a crowd loves — *any* crowd loves a free-for-all. I don't remember the final score: 15–11, 17–13. . . . Ted Seabrooke would have told me — indeed, Ted *had* told me — that I would *never* come out on top of a score like that. It was my last match in a Pittsburgh uniform, which I had worn for all of two days.

Whether they were disappointed or merely underimpressed, my parents were kind enough not to say. My mother was shocked to see how thin I was. I'd gotten much stronger in the wrestling room at Pitt, but I was nonetheless smaller than I'd been at Exeter; unlike Larry Palmer, I'd stopped growing when I was 15. My mom was worried about my weight. To that end, I was able to get some money from her — so that Caswell and Lee Hall and I could eat all the way back to Pittsburgh. I don't think I told my parents about the hundred-dollar taxi ride; I know I didn't tell them that I'd made up my mind to leave Pitt — I still didn't know where I would go.

I don't even remember if Lee Hall won the Freshman Easterns or if he lost in the finals; it wasn't like Lee to lose, but I vaguely recall that he had a difficult opponent — a Lehigh kid, as I remember him, but I'm on record for not remembering much. For example, I don't remember how Caswell did; in the end, like me, I think he won a couple of matches and lost a couple — I know he didn't make the finals, but he might have placed. (Caswell did everything in such a friendly, efficient, uncomplaining way; that's probably why I can't even be sure of his name.)

Back in Pittsburgh, I will never forget telling Coach Peery that I'd spent all the pocket money.

"You took a *taxi*?" Rex kept saying.

I had so much respect for Rex I couldn't tell him why I was leaving Pitt: specifically because I couldn't bear being a backup. Instead, I made up a story about missing a girlfriend back home; I thought this sounded more human — hence more forgivable. I didn't have a girlfriend "back home," or in Pittsburgh.

My *ex*-girlfriend was from Connecticut; she was spending the year in Switzerland. The only Creative Writing I'd managed to do at Pitt was a diary I kept; I was imagining that I would show my ex-girlfriend my diary — and thus win her back. Everything in the "diary" was made up; I hadn't exactly had the kind of year that made me want to write about it. I didn't know this at the time, but I had begun a traditional writer's task — namely, I was in the process of inventing myself. Before I could invent anything else, I needed to practice.

A Brief Conversation in Ohio

In Pittsburgh — notwithstanding my disappointment
in my wrestling — it had been a defeat of a deeper
kind to be abused in Freshman English, where I received the grade of C– and was told by an instructor
with less of a beard to shave than my own that my
overuse of the semicolon was archaic. I shall call him
Instructor C–, and if he is reading me still, which
would surprise me, there is no telling what he makes
of my semicolons today; if they were archaic in 1962,
they must be antiquated beyond redemption now.

But I stopped neither writing nor wrestling as a
result of these discouragements. I retreated to my
home state of New Hampshire, not necessarily to lick
my wounds. Even with my unimpressive grades at
Pitt, the University of New Hampshire was obliged to
admit me because of my in-state residency, and it
was there that I took my first Creative Writing class
by name. The teacher was a Southern novelist named
John Yount — an engaging, good-humored, and
good-hearted man who didn't bat an eye at my semicolons.

At the same time I became an extra coach in the
wrestling room at Exeter, and I competed "unat-
tached" in various "open" wrestling tournaments
around New England and New York State; the University of New Hampshire had no wrestling team.

The competition in so-called open tournaments
was a mixed bag: some of the entries were the better,
more mature high-school wrestlers; there were lots
of college freshmen and nonstarters on college
teams; and always a few older, postcollege competitors — some of these wrestlers were very good, often

the best in such tournaments, but others were . . . well, *too* old, or simply out-of-shape. I was in halfway-decent shape — not in Pittsburgh shape, but this wasn't Pittsburgh.

Although I was not attached to any team, I competed in my old Exeter uniform — with Ted Seabrooke's blessing. For takedowns, I had fair success with Warnick's arm-drag and Johnson's duck-under and with my own low, outside single-leg; defensively, on my feet — in the neutral position — I had a pretty good whizzer. Sherman Moyer had taught me the value of hand control; on top, I was hard to get away from but I was no pinner, and on the bottom I was difficult to hold down — although Moyer had managed to ride me until the clock ran out.

In lieu of cutting weight, I started *lifting* weights: if I couldn't make the cut to the 130-pound class, I would make myself strong enough to wrestle at 137 or 147. (In the open tournaments, the weight classes varied between collegiate and freestyle — sometimes I wrestled at 136½ or 137, other times at 147 or 149½.) A factor in what I weighed was beer; I turned 21 in the middle of the '63 wrestling season — at about the same time I gave up cigarettes, I took up beer.

Not surprisingly, the writers (and would-be writers) at the University of New Hampshire all smoked and drank; that I drove 45 minutes every day from Durham to Exeter for wrestling practice, and that I traveled on many weekends to wrestling tournaments, struck both me and my new writer friends as exceedingly unliterary. It was my earliest indication that my writing friends and my wrestling friends would rarely mix; for a brief period of time, I would give up the mixture myself — I was convinced that I could be a wrestler *or* a writer, but not both.

That March of '63, Ted Seabrooke and I drove out to Kent State University in Ohio to see the NCAA tournament. From the stands, I watched my old teammates at Pitt become All-Americans: Jim Harrison won the championship, Mike Johnson lost in the finals, Timothy Gay placed fifth, and Kenneth Barr was sixth. (I believe that the NCAA Division I tournament is the toughest in wrestling; it is both mentally and physically a tougher tournament than the Olympics — first of all, because of the tremendous pressure college wrestlers put on themselves to become All-Americans, but also because of how evenly matched many of the competitors are. In the 1995 tournament, there were six returning national champions; only two of them managed to defend their titles — and, out of 10 weight classes, only four of the number-one seeds finished first.)

A year away from Pittsburgh, I saw how far I stood from the top level of competition; it depressed me — I was 21, but I felt I'd failed at the one thing I'd been any good at. Worse than "failed" — I had *quit*. On our way home from Kent State, Ted told me that he'd talked with my Pitt coach, Rex Peery; Rex had been kind to me, as always — he had expressed his hope to Ted that I'd solved my "girlfriend problem."

"*What* 'girlfriend problem'?" Ted asked me.

I had to confess to Coach Seabrooke that I'd lied to Coach Peery about my reasons for leaving Pittsburgh. Mike Johnson had just finished second in the nation; yet I'd quit the Pitt team because I couldn't accept the role of spending four years as Johnson's workout partner. Far less honorable than being a backup to Mike Johnson was that I'd lied to Rex — I had made up a girlfriend, of all things.

"Johnny, Johnny," Ted Seabrooke said to me. (We were standing side by side at a urinal, still in Ohio.) "You don't have to give up wrestling because you're not the best wrestler," Ted told me. "You can still do it. And you're always going to love it — you can't help that."

But I didn't know that then. I had room in me to do, and to love, only what I thought I could be the best at, and John Yount had told me I could be a writer.

"So do it," Coach Seabrooke said.

It was Ted's idea that I should get out of New Hampshire; that I shouldn't be living at home and hanging out in the wrestling room of my old school — that if I were going to give up wrestling, I should give up more than that. I should get away — *far* away. Pittsburgh, of course, had been "away," but not far enough.

A Year Abroad

It was with John Yount's encouragement that I applied to a study-abroad program; as it turned out, the Institute for European Studies in Vienna admitted me. I went off to Europe feeling, for the first time, "like a writer."

I took 12 tutorial hours of German a week, but to this day I can speak the language only haltingly; I can barely understand German, when I'm spoken to, and reading German only serves to remind me of my dyslexia — all those verbs lurking at the end of the sentence, waiting to be reattached to the clauses they came from.

My favorite courses at the Institute for European Studies were taught by an Englishman named Edward Mowatt, with whom I studied (not necessarily in this order) Ludwig Josef Johann Wittgenstein and Greek Moral Philosophy. I also studied the Victorian Novel with Herr Doktor Felix Korninger from the University of Vienna. Professor Korninger was an Austrian who'd once taught at the University of Texas; he spoke English with a most original Texan-Austrian accent — a kind of conflation of Lyndon Baines Johnson and Arnold Schwartzenegger.

In Vienna, I shared an apartment on the Schwindgasse, next to the Polish Reading Room, with a fellow American named Eric Ross; he was from Chicago. Eric was tall and athletic, with honey-colored, curly hair; on skis, especially, he was a picture of Aryan perfection, but of course he was Jewish — and most savvy of the myriad, insidious forms of anti-Semitism in Austria. I knew nothing about anti-Semites, but I learned. I was short and dark and my last name was Irving — a Scots name, but common enough as a Jewish first name so that several Viennese anti-Semites were confused. (This is on a level of intelligence with thinking that John Milton was Jewish because of Milton Friedman, but — as Eric Ross was wise to point out — no one ever said anti-Semites were smart.) Eric and I developed a routine for exposing anti-Semites. Whether I was mistreated by a waiter or a shopkeeper, or by a fellow student at the University of Vienna, it was only necessary for the faintest hint of an anti-Semitic slur to emerge; I would not infrequently miss the slur — my German being as flawed as it was — but Eric, whose German was much better than mine, would instantly alert me to the insult.

"You're being treated like a Jew again," Eric would tell me.

Whereupon, pointing to Eric, I would deliver my well-rehearsed line to the offending anti-Semite: "*He's* the Jew, you idiot." ("*Er ist der Jude, Du Idiot.*") Eric always had to help me with the correct pronunciation, but we usually got our point across: Jew baiting was not merely distasteful — those with the inclination to do it were also stupid enough to think that they could tell who was Jewish and who wasn't.

Eric and I traveled to Istanbul together, and to Athens; we often went skiing together, too — in Kaprun. But while we both loved the experience of being on our own in Europe, we did not love — we *do* not love — Vienna. It is a small town; its notorious anti-Semitism is only part of a mean-spirited provincialism — an overall xenophobia, a suspicion (leading to hatred) of *all* outsiders. "*Das geht bei uns nicht,*" the Austrians say — "That doesn't go with us." "*Ausländer*" — a "foreigner" — is always a derogatory word. Viennese *Gemütlichkeit,* a tourist attraction, is the false sweetness of basically *unhöflich* people.

I was last in Vienna to promote the German translation of *A Prayer for Owen Meany,* and I got in trouble with the media for saying these things; at the time, the revelations about Kurt Waldheim's role in World War II appeared to have *enhanced* Waldheim's popularity in Vienna — and I said so. I doubt I'll go back to Vienna again.

When I was a student there, Freud's former apartment and office at 19 Berggasse was *not* open to the public; only the persistent efforts of Freud's

daughter finally forced the Austrian government to
let the modest *Wohnung* at 19 Berggasse stand for
what it is: a most moving museum of an intellectual
life interrupted by Nazi doctrine.

Freud was not mistaken to call Arthur Schnitzler
a "colleague" in the study of the "underestimated and
much-maligned erotic"; in my student days, this was
doubtless the source of my fondness for Schnitzler —
the "underestimated and much-maligned erotic,"
which Schnitzler often juxtaposed with the oppressive but slowly changing social order of fin-de-siècle
Vienna. But even *The Road into the Open* (1908) was
steeped in the *same* sexually oppressive atmosphere
that Eric Ross and I would encounter in Vienna more
than half a century later.

Observe young Baron Georg von Wergenthin
looking out a window. "Outside, the park was rather
empty. On a bench sat an old woman wearing an
outmoded coat with black glass pearls. A governess
walked by, a little boy on her hand, and another person, much smaller and in a hussar's uniform, with his
saber buckled on and a pistol at his side, walked
ahead, looked proudly around himself, and saluted
an invalid who came down the path smoking.
Deeper in the garden, around the kiosk, a few
people sat drinking coffee and reading newspapers.
The foliage was still rather thick, and the park
seemed oppressed, dusty, and on the whole more
summerlike than usual in late September." (Two
pages later, young Georg is thinking about "the mas-
querade at the Ehrenbergs" and remembering "Sissy's
fleeting kiss under the black lace of her mask.")

True, the small man in the hussar's uniform with
his saber and pistol was gone from the Stadtpark by
the time Eric Ross and I arrived in Vienna, but the

"oppressed" atmosphere was largely unchanged. Eric and I used to study in the evenings in a bar where the prostitutes waited for their customers out of the cold. Our landlady turned off the heat at night, and the coffeehouses frequented by students were too noisy for studying; besides, the Viennese students were too proper to be seen in a bar used by prostitutes — except for the one or two well-to-do students who would appear at the bar in order to *select* a prostitute. (These students were always embarrassed to be seen by Eric or me.) As for the prostitutes, they recognized from the beginning that Eric and I could not afford their more intimate company. Occasionally, there was an older one — my mother's age — who would help me with my German.

Baron von Wergenthin might first have attracted my interest in *The Road into the Open* because of his ceaseless fantasizing about women — and the ongoing difficulty of his relationships with them — but young Georg was also a Christian aristocrat whose principal friendships were with Jewish intellectuals, at a time when anti-Semitism was on the rise. By the time Eric Ross and I arrived in Vienna, anti-Semitism had not only risen, it had arrived — and it was intractable. It was also much more vulgar than my encounters with it in Schnitzler.

Witness Georg's meeting with Willy Eissler in the Stadtpark. It is *subtly* uncomfortable how Willy defends his Jewishness. He says: "The fact that I once had differences with Captain Ladisc cannot keep me from observing that he's always been a drunken pig. I have an insurmountable revulsion, irredeemable even by blood, against people who associate with Jews when it's to their advantage, but who begin to revile them as soon as they're outside on the steps.

One could at least wait until one got to the coffee-house."

Later, Baron von Wergenthin reflects that "he found it almost strange, as he often had before, that Willy was Jewish. The older Eissler, Willy's father, composer of charming Viennese waltzes and songs, distinguished art and antique collector and sometime dealer, with his giant's physique, had been known in his time as the foremost boxer in Vienna, and, with his long, full, gray beard and monocle, resembled more a Hungarian magnate than a Jewish patriarch. But talent, dilettantism, and an iron will had given Willy the affected image of a born cavalier. But what really distinguished him from other young people of his background and aspirations was the fact that he was content not to renounce his heritage; he pursued an explanation or reconciliation for every ambiguous smile, and in the face of pettiness or prejudice, by which he often appeared to be affected, he refused to make light of it whenever possible."

By the time Eric Ross and I arrived in Vienna, the anti-Semitism had long been administered by means more severe than the "ambiguous smile"; it had degenerated to base thuggery — it was impossible "to make light of it." Skinheads with swastika earrings, while not unusual, were not commonplace; what *were* commonplace were the shy citizens who looked away from the skinheads, pretending not to have seen them. As young, idealistic Americans, Eric and I could do no more than hold up a mirror to this inexplicable tolerance of intolerance. More than 30 years later, it is still a frequent topic of conversation between Eric and me: not simple intolerance but the tolerance of intolerance, which allows the intolerance to persist.

Eric Ross went into the advertising business in Chicago; then he moved to Crested Butte, Colorado, where he was a ski patrolman and a folksinger for many years. Eric still lives in Crested Butte, where he is a tireless contributor (both as an actor and a director) to the Crested Butte Mountain Theatre; and he's back writing ads again, when he's not writing letters to me — he's a most faithful correspondent. We try to see each other every year, together with our mutual best friend, David Warren. David is from Ithaca, New York — he was Eric's and my nearly constant companion in Vienna, and the best student among us.

Eric had the best motorcycle — a German Horex. However, the Horex lacked a kickstand, which for reasons peculiar to Eric was never replaced; the Horex was always falling down. My motorcycle was second-best among our three: a Yugoslavian Jawa — or maybe it was Czech? And David drove a terrible Triumph; it was always dying on him — it preferred stranding him on the autobahn to other places.

Anyway, for no good reason — except that I had gotten away (*far* away) from New Hampshire — I started to write. I had Ted Seabrooke and John Yount to thank for the move.

It was also John Yount who encouraged me to stay in Europe, at a later time (that same year) when I was homesick; I was missing, among other things, both wrestling and a girlfriend who would become my first wife. I had met Shyla Leary in Cambridge in the summer of '63, just before I left for Vienna — I was taking a crash course in German at Harvard summer school. It seems idiotic, but I think it's fairly common that we meet people of importance to us just before we are going away somewhere. Within a year, in the summer of '64, I would marry her — in Greece.

"Stay in Europe for a while," Mr. Yount wrote to me. "Melancholy is good for the soul."

Surely this was good and true advice, and beyond the call of duty of Creative Writing teachers. I see now that John Yount was, if not my first mentor, the first *writer* I was conscious of as a mentor; he made a world of difference to me — largely by impressing upon me that anything I did except writing would be unsatisfying. Even so, I didn't take his advice — I didn't stay in Europe.

I had tried another language, and I was uncomfortable with it; English was my *only* language, and — as a writer — I wanted it to be the language I lived with. Besides, Shyla and I had returned to Vienna from Greece — and she was already pregnant with Colin. I wanted to be a father, but only in my own country.

No Vietnam; No More Motorcyles

When I came back to the States, and to the University of New Hampshire, it was another writer who took me under his wing. Thomas Williams was much more to me than a teacher; his wife, Liz, would be the godmother of my first child, and Mr. Williams remained, until his death, my sternest and most passionate critic. Tom had a lifelong quarrel with my fondness for imitation — specifically, for imitating the narrative voices of many 19th-century novelists. He would not infrequently write in the margins of my manuscripts: "Who are you imitating now?" But his affection for me was genuine, as was mine for him; and his loyalty to me, when other critics would attack me, was steadfast. Tom Williams was a good friend, and it was on the strength of his reputation and his recommendation that I was given a teaching-writing fellowship to attend the Writers' Workshop at the University of Iowa. (Already married as an undergraduate, and with one child, I could not have afforded Iowa without the fellowship.) And it was Tom's agent who sold my first short story to *Redbook* for a whopping, at the time, $1,000. This sale occurred before I graduated from the University of New Hampshire, which caused me to be cordially loathed by my fellow students. But I was on my way to Iowa — what did I care?

That year in New Hampshire (my last) was a watershed for me. Not only did I become a published writer and a father, but the birth of my son Colin would change my draft status to 3A — "married with child" — which would forever isolate me from the dilemma facing my generation of American males; I would never have to make up my mind about Vietnam, because I couldn't be drafted. If Colin kept me out of Vietnam, the combination of being married and a father, *and* my return to the world of wrestling, kept me from experimenting with the most seductive hallmarks of my '60s generation: sex and drugs. I was a husband and a daddy and a jock — and, only recently, a writer.

I had just turned 23 when Colin was born. It was late March, which is not spring in New Hampshire. I remember driving my motorcycle home from the hospital. (A friend had driven Shyla to the hospital, because I'd been in class — in Tom Williams's Cre-

ative Writing class.) I remember watching out for the
patches of ice and snow that were still evident on the
roads; I drove home very slowly, put the motorcycle
in the garage, and never drove it again — I would
sell it that summer. It was a 750cc Royal Enfield,
black and chrome, with a customized tomato-red gas
tank the shape of a teardrop — I would never miss it.
I was a father; fathers didn't drive motorcycles.

The night Colin was born, George Bennett died
in the same hospital; I have called George my first
"critic and encourager" — he was my first *reader*. I
remember going back and forth in the hospital between Shyla and Colin and George. During the years
I'd grown up in Exeter, especially before I attended
the academy, George's son had been my best friend.
(I would dedicate my first novel *in memory of*
George, and to his widow and son.)

George Bennett took me to my first Ingmar
Bergman film; it would have been 1958 or '59 when I
saw *The Seventh Seal* — the movie was almost new
(it was released in the U.S. in '57). It's not psychologically complicated why, when Death came for
George, I saw Death as that relentless chess player in
the black robe (Bengt Ekerot) who defeats the
Knight (Max von Sydow) and claims the lives of the
Knight's wife and the Knight's squire, too.

I have since read that *The Seventh Seal* is a "medieval fantasy," and this I don't understand at all . . .
well, "medieval," maybe, although most of Bergman's work is timeless to me. But *The Seventh Seal* is
no "fantasy." That Death takes the Knight and allows
the young family to live . . . well, that was how it
happened to me, too. At the moment my son Colin
was born, George was gone.

In 1982, when Ingmar Bergman retired as a

filmmaker — with *Fanny and Alexander,* the stunning memoir of his childhood — I felt another loss. Bergman was the only major novelist making movies. My interest in the movies, which was never great, has grown fainter since his retirement. I hope that Mr. Bergman is happy in the theater (where he continues to direct), although I have difficulty seeing him there — my interest in the theater was never great either.

Not Even a Zebra

Upon my return from Europe, Ted Seabrooke had made me feel welcome in the Exeter wrestling room, but something had changed in me; I was so happy to be wrestling again I didn't care how I compared to the competition — I didn't enter a single tournament. I worked out, hard, every day; I coached the kids at Exeter — I thought more about *their* wrestling than I did about mine — and I became certified as a referee. (I'd always disliked referees until I became one.)

That winter of '65, there was an additional wrestling coach in the Exeter room — a retired Air Force lieutenant colonel, Cliff Gallagher. Cliff was the famous Ed Gallagher's brother. (Between 1928 and 1940, E. C. Gallagher coached Oklahoma State to 11 national team titles.) Born in Kansas, Cliff had wrestled at Oklahoma A & M — he was never beaten in a wrestling match — and he'd played football at Kansas State (he was a All-American halfback). Cliff had once held the world record in the 50-yard low hurdles, too, and he'd received a doctorate from

Kansas State in 1921 — in veterinary medicine, although he'd never been a practicing veterinarian. Cliff Gallagher was also a certified referee. We frequently refereed tournaments together.

As a wrestling coach, Cliff was a little dangerous; he showed the Exeter boys a great number of holds that had been illegal for many years — the key-lock, the Japanese wrist-lock, various choke-holds and other holds that dated from a time when it had been legal to coax your opponent to his back by applying pain or the threat of asphyxiation instead of leverage. Ted explained to me that he always allowed Cliff to demonstrate these holds to the boys; at some point, following Cliff's demonstration, Ted would quietly take the time to tell the boys: "Not that one." The boys, of course, were eager to learn anything new, and Cliff had much to teach that *I'd* never seen before; some of Cliff's holds were new to Ted, too.

We had to be on our toes in the Exeter wrestling room that year. There would be some kid twisting another kid's head off, and Ted or I would jump in and break it up. We'd always ask, "Did Cliff show you that?"

"Yes, sir," the boy would say. "I think it's called a Bulgarian head-and-elbow." Whatever it was called, Ted or I would put a stop to it, but we would never have criticized Cliff for his efforts — Cliff was having a great time, and we adored him. So did the kids — I'm sure they were putting the Bulgarian head-and-elbow to good use, probably in their dormitories.

As a referee, Cliff was completely reliable. He had all the right instincts for when to stop a potentially dangerous situation, for how to anticipate an injury before it happened; he always knew where the edge of the mat was — and which wrestler was using it, to what advantage — and he never called stalling on the wrong wrestler (he always knew who was stalling). It was a mystery to me how Cliff had memorized the rule book; as a referee, he permitted not a single illegal hold. (As a coach, Cliff Gallagher taught every move and hold he knew — legal or not.) Cliff taught me to be much better as a referee than I'd ever been as a wrestler. Refereeing is *all* technique; unlike wrestling, refereeing doesn't call upon superior athletic ability — or expose the lack thereof.

I will always remember a maniacally mismanaged high-school tournament in Maine — Cliff and I were the only actual wrestlers among our fellow referees. In the preliminary rounds, Cliff and I were also the only referees who penalized a headlock without the arm contained — if you lock up a man's head, you're supposed to include one of his arms in the headlock. To encircle your opponent's head — *just* his head — is illegal. For the benefit of the assembled coaches *and* our fellow referees, Cliff put on a clinic between rounds; he made special emphasis of the headlock *with* an arm. This information was dismaying to the other referees, and to most of the coaches. One of them said, "It's too late in the season to be showin' 'em somethin' new."

"It's not new, it's *legal,*" Cliff said.

"It's new, too," the guy said — I don't remember if he was a coach or a referee. In any case, he expressed the sentiment of the majority: they'd been using and accepting an illegal headlock all season — probably for years — and it was nothing but a nuisance to them to enforce the rule now.

"Johnny and I are calling the illegal headlock — is that clear enough?" Cliff told them. And so we did.

The points for a repeated illegal hold can mount

against a wrestler quickly. Repeated violations lead to disqualification. In no time, Cliff and I were penalizing *and* disqualifying half the state of Maine. (We "disqualified" a few coaches who protested, too.) In the semifinals, I also disqualified a heavyweight for deliberately throwing his opponent on top of the scorer's table; I had twice warned and penalized this wrestler for continuing to wrestle off the mat — after the whistle blew. I'd even asked his coach if the heavyweight in question was *deaf*.

"No, he's just a little stupid," his coach replied.

When I disqualified the heavyweight, his parents came out of the stands and confronted me in the middle of the mat. I had no trouble recognizing who they were — they didn't have to introduce themselves. At a glance, I could see they'd swum forth from the same gene pool for enormity that had spawned their son. Cliff saved me.

"If you understand nothing else, you can understand one rule," Cliff told the heavyweight's parents. "It's just *one* rule and I'm only going to tell you *once*." (I could see that he had their attention.) "This is a *mat*," Cliff said, pointing to where we were standing. "And *that*," Cliff said — pointing to the scorer's table where the heavyweight had thrown his opponent — "that is a goddamn table. In wrestling," Cliff said, "we do it on the *mat*. That's the rule." The heavyweight's parents shuffled away without a word. Cliff and I were alive until the finals.

The finals were at night. Scary people from the middle of Maine emerged in the night. (My good friend Stephen King doesn't make up *everything;* he knows the people I mean.) The fans for the finals that night made the disqualified heavyweight's parents seem mildly civilized. In rebellion over the illegal headlock, our fellow referees had gone home; Cliff and I alternated refereeing the weight classes for the finals. When he was refereeing, I was the mat judge; Cliff was the mat judge when I was out on the mat refereeing. A mat judge can (but usually doesn't) overrule a referee's call; in a flurry of moves, sometimes the mat judge sees something the referee misses — for example, illegally locked hands in the top position — and in the area of determining the points scored (or not) on the edge of the mat, before the wrestlers are out of bounds, the mat judge can be especially effective.

There can be 11 or 12 or 13 weight classes in a high-school wrestling tournament. Nowadays, in the New England Class A tournament, the lightest weight class is 103 pounds — there are 13 weight classes, ending with the 189-pounder and the heavyweight (under 275). But in high schools there is occasionally a 100-pound class — in some states today there is also a 215- or 220-pound class, in addition to 189 and 275 — and in Maine in '65 the heavyweight class was unlimited. (The weight class used to be *called* Unlimited.)

In the first three weight classes, Cliff and I gave out half a dozen penalty points for the illegal headlock — apparently a feature of Maine life — and Cliff bestowed one disqualification: for biting. Some guy was getting pinned in a crossface-cradle when he bit through the skin of his opponent's forearm. There was bedlam among the fans. What could possibly be more offensive to them than a no-biting rule? (There were people in the stands who looked like they bit other people every day.)

That night in Maine, Cliff Gallagher was 68. A former 145-pounder, he was no more than 10 pounds over his old weight class. He was pound-for-pound as strong as good old Caswell from Pitt. Cliff was mostly bald; he had a long, leathery face with remarkable ears — his neck and his hands were huge. And Cliff didn't like the way the crowd was reacting to his call. He went over to the scorer's table and took the microphone away from the announcer.

"No biting — is that clear enough?" Cliff said into the microphone. The fans didn't like it, but they quieted down.

We had a few more weight classes (and a lot more illegal headlocks) to get through; we kept alternating the matches, between referee and mat judge, and we kept blowing our whistles — in addition to the headlocks without an arm, there were over-scissors and full-nelsons and figure-four body-scissors and twisting knee-locks and head-butts, but there was no more biting. In the 177-pound class, I called the penalty that determined the outcome of the match; I thought the fans were going to rush me on the mat, and the coach of the penalized wrestler distinctly called me a "cocksucker" — normally another penalty, but I thought I'd better let it pass.

Cliff conferred with me while the crowd raged. Then he went to the microphone again. "No poking the other guy in his eyes over and over again — is that clear enough?" Cliff said.

It was Cliff who refereed the heavyweights, for which I was — for which I *am* — eternally grateful. The boy who'd been thrown on the scorer's table, and had thus been victorious in the semifinals, was a little the worse for wear; his opponent was a finger bender, whom Cliff penalized twice in the first period — patiently explaining the rule both times. (If you grab your opponent's fingers, you must grab all

four — not just two, or one, and not just his thumb.)
But the finger bender was obdurate about finger
bending, and the boy who'd been bounced off the
scorer's table was already . . . well, understandably,
sensitive. When his fingers were illegally bent, the
boy responded with a head-butt; Cliff correctly penalized him, too. Therefore, the penalty points were
equal as the second period started; so far, not one
legal wrestling move or hold had been initiated by
either wrestler — I knew Cliff had his hands full.

The finger bender was on the bottom; his opponent slapped a body-scissors and a full-nelson on
him, which drew *another* penalty, and the finger
bender applied an over-scissors to the scissors,
which amounted to another penalty against *him*.
Then the top wrestler, for no apparent reason, rabbit-
punched the finger bender, and that was that — Cliff
disqualified him for unsportsmanlike conduct.
(Maybe I should have *let* him be thrown on the
scorer's table without penalty, I thought.) Cliff was
raising the finger bender's arm in victory when I
spotted the losing heavyweight's mother; it was another easy gene-pool identification — this woman
was without question a heavyweight's mom.

In Maine that year — *only* in Maine — I had
heard us referees occasionally called "zebras." I presume this was a reference to our black-and-white-
striped shirts, and I presume that Cliff had previously
heard himself called a "zebra," too. Notwithstanding
our familiarity with the slur, neither Cliff nor I was
prepared for the particular assault of the heavyweight's mom. She lumbered manfully to the scorer's
table and ripped the microphone from the announcer's hands. She pointed at Cliff, who was

standing a little uncertainly in the middle of the mat when she spoke.

"Not even a zebra would fuck you," the mom said.

Despite the crowd's instinctive unruliness, they were as uncertain of how to respond to the claim made by the heavyweight's mother as Cliff Gallagher; the crowd stood or sat in stunned silence. Slowly, Cliff approached the microphone; Cliff may have been born in Kansas, but he was an old Oklahoma boy — he still walked like a cowboy, even in Maine.

"Is that clear enough?" Cliff asked the crowd.

It was a long way home from the middle of Maine, but all the way Cliff kept repeating, "Not even a zebra, Johnny." It would become his greeting for me, on the telephone, whenever he called.

That winter I took every refereeing job that I was offered. I didn't make much money, and I would never again see the likes of a tournament like that tournament in Maine. But the reason I was a referee at all, not to mention the reason I enjoyed it, was Cliff Gallagher. It was a great way to get back into wrestling.

"I told you — you're always going to love it," Ted Seabrooke said.

The Gold Medalist

In Iowa — I was a student at the Writers' Workshop from 1965 until 1967 — Vance Bourjaily befriended me, but Vance was not my principal teacher. For a brief moment I tried working with Nelson Algren, who — except for the unnamed Instructor C– from my unsuccessful days in Pittsburgh — represented my first encounter with a critic of an *un*constructive nature. I was attracted to Mr. Algren's rough charm, but he didn't much care for me or my writing. I was "too fancy" a writer for his taste, he told me; and, worse (I suspect), I was not a city boy who'd been schooled on the mean streets. I was a small-town boy and a private-school brat; I was even more privileged than Algren knew — I was a "faculty brat." The best tutor for a young writer, in Mr. Algren's clearly expressed view, was real life, by which I think he meant an *urban* life. In any case, my life had not been "real" enough to suit him; and it troubled him that I was a wrestler, not a boxer — the latter was superior to the former, in Mr. A.'s opinion. He was always good-natured in his teasing of me, but there was a detectable disdain behind his humor. And I was not a poker player, which I think further revealed to Algren the shallowness of my courage.

My friend the poet Donald Justice (a very *good* poker player, I'm told) once confided to me that Mr. Algren lost a lot of money in Iowa City — coming down from Chicago, as he did, and expecting to find the town full of rubes. He took me for a rube — and certainly I *was* — but he caused me no lasting wounds. Creative Writing, if honest at all, must be an occasionally unwelcoming experience. I appreciated Mr. Algren's honesty; his abrasiveness couldn't keep me from liking him.

I would not see Nelson Algren again until shortly before his death, when he moved to Sag Harbor and Kurt Vonnegut brought him to my house in Sagaponack for dinner. Again I liked him, and again he teased me; he was good at it. This time he claimed not to remember me from our Iowa days, although I went out of my way to remind him of our conversations; admittedly, since they had been few and brief, it's possible that Algren *didn't* remember me. But in saying goodnight he pretended to confuse me with *Clifford* Irving, the perpetrator of that notorious Howard Hughes hoax; he appreciated a good scam, Mr. Algren said. And when Vonnegut explained to him that I was not *that* Irving, Algren winked at me — he was still teasing me. (You shouldn't take a Creative Writing course, much less entertain the notion of becoming a writer, if you can't take a little teasing — or even a lot.)

But, thankfully, there were other teachers at Iowa. I was tempted to study with José Donoso, for I admired his writing and found him gracious — in every way that Nelson Algren was not. Then, upon first sight, I developed a schoolboy's unspoken crush on Mr. Donoso's wife; thereafter I could never look him in the eyes, which would not have made for a successful student-teacher relationship. And so my principal teacher and mentor at the Iowa Writers' Workshop became Kurt Vonnegut. (I once had a brawl in a pool hall — convincingly demonstrating, although never to Nelson Algren and not in his presence, that wrestling is superior to boxing — because a fellow student at Iowa, a boxer, had called Mr. Vonnegut a "science-fiction hack"; this false charge was made without the offending student's having read a single one of Kurt's books, "only the covers.")

Did Kurt Vonnegut "teach" me how to write? Certainly not; yet Mr. Vonnegut saved me time, and he encouraged me. He pointed out some bad habits in my early work (in my first novel-in-progress), and he also pointed out those areas of storytelling and characterization that were developing agreeably enough. I would doubtless have made these discoveries on my own, but later — maybe much later. And *time,* to young and old writers alike, is valuable.

Later, as a teacher — I taught at the Workshop from 1972 until 1975 — I encountered many future writers among my students at Iowa. I didn't "teach" Ron Hansen or Stephen Wright or T. Coraghessan Boyle or Susan Taylor Chehak or Allan Gurganus or Gail Harper or Kent Haruf or Robert Chibka or Douglas Unger how to write, but I hope I may have encouraged them and saved them a little time. I did nothing more for them than Kurt Vonnegut did for me, but in my case Mr. Vonnegut — and Mr. Yount and Mr. Williams — did quite a lot.

I'm talking about technical blunders, the perpetration of sheer boredom, point-of-view problems, the different qualities of first-person and third-person voice, the deadening effect of exposition in dialogue, the crippling limitations of the present tense, the intrusions upon narrative momentum caused by puerile and pointless experimentation — and on and on. You just say: "You're good at that." And: "You're not very good at this." These areas of complaint are so basic that most talented young writers will eventually spot their mistakes themselves, but perhaps at a time when a substantial revision of the manuscript might be necessary — or worse, after the book is published.

Tom Williams once told me that I had a habit of attributing mythological proportions and legendary status to my characters — he meant before my characters had *done* anything to earn such attribution. (The same could be said of García Márquez, but in my case Mr. Williams's criticism was valid.) And Kurt

Vonnegut once asked me if I thought there was something intrinsically funny about the verbs "peek" and "peer." (What could be "intrinsically funny" about *verbs?* I thought. But Mr. Vonnegut meant that I overused these verbs to a point of self-conscious cuteness; he was right.)

When I was a student at the Iowa Writers' Workshop, Gail Godwin was a student there, and the future (1989) National Book Award winner, John Casey, was in my class — Gail and John were "taught" by Kurt Vonnegut, too.

Mr. Casey recently reminded me that Ms. Godwin was, upon her arrival in Iowa City, already a writer to take seriously. Casey recalled how Gail defended herself in the parking lot of the English & Philosophy Building from the unwanted attentions of a lecherous fellow student, who shall remain nameless.

"Please leave me alone," Ms. Godwin warned the offending student, "or I shall be forced to wound you with a weapon you can ill afford to be wounded by in a town this small."

The threat was most mysterious, not to mention writerly, but the oafish lecher was not easily deterred. "And what might that weapon be, little lady?" the lout allegedly asked.

"Gossip," Gail Godwin replied.

Andre Dubus and James Crumley were also students at the Writers' Workshop then. I remember a picnic at Vance Bourjaily's farm, where a friendly pie-fight ensued; Dubus or Crumley, bare-chested and reasonably hairy, was struck in the chest by a Boston cream pie. Who threw the pie, and why, escapes my ever-failing memory — I swear I didn't do it. David Plimpton is a possible candidate. Plimpton and I were wrestling teammates at Exeter — he was the

team captain a year ahead of me — and our being together in Iowa seemed an unlikely irony to us both.
(Plimpton had wrestled at Yale.)

These were the days before the fabulous Carver-
Hawkeye Arena; the Iowa wrestling room was up
among the girders of the old fieldhouse. Dave Mc-
Cuskey was the coach; he was friendly to me, but
ever-critical of my physical condition. I was capable
of wrestling, hard, with Coach McCuskey's boys, but
only for three or four minutes; then I needed to sit
down and rest on the mat with my back against the
wrestling-room wall. McCuskey frowned upon this
behavior: if I wasn't in shape to go head to head with
his boys for "the full nine minutes," then I shouldn't
be wrestling at all. I was content to shoot takedowns
until I got tired; then I'd rest against the wall — and
then I'd shoot a few more takedowns. Coach Mc-
Cuskey didn't like me resting against the wall.

David Plimpton, who was as out-of-shape as I
was, also enjoyed sparring with Coach McCuskey's
Iowa wrestlers. Plimpton told me that McCuskey was
similarly disapproving of him. From Plimpton's and
my point of view, we were making a contribution:
we were offering our aging bodies as extra workout
partners for McCuskey's kids. But it was Coach Mc-
Cuskey's wrestling room; he set the tone — and I respected him. No resting against the wall. As a
consequence, my appearances (and Plimpton's) in
the Iowa wrestling room were sporadic — I went
there only when I wanted to punish myself.

A happy solution might have been for Plimpton
and me to wrestle together, but Plimpton had been a
191-pounder at Yale (when I'd been a 130-pounder
at Pitt); we'd both put on 15 or 20 pounds since then,

but we couldn't wrestle together — there was about a 60-pound difference between us.

Seven years later, when I would go back to Iowa to teach at the Writers' Workshop, the wrestling room was still in the girders of the old fieldhouse but the atmosphere in the room had changed. Gary Kurdelmeir, a former national champion for Iowa in 1958, was the head coach. In '72, Kurdelmeir's new assistant coach arrived in Iowa City — Dan Gable, fresh from a Gold-Medal performance in the Munich Olympics at 149½ pounds. In Kurdelmeir and Gable's wrestling room, there were lots of "graduate students" (as Plimpton and I had been in 1965–67) and other postcollege wrestlers. The years I taught at the Workshop (1972–75) were the beginning of Iowa's dominance of collegiate wrestling under Dan Gable. (As the head coach, Gary Kurdlemeir won two national team titles for Iowa — in '75 and '76 — but the head-coaching job would soon be Gable's; he won his first team championship in '78. J. Robinson, now the head coach at the University of Minnesota, became Gable's assistant.)

Brad Smith, Chuck Yagla, Dan Holm, Chris Campbell — they were all in the Iowa wrestling room at that time, and they would all become national champions. That wrestling room was the most intense wrestling room I have ever seen; yet Gable and Kurdlemeir were happy to have you there, contributing — even if you were good for no more than two minutes before you had to go rest against the wall. In that room, two minutes was all I was good for.

At several of Iowa's dual meets, I sat beside the former Iowa coach, Dave McCuskey, who was retired; as fellow spectators, Coach McCuskey and I had no philosophical differences of opinion. Everyone admired Gable: with three national collegiate titles at Iowa State (just *one* loss in his entire college career), he drew a crowd — not only at Iowa's matches but in the wrestling room. Everyone wanted to wrestle with him — if only for two minutes. In those years, I generally chose easier workout partners, but there were no easy workout partners in that Iowa room. Like everyone else, I couldn't resist the occasional thrill (and instant humiliation) of wrestling Dan Gable. I never scored a point on him, of course. In this failure, I was in good company: in the 1972 Olympics at Munich, where Gable won the Gold Medal, none of his opponents scored a point on him either.

To win the Olympics in freestyle wrestling without losing a single point is akin to winning the men's final at Wimbledon in straight sets, 6–0, 6–0, 6–0; or perhaps a four-game sweep of the World Series, while holding the losing team scoreless. It's rarer still that Gable's dominance as a wrestler has undergone the transition from competitor to coach with equal success: in 1995, Iowa won its fourth NCAA title of the last five years — and its fifteenth national championship of the last 21. In '95, Iowa also captured its 22nd straight Big 10 crown; I believe that's a record for consecutive collegiate championships — in any conference, in any sport. Out of 10 weight classes, the '95 Iowa team advanced seven wrestlers to the semifinal round of the NCAA tournament. Ever the perfectionist, Dan Gable was disappointed: Iowa's 150-pounder and 190-pounder were both defending national champions — in the finals, they both lost.

It's always the wrestling I remember; it marks the

years. My memories of being a student at the Iowa Writers' Workshop, and of being a teacher there, frequently intermingle; I even confuse my fellow students with my students. But I can manage to sort out the years (not only in Iowa) by the workout partners that I had, and by recalling who the coach was — and in which wrestling room I worked out. And possibly it is a testimony to the practical, businesslike atmosphere of the Writers' Workshop that I remember my student days and my teaching days as much the same. I felt fortunate to be at Iowa — in both capacities.

The Death of a Friend

Don Hendrie, Jr., who was a classmate of mine at Exeter, although I hardly knew him there, was another student at the Iowa Workshop (in my *student* days); he is the author of four novels and one collection of short stories — in addition to serving for several years as the director of the graduate writing program at the University of Alabama. The coincidence of my being at Iowa with Don Hendrie is an even more unlikely irony than my being there with David Plimpton, because, when Hendrie and I were students at Exeter, we both sought the affections of the same young woman; she married Hendrie, who in Iowa became my closest friend. Our children would grow up together. When I was teaching and coaching at a small college in Vermont, Hendrie would be teaching at a small college in New Hampshire — about an hour's distance. When he taught at Mount Holyoke College, I followed him there.

Hendrie had a habit of including the physical descriptions of his friends in his novels, where we would appear as characters under fictional names; this never offended me, because Hendrie's narrative voice was consistently teasing and affectionate. My last appearance in a Don Hendrie novel was as a character named Barry Kessler, a screenwriter, in *A Survey of the Atlantic Beaches*. He saw me as "a rabid, middle-aged athlete given to the long run and the heavy weight."

We had a lifelong argument about Oscar Wilde — Hendrie liked him, I don't. By the way, I bear no loathing for writers because they are minor; it isn't Wilde's being minor that troubles me. And my dislike of Wilde was never fueled by his homosexuality — that "gross indecency," as it was called in Britain at the time Wilde was sentenced to two years in prison, from which he never recovered. On the contrary, one has to like Oscar Wilde for championing "obscenity," as sodomy was then presumed to be. But what I hate about Wilde is that he was an inferior writer who delighted in aiming his one-liner wit at his superiors; did he so envy Dickens and Flaubert that he felt compelled to scorn them?

Wilde shouldn't have spent a day in jail for being "obscene," but posterity will relegate Wilde to where he belongs, which is where he can already be most widely found: in coffee-table books of harmless quotations. By comparison, Flaubert and Dickens still have actual *readers*. (What is ordinary about Wilde is that there's no shortage of writers whose lifestyles are more deserving of attention than their work.)

I say all this because the centenary of Oscar Wilde's wrongful imprisonment occurred as I was rewriting this memoir; predictably, the centenary was not allowed to pass without all manner of overpraise being heaped upon Wilde. Whereas I was prepared to read that "Wilde's imprisonment ranks as one of literature's greatest tragedies," I was *not* prepared to suffer the Wilde centenary hyperbole in silence; yet my friend Don Hendrie had died — there was no one else I wanted to argue about Oscar Wilde with.

Hendrie often found a means of furthering personal disputes in his fiction, which I accepted as a charming eccentricity. "Barry Kessler posed in the doorway with his hands on his hips," Hendrie wrote. "He wore running shoes, fresh white socks to his knees, filmy green shorts, and an immaculate T-shirt with the words 'Oscar Wilde Sucks' in diminutive letters over the breast pocket. A short man, narrow of waist, large of chest, he had the gone-craggy face of a former (and successful) child actor who had kept his confidence and improved upon it with a great deal of strenuous effort."

Don Hendrie died in March of '95, just two days before my son Colin's 30th birthday. Suffering from Parkinson's, Hendrie had lost his fine grasp of the language in a stroke four years earlier; his vocabulary had abandoned him. As a fellow writer, I admired how courageous and uncomplaining he was about losing his *words*. Only a month before he died, we were talking in my house in Vermont, and Hendrie — at a loss for the word he wanted — left the dinner table and walked into the kitchen. There he patiently patted the refrigerator. "*This* thing," he said, "where the food goes to be cold."

He had an automobile accident, in Maine, about a week or so later. When he was released from the hospital, he was frail and disoriented; in addition to the debilitation of the Parkinson's, something was wrong with his heart. He spent the night before he died at his ex-mother-in-law's house in Exeter with his elder son; they had breakfast together the next morning, and Hendrie died of a heart attack while walking around the block. He fell over on Front Street, the same street where I had grown up in my grandmother's house. (Hendrie wasn't a native of Exeter; he had attended the academy and married a town girl, but over the years Exeter had become a kind of home to him.)

It was Hendrie I sold my motorcycle to, when I became a father. We were married within a couple of years of each other; I was an usher at his wedding, in Exeter — the wedding-reception was at the Exeter Inn, which is also on Front Street, where he died. (We were divorced within a couple of years of each other, too.)

I miss him. And when I think of him, I see him as a student at Iowa when I was a student, too, and we would read aloud what we'd written to each other, and say things of small importance — such as, "Oscar Wilde sucks" — which, of course, were things we thought were of no small importance then.

I was newly married, and recently a father for the first time; Hendrie was in love, and about to be married — and soon to be a father, too. And, as writers — actually, would-be writers — we were just getting started. We both had jobs in the university library, restacking the returned books. We both had football-season jobs, selling pennants and buttons and stadium cushions and cowhorns and bells at the Iowa home games. We both worked as waiters in a nauseating restaurant out on the Coralville strip. The point is, Hendrie and I saw each other every day, and we were doing a variety of mindless things, but every day we were excited, because we were going to be writers. That's how I want to remember him.

What Vonnegut Said

I don't remember my fellow student Tom McHale, the future author of *Farragan's Retreat* and *Principato*. I must have met him in Iowa City, but I never really knew him, nor do I recall McHale's "terrific Belgian girlfriend"; the description is John Casey's — John has expressed his surprise that I fail to remember her. (Tom McHale died, an apparent suicide, in 1982; some say he had a heart attack.)

I do remember Jonathan Penner — tall and particularly striking-looking in profile. I recall him running laps on the indoor track, where I ran every day; in my memory, Penner was a strong and tireless runner — and a lot faster than I was. But my principal attentions at Iowa were given to my developing writing; in writers' memories, real people are often not as clear as our created characters. It wouldn't surprise me if Penner were to ring me up, upon reading this, and tell me that he never ran at all — not one lap. (It would amaze me, however, to hear that Jonathan Penner is a *short* person.)

Of course I could phone Andre Dubus and ask him if it was his chest or Crumley's that was splattered with Boston cream pie; I could call David Plimpton and ask him if he threw the pie, and whose chest he hit. But I believe the gaps and even the errors in my memory are truthfulness of another kind: what we fiction writers forget, or what we get wrong, is part of what a "memoir" means to us. (I do recall that

Plimpton caused both envy and indignation by selling a short story to one of those magazines that are routinely concealed from wives and children, and that he spent the money on a shotgun, which prompted one sour fellow student to express the hope that Plimpton would use his new weapon on himself.)

And what of my classmates at Iowa who did *not* become writers? One of them is a high-school English teacher, and one of them is a law-school professor, and another one is a clinical psychologist. (The psychologist is David Plimpton.)

In addition to the many published writers among my students at Iowa, my two best students at Bread Loaf, Patty Dann and Elisabeth Hyde, and my best student at Brandeis, Carol Markson, are working novelists. But what about those Creative Writing students of mine — not only at Iowa but elsewhere — who did *not* go forth to take the literary world by storm? One of them is a highly respected editor in a venerable New York publishing house; another makes a rather good living writing Westerns; a third is the headmaster of a distinguished private school; many are English teachers, at both the high-school and the college level; and last but not least — in fact, this is someone I am particularly proud of — is a champion-class female bodybuilder, Karen Andes, who has written a book about strength conditioning for women. I was not of much help to Karen with her first novel, which remains unpublished, but I was the first person who took her to a gym and put a dumbbell in her hand. Now I am learning from her, for — at my age (I am 53) — a book about strength conditioning for female bodybuilders is considerably above my present capacities.

Yet what I remember best about being a student

at Iowa was that sense of myself as being married, and being a father. It separated me from the majority of the other students; they had the time to talk about writing — my impression was that they talked about it endlessly. Except with Hendrie, I had no time for talking; I taught only one undergraduate writing course but I had three part-time jobs. When I wasn't working, I was either looking after my son Colin or I was writing.

We didn't have a television. When there was something of interest on TV, I put Colin in the stroller and walked around the block to the Vonneguts' house. It was in Kurt's house that I watched the Six Day War, holding Colin on my lap. It was on the occasion of another television event, with Colin again on my lap or destroying some household possession of the Vonneguts', that I remember having a conversation with Kurt about what I would *do* to support my writing habit.

Teachers and coaches had been good to me, Kurt included. I presumed I would get a teaching job, and I would coach wrestling. I certainly had no illusions about my writing being self-supporting. I told Kurt that I wasn't going to make myself miserable by even imagining that I would make a living from my *writing*.

"You may be surprised," Vonnegut told me. "I think capitalism is going to treat you okay."

The Ph.D. Vote

My first teaching job was at Windham College (now defunct) in Putney, Vermont. Windham was one of those colleges that prospered, briefly, during the time of the Vietnam War; it was richly populated with students who wouldn't have been students if they hadn't been trying to stay out of Vietnam, but some of these nonstudents were the best Creative Writing students I ever had — and one real student among them was my future business manager, Willard Saperston. When the war was over, Windham folded, but by then I had already resigned.

There was no wrestling team at Windham when I came there. I prevailed upon the college to buy a wrestling mat, which I installed in a former storage room of the fieldhouse, where I coached wrestling as a so-called club sport. About a half-dozen former high-school wrestlers, including a couple of Vietnam vets, were the core of the club; compared to every wrestling room I had ever worked out in, it was unsatisfactory, but I had my workout partners — I couldn't complain.

When the college went belly-up and auctioned all of its portable holdings, I went to the auction with the hope that I could buy the wrestling mat. But the mat was sold to a college down South as part of a package of athletic equipment — the whirlpool baths from the training room, and three sets of Universal Gyms, and all the free weights from the weight room. I don't think the buyer even wanted the mat — the college down South didn't offer wrestling as a sport — but I was unable to extricate the mat from the overall package.

Notwithstanding Windham's collapse, Putney was a good home for my children, and my primary residence for the 18 years of my first marriage; my ex-wife, Shyla, still lives there. The same Windham student who would become my business manager was also handy as a carpenter; on my Putney property, Willard Saperston converted a tool shed — one of the small outbuildings beside the barn — into an office for me. I would write the better part of five novels in that tiny box of a building, which Shyla has now restored to what it originally was: a tool shed. As I've said, Willard Saperston, who created my first office, now "manages" my money. (I sense a kind of symmetry to this story, not unlike my old friend Don Hendrie dying within sight of the inn where he had his wedding reception and the house where I was born.)

And despite Windham's relatively short life, I would keep coming back to Putney. I went away for a year, to Vienna — where my second son, Brendan, was born in 1969 — and I was three years away from Putney when I returned to Iowa to teach at the Workshop; there was another year away, when I first taught at Mount Holyoke; and another, when I taught at Brandeis. But in between those times away, I was in Putney, writing in the tool shed.

For the writing of my first four novels (*The World According to Garp* was my fourth) I usually had a full-time job — the two exceptions being an award from the Rockefeller Foundation (they don't give grants to individual writers anymore) and a Guggenheim Fellowship. I had only two years of being a full-time writer between 1967 and 1978; yet, in those 11 years, I wrote and published four novels.

There was one other year when I didn't teach Creative Writing or coach wrestling: that was when I took time off to write a screenplay of my first novel, *Setting Free the Bears*. In that year, I was never once paid at the agreed-upon time — I sent desperate telegrams from Vienna to Los Angeles, begging for the next installment of my screenwriting fee. Worse, I had no time for my day job, which was to write a second novel; and the screenplay, after five drafts, was never made into a film. The point being: this was less of a *writing* year than any year in which I taught and coached full-time.

A footnote: the fellowship I received from the National Endowment for the Arts, to complete my third novel, was not enough money for a family of four, which I was supporting, to live on for a single summer; I spent the "fellowship" to rebuild the only bathroom in the Putney house — and I took a summer job. I'm not complaining about having to get a job, *or* about the NEA — the NEA was only giving me what the NEA could afford.

I've heard many of my fellow writers say that a writer must make it on his own and not lean on the university for assistance; they say that a writer who teaches for his daily bread — so that he's not putting financial burdens on his writing — is not a real writer . . . only hedging his bets. But in my own experience I *wanted* my writing to be free from the pressure to publish it too soon — free from the need to make a living from it. Friends who were constantly interrupting their novels-in-progress to write for magazines, or who published novels badly in need of rewriting because they needed the advances, have suffered the constraints of time and money as, truly, I never did.

Nowadays, nothing angers me as much (from my fellow writers) as to see those fortunate souls who are self-supporting in the writing business make their insensitive pronouncements at various Creative Writing programs across the United States. In the presence of good writers who teach for a living, these best-selling authors are fond of denouncing the university as too-safe a haven; they frequently urge student writers to make it on their own — even, hypocritically, to starve a little. This is *idle* hypocrisy, of course; it is doubly hard to tolerate when the proselytizing author is expensively well-tailored and riding a multibook contract in 25 languages.

Creative Writing courses are an economic necessity for writers in this country; for the writers who teach them, they are essential to their lives *as writers*. And for those few students who truly benefit from them, they are a gift of encouragement and time; writers — young writers, particularly — need more of both.

There is a quandary here, however: not every writer can or should teach Creative Writing. Many of my writer friends are simply too standoffish for the requisite social contact of the job; some are preternaturally uncomfortable in the presence of "young people" — many more are too thin-skinned to endure the nastiness of English Department politics.

I once was a member of an English Department (at Windham) wherein a senior full professor proposed that any department member without a Ph.D. should not be permitted to vote on matters concerning the curriculum. I was the *only* member of that English Department without a Ph.D., and so I sought to defend myself by saying that I agreed; I even flattered my colleagues by telling them that the writing of a Ph.D. thesis was a "massive" accomplishment. I thought it fair to warn them, however, that I was soon going to publish my first novel, which they would surely accept as an undertaking equal to their theses; I would wait to have a vote in the department until my novel was published.

I felt it also fair to warn them that I intended to write a second novel, and a third — and, if I were able, many more after those — and that with the publication of each novel I expected to be granted an additional vote. To my surprise, my argument was not met with the good humor with which I had delivered my defense, but the proposition — that only Ph.D.s be permitted to vote on matters pertaining to the curriculum — was narrowly defeated.

Many writers I know would rather write nonstop for magazines or newspapers than subject themselves to the pompous lunacy of academics. But, in my case, I got up early to write — having children in the house helps. I met with my students in an organized fashion, I daydreamed through English Department meetings, and then I went to the wrestling room — to a great number and variety of wrestling rooms — and I forgot about everything for two hours. Fortunately for me, this meant I hurried my writing for no one. And I could turn a deaf ear to that contact with the university community which I know is truly odious and intolerable to many writers. The point being: writers *usually* need to support themselves by means other than that writing which they most desire to do. And the economics of being a writer aren't getting any better — except for the lucky few, like me.

My First Novel

In 1968 I was paid an advance of $7,500 for my first novel, which Random House published in 1969. Joe Fox was my editor. Still at Random House, and still my in-house editor there, Mr. Fox told me that the average advance for a literary first novel today — "with expectations similar to the expectations that I had for *Setting Free the Bears*" — is $12,500. (Richard Seaver, my editor at Arcade, disputes Mr. Fox's figures; Mr. Seaver argues that the more common figure today is *still* $7,500.)

In 1968, with a wife and one child, I could *almost* have lived for a year on $7,500, but the pressures this would have put on me to too-hastily produce a second novel were unwelcome. I kept my teaching and coaching jobs, and I wrote my second novel — and my third and fourth — at a restrained pace.

Trust me: it was more possible for a family of three to live on $7,500 in 1968 than it is even imaginable for a family of three to survive on $12,500 today — for the moment assuming that Joe Fox's higher figure for an "average advance" is correct. And what did *Setting Free the Bears* actually sell? About 8,000 hardcover copies — a good number for that time, far exceeding both my publisher's and my own expectations. A first printing of a novel of a similar kind, today, would run between 7,500 and 10,000 copies — with the notable difference that, *today,* a sale of 8,000 copies would make neither the publisher nor the author feel at all as secure as Joe Fox and I were made to feel in 1969.

(I never expected, not quite 10 years later, that *The World According to Garp* would enable me to support myself by my writing alone. I don't miss teaching Creative Writing — it was hard and time-consuming work. But it was honorable, worthwhile work, and of use to my students — if only to a few of them.)

In a separate conversation I asked Mr. Fox if he would publish *Setting Free the Bears* if it came across his desk at Random House today. My friend Joe hesitated, just a moment too long, before saying, "Well, yes, *but* . . ." I think the answer is no.

My Two Champions

I taught Creative Writing, at one place or another, for a total of 11 years; yet I continued to coach wrestling long after the publication of *The World According to Garp* freed me of the financial need for an outside job. I coached until 1989, when I was 47, not only because I preferred coaching to teaching but for a variety of other reasons; the foremost reason was the success of my two elder sons in the sport — they were better wrestlers (and better athletes) than I had been, and coaching them meant more to me than my own modest accomplishments as a competitor.

Colin, who wrestled at Northfield Mount Hermon, was a prep-school All-American at 152 pounds — at the annual Lehigh tournament in 1983. Colin also won the New England Class A title at 160 pounds in '83; ironically, he pinned a guy from Exeter in the finals. Colin was voted the Outstanding Wrestler in the Class A tournament, for which he received the Ted Seabrooke Memorial trophy. I would have been happier if Ted had been alive to see Colin win the championship. Ted had seen Colin wrestle only once, when Colin was just starting the sport.

"He's got much longer arms than *you* ever had," Coach Seabrooke told me. "You ought to show him a crossface-cradle." By the time Colin was a Class A

Champion and an All-American, he was pinning half his opponents with a crossface-cradle.

At six feet two and a half, Colin was tall for a middleweight. I think that his college coach was well intentioned but mistaken to put Colin on a weight-lifting program in order to beef him up to the 177-pound class, and then to 190. Colin was not a natural light heavyweight; he was at his best as a *tall* middleweight. Nowadays — Colin is 30 years old — he stays out of the weight room and rides a mountain bike; he's a very lean 175.

His younger brother Brendan was, like me, a lightweight; *un*like me, Brendan was a *tall* lightweight — at five feet eleven and a half, Brendan is so thin that he looks like a six-footer. (I'm only five feet eight, "normal" for a lightweight.) Unremarkably, both Colin and Brendan grew up in wrestling rooms; rolling around on a mat was second nature to them — I remember that Brendan learned to walk on a wrestling mat. Unlike Colin, who didn't start competing as a wrestler before his prep-school years, Brendan had already won six junior-school New England tournaments before his prep-school career began. (Brendan won his first wrestling tournament at the weight of 82½ pounds.) By the time Brendan was wrestling for Vermont Academy, the other wrestlers — and, especially, the other coaches — in the New England Class A league were watching him closely to see if he would live up to the reputation of being Colin Irving's little brother; this was a burden for Brendan, largely because his proneness to injury was unlike anything Colin had ever suffered.

Brendan placed third in the New England Class A tournament his sophomore year at Vermont Academy; it was a good finish to a bad season for him, because the tournament was only a month after he'd had knee surgery for torn cartilage — he'd missed most of the '87 season. In '88, he was seeded second in the Class A tournament; he'd had an undefeated dual-meet season, excepting two losses to injury-default. Then, in the semifinals of the tournament, he reinjured the knee and was pinned by a boy he'd pinned earlier in the season; the injury forced him to drop out of the Class A's — and he reinjured the same knee at the Navy wrestling camp in Annapolis that summer. He spent the rest of the summer and the fall in physical therapy.

Colin lost a close match in the Class A finals his junior year — to a boy he'd beaten easily in the dual-meet season. Colin didn't win the New England Class A title until his senior year. Brendan's senior year began badly. A separated shoulder and a torn rotator-cuff tendon eliminated him from a Christmas tournament. Brendan was the 1989 team captain at Vermont Academy, but he would spend the heart of the season on the bench. When his shoulder healed, he was back in the lineup for three matches; he won all three — then he sat out another three weeks with mononucleosis. (Then he knocked out a front tooth.)

The week before the New England Class A's, Brendan was wrestling at St. Paul's when the St. Paul's wrestler, who was losing at the time and re-peatedly being put in a crossface-cradle, bent back two of Brendan's fingers on his right hand and broke them at the big knuckle joints. Under the finger-bending rule (all four or none), Brendan won the match, despite having to default with the injury. But the damage had been done: the fingers wouldn't heal by the time of the tournament — Brendan would wrestle at the Class A's with two broken fingers.

To add insult to injury, the mother of the St. Paul's wrestler objected to the referee's decision to award the match to Brendan because of her son's illegal hold; when a wrestler is injured by an illegal hold, and cannot continue wrestling, he wins. But the St. Paul's mother declared that Brendan had been injured prior to the match; she'd seen a Band-Aid on one of his fingers — one of the now-broken fingers. (Brendan had skinned a knuckle while scraping the ice off his car's windshield that morning, on his way to weigh in.) I had to restrain myself from sending the St. Paul's mother a videocassette of the match. The St. Paul's wrestler not only clearly broke Brendan's fingers; with his other hand, Brendan was pointing to his bent fingers — to draw the referee's attention to the foul — when the two fingers broke. The ref had made the right call, but he should have spotted the injury-in-progress — he could have prevented it.

Given the accumulation of Brendan's injuries, and his small number of matches in the '89 season, the seeding committee at the New England Class A tournament was entirely justified in seeding Brendan no higher than fifth in the 135-pound class; there were seven other wrestlers in the weight class with winning records. As his coach — I was an assistant coach at Vermont Academy for one year and the head coach for Brendan's last two seasons — I had contemplated moving Brendan up to the 140-pound class. In previous seasons, Brendan had pinned the two best wrestlers who would be the finalists in that weight class; in the 1989 Class A's, 140 was a weaker weight than 135. But Brendan, who was always admirably stubborn — even as a small child — insisted that 135 was *his* weight class; he didn't want to move up. (No wrestler wants to move *up* a weight class.)

The New England Class A tournament was at Exeter that year — in the new gym, where I'd never wrestled. (I have no idea what the pit is used for now.) I had a good team at little Vermont Academy in '89. In the Class A team standings, we would finish third — behind Deerfield and Exeter, two much bigger schools. I would send three Vermont Academy wrestlers to the finals, and two of them would win — Brendan was one of Vermont's two champions. He pinned the number-four seed from Northfield Mount Hermon in the quarterfinals, he pinned the number-one seed from Hyde in the semifinals, and he pinned the number-two seed from Worcester in the finals; he stuck his broken fingers, which were rebroken in the semifinals, in a bucket of ice between the rounds.

Tom Williams, who would die of cancer in three years, came to the tournament. Colin was there. My wife, Janet, was there; for two years, she'd not missed a match of Brendan's — and she'd taken what seemed, at the time, to be an excessive number of photographs. (As time passes, I'm grateful for every picture.) My mother had come up from Florida to see the tournament. And my old Exeter teammate, Charles C. ("Brute") Krulak — *General* Krulak — had come to see Brendan, too. Chuck had seen Brendan win the Lakes Region tournament (now known as the Northern New England tournament) the previous year; he'd promised Brendan that he would come to see him wrestle in the New England Class A's — but only if Brendan would promise to win the tournament. Brendan had promised, and Brendan had done it. (To be truthful, I'd always known he *could*. But he'd been so banged-up, I didn't think he *would*.)

I had spent so many hours of my life at wrestling

The Phillips Exeter Academy wrestling team, 1961—Captain John Irving (front row, center). Irving's regular workout partners were Mike McClave (front row, second from right) and Al Keck (front row, second from left). Larry Palmer, who ate the famous half-pound piece of toast, is seated to Irving's right. The man in the coat and tie is Coach Ted Seabrooke. PHOTO: '61 PEAN

John Irving (on top) at 133 pounds in '61. Despite two undefeated dual-meet seasons, he never won a New England title. PHOTO: '61 PEAN

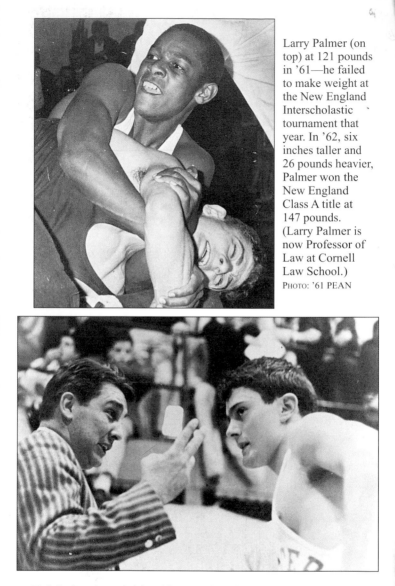

Larry Palmer (on top) at 121 pounds in '61—he failed to make weight at the New England Interscholastic tournament that year. In '62, six inches taller and 26 pounds heavier, Palmer won the New England Class A title at 147 pounds. (Larry Palmer is now Professor of Law at Cornell Law School.) PHOTO: '61 PEAN

Ted Seabrooke coaching 137-pounder Al Keck in '61. The fans are draped on the rails of the overhanging wooden track that circumscribed "the pit" at Exeter. PHOTO: '61 PEAN

Cliff Gallagher coaching in the Exeter wrestling room in 1966. It must be before practice, because the door to the wrestling room is partially open and there are so few bodies rolling around; Cliff always came to practice early. The boy sitting on the mat must be a first-year wrestler— he's not wearing wrestling shoes. PHOTO: BRADFORD F. HERZOG

In the University of Iowa wrestling room, 1973: Dan Gable catches John Irving with a foot-sweep. PHOTO: GARY WINOGRAD

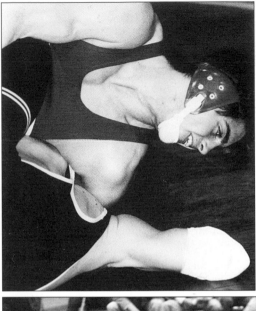

Irving's son Colin,
a 1983 prep-school
All-American
for Northfield
Mt. Hermon at
152 pounds—
Colin was also the
160 pound
New England
Class A Champion
in '83.
PHOTOGRAPHER UNKNOWN

Colin Irving completing an upper-body throw in the '83 New England Class A finals. Both the referee and the mat judge (upper left) are anticipating the pin. PHOTO: C.F.N.I.

Colin driving his Exeter opponent's shoulders to the mat in the 160-pound finals. PHOTO: C.F.N.I.

A legal headlock: the head encircled with an arm contained—in this case, Colin has his opponent's head and *both* his arms contained. Colin's pin in the finals at 1:45 of the first period won him the Ted Seabrooke Memorial Trophy for the Outstanding Wrestler in the '83 New England Class A tournament. PHOTO: C.F.N.I.

Summer '84: brothers—Colin with Brendan in Bridgehampton, New York. Colin is 19, and at his heaviest—about 195 pounds. Brendan is 14; he weighs about 105 pounds.

PHOTO: MARY ELLEN MARK

Brendan Irving (right), a tall 135-pounder with a proneness to injury: knee surgery in '87; reinjured the knee in '88; in '89, a separated shoulder, a torn rotator cuff, a lost front tooth, two broken fingers (right hand), mononucleosis, and a championship title.

PHOTO: STEVE IRVING

Brendan (black headgear) going for the pin: between 1984 and 1989, he won over 90 percent of his matches by a fall. Brendan was captain of the Vermont Academy team in '89. PHOTO: JANET IRVING

The semifinals: Brendan Irving, seeded fifth at 135 pounds, pins the number-one seed at 4:40 of the third period. Brendan pinned all his opponents in the '89 New England Class A tournament.
PHOTO: JANET IRVING

Coach Irving embracing son Brendan, seconds after Brendan won the '89 New England Class A title at 135 pounds—by a fall in 4:52 of the third period.

PHOTOGRAPHER UNKNOWN

At 31 pounds, Everett looks like a future middleweight.

PHOTO: COOK NEILSON

tournaments, and so many more hours in wrestling rooms. After Exeter and Pittsburgh and Iowa and Windham, there were the hours in the wrestling room at Amherst College and at the Buckingham Browne & Nichols School — and at Harvard, at the New York Athletic Club, at Northfield Mount Hermon, and at Vermont Academy, too. It was the perfect closure . . . that it should end at Exeter, where it began. I knew I would still be a visitor to the occasional wrestling room, and that I would still put on the shoes — if only to roll around on the mat with Colin or Brendan, or with another old *ex*-wrestler of my generation — but my life in wrestling effectively ended there.

I put my Vermont Academy wrestlers on the team bus with my co-coach, Mike Kennelly, and I asked Mike and the team to forgive me for not riding on the bus with them one last time. I wanted to ride back to Vermont in Colin's car, with Colin and Brendan. On the long drive home (we were still somewhere in New Hampshire), Colin picked up a speeding ticket — shortly after delivering a lecture to Brendan and me about the infallibility of his new radar-detection system. But we could laugh about the ticket. Brendan, like his brother before him, had won the New England Class A title. It was the happiest night of my life.

My Last Weigh-in

I suppose I could mope around, wishing that my wrestling career, as a competitor, had ended half as happily as my life as a coach. But I think I've been lucky: I've always taken more pleasure from my children than I have from myself; I enjoy my children, and I try not to drive them — I drive myself.

In 1976, I was in the middle of *The World According to Garp,* and I was struggling with it — the novel had three first chapters, and I couldn't decide whether Garp or his mother was the main character. I had applied for a Guggenheim, but I didn't know that this time I was going to get one — I'd applied and *hadn't* gotten one before. I was teaching at Mount Holyoke — an all-women's college in South Hadley, Massachusetts — and I was working out in the wrestling room at Amherst College.

Henry Littlefield was the coach at Amherst then; Henry was a heavyweight — everything about him was grand. He was more than expansive, he was eloquent; he was better than good-humored, he was jolly. Henry was very rare, a kind of Renaissance man among wrestling coaches, and the atmosphere in the Amherst wrestling room was, to Henry's credit, both aggressive and good-natured — a difficult combination to achieve.

I was living in a faculty house on the edge of the Mount Holyoke athletic fields — Colin and Brendan had a great "yard" to play in, and the college pool to swim in. I arranged my classes so that I could run or use the weight room at the Mount Holyoke gym in the early morning; I would write for a couple of hours at midday — and again, late at night, after the children were in bed. In the afternoons, I would drive to the Amherst wrestling room; I often took Colin with me — he was 10 and 11 that wrestling season.

I weighed 162 when that season began; there

was a postseason open tournament at Springfield College, and I intended to enter it at 136½ pounds. I was 34; the weight came off a little harder than it once had. After three months, I was holding my weight pretty easily at 142; the rest, as wrestlers frequently say, was "just water." That was all I was drinking in those months — just water. I had half a grapefruit with a teaspoon of honey for breakfast, and usually an apple or a banana; I had a bowl of oatmeal with a teaspoon of maple syrup for lunch; for dinner, I had some steamed fish and vegetables — lots of vegetables.

The last week before the tournament I was consistently weighing under 140, but I couldn't get under 138 — that was the "water." Then I got sick; I had bronchitis, and the antibiotic was intolerable on my empty stomach. The doctor told me I had to eat to save my stomach, or give up the antibiotic; I couldn't give up the antibiotic because I couldn't wrestle with bronchitis. I tried to soothe my stomach with a little yogurt, or some skim milk. I felt better, but in two days I weighed 145. I couldn't make the 136½-pound class, although I knew it was my best wrestling weight. The next weight class was 149½; I started eating more oatmeal, and I added some rice to the steamed fish and vegetables.

At Springfield I weighed in at 147, with all my clothes on — and I'd eaten breakfast before the weigh-ins. The other contenders at 149½ were stripped naked; they exhaled their last breath before stepping on the scales. I tried not to notice how big they were. I was in the training room, getting taped — I had had a "loose" left pinky finger all season; it kept dislocating at the big knuckle joint — and

Colin was looking grim. He was just beginning to get interested in wrestling; he had watched every detail of the weigh-ins.

"What are you thinking, Colin?" I asked him.

"You look like a thirty-six-pounder, Dad," Colin said.

I had never thought of the tournament at Springfield as my last tournament; all I'd hoped was to win one or two matches — and maybe place. It hadn't occurred to me that *watching* me lose might be painful for Colin. For Brendan, who was only six that spring, watching me wrestle, win or lose, was no big deal. Colin was old enough to realize that losing a wrestling match took a lot more out of me than losing a couple of sets of weekend tennis to a friend.

I drew a wild man in the first round. "Talent is overrated," Ted Seabrooke used to say. The guy was talented, and very dangerous, but he was also stupid. I was overcautious in the first period; I pulled out of a couple of sure takedowns because I was afraid of an upper-body throw that the wild man appeared to like in the underhook position — I came out ahead on takedowns, anyway. It was in the top position that the wild man was most dangerous. He was a leg man, and he hit me with a cheap tilt off a cross-body ride. (I was lucky it was only the tilt I got caught in; what the leg man was looking for was a bent-leg Turk — very uncomfortable.) I'd been leading 6–3, but the near-fall tied it up at 6–6 — and I was still on the bottom. Off the whistle, the leg man put in his near leg for the cross-body ride again, but this time I drilled his head into the mat before he could tie up my far arm; it was a most basic defense against a cross-body ride. Ted Seabrooke had warned me that the move wouldn't work against a *good* leg man, but this guy wasn't good — he was sloppy.

At first I thought I'd given him a concussion, but the wild man needed only 45 seconds of injury time to clear his head. He was angry at me. It's stupid to be angry at your opponent when you wrestle; also, my move had been perfectly legal — it was a Ted Seabrooke move, not a Cliff Gallagher move.

The referee had blown the whistle for the injury without giving me points for my reversal, so the score was still 6–6 — and I was still on the bottom. Off the whistle, Talented-but-Stupid put in his near leg again; once again, I protected my far arm and drilled his head into the mat. This time, the wild man needed a full minute to clear his head; thus he ran out of injury time — I won by injury default. The leg man was still angry; I could tell he thought he would have won the match if only I hadn't kept banging his head into the mat. I tend to think that he would have won, too; he seemed tireless to me — Tireless-but-Stupid. The wild man told me he hoped he would see me in one of the consolation rounds. If I lost in one of the championship rounds, at any time before the finals, I would drop down to the wrestle-backs, to the consolation brackets. It was conceivable that, if the leg man kept winning consolation matches, we would meet again. I hoped not.

("There is no such thing as *half* a cross-body ride," Coach Seabrooke used to say. "If you put a leg in, you've got to get hold of something else — unless you *want* to get your head drilled into the mat.")

In the locker room, the wild man with the headache was slamming lockers and kicking benches. I tried to stay away from him, but he followed me into the training room, where I had to have my "loose" left pinky finger retaped.

"I don't like anybody fuckin' with my head!" the leg man told me.

I felt old — I felt like a coach, not like a wrestler. Quoting Ted Seabrooke, I said: "If you put a leg in, you've got to get hold of something else — unless you *want* to get your head drilled into the mat."

"Shit!" the wild man shouted. (An inexplicable utterance — on a level of intelligence with *half* a cross-body ride.)

I was glad that Colin was in the stands with Brendan. Don Hendrie was in the stands with his children, too. When I was retaped, I went back up on the floor of the gym where the mats were laid out. A couple of Amherst wrestlers were also entered in the tournament; I watched their matches — all day, we would take turns coaching each other.

The toughest-looking kid in my weight class was a guy from the Coast Guard Academy; he was very slick on his feet, and he liked the high-crotch series for takedowns — my best defense, my whizzer, was worthless against a high-crotch. I knew I would have trouble with the guy from the Coast Guard, but I made the mistake of looking ahead, in the brackets, to my match with him; I overlooked the guy I had to wrestle in the next round.

He was someone in the military. He told me later he'd been stationed in Germany and had wrestled a lot of Greco-Roman matches over there; at the time, I think, he was stationed somewhere in New Jersey. I had my mind on the guy from the Coast Guard Academy, an error in concentration — and further indication, to me, that it was time to be a coach and not a wrestler. I gave up a couple of avoidable takedowns in the first period. Trailing by only three points in the second, I panicked too early and took an out-of-position shot at a takedown; he countered me to my back. When I fought off my back, I was trailing by seven points. Now it was time to panic. I managed an escape before the end of the period, but I couldn't complete a takedown before the buzzer; starting the third, I was six points behind. I got another escape, and a takedown, and he was hit with a penalty point for stalling; I rode him out, in the final period (I picked up another point for riding time), but I was aware of myself as a 36-pounder trying to turn a 49-pounder — he was too big to turn. I lost by a point. It was a respectable match, but I'd given it away in the first period. "Mental mistakes," Coach Seabrooke would have told me.

I dropped down into the consolation brackets and was pinned in my first match. I had scored with a snap-down in the first period — I was leading 2–1, because the guy had escaped from me following my takedown, when I got caught in a nice upper-body move: a bear hug with an inside trip. I was pinned before I could get my breath back. When I went to the training room, to get untaped, I saw that my left pinky finger was pointing straight up from the back of my hand; it was dislocated at the big knuckle joint again, but I was unaware of when or how it had happened. The trainer popped the finger back in place.

I was sitting on the training table, with my left hand packed in ice, when my opponent from the second round — the guy who'd been stationed in Germany and who was still in the military in New Jersey — came into the training room to ice his neck. He'd run into the guy from the Coast Guard Academy in the semifinals — he'd lost — and he wanted to know about the guy who'd just pinned me; he was a boy from Springfield College. I told the military man to watch out for the bear hug with the inside trip.

I still wasn't thinking that this was my last tournament; I didn't feel bad, although I was angry at myself for getting pinned. Then the military man and I shook hands, and I wished him luck the rest of the way; since I'd been eliminated from the tournament, and my children were there, I thought it was time to take the children home. I felt like having a beer, and eating as much as my shrunken stomach would hold.

In parting, the military man said: "Nice match, sir."

That was all. That was it. He meant me no harm. But the damage was done. He was probably 24, and I was 34, but when he called me "sir," I felt older than I feel now, at 53; I felt ancient. It was time to be a coach, but not a wrestler.

Later, I phoned Ted Seabrooke. (At the time, Ted's death was four years away; he'd been sick, but I had no idea how bad things were going to get for him — I doubt that he knew either.) I gave Ted the results of the tournament, and I told him that I'd decided to call an end to competing as a wrestler — I told him the "sir" story.

"Johnny, Johnny," Coach Seabrooke said. "If the guy's in the military, he calls *everyone* 'sir.'" Incredibly, that hadn't occurred to me. But the damage had been done.

It was the last time I would weigh in. Only a week before the tournament, I'd weighed 138 pounds. At the tournament, I'd weighed 147 — in all my clothes. When I weighed myself after Easter dinner, that same spring of '76, I weighed 165 pounds — my "natural" weight. (I weigh 167 pounds today.)

I remember that, 12 days after Brendan won the Class A title at 135 pounds, we were in a gym in Anguilla in the British West Indies. I was riding the stationary bike and Brendan was fooling around with the treadmill, making it go as fast as it could — and then trying to jump on it, and stay on it, while it was running. There were scales in the locker room; before we went for a swim, Brendan stripped down and weighed himself. Only 12 days earlier, I had seen him weigh in at 134½ pounds — now he weighed 152. That was six years ago. It was only yesterday that I called Brendan in Colorado.

"What do you weigh?" I asked him. (Wrestlers always ask this question.)

There was a pause while Brendan left the phone to weigh himself, and I overheard the O. J. Simpson trial on CNN — all the way from Colorado. (I was phoning from Vermont.) Then Brendan came back to the phone.

"One-fifty-two," he told me.

(As of this writing, my third son, Everett, who was born in Rutland, Vermont, in October of '91, is three-and-a-half years old; he weighs 31 pounds. It is my observation that Everett is tall for his age, and his weight is slightly below average for his height. His hands look large, compared to the rest of him. If I had to hazard a guess, I'd say he looks like a future middleweight.)

Merely a Human Being

My involvement with wrestling has been widely misunderstood, even among my friends. John Cheever was a friend to me when we both taught at Iowa; he was a fan of Italian cooking, as I am, and we used to watch Monday Night Football at my house in Iowa City over a dish of pasta. Cheever once wrote a letter to Allan Gurganus in which he said: "John has always struck me as having been saddened by the discovery that to have been captain of the Exeter wrestling team was a fleeting honor."

Mr. Cheever was terribly correct, and often right about many things: he once warned me that it was a weakness in my writing that I described sexual acts and people consuming food, for these things were best enjoyed when not described; yet he mistook whatever had "saddened" me for the wrestling, the honors of which were never "fleeting" to me. Long after I stopped competing — and after I stopped coaching, too — the discipline remained. (My life in wrestling was one-eighth talent and seven-eighths discipline. I believe that my life as a writer consists of one-eighth talent and seven-eighths discipline, too.)

Nor am I inclined to complain about my wrestling-related surgeries — both knees, my right elbow, my left shoulder. Of the four operations, only the shoulder was major; a detached rotator-cuff tendon is no fun. But even the injuries that led to these surgeries are of lasting (not "fleeting") honor to me. My first knee (torn cartilage) was injured when I was fooling around with J. Robinson in the workout room at the Meadowlands Arena, during a break between sessions at the 1984 NCAA tournament; my other knee was hyperextended when I was wrestling with one of Brendan's teammates at Vermont Academy in '88 — a good kid named Joe Black. (Joe was a three-time New England Class A Champion at 160 and 171 pounds.) Sometime between the knee injuries, my elbow was hyperextended at the New York Athletic Club — I was working out with Colin. And my shoulder succumbed, more gradually, to an accumulation of separations and rotator-cuff tears; what finally detached the supraspinatus tendon from the humerus wasn't a wrestling injury at all — rather, I fell off a children's slide with Everett in my arms (he was two), and in an effort to cover him up, and not land on him, I landed on my bad shoulder. Everett, who landed on my chest, was fine. (Had Coach Seabrooke been present to observe the fall, he would have reminded me that my standing side-roll had always been better executed to the right than to the left.)

I have no doubt that I have learned more from wrestling than from Creative Writing classes; good writing means *re*writing, and good wrestling is a matter of re*doing* — repetition without cease is obligatory, until the moves become second nature. I have never thought of myself as a "born" writer — anymore than I think of myself as a "natural" athlete, or even a good one. What I am is a good *re*writer; I never get anything right the first time — I just know how to revise, and revise.

And for me to continue coaching wrestling, when there was no longer any financial need, was not a strain; coaching was never as time-consuming as teaching. At the prep-school level, where I chiefly coached, wrestling is a seasonal sport; and neither my presence in the gym nor the hours riding on the team bus took anything away from that part of me that was a writer — on the contrary, wrestling was an escape from writing; it was a release — whereas *talking* about writing, as one must to "teach" it, exercised many of the same muscles I needed for my own work.

Another factor, the videocassette recorder, has entered the world of coaching — the coaching of *any* sport. To my knowledge, there is no such handy tool available for Creative Writing classes. For example: my 189-pounder walks dejectedly off the mat, once more a loser, and once again because every time he stands up to escape from the bottom position his elbows are flailing a foot away from his rib cage — therefore, he is easily tight-waisted and thrown to his face. When I would invariably point out to him that even an object as large as his head could have passed through the space left between his elbows and his ribs (during his feeble standup attempt), he would say, "My elbows were tight to my sides, Coach — he just *did* something to them!"

But then would come the next day's film session, where, in front of his snickering teammates, I would show my 189-pounder the footage of his pathetic standup (with his elbows flapping as far from his body as a chicken's clipped wings in mock flight). I would slow-motion it, I would rewind it and slow-motion it again; in later years I could freeze-frame it, too — and that would be the end of arguing with him (until, naturally, he did it again). But I had a backup: the camera made my criticism valid.

There is no such indisputable backup in Creative Writing classes; frequently the student who perpetrates the deeply flawed story is adored and supported by his or her peers. A teacher's triumphs are few. You say: "When the father drops dead with an apple in his mouth while urinating on the front fender of his mother-in-law's car . . . uh, well, I just had trouble *seeing* it." Whereupon the student breaks into tears and confesses that this actually happened to her own father, in exactly the way she described it; and there then must follow, always unsatisfactorily, the timeless explanation that "real life" must be made to *seem* real — it is not believable solely for the fact that it *happened*. The truth is, the imagination can select more plausible details than those incredible-but-true details that we remember.

This is a tough sell to students rooted in social realism, and young writers without the imagination to move beyond autobiographical fiction — namely, to that host of first novelists who treat a novel as nothing but a thinly masked rendition of their lives up to that point.

Nor are the earliest efforts young writers make to *escape* autobiographical fiction necessarily successful. A student of mine at Iowa — a brilliant fellow, academically; he would go on to earn a Ph.D. in something I can't even pronounce or spell — wrote an accomplished, lucid short story about a dinner party from the point of view of the hostess's fork.

If you think this sounds fascinating, my case is already lost. Indeed, the young writer's fellow students worshiped this story and the young genius who wrote it; they regarded my all-too-apparent indifference to the fork story as an insult not only to the author but to all of them. Ah, to *almost* all of them, for I was saved by a most unlikely and usually most silent member of the class. He was an Indian from Kerala, a devout Christian, and his accent and word order caused him to be treated dismissively — as someone who was struggling with English as a second language, although this was not the case. English was his first language, and he spoke and wrote it very well; the unfamiliarity of his accent and the cadence, even of his written sentences, made the other students regard him lightly.

Into the sea of approval that the fork story was receiving, and while my "but . . ." was repeatedly drowned out by the boisterous air of celebration in the class, the Indian Christian from Kerala said, "Excuse me, but perhaps I would have been moved if I were a fork. Unfortunately, I am merely a human being."

That day, and perhaps forever after, *he* should have been the teacher and I should have given my complete attention to him. He is not a writer these days, except on the faithful Christmas cards he sends from India, where he is a doctor. Under the usual holiday greetings, and the annual photograph of his increasing family, he writes in a firm, readable hand: "Still merely a human being."

On my Christmas cards to him, I write: "Not yet a fork."

(I used to say this to my students in Creative Writing: the wonderful and terrifying thing about the first page of paper that awaits the first sentence of your next book is that this clean piece of paper is completely unimpressed by your reputation, or lack thereof; that blank page has not read your previous work — it is neither comparing you to its favorite among your earlier novels nor is it sneering in memory of your past failures. That is the absolutely exhilarating and totally frightening thing about beginning — I mean each and every new beginning. That is when even the most experienced teacher becomes a student again and again.)

And what about the fork author — where is he today? In Boston, I believe; more pertinent, he's a published novelist — and a good one. I much admired his first novel, and was overall relieved to see that the characters in it were human beings — no cutlery among them.

Alas, these generally pleasant memories should not conceal the fact that I must have played the Nelson Algren role to more than one of my writing students. I'm certain that I've hurt the feelings of young writers who were more serious and gifted than I judged them to be. But just as Mr. Algren didn't harm me by his blunt and (I think) unfair assessment, I doubt that I have harmed any *real* writers; real writers, after all, had better get used to being misunderstood.

When it happens to me, I just remind myself of what Ted Seabrooke told me: "That you're not very talented needn't be the end of it."

The Imaginary Girlfriend (1995)

AUTHOR'S NOTES

A few pages of this memoir were written as a letter to John Baker, Editorial Director at *Publishers Weekly;* John published parts of my letter to him in an article he wrote for *PW* (June 5, 1995). Portions of my remembrance of Don Hendrie were published in the form of an obituary for Hendrie that I wrote for *The Exeter Bulletin* (Fall 1995). And an excerpt from "The Imaginary Girlfriend" appeared in a fall '95 issue of *The New Yorker.*

I am grateful to Deborah Garrison at *The New Yorker* and to my wife, Janet, for their editorial response to an earlier draft of this autobiography, which was called "Mentors" and (believe it or not) contained fewer than 10 pages about wrestling. Deb and Janet ganged up on me; they said, in effect, "Are you kidding? Where's the wrestling?"

The reason this memoir was written at all is because I had shoulder surgery a week before Christmas, 1994. I was completely unprepared for how many hours a day, and for how many months, I would be rehabilitating my shoulder; I had anticipated an easier recovery. I knew there would be a little bone sawing in the area of the acromion-clavicular joint, and I knew I had a torn rotator-cuff tendon; I *didn't* know that the tendon was detached from the humerus — nor did the surgeon, until he got in there.

With four hours of physical therapy a day, for four months, I didn't feel the time was right for me to begin a new novel, which I'd planned to begin after Christmas; I had about 200 pages of notes for the novel, and a halfway-decent first sentence, but the shoulder rehabilitation was too distracting.

One day in January of '95 I was making a nuisance of myself in my wife's office; I was aimlessly bothering Janet and her assistant — poking my nose into the pile of manuscripts that are always waiting to be read in the office of a literary agent. The stitches had only recently been removed from my shoulder and I had just begun the requisite physical therapy; I was still wearing a sling, and I was bored.

Janet doesn't like it when I hang around her office. "Why don't you get out of here?" she said. "Go write a novel."

Summoning my most self-pitying voice, I said, "I can't write a novel with one arm and four hours a day of rehabilitation."

"Then go write a memoir, or something," Janet said. "Just get out of here."

My goal was to write an autobiography of 100 pages in four months. It took five months, and the finished manuscript was 101 pages — not counting the photographs.

And so the winter of '95 was one of recovery (April counts as a winter month in Vermont). I would see the physical therapist first thing in the morning; she would "manipulate" my shoulder and prescribe the stretching exercises and the weight lifting that she wanted me to do in the afternoon. I would write my memoir in the middle of the day; in the late afternoon or early evening I would go to my wrestling room and follow the orders of the physical therapist.

To explain "my" wrestling room — it is about 25 feet from my office in the Vermont house. (Between the office and the wrestling room is a small locker room: a toilet, three sinks, two showers, a sauna.) My wrestling mat is equivalent to the in-bounds area of a regulation mat. About a dozen jump ropes, of varying lengths, hang from pegs at one end of the room; at the other end is an area for weight lifting — a couple of weight benches and two racks of free weights. There's also a stationary bike and a treadmill, and lots of shelves for knee pads, elbow pads, head gear, spools of tape — and about a dozen pairs of wrestling shoes, in a somewhat limited range of sizes. (Brendan's feet are only a little bigger than mine; Colin's are only a little bigger than Brendan's.)

There are over 300 photographs on the walls; there aren't many of me, and even fewer of Everett — and not a lot of room remaining for the photos of Everett, which I presume will come. Most of the pictures are of Colin and Brendan, together with the bracket sheets from the tournaments they won. There are twelve medals, five trophies, and one plaque; only the plaque is mine. I never won any medals or trophies, because I never won a wrestling tournament.

I didn't really "win" the plaque. In 1992, I was selected as one of the first 10 members in the Hall of Outstanding Americans by the National Wrestling Hall of Fame in Stillwater, Oklahoma. These "Outstanding Americans" were not necessarily outstanding wrestlers, although a few of them were; we were all chosen for being outstanding at something else, and for having also (in our fashion) wrestled.

I am honored to be a member of the National Wrestling Hall of Fame, although I'm embarrassed to have gained entry through the back door — meaning for my other accomplishments, *not* my wrestling or my coaching. I feel privileged to have been in the same wrestling room with some of the wrestling and coaching members of the Hall of Fame — George Martin, Dave McCuskey, Rex Peery, Dan Gable.

You may be surprised to learn of a couple of other "Outstanding Americans" whom the National Wrestling Hall of Fame has honored: Kirk Douglas and General H. Norman Schwarzkopf. I'm surprised that, as of this writing, my fellow novelist Ken Kesey *hasn't* been selected as a member; Mr. Kesey's wrestling credentials are a whole lot better than mine. He is still ranked as one of the top 10 wrestlers (most career wins) at the University of Oregon, where he graduated in '57. And in '82, at the age of 47, Kesey won the AAU Masters Championships at 198 pounds.

I suspect that after the Senate confirms General Charles C. ("Brute") Krulak's promotion to four-star rank, and General Krulak is officially serving on the Joint Chiefs of Staff, the new Commandant of the Marines will also become a member in the Hall of Outstanding Americans at Stillwater. Described by *The New York Times* as "a diminutive dynamo of a man" — he was a 121-pounder at Exeter and a 123-pounder at Navy — Chuck was a platoon leader and company commander during two tours of duty in the Vietnam War, and later served as commander of the counterguerrilla-warfare school in Okinawa. Thereafter, General Krulak was commanding general of the Marine Corps Combat Development Command in Quantico, Virginia, and — just prior to President Clinton's nominating him as the next Commandant of the Marines — Krulak commanded 82,000 marines and

600 combat aircraft in the Pacific. (In the event of war in Korea or the Persian Gulf, General Krulak would have commanded all the marines there.) But as a member of the National Wrestling Hall of Fame, which I assume he will be, Chuck Krulak will probably feel as I do: namely, that the honor is undeserved.

Thus my plaque from the National Wrestling Hall of Fame occupies the far corner of a shelf in my wrestling room, where it stands a little sheepishly, looking unearned beside the hardware and the ribbons that Colin and Brendan won outright. I go to such lengths to describe the territory of my wrestling room and its proximity to my office because I want you to understand that the distance between my writing and my wrestling is never great; indeed, in the winter I was writing "The Imaginary Girlfriend," the distance was only 25 feet.

For four months, I didn't venture farther than that 25-foot path — with two exceptions. The first was a trip to Aspen in the middle of March. I spent less than a week with Colin and Brendan in Colorado. I couldn't ski; I went to the gym and repeated the rehabilitation exercises that my physical therapist in Vermont had given me, and I paddled around in the heated pool and the hot tub with Everett. I had some very pleasant dinners with the Salters, Kay and Jim, and then it was back to Vermont to finish the "Girlfriend" — only I couldn't finish it; not before leaving for France in April, for the French translation of *A Son of the Circus*.

After most of my interviews in Paris, in the lobby of the Hotel Lutétia, a photographer would drag me to a small plot of greenery (less than a park) off the boulevard Raspail and attempt to position me beside a statue of the French novelist François Mauriac. I refused to be photographed beside the statue of Mauriac, largely because the statue is 15 feet tall — you may recall that I'm only five feet eight — but also because I thought that Mauriac looked extremely undernourished and depressed. Possibly he was mortified to be photographed alongside every visiting author who was staying at the Lutétia.

That was Paris: I was brooding about not having finished "The Imaginary Girlfriend" before I had to leave for France, and I was constantly and unsubtly being compared to Mauriac. One of his critics once said that God surely disapproved of what Mauriac had written, to which Mauriac admirably responded: "God doesn't care at all — what we write — but when we do it right, He can use it." (I kept telling one photographer after another that God couldn't possibly find a use for a photograph of John Irving with François Mauriac, but the photographers were uncomprehending; one of them misinterpreted my refusal to be photographed with Mauriac as a sure sign of religious zealotry.)

Back in Vermont, April dragged on — so did the "Girlfriend." In May I spent less than a week with Colin and Brendan in California. By then, my rehabilitation exercises were only two hours a day, and I discovered that I could once again carry Everett on my shoulders; we took him to Disneyland, where, admittedly, Colin and Brendan carried him around more often and more easily than I did. On the plane back East from L.A., I was still revising "The Imaginary Girlfriend," which I wouldn't finish before June.

An intractable phenomenon of writing an autobiography is that you begin to miss the people you are writing about; I don't ever miss the characters in my novels, although some of my readers have told me that *they* miss them. I found myself wanting to call up people I hadn't seen or spoken to in more than 30 years. In most cases, the motivation was more than nostalgia; I couldn't remember all the details — what was so-and-so's weight class, and did he win a Big 10 title, or did he even *place?*

I called Kay Gallagher, Cliff's widow, a couple of times. Cliff had done so many things I couldn't keep them all straight. It was nice to talk to Kay, but it made me miss Cliff.

As for coincidence, the novelist's companion, Don Hendrie's death (in March) coincided precisely with that point in my autobiography where Hendrie was to make his first appearance. My friend Phillip Borsos also died last winter; he was the movie director who made *The Grey Fox,* and with whom I'd been trying to make the film of *The Cider House Rules* — for almost 10 years. Phillip was only 41; his death (cancer), in addition to its own sadness, called back to mind the death of Tony Richardson. (Tony directed *The Hotel New Hampshire* — he died of AIDS in 1991. My friend George Roy Hill, now debilitated with Parkinson's, directed *The World According to Garp.*) Tony used to call me rather late at night and ask me if I'd read anything good lately; he was a voracious reader. Thinking of Tony often puts me in a mood to call people, too. As I was coming to the end of "The Imaginary Girlfriend," I was calling people left and right.

On Memorial Day weekend, I called my old friend Eric Ross in Crested Butte. While I'd been in France, avoiding the Mauriac photo opportunities, Eric had been golfing in Ireland with a bad case of gout. I have never golfed, nor had gout, but the combination struck me as a cruel and comedic affliction.

Thus inspired, I decided to call Vincent Buonomano. I speculated, stupidly, that after Buonomano had graduated from Mount Pleasant High School, he'd never left the Providence area. I called information in Rhode Island and was informed that there was only one Vincent Buonomano in the environs of Providence; actually, he lived in Warwick. I made the call.

A girl answered; she sounded like a teenager. I asked for Vincent Buonomano. The girl said, "Who's calling?"

"He probably doesn't remember me," I said. "I haven't seen him since he was in high school."

She went off screaming for him. "Dad!" Or maybe she said, "Daddy!" I had the impression of a large house and a large family.

Mr. Buonomano was very friendly to me on the phone, but he wasn't the same Vincent Buonomano who'd pinned me in the pit — with less than a minute remaining in the third period. The nice man on the phone said that he occasionally got calls for the other Buonomano, the wrestler, and once some bills for "the wrestler" had been sent to the wrong Buonomano's address. The Mr. Buonomano who talked to me told me that he thought the Buonomano I was looking for had gone to college and was now a physician — because one of the bills was seeking repayment of a student loan, and because one of the bills was addressed to a Dr. Vincent Buonomano. (I speculated that he specialized in necks.) But I couldn't find him. He had slipped away, surely never remembering me.

It made me so sad I simply had to call Anthony Pieranunzi. There was a greater likelihood that Pieranunzi would remember me, I thought: our matches had been close. But the operator told me that there was no Anthony Pieranunzi in East Providence, and only one in Providence; it had to be him, I was certain — I called immediately. An extremely likable woman answered the phone. I instantly remembered Pieranunzi's girlfriend. (It's possible she was his sister — she was a knockout, anyway.) I imagined I was talking to the high-school sweetheart of my archrival — now a devoted wife of some 30-plus years.

I said something truly stupid, like: "Is this the home of Anthony Pieranunzi, the wrestler?"

The woman laughed. "Lord, no," she said. She'd heard of the wrestler; there had been other phone calls — and, of course, bills sent to the wrong address. (Bills had become a common theme — they were perpetually being sent to the wrong address.) The woman told me that someone had once called her husband and asked him if he was *the* Anthony Pieranunzi. It was *the* Anthony Pieranunzi I was looking for, of course. But he had slipped away with Vincent Buonomano, neither of them ever knowing how important they were to me.

I felt like talking to a friend.

Following a conversation with Sonny Greenhalgh, which deteriorated into a dispute concerning whether John Carr had wrestled at 147 pounds or at 157, I decided to call John Carr. The conversation with Sonny, as with most conversations with Sonny, entailed a fair amount of Sherman Moyer. To this day, it stands as an outrage in Sonny's life that he lost twice, in the same season, to Moyer — although this was 33 years ago. (Sonny was an All-American;

Moyer wasn't. I'm guessing that this is what makes the losses unacceptable to Sonny.) To this day, my sympathy for Sonny is moderated by the fact that, at the time, I was cheering for Moyer, who was my teammate; I didn't know Sonny then, except that I knew he was a highly regarded 130-pounder at Syracuse. My sympathy for Sonny's two losses to Moyer is also lessened by the fact that I wrestled Moyer every day for an entire wrestling season; as such, I lost to him every day — a mere *two* defeats at the hands of Moyer seems like no disgrace and no special hardship to *me*. Sonny and I *always* talk about this, notwithstanding the fact that we have other things in common to talk about. (I coached Sonny Greenhalgh's son, Jon, when Jon was a teammate of Brendan's at Vermont Academy; Jon Greenhalgh won a New England title in 1989.)

But this time my conversation with Sonny concerned John Carr — was he a 147-pounder or a 157-pounder? What turned the talk to Carr was that Sonny had heard that Carr's dad had died, and I remembered Mr. Carr fondly — from the time he'd enthusiastically stepped in and coached me at West Point. By the time I got off the phone with Sonny, there was another thing I wanted to talk to John Carr about: I knew he'd won a New England title the year before we both went to Pittsburgh, but I couldn't remember if he'd been a PG at Andover or at Cheshire — in both cases, in my memory, the uniforms were blue.

At the New England tournament that year, the Outstanding Wrestler award was given to Anthony Pieranunzi, the presently elusive East Providence standout, who'd kept me from winning a New England title; John Carr arguably deserved the award.

Pieranunzi was good, but the talk in the locker room suggested that Carr was better; I don't really know, because I never wrestled Carr. And that was why I believed Carr had wrestled at 157 pounds: if he'd wrestled at 147, I *would* have wrestled him — he would have been a workout partner, at least a few times. (As a 130-pounder, I used to work out with the 147-pounders occasionally, but the 157-pounders were too big.)

When I called information, the operator informed me that there were seven guys named John Carr in the Wilkes-Barre area of Pennsylvania, but it didn't take long to track him down. I talked to the wife of the wrong John Carr, and to four or five other wrong John Carrs, too; they *all* said, "Oh, you want the wrestler." Or: "You want the coach."

By the time I got him, it was all over town that I was looking for him; he was expecting my call. Carr remembered me, but not my face; he couldn't put me with a face, he said. I'm not surprised; in fact, I was surprised he remembered me at all — as I said, we never wrestled each other and my wrestling was hardly anything worth *watching*. If John Carr had had a minute to watch the other wrestlers in the Pitt wrestling room, there were a lot of better guys to watch than me.

I was right: Carr had been a 157-pounder, and he told me he'd been a PG at Cheshire when he won the New England's — *not* at Andover. I told him I was sorry to hear about his dad. Carr wasn't coaching anymore; he complained that the influence of freestyle (international) wrestling had hurt high-school and collegiate (or folkstyle) wrestling. For one thing, there was not enough pinning — wrestling wasn't as aggressive as it used to be, John Carr said. I share his view. I was never a fan of freestyle. As I once heard Dan Gable say of collegiate wrestling: "If you can't get off the bottom, you can't win." (In freestyle, you don't have to be able to get off the bottom; the referee blows his whistle and *lets* you off the bottom — you can spend almost the whole match in the neutral position, on your feet. And so I knew what John Carr was thinking: he was thinking, How tough is *that?* In a freestyle match, I *might* have been able to beat Sherman Moyer; it was when I was on the bottom that Moyer killed me.)

Carr told me that Mike Johnson was still coaching at Du Bois, and that Warnick's kid — or one of Warnick's kids — had been pretty successful on the mat at West Point. I remembered seeing the name Warnick in the Army lineup and wondering if this was a child of the Warnick who'd arm-dragged me to death in my one winter at Pittsburgh. After John Carr and I said goodnight, and I hung up the phone, I realized that I'd not asked him if Warnick's kid had learned his father's killer arm-drag. I almost called Carr back. But when I start the phone calls, especially at night, I have to stop somewhere. If I keep going, I get in a mood to call *everybody*.

Of course I'd like to call Cliff Gallagher — if only to hear him say, "Not even a zebra, Johnny." And I often think about calling Ted Seabrooke, before I remember that I can't. Ted wasn't a big talker — not compared to Cliff — but Ted was insightful at interrupting me, and at contradicting me, too. I'd be saying something and he'd say, "That sounds pretty stupid to me." Or: "Why would you want to do that?" And: "Do what you know how to do." Or: "What's worked for you before?" Cliff used to say that Ted could clear the air.

It still seems unacceptable that both Ted and Cliff are dead, although Cliff (given normal life expectancy) would almost surely be dead by now — Cliff was born in 1897, which would make him all of 98, if he were alive today. I think it broke Cliff's heart that Ted died first — Ted died young. And Ted fooled us: after the diabetes, which he got control of, he had some healthy years; then the cancer came and killed him in the fall of 1980. He was 59.

For Coach Seabrooke's memorial service in Phillips Church, there were more wrestlers than I ever saw in the Exeter wrestling room. Bobby Thompson, one of Exeter's ex-heavyweights — and arguably the biggest-ever New England Class A Champion in the Unlimited class — sang "Amazing Grace." (Bobby is the school minister at Exeter today.)

It was an outrage to all his wrestlers that Ted was dead. He'd seemed indomitable to us. He had twice been struck by lightning, while playing golf; both times he'd survived. Both times he'd said, "It's just one of those things."

After Ted's memorial service, I remember Cliff Gallagher grabbing me with a Russian arm-tie and whispering in my ear: "It should have been me, Johnny — it should have been me." My arm was sore for days. Cliff had a nasty Russian arm-tie. At the time, Cliff was 83.

I don't lead a hectic life. It's not every night, or every week — or even every month — that I feel the need to "clear the air." Most nights, I don't even look at the telephone. Other times, the unringing phone seems to summon all the unreachable people in the past. I think of that poem of Rilke's, about the corpse: "*Und einer ohne Namen/ lag bar und reinlich da und gab Gesetze*" ("And one without a name/ lay clean and naked there, and gave commands"). That is the telephone on certain nights: it is the unreachable past — the dead demanding to give us advice. On those nights, I'm sorry I can't talk to Ted.

My Dinner at the White House

Here's what happened when Dan Quayle invited me to dinner. My wife accused me of covert right-wing activities; Janet speculated that she'd married a closet Republican, or a secret golfer. I promised her that I didn't *know* Dan — I'd never even met him. Then we both calmed down and read the rest of Mr. Quayle's letter. Everything was correctly spelled, which was both a shock and a disappointment, but it was only a *pro forma* invitation — not nearly as "personal" a letter as it had appeared at first glance. It was also an embarrassing mistake: I'm a registered Democrat and Janet is a Canadian citizen; here we were being invited to become members of something called the Republican Inner Circle. We understand it's easy to get on the wrong mailing list; nevertheless, we were tempted to join. Since we moved to Vermont (in 1990), neither the Democrats nor the Canadians have invited us to be members of *anything*.

But, alas, Janet questioned my motivation for accepting a dinner invitation from the Vice President. I do admit that the letter from Dan Quayle was a trifle vague. We weren't sure if money or celebrity was the desired result; yet it appeared that we would get to dine at the White House — at no charge. Furthermore, it was implied that the Republican Inner Circle was of an intimate size, suggesting that we might even expect close conversation with the Vice President *and* the President.

After the President's puking incident in Japan, we knew it was dangerous to be seated *too* close to Mr.

Bush while he was eating; we wanted no part of that. Nevertheless, it's about a 10-hour drive to Washington from Vermont; to eschew eating in proximity to the President, for fear of projectile vomiting, was weighed against the potential boredom of dining near the Vice President. Coming all the way from Vermont, we wondered if the level of Mr. Quayle's "close conversation" would be a just reward. My repertoire of golfing tales is somewhat small; a night comparing greens fees struck me as less than exciting. On the other hand, Janet and I wouldn't have minded an evening's chat with *Mrs.* Quayle, but we didn't think it was our place to suggest a seating plan that would land us next to Marilyn.

In light of what's happened — I mean that there are Democrats at least temporarily occupying the White House — you can imagine how much Janet and I regret that we turned down Dan Quayle's invitation to dine at the White House with the Republican Inner Circle. What a blown opportunity! But I'd had a funny evening at the White House before; I wasn't sure I had the stamina to repeat it.

President Reagan invited me to dinner, several times. At first I declined — I'm sorry to say, with childish bad manners. I said stupid, rude things. ("No thanks. I'm eating with the homeless that night." Juvenilia like that.) Then, after the third invitation, it occurred to me that the Republicans were obdurate in their sense of who their friends were, or who they *wanted* for friends; I also realized that if the Democrats were ever in office, they might be too busy invigorating the economy to invite me to dinner. If I wanted to go to dinner at the White House, I thought I'd better accept Mr. Reagan's invitation. How was I to know I'd get another?

So I went. The occasion was your usual state dinner, about 200 people — this one for Mr. and Mrs. Algeria. To my surprise, I was seated at the President's table with only five other stunned individuals. There was a nervous lady from Ohio; she'd written Mr. Reagan his favorite fan letter of the week, although neither the President nor his fan would tell the rest of us what the letter had said. Also among us was a Rhode Island woman they called Attila the Nun (in a very attractive, all-gray outfit) and the former New York Jets quarterback — and a personal hero of mine — Joe Namath. Mr. Namath enlivened the conversation by stating that "only in the United States" could such a thing be happening to him — namely, that he was having dinner with the President of the United States. I let it pass.

But, throughout our dinner, Mr. Namath repeated and repeated his observation, until I finally said, "Well, of course, it's highly unlikely that you'd be having dinner with the President of the United States in any country *other* than the United States." Everyone looked at me as if I were a real jerk; only Mr. Reagan got the joke, and he was also kind enough to point out why my effort at humor had failed.

"It's your timing *and* your delivery," the President said.

Then the fan of the week from Ohio asked the President to tell us the "funniest thing" that ever happened to him. Mr. Reagan didn't hesitate.

"We were at the Brown Derby," the President said. But suddenly Mr. Reagan realized that Mrs. Algeria, and her interpreter, were also at our small dinner table. (Actually, the interpreter sat in a less comfortable chair *behind* Mrs. Algeria; it seemed incredibly impolite that he wasn't served any food.) Mr.

Reagan was worried that Mrs. Algeria might not be well schooled in California entertainment spots. Thus the President explained: "The Brown Derby is a famous restaurant where movie people go." This was communicated to Mrs. Algeria through her interpreter.

After a brief exchange, the interpreter said, "She knows."

Mr. Reagan continued. He said he was at the Brown Derby one night with his friend Bing Crosby and a comedian named Bishop (*not* Frank Sinatra's pal) — and here the President paused to tell Mrs. Algeria that Bing Crosby was a famous American singer, "dead now."

As one might expect, the interpreter — after another brief exchange — said, "She knows."

And so it continued, with Mr. Reagan moving ahead to the part about the dwarf. Apparently, there often was a dwarf at the Brown Derby — and an objectionable little person he was. It was also true that the comedian named Bishop, who was dining with Mr. Crosby and Mr. Reagan, suffered a slight speech defect, which the President said was a contributing factor to Bishop's lack of fame and fortune. Bishop was a stutterer.

Thus it came to pass that the dwarf, who was obnoxious, presented himself at the Reagan-Crosby-Bishop gathering by placing his head on their dinner table. The table was about the right height, level to the dwarf's head, and thereupon Bishop (with the stutter) asked: "Did some-some-some-*some*one order John-John-John the *Baptist?*"

No one at our White House table reacted, and so the President explained his joke to Mrs. Algeria.

"John the Baptist? The Bible? Got his head cut off? Had it served on a platter? You get it?"

Whereupon, without a word to Mrs. Algeria, the interpreter said, "She knows."

That was the kind of evening it was. When I had to go to the men's room, a U.S. Marine escorted me there, and he stayed to watch me pee — to make sure that was all I was going to do, I guess. I was feeling disappointed in myself for failing to represent the literary community with the sort of rebellious spirit that I imagine this community prefers. My very faint rebellion was indicated only by the fact that I wore a silver tie; all the other men had interpreted the "black tie" announcement on the invitation literally. And in my case, I must confess, I'd packed in the early morning, not in very good light; I'd actually thought my tie *was* black until I saw it in the well-lit hotel room where I dressed for dinner. I never would have chosen that tie if I'd been able to see it properly; it was the sort of unnatural silver of a fish's underbelly, the kind of tie an oafish high-school student might wear to his first prom.

And as at a prom, on my night at the White House — and befitting a Hollywood party — there was dancing after dinner. I was standing as close as possible to a very attractive young actress; it's an indication of my age that I'm doomed to remember her as Alan Ladd's beautiful daughter. I'm sure she has a first name, and I'm not at all sure that she really *is* Alan Ladd's daughter; that's just how I think of her. Now that I'm creeping past 50, it occurs to me that she might even be his *granddaughter,* or no relation to him at all. Anyway, she was Alan Ladd's daughter to *me,* and she was wearing the kind of dress that made most of the men want to stand as close to her as possible. When her dress fell the rest of the way off, you just wanted to be there. Naturally, there wasn't another woman within 25 yards of her — Ms. Ladd looked absolutely terrific. And then the music started, and George P. Shultz, who (like the rest of us) had his eye on Ms. Ladd, began to walk very rapidly and purposefully in her direction.

"Oh, God — who's this old coot coming at me?" Ms. Ladd asked. (Or words to that effect.)

With just a hint of indignation that implied to Ms. Ladd that she should be *honored,* a gray-haired gentleman said, "That, my dear, is the Secretary of State."

I was determined to stick up for Ms. Ladd, so I said to the gray-haired gentleman, "Well, he's not going to ask *you* to dance, is he?" But this was no better received than my witty remark to Joe Namath. The Secretary of State danced away with Ms. Ladd, and I never saw her again; it must have been my tacky silver tie.

Like a typical country boy, I went home early. When I left, the President and Mrs. Reagan were still dancing; they're simply fabulous dancers. Back in my hotel, I realized I'd not seen Joe Namath dance all night — probably because of his football knees.

This is the full extent of my White House history, and while my wife and I were weighing the pros and cons of Dan Quayle's invitation, we saw the news in *USA Today* — Dan Quayle had also invited the late Leonard Bernstein. We were floored. We don't know for sure, but we're inclined to believe that, when he was alive, Leonard Bernstein generally preferred Democrats. Now that he was dead, it was true that Mr. Bernstein's absolute party preference could not be ascertained. But how did we feel about being invited to drinks and dinner with a bunch of *dead* people? (We presume that Mr. Bernstein wasn't the *only* dead person who was asked.) I said to Janet that, more and more, this was shaping up to be *not* our kind of party.

So we declined. We hope we were polite, but we couldn't resist saying that Mr. Irving was a Democrat and his wife wasn't a U.S. citizen, and that, furthermore, we were both *alive*. If that doesn't disqualify us from the Republican Inner Circle, nothing will.

My Dinner at the White House (1992)

AUTHOR'S NOTES

For reasons I can't remember — possibly I developed a compelling interest in a moral showdown between two men of wavering principles — I kept a kind of election diary in the months leading up to and including the 1992 presidential election. Here's an excerpt from that diary: "With only 12 days to go before the election, President Bush was photographed walking toward his helicopter in Atlantic City. The picture, which appeared on the front page of *The New York Times,* shows the President walking backward; we presume he's giving one last wave to his supporters. The white of his raincoat stands out against the gray of the tarmac. Six Secret Servicemen surround him, all in dark suits, all walking forward, but — in Secret Service fashion — two of the men are looking over their shoulders. The shadows of the men are slanted to the left, as if giving further evidence to the President's allegations that the press is biased in a liberal direction — against him."

Well, this is old news — as we know now, the *other* waverer won. I voted for him; I would do so again. Contrary to accusations you may have heard, Bill Clinton is no liberal; as a lifelong Democrat, I consider President Clinton to most resemble a moderate, decent-minded Republican — he's not nearly as dangerous and deceitful as those Republicans who most virulently oppose him — but he *is* a waverer (and *not* because he didn't go to Vietnam). Nevertheless, I enjoyed keeping my '92 election diary; there were so many stupid things to keep track of — for example, it was in Ridgefield, New Jersey, where President Bush suffered a memorable slip of the tongue. He told a crowd of 15,000 that he appreciated their "lovely recession." Of course he'd meant to say "reception," but he was exhausted. "Character counts," Mr. Bush kept saying. "Character matters."

It is only necessary to remember that Mr. Bush was also the candidate who ran against Ronald Reagan for the nomination of the Republican party in 1980, and who (at the time) was pro-choice; he was also opposed to giving any aid to Mr. Reagan's beloved "freedom fighters" in Nicaragua — and it was George Bush who first called Mr. Reagan's supply-side economics "voodoo." Had being Reagan's Vice President changed him? Now firmly anti-abortion, and a born-again convert to the trickle-down economic theories of the former actor, Mr. Bush suffered no loss of face in delivering one of the most egregious lies of the '92 election. Bush actually urged Clinton to "come clean" about his student trip to Moscow — "just as I have [come clean] about Iran-Contra." But if George Bush had "come clean" about his role in the Iran-Contra affair, then Bill Clinton could tell everyone that he'd *fought* in Vietnam.

I know — more old news. It may be of greater interest to my readers to learn if I have been invited to President Clinton's White House. Yes — in fact, twice. Both times I was unable to accept: the first time I'd made plans to take a trip with my children, the second time I was in Europe. I hope the Clintons ask me again. (It seems increasingly unlikely.) President Bush never invited me, but I wasn't surprised; I was only surprised to hear the reason — and from no less an authority on dinner invitations to the White House than *Mrs.* Bush.

I ran into Barbara Bush at a black-tie event in New York City, following her husband's return to private life. Mrs. Bush and my wife (the Canadian) were talking; Mrs. Bush was surprised to learn that I was an American. Because I was one of her favorite authors, Barbara assured me, she had tried to have me invited to dinner at the White House; someone on George's staff had told her that it wouldn't be appropriate to invite me to dine at the taxpayers' expense — because I was a *Canadian!* (Apparently, the same someone on George's staff failed to convey this misinformation to Dan Quayle; poor Dan was of the opinion that I was fair game for the Republican Inner Circle.)

After this little misunderstanding was cleared up, Barbara told me that she and George would be happy to have Janet and me to dinner; and that, vaguely, was how the matter was left. Janet and I are still wondering if Mrs. Bush meant Maine or Texas. (We still haven't been asked.)

"My Dinner at the White House," which in an earlier draft contained about 50 pages of my election-year diary, was originally published in Canada — in the February 1993 issue of *Saturday Night.* (Neither Bill Clinton nor George Bush would want to have dinner with me if they read the *Saturday Night* version.)

It was for the benefit of Canadian readers that I included a small geography lesson in the original essay. I wrote: "My wife and I live in the low mountains of southern Vermont; we are a four-hour drive from New York City, which is directly south of us, and a four-hour drive from Montreal, Quebec, which is directly north of us. Both our Canadian and our American friends would be inclined to describe our location as 'nowhere,' or 'the wilderness,' but you would be mistaken to think that we are at all shut off from the world. Why? Because here is what you do if you live in Vermont: you find a pretty piece of land, you build a tasteful house, and then you stick a giant TV satellite dish in a prominent position — such as in your nearest neighbor's face. Our dish is black, resembling the giant ear of a dinosaur species of bat. That's what you need, if you want 75 channels of sex and violence and sports — and we do."

In an essay for a Canadian audience, it was also necessary for me to explain the American passion for bumper stickers, which is always exacerbated in an election year. In Vermont, I LIKE IKE was a prominent bumper sticker in the '92 election — an expression either of nostalgia or of general displeasure with the choice between Clinton or Bush, or both. In my diary I noted: "Bumper-sticker lovers must regret the passing of President Bush's occasion to vomit in Japan. Even in Vermont, there were UPCHUCK IN ASIA! bumper stickers for a while — they didn't last — and many local wits subscribed to the theory that this moment of sudden illness was the most decisive, most straightforward foreign policy that Mr. Bush had enacted since taking office. Democrats hoped that this brief barf might be the only thing we would remember about George Bush, but — to judge the passing importance of the event by the speed with which it vanished from Vermont bumper stickers — the barfing episode was quickly forgotten. Perhaps the prospect of a President who travels to foreign countries and vomits on their leaders is an idea ahead of its time, although suggestions spring readily to mind. . . . I mean, regarding where Mr. Bush should have traveled next. Anyway, the puking-related bumper stickers simply disappeared, whereas the President's ill-fated READ MY LIPS was still very visible on car bumpers, and still hurting him, in November."

Naturally, no diary of incidents contributing to the '92 election could be complete without a modest anthology of Dan Quayle jokes. By June of '92, about the only group Quayle could address — if he wanted to be free of hecklers — was an anti-abortion meeting where he followed up his attack on Murphy Brown, the fictional character in the television series, with more hot-blooded rhetoric. (An unwed mother was a poor role model for our society, Quayle had said.) He would press his case, the Vice President declared, "even though the cultural elites in some of our newsrooms, sitcom studios and faculty lounges may not like it." This was the same level of anti-intellectual buffoonery that had been used to portray Governor Dukakis (in the 1988 election) as a creation of the "Harvard boutique." But in June of '92, Clinton sent the signal that he would not be baited to discuss abortion or other "family values" on this level; to the disappointment of many Democrats, Clinton would fail to mention abortion sufficiently on *any* level, yet his cool response to Quayle set a tone. "I'm getting tired of people who have the responsibility for the American people — like the Vice President — pretending that the only problem we have is the absence of values," Clinton said.

Not even Ross Perot would bother to fight with Dan Quayle. "If anybody in the world should be able to understand the Murphy Brown story, it's the Republican party in the White House, because their

whole lives are driven by *ratings,*" Mr. Perot declared. "Murphy Brown had the baby the way she
had it to get *ratings.*"

President Bush, after agreeing with Quayle's negative response to Murphy Brown — for having a
baby when she wasn't married — added only that
"having a child out of wedlock is a better choice than
having an abortion." But the big news was, no one
really cared.

It is rare in American politics when a belligerent
fool can't manage to stir up a hornet's nest by making an insensitive remark or two. Yet Dan Quayle
went on and on being insensitive, and all he inspired
was a plethora of political cartoons.

"If we don't succeed, we run the risk of failure,"
the Vice President had said in November of '89.

In a Hardee's restaurant in Chicago, in August of
'90, Quayle had greeted a woman and tried to shake
her hand. "I'm Dan Quayle. Who are you?" the Vice
President had asked. "I'm your Secret Service agent,"
the woman had replied.

That same year, in California, the Vice President
had announced: "I love California. I grew up in
Phoenix. A lot of people forget that."

But Quayle could be more mystifyingly stupid
than that. "I have made good judgments in the past,"
he'd once said. "I have made good judgments in the
future," the Vice President had added.

As for family-oriented issues, nothing he would
say about Murphy Brown could compete with this
classic Quayle remark in December of '91: "Republicans understand the importance of bondage between
mother and child," the Vice President had informed
us. (And we thought Henry Kissinger spoke English
as a second language!)

And so, when Quayle attacked a fictional character for being an unwed mother, nothing really happened except that the media went wild for a week. When the flap died down, nobody's mind had been changed — least of all, Dan Quayle's.

At the time, however, Quayle's bullying idiocy about "family values" affected *me* more than the polls, for it occurred not long after Dan had invited me to dine with the Republican Inner Circle and I'd declined the invitation. I had developed the habit of pacing in my office, mumbling "I have made good judgments in the future." Clearly I was beginning to regret that I hadn't gone to the White House to eat with Dan and his friends.

I remember, too, that a kind of melancholy attended the week before the election. Janet and I were in New York one night when something triggered the security system in our Vermont house; the alarm sounded. A policeman searched the house for an intruder but found only a partially deflated helium balloon. The balloon said HAPPY BIRTHDAY! and the motion detector had responded to its errant behavior in the rising hot air from the furnace. We came home to find the balloon weighted down to the floor; for this purpose, the policeman had used our one-year-old's favorite toy — a three-foot-tall version of Big Bird, the *Sesame Street* character. (Television is the source of so much American life.) The helium balloon was tied around Big Bird's neck. Was this an omen? Was Big Bird a Republican or a Democrat? He looked like an Independent to me. ("Which one of the three candidates as young men would you want your daughter to marry?" Ross Perot had asked. "Ears and all," he'd added — definitely a Big Bird kind of character.)

Another night, when we were back home from New York, the phone rang at 5:00 in the morning and a man from the alarm company informed me that the heat detector in my security system indicated that the temperature was below freezing in my house. I told him I was perfectly comfortable, and that the house was adequately heated — the security system was screwed up, I said. But when I couldn't fall back to sleep, I went downstairs and discovered that an outside door had blown open in the wind. The thermostat for the heat detector had been exposed to the cold air, and the front hall was full of dead leaves. A gray squirrel was sitting on the threshold of the open door; it looked uncertain — trying to make up its mind whether or not to come inside.

This was disconcerting enough to compel me to watch the early-morning news. At a rally in Michigan, President Bush called Al Gore "crazy" — and Bush had this to say for the Clinton-Gore ticket: "My dog Millie knows more about foreign affairs than these two bozos!" Later, a "news analyst" (I think this means a journalist) was whining about Bush's calling Clinton and Gore "bozos"; the issue was whether or not the demeaning word ("bozos") was Presidential. "Presidential" is an adjective we suffer over — thankfully, only every four years. If the President said it, whatever it was, I say it's Presidential.

Thus inspired, I kept the following election-day diary.

"I wake up at 6:00 to the sound of hail on the roof, and on the slate terrace; the trees are completely shrouded in ice — very ominous. I go back to bed and hear two or three thuds against the north wall — also very ominous. This usually means that grouse have been flushed from the woods and have failed to clear the house, which is three floors high, with a steep roof. The sound of the birds killing themselves also wakes up our one-year-old.

"The three of us get up. I make coffee and watch the All-News channel, then CNN. Am informed that the polls open at 7:00. Drink one cup of coffee, then drive off to the elementary school — our local voting place. We live on a mountain; there's a dirt driveway and two dirt roads before you get to the paved road. On the mountain, it's sleeting; in the valley, it's raining — there's no ice on the trees in the valley.

"They're setting up the voting booths in the elementary-school gym; I'm told the polls don't open till 10:00. Several Republican-looking people are already there, looking obdurate. I mean by 'Republican-looking' that they appear to be wealthy and retired. 'I can wait all day,' one of the elderly gentlemen says.

"A young woman is setting up hot plates for split-pea soup and baked beans; the coffee urn is already plugged in, and there's a long table piled with cookies and pies. In Vermont, every public event comes with this kind of food. I drive home, drink half-a-dozen cups of coffee, get so wired that all I can think of doing is raking leaves — an arduous task in an ice storm. But by 9:00 the sleet has turned to rain, even on the mountain. I find the three dead grouse; they're too big to 'rake.' I make a mental note to come back for them with a shovel — maybe tomorrow. If Bush wins, I decide I'll *feel* like shoveling dead grouse. If Clinton wins, I won't *mind* shoveling dead grouse. If Perot wins, I'll let them rot until spring — if Perot wins, *everything* will rot.

"At 9:00 I begin to read a Chekhov short story; in five minutes, I decide I've already read it. I turn on the All-News channel. Some town in New Hampshire has already closed its polls. All 37 registered voters have voted — 25 for Bush, 10 for Perot, 2 for Clinton. There's a brief interview with the town ballot-counter, a startled-looking man who resembles Christopher Lloyd in his *Back to the Future* phase. 'We didn't think we had any Democrats in town,' he says. He looks worried, as if the two votes for Clinton were too many.

"I find a shovel and bury the three dead grouse in the woods, talking to them all the while as if they were Republicans. The grouse, of course, are accepting of this criticism. Suddenly it's 10:15!

"I jump in the car and race to the elementary school. The parking lot is full and I have to wait in line for 45 minutes. Is this a good sign? Are these people fed up with George or frightened of Bill? In Vermont, a dozen people are running for President; I've never heard of nine of them. There's also a space on the ballot so you can write in the name of a Presidential candidate of your own — or your own name, for that matter. I vote for all the Democrats on the ballot, even for Justice of the Peace, but I make an exception for Bernie Sanders, Vermont's favorite Socialist; Bernie is seeking a second term in Congress, in the House of Representatives, for the Liberty Union party. I decide, spur-of-the-moment, to vote for Bernie. It occurs to me that we may not have any other Socialists in the House.

"I come home all hopped-up and unable to write; I regret that I've already buried the three dead grouse — stupid birds! Decide to walk in the wet woods; change my mind because the bow-and-arrow season (for deer) has started — don't want to be skewered by a crazed bow hunter. I think about trying the Chekhov story again, but I can't discover which bathroom I've left the book in; the damn house has six bathrooms. I sit in my office, not writing, watching squirrels leaping in the trees. If you watch squirrels long enough, you'll see one fall — especially after ice storms. I decide to watch them until *two* squirrels fall — about an hour. Not much else is happening in nature today: no deer out the windows, no wild turkey. There are only the squirrels, and the three dead grouse; their graves, fortunately, are not in view from my office.

"If Bush loses, there's someone in Arizona I'd like to call, so that I can gloat. But the person may be dead, and I never knew his name. In 1988 I was invited to speak at a fund-raising event for Planned Parenthood in Phoenix. (Dan, if you're reading this, Phoenix is in Arizona.) I gave a rousing speech in favor of abortion rights, and lambasting George Bush — from an exclusively Planned Parenthood perspective, mind you. I said you couldn't be a member of Planned Parenthood and vote for George Bush — Michael Dukakis was the alternative, then. The speech was rather coolly received. A woman told me that most of the women were Planned Parenthood members, but most of their husbands were Republicans who supported Planned Parenthood — 'only financially' — because they didn't want the Hispanic vote to one day outnumber the vote of the retired community. In other words, they supported Planned Parenthood for Mexican-Americans — and the Republican party for their every other need. They supported Planned Parenthood only out of their fear that the Mexican-Americans were outreproducing them! This pissed me off; I wished someone had warned me before my speech — then I could have been directly insulting to these particular Republicans.

"It was in this mood that I went to the men's room, where I was accosted by an elderly, infirm Republican who used one of those aluminum walkers. He shuffled over to the urinal and glared at me, which I found fairly inhibiting.

"'What's a writer like you make a year?' he asked me. 'Half a million? More?'"

"'About that,' I answered cautiously.

"'Then you ought to be a Republican, you idiot!' the old gentleman said. He was certainly right in one sense. Before Ronald Reagan was elected, when Jimmy Carter was in the White House, my personal income was taxed to the maximum — I was in the highest bracket. After Reagan took office — and for the next 12 years — my taxes dropped about 40 percent on personal income. There were lots of friendly loopholes — meaning tax deductions for rich people. Even so, I explained to the old fart with the walker that I didn't vote solely out of self-interest.

"'Then you're a damn fool!' he told me. 'What other, dumb-ass reason to vote *is* there?' I was on the verge of hinting that the gentleman might be too old a dog to learn new tricks, but that perhaps it wasn't too late for him to develop a social conscience . . . only I never said any of this. At that moment, both the elderly gentleman and I noticed that he'd peed all over his walker. Political agitation had doubtless affected his aim. There seemed to be nothing I could add to the conversation." (Or to my diary.)

President Bush became the first incumbent to win less than 40 percent of the popular vote since Herbert Hoover lost to Franklin Delano Roosevelt in

1932 — another year when the economy was a crucial issue. Bush was gentlemanly in accepting the loss; frankly, I thought he looked relieved. Perhaps he knew what he was going to do on Christmas Eve. At that time of the year when we are most inclined to exhibit some form of goodwill toward our fellowman, Bush would issue a presidential pardon to Caspar Weinberger — the ultimate gesture of *not* "coming clean" about the Iran-Contra affair. Even in defeat, Bush would be Bush — cynical to the core.

As for Independent Ross Perot, he finished with 19 percent of the popular vote — ears and all. Perot made the strongest third-party showing since Teddy Roosevelt ran on the Bull Moose ticket in 1912; Teddy captured 27 percent of the vote, which the Democrat, Woodrow Wilson, won.

Old news. Politics becomes old news quickly. My election-year diary is of limited and fast-fading interest, but my dinner at the White House with Ronald Reagan will stay with me. I was shortsighted not to accept Dan Quayle's invitation to dine with the Republican Inner Circle; I'm certain that something wonderful or terrible or both would have happened — at least it would have been memorable. In comparison to what that occasion might have been like, of what lasting interest is it that I think Bill Clinton is a waverer, and/or that I will almost certainly vote for him again — or for *any* Democrat over *any* Republican? We all have our opinions concerning what or who is ruining our country; right-wing conservatives are at the top of my list. As a novelist, my political opinions *or* yours aren't half as interesting to me as what happens at a good dinner party.

Does it matter that I personally like Mrs. Clinton better than Bill? I don't think Hillary is a waverer; I doubt she would have let Dr. Elders slip away. Dr. Elders was a favorite of mine; it was deeply disappointing to me that the President didn't *beg* her to stay as our Surgeon General. (Anyone who thinks that condoms and masturbation are the *worst* things to introduce to young people is standing at a low point of social responsibility and historical accuracy, not to mention common sense; yet those who attacked Dr. Elders won that round.)

By the time this book is published, a new election-year hysteria will already be gripping the country. I find it instructive to look at my diary of only four years ago — how dated and irrelevant it is! Look around you today, right now: what the candidates and their supporters (or detractors) are saying occupies the mainstream of the media's attention; all this energy — both the promises and the accusations — will quickly become dated and irrelevant, too. The passion of our political convictions can be as misleading as sexual desire, and as short-lived. What lasts longer is a good story. The only time I went to the White House, I had a great time. I should have gone again.

FICTION

INTERIOR SPACE

George Ronkers was a young urologist in a university town — a lucrative situation nowadays; the uninformed liberality of both the young and old college community produced a marvel of venereal variety. A urologist had plenty to do. Ronkers was affectionately nicknamed by a plethora of his clientele at Student Health. "Raunchy Ronk," they said. With deeper affection, his wife called him "Raunch."

Her name was Kit; she had a good sense of humor about George's work and a gift for imaginative shelter. She was a graduate student in the School of Architecture; she had a teaching assistantship, and she taught one course to undergraduate architecture students called "Interior Space."

It was her field, really. She was completely responsible for all the interior space in the Ronkers home. She had knocked down walls, sunk bathtubs, arched doorways, rounded rooms, ovaled windows; in short, she treated interior space as an illusion. "The trick," she would say, "is not letting you see where one room ends and another begins; the concept of a *room* is defeating to the concept of *space;* you can't make out the boundaries. . . ." And so on; it was her field.

George Ronkers walked through his house as if it were a park in a foreign but intriguing city. Theories of space didn't bother him one way or another.

"Saw a girl today with seventy-five warts," he'd say. "Really an obvious surgery. Don't know why she came to *me*. Really should have seen a *gynecologist* first."

The only part of the property that Ronkers considered *his* field was the large, lovely black walnut tree beside the house. Kit had spotted the house first; it belonged to an old Austrian named Kesler whose wife had just died. Kit told Ronkers it was repairable inside because the ceilings were at least high enough. But Ronkers had been sold on account of the tree. It was a split-trunked black walnut, growing out of the ground like two trees, making a high, slim V. The proper black walnut has a tall, graceful, upshooting style — the branches and the leaves start about two stories off the ground, and the leaves are small, slender, and arranged very closely together; they are a delicate green, turning yellow in October. The walnuts grow in a tough, rubbery pale-green skin; in the fall they reach the size of peaches; the skins begin to darken — even blackening in spots — and they start to drop. Squirrels like them.

Kit liked the tree well enough, but she was ecstatic telling old Herr Kesler what she was going to do with his house after he moved out. Kesler just stared at her, saying occasionally, "Which wall? *That* wall? You're going *this* wall to down-take, yes? Oh, the *other* wall too? Oh. Well . . . what will the ceiling up-hold? Oh . . ."

And Ronkers told Kesler how *much* he liked the black walnut tree. That was when Kesler warned him about their neighbor.

"*Der Bardlong,*" Kesler said. "He wants the tree down-chopped but I never to him listened." George Ronkers tried to press old Kesler to explain the motives of his would-be neighbor Bardlong, but the Austrian suddenly thumped the wall next to him with the flat of his hand and cried to Kit, "Not *this* wall too, I hope not! Ah, this wall I always *enjoyed* have!"

Well, they had to be delicate. No more plans out loud until Kesler moved out. He moved to an apartment in another suburb; for some reason, he dressed for the occasion. Like a Tyrolean peasant, his felt Alpine hat with a feather in it and his old white knees winking under his lederhosen, he stood in a soft spring rain by his ancient wooden trunks and let George and Kit hustle the furniture around for him.

"Won't you get out of the rain, Mr. Kesler?" Kit asked him, but he would not budge from the sidewalk in front of his former house until all his furniture was in the truck. He was watching the black walnut tree.

Herr Kesler put his hand frankly on Kit's behind, saying to her, "Do not let *der pest Bardlong* the tree down-chop, okay?"

"Okay," said Kit.

George Ronkers liked to lie in bed in the spring mornings and watch the sun filter through the new green leaves of his black walnut tree. The patterns the tree cast on the bed were almost mosaic. Kit had enlarged the window to accommodate more of the tree; her term for it was "inviting the tree in."

"Oh, Raunch," she whispered, "isn't it lovely?"

"It's a lovely tree."

"Well, I mean the *room* too. And the window, the elevated sleeping platform . . ."

"*Platform?* I thought it was a bed."

There was a squirrel who came along a branch very near the window — in fact, it often brushed the screen with its tail; the squirrel liked to tug at the new nuts, as if it could anticipate autumn.

"Raunch?"

"Yup . . ."

"Remember the girl with seventy-five warts?"

"*Remember* her!"

"Well, Raunch . . . *where* were the warts?"

And *der pest Bardlong* gave them no trouble. All that spring and hot summer, when workmen were removing walls and sculpting windows, the aloof Mr. and Mrs. Bardlong smiled at the confusion from their immaculate grounds, waved distantly from their terraces, made sudden appearances from behind a trellis — but always they were neighborly, encouraging of the youthful bustle, prying into nothing.

Bardlong was retired. He was *the* Bardlong, if you're at all familiar with the shock-absorber and brake-systems magnate. In the Midwest, you maybe have seen the big trucks.

BARDLONG STOPS YOU SHORT!
BARDLONG TAKES THAT SHOCK!

Even in retirement, Bardlong appeared to be absorbing whatever shock his new neighbors and their renovations might have caused him. His own house was an old red-brick mansion, trimmed tastefully with dark green shutters and overcrawling with ivy. It imitated a Georgian version of architecture; the front of the house was square and centered with tall, thin downstairs windows. The depth of the house was considerable; it went back a long way, branching into terraces, trellises, rock gardens, manicured hedges, fussed-over flower beds, and a lawn as fine as a putting green.

The house took up a full corner of the shady, suburban street. Its only neighbor was the Ronkerses' house, and the Bardlongs' property was walled off from George and Kit by a low slate-stone wall. From their second-floor windows, George and Kit looked down into the Bardlongs' perfect yard; their tangle of bushes and unkempt, matted grass was a full five feet above the apparent dike that kept their whole mess from crushing Bardlong as he raked and pruned. The houses themselves were queerly close together, the Ronkerses' having once been servant quarters to the Bardlongs', long before the property was divided.

Between them, rooted on the raised ground on the Ronkerses' side of the slate-stone wall, was the black walnut tree. Ronkers could not imagine whatever had prodded old Herr Kesler to think that Bardlong wanted the demise of the tree. Perhaps it had been a language problem. The tree must have been a shared joy to Bardlong. It shaded *his* windows, too; its stately height towered over his roof. One veer of the V angled over George and Kit; the other part of the V leaned over Bardlong.

Did the man not care for unpruned beauty?

Possibly; but all summer long, Bardlong never complained. He was there in his faded straw hat, gardening, simply puttering, often accompanied by his wife. The two of them seemed more like guests in an elegant old resort hotel than actual residents. Their dress, for yard work, was absurdly formal — as if Bardlong's many years as a brake-systems business-man had left him with no clothes other than business suits. He wore slightly out-of-style suit trousers, with suspenders, and slightly out-of-style dress shirts — the wide-brimmed straw hat shading his pale, freckled forehead. He was complete with an excessively sporty selection of two-toned shoes.

His wife — in a lawn-party dress and a cream-white Panama with a red silk ribbon around the bun at the back of her nail-gray hair — tapped her cane at bricks in the terrace that might dare to be loose. Bardlong followed her with a tiny, toylike pull-cart of cement and a trowel.

They lunched every midafternoon under a large sun umbrella on their back terrace, the white iron lawn furniture gleaming from an era of hunt breakfasts and champagne brunches following a pampered daughter's wedding.

A visit of grown-up children and less grown-up grandchildren seemed to mark the only interruption to Bardlong's summer. Three days of a dog barking and of balls being tossed about the pool-table symmetry of that yard seemed to upset the Bardlongs for a week following. They anxiously trailed the children around the grounds, trying to mend broken stalks of flowers, spearing on some garden instrument the affront of a gum wrapper, replacing divots dug up by the wild-running dog who could, and had, cut like a halfback through the soft grass.

For a week after this family invasion, the Bardlongs were collapsed on the terrace under their sun umbrella, too tired to tap a single brick or repair a tiny torn arm of ivy ripped from a trellis by a passing child.

"Hey, Raunch," Kit whispered. "Bardlong takes that shock!"

"Bardlong stops you short!" Ronkers would read off the trucks around town. But never did one of those crude vehicles so much as approach the fresh-painted curb by Bardlong's house. Bardlong was, indeed, retired. And the Ronkerses found it impossible to imagine the man as ever having lived another way. Even when his daily fare had been brake systems and shock absorbers, the Ronkerses couldn't conceive of Bardlong having taken part.

George once had a daydream of perverse exaggeration. He told Kit he had watched a huge BARD-LONG STOPS YOU SHORT! truck dump its entire supply in Bardlong's yard: the truck with its big back-panel doors flung wide open, churning up the lawn and disgorging itself of clanking parts — brake drums and brake shoes — and great oily slicks of brake fluid, rubbery, springing shock absorbers mashing down the flower beds.

"Raunch," Kit whispered.

"Yup . . ."

"Were the warts actually *in* her vagina?"

"In it, on it, all around it. . . ."

"*Seventy-five!* Oh, Raunch, I can't imagine it."

They lay in bed dappled by the late summer sun, which in the early morning could scarcely penetrate the thick weave of leaves fanned over their window by the black walnut tree.

"You know what I love about lying here?" Ronkers asked his wife. She snuggled up to him.

"Oh no, tell . . ."

"Well, it's the *tree*," he said. "I think my first sexual experience was in a tree house and that's what it's like up here. . . ."

"You and the damn tree," Kit said. "It might be my *architecture* that makes you like that tree so much. Or even *me*," she said. "And *that's* a likely story — I can't imagine you doing it in a tree house, frankly — that sounds like something one of your dirty old patients told you. . . ."

"Well, actually it was a dirty *young* one."

"You're awful, Raunch. My God, seventy-five *warts* . . ."

"Quite a lot of surgery for such a spot, too."

"I thought you said Tomlinson did it."

"Well, yes, but I *assisted*."

"You don't *normally* do that, do you?"

"Well, no, but this wasn't *normal*."

"You're really awful, Raunch. . . ."

"Purely medical interest, professional desire to learn. You use a lot of mineral oil and twenty-five percent podophyllin. The cautery is delicate. . . ."

"Turds," Kit said.

But summer soon ends, and with the students back in town Ronkers was too busy to lie long abed in the mornings. There are a staggering host of urinary-tract infections to be discovered in all corners of the globe, a little-known fringe benefit of the tourist trade; perhaps it is the nation's largest unknown summer import.

A line of students waited to see him each morning, their summer travel ended, their work begun in earnest, their peeing problems growing more severe.

"Doc, I think I picked this up in Izmir."

"The question is, how much has it gotten around *since?*"

"The trouble," Ronkers told Kit, "is that they all know perfectly well, at the first sign, what it is they've got — and, usually, even from *whom*. But almost all of them spend some time waiting for it to go away — or passing it on, for Christ's sake! — and they don't come to me until they can't *stand* it anymore."

But Ronkers was very sympathetic to his venereal patients and did not make them feel steeped in sin or wallowing in their just rewards; he said they should not feel guilty for catching anything from ab-

solutely anybody. However, he was tough about insisting that they inform the original hostess — whenever they knew her. "She may not *know*," Ronkers
would say.

"We are no longer communicating," they'd say.

And Ronkers would charge, "Well, she's just
going to be passing it on to someone else, who in
turn . . ."

"Good for them!" they'd holler.

"No, *look*," Ronkers would plead. "It's more serious than that, for *her*."

"Then *you* tell her," they'd say. "I'll give you her
number."

"Oh, *Raunch!*" Kit would scream. "Why don't
you make *them* do it?"

"How?" Ronkers would ask.

"Tell them you won't *fix* them. Tell them you'll
let them pee themselves *blind!*"

"They'd just go to someone else," Ronkers would
say. "Or they'd simply tell me that they've already
told the person — when they haven't, and never in-
tend to."

"Well, it's absurd, *you* calling up every other
woman in the damn town."

"I just hate the long-distance ones," Ronkers
would say.

"Well, you can at least make *them* pay for the
calls, Raunch!"

"Some of these students don't have any money."

"Tell them you'll ask their *parents* to pay, then!"

"It's tax-deductible, Kit. And they're not all students, either."

"It's awful, Raunch. It really is."

"How much higher are you going to make this
damn sleeping platform?"

"I like to make you work for it, Raunch."

"I know, but a *ladder,* my God . . ."

"Well, it's up in your favorite tree, right? And you like that, I'm told. And anyone who gets me has got to be athletic."

"I may get maimed trying."

"Raunch! Who are you calling *now?*"

"Hello?" he said to the phone. "Hello, is this Miss Wentworth? Oh, *Mrs.* Wentworth, well . . . I guess I would like to speak to your *daughter,* Mrs. Wentworth. Oh. You don't *have* a daughter? Oh. Well, I guess I would like to speak to *you,* Mrs. Wentworth. . . ."

"Oh, Raunch, how *awful!*"

"Well, this is Dr. Ronkers. I'm a urologist at University Hospital. Yes, *George* Ronkers. Dr. George Ronkers. Well . . . hi. Yes, *George.* Oh, *Sarah,* is it? Well, Sarah . . ."

And with the end of the summer there came an end to the rearrangements of the Ronkerses' interior space. Kit was through with carpentry and busy with her teaching and her schoolwork. When the workmen left, and the tools were carried off, and the dismantled walls no longer lay heaped in the Ronkerses' yard, it must have become apparent to Bardlong that reconstruction — at least for this year — was over.

The walnut tree was still there. Perhaps Bardlong had thought that, in the course of the summer building, the tree would go — making way for a new wing. He couldn't have known that the Ronkerses were rebuilding their house on the principle of "inviting the tree in."

With autumn coming on, Bardlong's issue with

the black walnut tree grew clear. Old Herr Kesler had not been wrong. George and Kit had a premonition of it the first cool, windy night of the fall. They lay on the sleeping platform with the tree swirling around them and the yellowing leaves falling past them, and they heard what sounded like a candlepin bowling ball falling on their roof and thudding its way down the slope to score in the rain gutter.

"Raunch?"

"That was a goddamn *walnut!*" Ronkers said.

"It sounded like a brick out of the chimney," Kit said.

And through the night they sat bolt upright to a few more: when the wind would loose one or, toward morning, a squirrel would successfully attack one, *whump!* it would strike, and roll *thunker-thunker-thunker-thunker dang!* into the clattering rain gutter.

"That one took a squirrel with it," Ronkers said.

"Well," said Kit, "at least there's no mistaking it for a prowler. It's too obvious a noise."

"Like a prowler dropping his instruments of burglary," Ronkers said.

Whump! thunker-thunker-thunker-thunker dang!

"Like a prowler shot off the roof," Kit groaned.

"We'll get used to it, I'm sure," Ronkers said.

"Well, Raunch, I gather Bardlong has been slow to adapt. . . ."

In the morning Ronkers noticed that the Bardlong house had a slate roof with a far steeper pitch than his own. He tried to imagine what the walnuts would sound like on Bardlong's roof.

"But there's surely an attic in that house," Kit

said. "The sound is probably muffled." Ronkers could not imagine the sound of a walnut striking a slate roof — and its subsequent descent to the rain gutter — as in any way "muffled."

By mid-October the walnuts were dropping with fearful regularity. Ronkers thought ahead to the first wild storm in November as a potential blitzkrieg. Kit went out to rake a pile of the fallen nuts together; she heard one cutting loose above her, ripping through the dense leaves. She thought against looking up — imagining the ugly bruise between her eyes and the blow on the back of her head (driven into the ground). She bent over double and covered her head with her hands. The walnut narrowly missed her offered spine; it gave her a kidney punch. *Thok!*

"It *hurt*, Raunch," she said.

A beaming Bardlong stood under the dangerous tree, watching Ronkers comfort his wife. Kit had not noticed him there before. He wore a thick Alpine hat with a ratty feather in it; it looked like a reject of Herr Kesler's.

"Kesler gave it to me," Bardlong said. "I had asked for a *helmet*." He stood arrogantly in his yard, his rake held like a fungo bat, waiting for the tree to pitch a walnut down to him. He had chosen the perfect moment to introduce the subject — Kit just wounded, still in tears.

"You ever hear one of those things hit a slate roof?" Bardlong asked. "I'll call you up the next time a whole clump's ready to drop. About three A.M."

"It *is* a problem," Ronkers agreed.

"But it's a *lovely* tree," Kit said defensively.

"Well, it's *your* problem, of course," Bardlong said, offhanded, cheerful. "If I have the same problem with my rain gutters this fall as I had last, I *may* have to ask you to remove the part of your tree that's over *our* property, but you can do what you want with the rest of it."

"*What* rain gutter problem?" Ronkers asked.

"It must happen to *your* rain gutters, too, I'm sure. . . ."

"*What* happens?" asked Kit.

"They get full of goddamn walnuts," Bardlong said. "And it rains, and rains, and the gutters don't work because they're clogged with walnuts, and the water pours down the side of your house; your windows leak and your basement fills with water. That's all."

"Oh."

"Kesler bought me a mop. But he was a poor old foreigner, you know," Bardlong said confidingly, "and you never felt like getting *legal* with him. You know."

"Oh," said Kit. She did not like Bardlong. The casual cheerfulness of his tone seemed as removed from his meaning as the shock-absorber trade was from those delicately laced trellises in his yard.

"Oh, I don't mind raking up a few nuts," Bardlong said, smiling, "or waking up a few times in the night, when I think storks are crash-landing on my roof." He paused, glowing under old Kesler's hat. "Or wearing the protective gear," he added. He doffed the hat to Kit, who at the moment she saw his lightly freckled dome exposed was praying for that unmistakable sound of the leaves ripping apart above. But Bardlong returned the hat to his head. A walnut began its descent. Kit and George crouched, hands over their heads; Bardlong never flinched. With considerable force the walnut struck the slate-stone wall between them, splitting with a dramatic *kak!* It was as hard and as big as a baseball.

"It's sort of an *exciting* tree in the fall, really," Bardlong said. "Of course, my wife won't go near it this time of year — a sort of prisoner in her own yard, you might say." He laughed; some gold fillings from the booming brake-systems industry winked in his mouth. "But that's all right. No price should be set for beauty, and it *is* a lovely tree. *Water damage,* though," he said, and his tone changed suddenly, "is *real* damage."

Bardlong managed, Ronkers thought, to make "real" sound like a legal term.

"And if you've got to spend the money to take down half the tree, you better face up to taking it all. When *your* basement's full of water, that won't be any joke." Bardlong pronounced "joke" as if it were an obscene word; moreover, the implication in Bardlong's voice led one to suspect the wisdom in thinking *anything* was funny.

Kit said, "Well, Raunch, you could just get up on the roof and sweep the walnuts out of the rain gutters."

"Of course *I'm* too old for that," Bardlong sighed, as if getting up on his roof was something he *longed* to do.

"Raunch, you could even sweep out Mr. Bardlong's rain gutters, couldn't you? Like once a week or so, just at this time of the year?"

Ronkers looked at the towering Bardlong roof, the smooth slate surface, the steep pitch. Headlines flooded his mind: DOCTOR TAKES FOUR-STORY FALL! UROLOGIST BEANED BY NUT! CAREER CUT SHORT BY DEADLY TREE!

No, Ronkers understood the moment; it was time to look ahead to the larger victory; he could only win half. Bardlong was oblique, but Bardlong was clearly a man with a made-up mind.

"Could you recommend a tree surgeon?" Ronkers asked.

"Oh, *Raunch!*" said Kit.

"We'll cut the tree in half," Ronkers said, striding boldly toward the split trunk, kicking the bomb-debris of fallen walnuts aside.

"I think about *here,*" Bardlong said eagerly, having no doubt picked the spot years ago. "Of course, what *costs,*" he added, with the old shock-absorber seriousness back in his voice, "is properly roping the overhanging limbs so that they won't fall on my roof." *I hope they fall* through *your roof,* Kit thought. "Whereas, if you cut the whole tree down," Bardlong said, "you could save some time, and your money, by just letting the whole thing fall along the line of the wall; there's room for it, you see, before the street. . . ." The tree spread over them, obviously a *measured* tree, long in Bardlong's calculations. A terminal patient, Ronkers thought, perhaps from the beginning.

"I would like to keep the part of the tree that doesn't damage your property, Mr. Bardlong," Ronkers said; his dignity was good; his distance was cool. Bardlong respected the sense of business in his voice.

"I could arrange this for you," Bardlong said. "I mean, I know a good tree outfit." Somehow, the "outfit" smacked of the fleet of men driving around in the Bardlong trucks. "It would cost you a little less," he added, with his irritatingly confiding tone, "if you let me set this up. . . ."

Kit was about to speak but Ronkers said, "I

would really appreciate that, Mr. Bardlong. And we'll just have to take our chances with *our* rain gutters."

"Those are new windows," Kit said. "They won't leak. And who cares about water in the old basement? God, I don't care, I can tell you. . . ."

Ronkers tried to return Bardlong's patient and infuriatingly *understanding* smile. It was a Yes-I-Tolerate-My-Wife-Too smile. Kit was hoping for a vast unloading from above in the walnut tree, a downfall which would leave them all as hurt as she felt they were guilty.

"Raunch," she said later. "What if poor old Mr. Kesler sees it? And he *will* see it, Raunch. He comes by, from time to time, you know. What are you going to tell him about selling out his tree?"

"I didn't sell it out!" Ronkers said. "I think I saved what I could of the tree by letting him have his half. I couldn't have stopped him, legally. You must have seen that."

"What about poor Mr. Kesler, though?" Kit said. "We *promised*."

"Well, the tree will still be here."

"Half the tree . . ."

"Better than none."

"But what will he think of us?" Kit asked. "He'll think we agree with Bardlong that the tree is a nuisance. He'll think it will only be a matter of time before we cut down the rest."

"Well, the tree *is* a nuisance, Kit."

"I just want to know what you're going to say to Mr. Kesler, Raunch."

"I won't have to say anything," Ronkers told her. "Kesler's in the hospital."

She seemed stunned to hear that, old Kesler always having struck her with a kind of peasant hearti-

ness. Those men must live forever, surely. "Raunch?"
she asked, less sure of herself now. "He'll get *out* of
the hospital, won't he? And what will you tell him
when he gets out and comes around to see his tree?"

"He won't get out," Ronkers told her.

"Oh *no*, Raunch . . ."

The phone rang. He usually let Kit answer the
phone; she could fend off the calls that weren't serious. But Kit was deep in a vision of old Kesler, in his
worn lederhosen with his skinny, hairless legs.

"Hello," Ronkers told the phone.

"Dr. Ronkers?"

"Yes," he said.

"This is Margaret Brant." Ronkers groped to place
the name. A young girl's voice?

"Uh . . ."

"You left a message at the dorm to have me call
this number," Margaret Brant said. And Ronkers remembered, then; he looked over the list of the
women he had to call this week. Their names were
opposite the names of their infected partners-in-fun.

"Miss Brant?" he said. Kit was mouthing words
like a mute: *Why* won't old Mr. Kesler ever get out of
the hospital? "Miss Brant, do you know a young man
named Harlan Booth?"

Miss Brant seemed mute herself now, and Kit
whispered harshly, "*What?* What's wrong with him?"

"Cancer," he whispered back.

"Yes. *What?*" said Margaret Brant. "Yes, I know
Harlan Booth. What is the matter, please?"

"I am treating Harlan Booth for gonorrhea, Miss
Brant," Ronkers said. There was no reaction over the
phone. "Clap?" Ronkers said. "Gonorrhea? Harlan
Booth has the clap."

"I know what you mean," the girl said. Her voice

had gone hard; she was suspicious. Kit was turned away from him so that he couldn't see her face.

"If you have a gynecologist here in town, Miss Brant, I think you should make an appointment. I could recommend Dr. Caroline Gilmore; her office is at University Hospital. Or, of course, you could come to see me. . . ."

"Look, who *is* this?" Margaret Brant said. "How do I know you're a doctor? Someone just left a phone number for me to call. I never had anything to do with Harlan Booth. What kind of dirty joke is this?"

Possible, thought Ronkers. Harlan Booth had been a vain, uncooperative kid who had very scornfully feigned casualness when asked who else might be infected. "Could be a lot of people," he'd said proudly. And Ronkers had been forced to press him to get even one name: Margaret Brant. Possibly a virgin whom Harlan Booth disliked?

"You can call me at my home phone after I hang up," Ronkers said. "It's listed in the book: Dr. George Ronkers . . . and see if it's not the same number you have now. Or else I can simply apologize for the mistake; I can call up Harlan Booth and tell him off. And," Ronkers gambled, "you can examine yourself for any discharge, especially in the morning, and see if there's any inflammation. And if you think there's a possibility, you can certainly see *another* doctor and I'll never know. But if you've had relations with Harlan Booth, Miss Brant, I . . . ."

She hung up.

"Cancer?" Kit said, her back still to him. "Cancer of what?"

"Lungs," Ronkers said. "The bronchoscopy was positive; they didn't even have to open him up."

The phone rang again. When Ronkers said hello,

the party hung up. Ronkers had a deplorable habit of visualizing people he had spoken with only on the phone. He saw Margaret Brant in the girls' dormitory. First she would turn to the dictionary. Then, moving lights and mirrors, she would *look* at herself. What *should* it look like? she would be wondering. And perhaps a trip to the rack of medical encyclopedias in the library. Or, last, a talk with a friend. An embarrassing phone call to Harlan Booth? No, Ronkers couldn't see that part.

He could see Kit examining her walnut bruise in the multi-imaged mirror that was suspended beside the inverted cone — also suspended — that was the flue for the open-pit fireplace in their bedroom. One day, Ronkers thought, I will fall off the sleeping platform into the open-pit fireplace and run screaming and burning through the bedroom, seeing myself times five in that multi-imaged mirror. Jesus.

"One walnut sure makes a lot of bruises," Ronkers said sleepily.

"Please don't touch it," Kit said. She had wanted to bring up another subject tonight, but her enthusiasm had been stolen.

Outside, the doomed tree — the would-be amputee — brushed against their window the way a cat brushes against your leg. In that high room, the way the wind nudged under the eaves made sleep feel precarious — as if the roof might be suddenly lifted off the house and they'd be left there, exposed. The final phase of achieving perfect interior space.

Sometime after midnight, Ronkers was called to the hospital for an emergency. An old woman, whose entire urinary system Ronkers had replaced with bags and hoses, was suffering perhaps her last malfunction. Five minutes after he left the house, Kit answered the phone. It was the hospital saying that the woman had died and there was no need to hurry.

George was gone two hours; Kit lay awake. She had so much she wanted to say when George got back that she was overwhelmed with where to begin; she let him fall asleep. She had wanted to discuss once more whether and when they would have children. But the night seemed so stalked by mayhem that the optimism of having babies struck her as absurd. She thought instead of the cool aesthetics, the thin economy, which characterized her leanings in the field of architecture.

She lay awake a long time after George fell asleep, listening to the restless rubbing of the tree, hearing the patternless, breakaway falls of the walnuts hurtling down on them — dropping into their lives as randomly as old Herr Kesler's cancer, as Margaret Brant's possible case of clap.

In Ronkers's office, waiting for him even before his receptionist had arrived, was a bird-boned girl with a yogurt-and-wheat-germ complexion who couldn't have been more than 18; her clothes were expensive-looking and conservative — a steel-toned suit her mother might have worn. A cream-colored, softly scented scarf was at her throat. Ronkers thought she was beautiful; she looked as if she'd just stepped off a yacht. But, of course, he knew who she was.

"Margaret Brant?" he asked, shaking her hand. Her eyes were a complement to her suit, an eerie dawn-gray. She had a perfect nose, wide nostrils in which, Ronkers thought, hair would not dare to grow.

"Dr. Ronkers?"

"Yes. Margaret Brant?"

"Of course," she sighed. She eyed the stirrups on Ronkers's examining table with a bitter dread.

"I'm awfully sorry, Miss Brant, to have called you, but Harlan Booth was not the most cooperative patient I've ever had, and I thought — for your own good — since *he* wouldn't call you, I should." The girl nodded, biting her lower lip. She absently removed her suit jacket and her English buckle shoes; she moved toward the examining table and those gleaming stirrups as if the whole contraption were a horse she was not sure how to mount.

"You want to *look* at me?" she asked, her back to Ronkers.

"Please relax," Ronkers begged her. "This isn't especially unpleasant, really. Have you had any discharge? Have you noticed any burning, any inflammation?"

"I haven't noticed *anything,*" the girl told him, and Ronkers saw she was about to burst into tears. "It's very unfair!" she cried suddenly. "I've always been so careful with . . . sex," she said, "and I really didn't allow very much of *anything* with Harlan Booth. I *hate* Harlan Booth!" she screamed. "I didn't know he had anything wrong with him, of course, or I never would have let him *touch* me!"

"But you *did* let him?" Ronkers asked. He was confused.

"*Touch* me?" she said. "Yes, he touched me . . . *there,* you know. And he kissed me, a *lot.* But I wouldn't let him do anything *else!*" she cried. "And he was just *awful* about it, too, and he probably knew then that he was giving me *this!*"

"You mean, he just *kissed* you?" Ronkers asked, incredulous.

"Well, *yes.* And *touched* me, you know," she said,

blushing. "He put his hand in my pants!" she cried. "And I *let* him!" She collapsed against the bent-knee part of one stirrup on the examining table and Ronkers went over to her and led her very gently to a chair beside his desk. She sobbed, with her little sharp-boned fists balled against her eyes.

"Miss Brant," Ronkers said. "Miss Brant, do you mean that Harlan Booth only touched you with his *hand?* You didn't have *real* sexual intercourse . . . Miss Brant?"

She looked up at him, shocked. "God, *no!*" she said. She bit the back of her hand and kept her fierce eyes on Ronkers.

"Just his *hand* touched you . . . *there?*" said Ronkers; he pointed to the lap of her suit skirt when he said "there."

"Yes," she said.

Ronkers took her small face in his hands and smiled at her. He was not very good at comforting or reassuring people. People seemed to misread his gestures. Margaret Brant seemed to think he was going to kiss her passionately on the mouth, because her eyes grew very wide and her back stiffened and her quick hands came up under his wrists, trying to shove him away.

"Margaret!" Ronkers said. "You *can't* have the clap if that's all that happened. You don't often catch a venereal disease from someone's *hand.*"

She now held his wrists as though they were important to her. "But he *kissed* me, too," she said worriedly. "With his *mouth,*" she added, to make things clear.

Ronkers shook his head. He went to his desk and gathered up a bunch of medical pamphlets on venereal disease. The pamphlets resembled brochures from travel agencies; there were lots of pictures of people smiling sympathetically.

"Harlan Booth must have wanted me to embarrass you," Ronkers said. "I think he was angry that you wouldn't let him . . . *you* know."

"Then you don't even have to *look* at me?" she asked.

"No," Ronkers said. "I'm sure I don't."

"I've never *been* looked at, you know," Margaret Brant told him. Ronkers didn't know what to say. "I mean, *should* I be looked at? — sometime, you know. Just to see if everything's all right?"

"Well, you might have a standard examination by a gynecologist. I can recommend Dr. Caroline Gilmore at University Hospital; a lot of students find her very nice."

"But *you* don't want to look at me?" she asked.

"Uh, no," Ronkers said. "There's no need. And for a standard examination, you should see a gynecologist. I'm a urologist."

"Oh."

She looked vacantly at the examining table and those waiting stirrups; she slipped into her suit jacket very gracefully; she had a bit more hardship with her shoes.

"Boy, that Harlan Booth is going to *get* it," she said suddenly, and with a surprising authority in her small, sharp voice.

"Harlan Booth has already *got* it," Ronkers said, trying to lighten the situation. But tiny Margaret Brant looked newly dangerous to him. "Please don't do anything you'll regret," Ronkers began weakly. But the girl's clean, wide nostrils were flaring, her gun-gray eyes were dancing.

"Thank you, Dr. Ronkers," Margaret Brant said

with icy poise. "I very much appreciate your taking the trouble, and putting up with the embarrassment, of calling me." She shook his hand. "You are a very brave and *moral* man," she said, as if she were conferring military honors on Ronkers.

Watch out, Harlan Booth, he thought. Margaret Brant left Ronkers's office like a woman who had strapped on those stirrups for a ride on the examining table — and won.

Ronkers phoned up Harlan Booth. He certainly wasn't thinking of warning him; he wanted some right names. Harlan Booth took so long to answer the phone that Ronkers had worked himself up pretty well by the time Booth said a sleepy "Hello."

"You lying bastard, Booth," Ronkers said. "I want the names of people you've actually slept with — people who actually might have been exposed to your case, or from whom you might even have *gotten* it."

"Oh, go to hell, Doc," Booth said, bored. "How'd you like little Maggie Brant?"

"That was dirty," Ronkers said. "A rather young and innocent girl, Booth. You were very mean."

"A little prig, a stuck-up rich bitch," Harlan Booth said. "Did you have any luck with her, Doc?"

"Please," Ronkers said. "Just give me some names. Be kind, you've got to be kind, Booth."

"Queen Elizabeth," Booth said. "Tuesday Weld, Pearl Buck . . ."

"Bad taste, Booth," Ronkers said. "Don't be a swine."

"Bella Abzug," Booth said. "Gloria Steinem, Raquel Welch, Mamie Eisenhower . . ."

Ronkers hung up. *Go get him if you can, Maggie Brant; I wish you luck!*

There was a crush of people in the waiting room outside his office; Ronkers peered out the letter slot at them. His receptionist caught the secret signal and flashed his phone light.

"Yes?"

"You're supposed to call your wife. You want me to hold up the throng a minute?"

"Thank you, yes."

Kit must have picked up the phone and immediately shoved the mouthpiece toward the open window, because Ronkers heard the unmistakably harsh *yowl* of a chain saw (maybe, *two* chain saws).

"Well," Kit said, "this is some tree outfit, all right. Didn't Bardlong say he'd fix us up with a good *tree* outfit?"

"Yes," Ronkers said. "What's wrong?"

"Well, there are three men here with chain saws and helmets with their names printed on them. Their names are Mike, Joe, and Dougie. Dougie is the highest up in the tree right now; I hope he breaks his thick neck. . . ."

"Kit, for God's sake, what's the matter?"

"Oh, Raunch, they're not a *tree* outfit at all. They're Bardlong's men — you know, they came in a goddamn BARDLONG STOPS YOU SHORT truck. They'll probably kill the whole tree," Kit said. "You can't just hack off limbs and branches without putting that *stuff* on, can you?"

"Stuff?"

"Goop? Gunk?" Kit said. "You know, that gooey black stuff. It *heals* the tree. God, Raunch, you're supposed to be a *doctor,* I thought you'd know something about it."

"I'm not a *tree* doctor," Ronkers said.

"These men don't even look like they know what

they're doing," Kit said. "They've got ropes all over the tree and they're swinging back and forth on the ropes, and every once in a while they buzz something off with those damn saws."

"I'll call Bardlong," Ronkers said.

But his phone light was flashing. He saw three patients in rapid order, gained four minutes on his appointment schedule, peeked through the letter slot, pleaded with his receptionist, took three minutes off to call Bardlong.

"I thought you were hiring *professionals,*" Ronkers said.

"These men are *very* professional," Bardlong told him.

"Professional *shock-absorber* men," Ronkers said.

"No, no," Bardlong said. "Dougie used to be a tree man."

"Specialized in the walnut tree, too, I'll bet."

"Everything's fine," Bardlong said.

"I see why it costs me less," Ronkers said. "I end up paying *you.*"

"I'm retired," Bardlong said.

Ronkers's phone light was flashing again; he was about to hang up.

"Please don't worry," Bardlong said. "Everything is in good hands." And then there was an ear-splitting disturbance that made Ronkers sweep his desk ashtray into the wastebasket. From Bardlong's end of the phone came a rending sound — glassy, baroque chandeliers falling to a ballroom floor? Mrs. Bardlong, or some equally shrill and elderly woman, hooted and howled.

"Good *Christ!*" Bardlong said over the phone. And to Ronkers he hastily added, "Excuse me." He hung up, but Ronkers had distinctly heard it: a splintering of wood, a shattering of glass, and the yammer of a chain saw "invited in" the house. He tried to imagine the tree man, Dougie, falling with a roped limb through the Bardlongs' bay window, his chain saw still sawing as he snarled his way through the velvet drapes and the chaise longue. Mrs. Bardlong, an ancient cat on her lap, would have been reading the paper, when . . .

But his receptionist was flashing him with mad regularity, and Ronkers gave in. He saw a four-year-old girl with a urinary infection (little girls are more susceptible to that than little boys); he saw a 48-year-old man with a large and exquisitely tender prostate; he saw a 25-year-old woman who was suffering her first bladder problem. He prescribed some Azo Gantrisin for her; he found a sample packet of the big red choke-a-horse pills and gave it to her. She stared at them, frightened at the size.

"Is there, you know, an *applicator?*" she asked.

"No, no," Ronkers said. "You take them *orally.* You *swallow* them."

The phone flashed. Ronkers knew it was Kit.

"What happened?" he asked her. "I *heard* it!"

"Dougie cut right through the limb *and* the rope that was guiding the limb away from the house," Kit said.

"How exciting!"

"Poked the limb through Bardlong's bathroom window like a great pool cue . . ."

"Oh," said Ronkers, disappointed. He had hoped for the bay. . . .

"I think Mrs. Bardlong was in the bathroom," Kit said.

Shocked at his glee, Ronkers asked, "Was anyone hurt?"

"Dougie sawed into Mike's arm," Kit said, "and I think Joe broke his ankle jumping out of the tree."

"God!"

"No one's badly hurt," Kit said. "But the tree looks *awful;* they didn't even finish it."

"Bardlong will have to take care of it," Ronkers said.

"Raunch," Kit said. "The newspaper photographer was here; he goes out on every ambulance call. He took a picture of the tree and Bardlong's window. Listen, this is *serious,* Raunch: Does Kesler get a newspaper on his breakfast tray? You've got to speak to the floor nurse; don't let him see the picture, Raunch. Okay?"

"Okay," he said.

Outside in the waiting room the woman was showing the Azo Gantrisin pills to Ronkers's receptionist. "He wants me to *swallow* them. . . ." Ronkers let the letter slot close slowly. He buzzed his receptionist.

"Entertain them, please," he said. "I am taking ten."

He slipped out of his office through the hospital entrance and crossed through Emergency as the ambulance staff was bringing in a man on a stretcher; he was propped up on his elbows, his ankle unbooted and wrapped in an ice pack. His helmet said JOE. The man who walked beside the stretcher carried his helmet in his one good hand. He was MIKE. His other hand was held up close to his breast; his forearm was blood-soaked; an ambulance attendant walked alongside with his thumb jammed deep into the crook of Mike's arm. Ronkers intercepted them and took a look at the cut. It was not serious, but it was a messy, ragged thing with a lot of black oil and sawdust in it. About 30 stitches, Ronkers guessed, but the man was not bleeding too badly. A tedious debridement, lots of Xylocaine . . . but Fowler was covering Emergency this morning, and it wasn't any of Ronkers's business.

He went on to the third floor. Kesler was in 339, a single room; at least a private death awaited him. Ronkers found the floor nurse, but Kesler's door was open and Ronkers stood with the nurse in the hall where the old man could see them; Kesler recognized Ronkers, but didn't seem to know *where* he recognized Ronkers from.

"*Kommen Sie hinein, bitte!*" Kesler called. His voice was like speech scraped on a file, sanded down to something scratchier than old records. "*Grüss Gott!*" he called.

"I wish I knew some German," the nurse told Ronkers.

Ronkers knew a little. He went into Kesler's room, made a cursory check on the movable parts now keeping him alive. The rasp in Kesler's voice was due to the Levin tube that ran down his throat to his stomach.

"Hello, Mr. Kesler," Ronkers said. "Do you remember me?" Kesler stared with wonder at Ronkers; they had taken out his false teeth and his face was curiously turtlelike in its leatheriness — its sagging, cold qualities. Predictably, he had lost about 60 pounds.

"*Ach!*" Kesler said suddenly. "*Das house ge-bought?* You . . . *ja!* How goes it? Your wife the walls down-took?"

"Yes," Ronkers said, "but you would like it. It's very beautiful. There's more window light now."

"*Und der Bardlong?*" Kesler whispered. "He has not the tree down-chopped?"

"No."

"*Sehr gut!*" Herr Kesler said. That is pronounced *zehr goot*. "*Gut boy!*" Kesler told Ronkers. *Goot buoy*. Kesler blinked his dull, dry eyes for a second and when they opened it was as if they opened on another scene — another time, somewhere. "*Frühstück?*" he asked politely.

"That means breakfast," Ronkers told the nurse. They had Kesler on a hundred milligrams of Demerol every four hours; that makes you less than alert.

Ronkers was getting out of the elevator on the first floor when the intercom paged "Dr. Heart." There was no Dr. Heart at University Hospital. "Dr. Heart" meant that someone's heart had stopped.

"Dr. Heart?" the intercom asked sweetly. "Please come to 304. . . ."

Any doctor in the hospital was supposed to hurry to that room. There was an unwritten rule that you looked around and made a slow move to the nearest elevator, hoping another doctor would beat you to the patient. Ronkers hesitated, letting the elevator door close. He pushed the button again, but the elevator was already moving up.

"Dr. Heart, room 304," the intercom said calmly. It was better than urgently crying, "A doctor! Any doctor to room 304! Oh, my God, *hurry!*" That might disturb the other patients and the visitors.

Dr. Hampton was coming down the floor toward the elevator.

"You still having office calls?" Hampton asked Ronkers.

"Yup," Ronkers said.

"Go back to your office, then," Hampton said. "I'll get this one."

The elevator had stopped on the third floor; it

was pretty certain that "Dr. Heart" had already arrived in 304. Ronkers went back to his office. It
would be nice to take Kit out to dinner, he thought.

At the Route Six Ming Dynasty, Kit ordered the sweet
and sour bass; Ronkers chose the beef in lobster
sauce. He was distracted. He had seen a sign in the
window of the Route Six Ming Dynasty, just as they'd
come in the door. It was a sign about two feet long
and one foot high — black lettering on white shirt
cardboard, perhaps. It looked perfectly natural there
in the window, for it was about the expected size —
and, Ronkers falsely assumed, about the expected
content of a sign like TWO WAITRESSES WANTED.

Ronkers was distracted only now, as he sipped a
drink with Kit, because only now was the *real* content of that sign coming through to him. He thought
he was imagining it, so he excused himself from the
table and slipped outside the Route Six Ming Dynasty
to have another look at the sign.

Appallingly, he had *not* imagined it. There,
vividly in a lower corner of the window, plainly in
view of every customer approaching the door, was a
neatly lettered sign, which read: HARLAN BOOTH HAS
THE CLAP.

"Well, it's *true,* isn't it?" Kit asked.

"Well, yes, but that's not the point," Ronkers
said. "It's sort of unethical. I mean, it *has* to be Margaret Brant, and I'm responsible for releasing the information. That sort of thing should be confidential,
after all."

"Turds," said Kit. "Good for Margaret Brant! You
must admit, Raunch, if Harlan Booth had played fair
with you, the whole thing wouldn't have happened. I
think he deserves it."

"Well, of course he *deserves* it," Ronkers said, "but I wonder where *else* she put up signs."

"Really, Raunch, just let it be. . . ."

But Ronkers had to see for himself. They drove to the Student Union. Inside the main lobby, Ronkers searched the giant bulletin board for clues.

'70 BMW, LIKE NEW . . .

RIDERS WANTED TO SHARE EXPENSES AND DRIVING TO NYC, LV. THURS., RETURN MON. EVE., CALL "LARRY," 351-4306. . . .

HARLAN BOOTH HAS THE CLAP. . . .

"My God."

They went to the auditorium; a play was in progress. They didn't even have to get out of their car to see it: a NO PARKING sign had been neatly covered and given the new message. Kit was hysterical.

The Whale Room was where a lot of students drank and played pool and danced to local talent. It was a loud, smoke-filled place; Ronkers had several emergency calls a month involving patients who had begun their emergency in the Whale Room.

Somehow, Margaret Brant had warmed the bartender's heart. Above the bar mirror, above the glowing bottles, above the sign saying CHECKS CASHED FOR EXACT AMOUNT ONLY, were the same neat and condemning letters now familiar to Ronkers and Kit. The Whale Room was informed that Harlan Booth was contagious.

Fearing the worst, Ronkers insisted they take a drive past Margaret Brant's dorm — a giant building, a women's dormitory of prison size and structure. Ivy did not grow there.

In the upcast streetlights, above the bicycle racks — seemingly tacked to every sill of every third-floor window — a vast sewn-together bedsheet stretched across the entire front of Catherine Cascomb Dormitory for Women. Margaret Brant had friends. Her friends were upset, too. In a massive sacrifice of linen and labor, every girl in every third-floor, front-window room had done her part. Each letter was about five feet high and single-bed width.

"Fantastic!" Kit shouted. "Well done! Good show! Let him have it!"

"Way to go, Maggie Brant," whispered Ronkers reverently. But he knew he hadn't seen the end of it.

It was 2:00 A.M. when the phone rang, and he suspected it was not the hospital.

"Yes?" he said.

"Did I wake you up, Doc?" said Harlan Booth. "I sure *hope* I woke you up."

"Hello, Booth," Ronkers said. Kit sat up beside him, looking strong and fit.

"Call off your goons, Doc. I don't have to put up with this. This is harassment. You're supposed to be *ethical,* you crummy doctors."

"You mean you've seen the signs?" Ronkers asked.

"*Signs?*" Booth asked. "*What* signs? What are you talking about?"

"What are *you* talking about?" Ronkers said, genuinely puzzled.

"You know goddamn well what I'm talking about!" Harlan Booth yelled. "Every half-hour a broad calls me up. It's two o'clock in the morning, Doc, and every half-hour a broad calls me up. *A different* broad, every half-hour, you know perfectly well . . ."

"What do they say to you?" Ronkers asked.

"Cut it out!" Booth yelled. "You know damn well

what they say to me, Doc. They say stuff like 'How's your clap coming along, Mr. Booth?' and 'Where are you spreading your clap around, Harlan old baby?' You *know* what they say to me, Doc!"

"Cheer up, Booth," Ronkers said. "Get out for a breath of air. Take a drive — down by Catherine Cascomb Dormitory for Women, for example. There's a lovely banner unfurled in your honor; you really ought to see it."

"A *banner?*" Booth said.

"Go get a drink at the Whale Room, Booth," Ronkers told him. "It will settle you down."

"*Look,* Doc!" Booth screamed. "You call them off!"

"I didn't call them on, Booth."

"It's that little bitch Maggie Brant, isn't it, Doc?"

"I doubt she's operating alone, Booth."

"Look," Booth said. "I can take you to court for this. Invasion of privacy. I can go to the papers. I'll go to the *university* — expose Student Health. You've got no right to be this unethical."

"Why not just call Margaret Brant?" Ronkers suggested.

"*Call* her?"

"And apologize," Ronkers said. "Tell her you're sorry."

"*Sorry?!*" Booth shouted.

"And then come give me some names," Ronkers said.

"I'm going to every newspaper in the state, Doc."

"I'd love to see you do that, Booth. They would crucify you. . . ."

"Doc . . ."

"Give yourself a real lift, Booth. Take a drive by Catherine Cascomb Dormitory for Women. . . ."

"Go to hell, Doc."

"Better hurry, Booth. Tomorrow they may start the bumper sticker campaign."

"Bumper stickers?"

"'Harlan Booth has the clap,'" Ronkers said. "That's what the bumper stickers are going to say. . . ."

Booth hung up. The way he hung up rang in Ronkers's ear for a long time. The walnuts dropping on the roof were almost soothing after the sound Booth had made.

"I think we've got him," Ronkers told Kit.

"'*We*,' is it?" she said. "You sound like you've joined up."

"I *have*," Ronkers said. "I'm going to call Margaret Brant first thing in the morning and tell her about my bumper-sticker idea."

But Margaret Brant needed no coaching. In the morning when Ronkers went out to his car, there was a freshly stuck-on bumper sticker, front and back. Dark blue lettering on a bright yellow background; it ran half the length of the bumper.

HARLAN BOOTH HAS THE CLAP

On his way to the hospital, Ronkers saw more of the adorned cars. Some drivers were parked in gas stations, working furiously to remove the stickers. But that was a hard, messy job. Most people appeared to be too busy to do anything about the stickers right away.

"I counted thirty-four, just driving across town," Ronkers told Kit on the phone. "And it's still early in the morning."

"Bardlong got to work early, too," Kit told him.

"What do you mean?"

"He hired a real *tree* outfit this time. The tree surgeons came right after you left."

"Ah, real tree surgeons . . ."

"They have helmets, too, and their names are Mickey, Max, and Harv," Kit said. "And they brought a whole tub of that black healing stuff."

"*Dr. Heart,*" said Ronkers's receptionist, cutting in. "*Dr. Heart, please, to 339.*"

"Raunch?"

But the receptionist was interrupting because it was so early; there just might not be another doctor around the hospital. Ronkers came in early, often hours ahead of his first appointment — to make his hospital rounds, yes, but mainly to sit in his office alone for a while.

"I've got to go," he told Kit. "I'll call back."

"Who's Dr. Hart?" Kit asked. "Somebody new?"

"Yup," Ronkers said, but he was thinking: No, it's probably somebody *old*.

He was out of his office, and half through the connecting tunnel which links the main hospital to several doctors' offices, when he heard the intercom call for Dr. Heart again and recognized the room number: 339. That was old Herr Kesler's room, Ronkers remembered. Nurses, seeing him coming, opened doors for him; they opened doors in all directions, down all corridors, and they always looked after him a little disappointed that he did not pass through *their* doors, that he veered left instead of right. When he got to Kesler's room, the cardiac-resuscitation cart was parked beside the bed and Dr. Heart was already there. It was Danfors — a better Dr. Heart than Ronkers could have been, Ronkers knew; Danfors was a heart specialist.

Kesler was dead. That is, technically, when your heart stops, you're dead. But Danfors was already holding the electrode plates alongside Kesler's chest; the old man was about to get a tremendous jolt. Ah, the new machines, Ronkers marveled. Ronkers had once brought a man from the dead with 500 volts from the cardioverter, lifting the body right off the bed, the limbs jangling — like pithing a frog in Introductory Biology.

"How's Kit, George?" Danfors asked.

"Just fine," Ronkers said. Danfors was checking the IV of sodium bicarbonate running into Kesler. "You must come see what she's done to the house. And bring Lilly."

"Right-O," said Danfors, giving Kesler 500 volts.

Kesler's jaw was rigid on his chest and his toothless gums were clenched together fast, yet he managed to force a ghastly quarter-moon of a smile and expel a sentence of considerable volume and energy. It was German, of course, which surprised Danfors; he probably didn't know Kesler was an Austrian.

"*Noch ein Bier!*" Kesler ordered.

"What'd he say?" Danfors asked Ronkers.

"One more beer," Ronkers translated.

But the current, of course, was cut. Kesler was dead again. Five hundred volts had woken him up, but Kesler did not have enough voltage of his own to keep himself awake.

"Shit," Danfors said. "I got three in a row with this thing when the hospital first got it, and I thought it was the best damn machine alive. But then I lost four out of the next five. So I was four-and-four with the thing; nothing is foolproof, of course. And now this one's the tie breaker." Danfors managed to make his record with the heart machine sound like a losing season.

Now Ronkers didn't want to call Kit back; he knew Kesler's death would upset her. But she called him before he could work it out.

"Well, well," Ronkers said.

"Raunch?" Kit asked. "Kesler didn't see the paper, did he? They put the picture right on the front page, you know. You don't think he saw it, do you?"

"For a fact, he did not see it," Ronkers said.

"Oh, good," she said. She seemed to want to stay on the phone, Ronkers thought, although she wasn't talking. He told her he was awfully busy and he had to go.

Ronkers was in a cynical mood when he sat down to lunch with Danfors in the hospital cafeteria. They were still on the soup course when the intercom pleasantly asked for Dr. Heart. Since he was a heart specialist, Danfors answered most of the Dr. Heart calls in the hospital whenever he was there, even if someone beat him to the elevator. He stood up and drank his milk down with a few swift guzzles.

"*Noch ein Bier!*" Ronkers said.

At home, Kit — the receiver of messages, the composer of rooms — had news for him. First, Margaret Brant had left word she was dropping the Harlan Booth assault because Booth had called and begged her forgiveness. Second, Booth had called and left Kit a list of names. "Real ones," he'd said. Third, something was up with Bardlong and the infernal tree. The tree surgeons had alarmed him about something, and Bardlong and his wife had been poking about under the tree, along their side of the slate-stone wall, as if inspecting some new damage — as if plotting some new attack.

Wearily, Ronkers wandered to the yard to confront this new problem. Bardlong was down on the ground on all fours, peering deep into the caves of his slate-stone wall. Looking for squirrels?

"After the men did such a neat job," Bardlong announced, "it came to their attention that they should really have taken the whole thing down. And they're professionals, of course. I'm afraid they're right. The whole thing's got to come down."

"Why?" Ronkers asked. He was trying to summon resistance, but he found his resistance was stale.

"The roots," Bardlong said. "The roots are going to topple the wall. The *roots,*" he said again, as if he were saying, *the armies! the tanks! the big guns!* "The roots are crawling their way through my wall." He made it sound like a conspiracy, the roots engaged in strangling some stones, bribing others. They crept their way into revolutionary positions among the slate. On signal, they were ready to upheave the whole.

"That will surely take some time," Ronkers said, thinking, with a harshness that surprised him: That wall will outlive *you,* Bardlong!

"It's already happening," Bardlong said. "I hate to ask you to do this, of course, but the wall, if it crumbles, well . . ."

"We can build it up again," Ronkers said. Ah, the *doctor* in him!

As illogical as cancer, Bardlong shook his head. Not far away, Ronkers saw, would be the line about hoping not to get "legal." Ronkers felt too tired to resist *anything.*

"It's simple," said Bardlong. "I want to keep the wall, you want to keep the tree."

"Walls can be rebuilt," Ronkers said, utterly without conviction.

"I see," Bardlong said. Meaning what? It was like the 500 volts administered to Kesler. There was a real effect — it was visible — but it was not effective at all. On his gloomy way back inside his house Ronkers pondered the effect of 500 volts on Bardlong. With the current on for about five minutes.

He also fantasized this bizarre scene: Bardlong suddenly in Ronkers's office, looking at the floor and saying, "I have had certain . . . relations, ah, with a lady who, ah, apparently was not in the best of . . . health."

"If it would, Mr. Bardlong, spare you any embarrassment," Ronkers imagined himself saying, "I could of course let the, ah, lady know that she should seek medical attention."

"You'd do that for me?" Bardlong would cry then, overcome. "Why, I mean, I would, ah . . . pay you for that, anything you ask."

And Ronkers would have him then, of course. With a hunting cat's leer, he would spring the price: "How about half a walnut tree?"

But things like that, Ronkers knew, didn't happen. Things like that were in the nature of the stories about abandoned pets limping their way from Vermont to California, finding the family months later, arriving with bleeding pads and wagging tails. The reason such stories were so popular was that they went pleasantly against what everyone knew *really* happened. The pet was squashed by a Buick in Massachusetts — or, worse, was perfectly happy to remain abandoned in Vermont.

And if Bardlong came to Ronkers's office, it would be for some perfectly respectable aspect of age finally lodging in his prostate.

"Kesler's dead, Kit," Ronkers told her. "His heart stopped, saved him a lot of trouble, really; he would have gotten quite uncomfortable."

He held her in the fabulous sleeping place she had invented. Outside their window the scrawny, pruned tree clicked against the rain gutter like light bones. The leaves were all gone; what few walnuts remained were small and shriveled — even the squirrels ignored them, and if one had fallen on the roof it would have gone unnoticed. Winter-bare and offering nothing but its weird shadows on their bed and its alarming sounds throughout their night, the tree seemed hardly worth their struggle. Kesler, after all, was dead. And Bardlong was so *very* retired that he had more time and energy to give to trivia than anyone who was likely to oppose him. The wall between Ronkers and Bardlong seemed frail indeed.

It was then that Ronkers realized he had not made love to his wife in a very long time, and he made the sort of love to Kit that some therapist might have called "reassuring." And some lover, Ronkers thought later, might have called dull.

He watched her sleep. A lovely woman; her students, he suspected, cared for more than her architecture. And she, one day, might care more for them — or for *one* of them. Why was he thinking *that?* he wondered; then he pondered his own recent sensations for the X-ray technician.

But those kinds of problems, for Kit and him, seemed years away — well, *months* away, at least.

He thought of Margaret Brant's sweet taste of revenge; her mature forgiveness surprised and encouraged him. And Harlan Booth's giving in? Whether he was converted — or just trapped, and evil to the core — was quite unknowable at the moment. Whether *anyone* was . . . Ronkers wondered.

Danfors's season with the heart machine now stood at four-and-six. What sort of odds were those in favor of human reproduction — Ronkers's and Kit's, especially? . . . And even if all the high school principals and parents in the world were as liberal and humorous and completely approachable concerning venereal disease as they might be sympathetic toward a football injury, there would *still* be rampant clap in the world — and syphilis, and worse.

Kit slept.

The brittle tree clacked against the house like the bill of a parrot he remembered hearing in a zoo. Where was that? *What zoo?*

In an impulse, which felt to Ronkers like resignation, he moved to the window and looked over the moonlit roofs of the suburbs — many of which he could see for the first time, now that the leaves were all gone and a winter view was possible. And to all the people under those roofs, and more, he whispered, wickedly, "Have fun!" To Ronkers, this was a kind of benediction with a hidden hook.

"Why *not* have children?" he said aloud. Kit stirred, but she had not actually heard him.

Interior Space (1980)

AUTHOR'S NOTES

"Interior Space" was first published in *Fiction* (vol. 6, no. 2, 1980). It is my second-favorite among the very few short stories I have written; I have written more novels (eight) than short stories — I believe that will always be the case. I remember that I wrote the first draft of this story sometime in 1974, probably before I began *The World According to Garp* (1978); for forgotten reasons, the story languished in a bottommost drawer for five or six years before I took it out and finished it.

I admit that a certain confusion regarding the subject of this story may lie at the heart of why the story "languished" for so long, and why I was quite surprised when it won an O. Henry Award. "Interior Space" began as a story about a false case of gonorrhea, but Mr. Kesler's cancer stole the stage. All along, it was the death of the *tree* that most interested me. In the end, it is a story about marriage, and — more important — about the necessary optimism that is required of thoughtful, observant people who decide (despite what they *know*) to have children.

I see now, too, that in "Interior Space" I was testing a line that would (with revision) become the last line of *The World According to Garp:* "In the world according to Garp, we are all terminal cases." Here it is the tree that is a "terminal patient."

BRENNBAR'S RANT

My husband, Ernst Brennbar, worked steadily on his second cigar and his third cognac. A slow, rising heat flushed his cheeks. His tongue felt lazy and overweight. He knew that if he didn't try to speak soon, his mouth would loll open and he'd belch — or worse. A bear of guilt shifted in his stomach and he remembered the bottle of '64 Brauneberger Juffer Spätlese that had accompanied his ample portion of *truite Metternich*. His red ears throbbed a total recall of the '61 Pommard Rugiens that had drowned his *boeuf Crespi*.

Brennbar looked across the wasted dinner table at me, but I was lost in a conversation about minority groups. The man speaking to me appeared to be a member of one. For some reason, the waiter was included — perhaps as a gesture meant to abolish class distinctions. Possibly the man who spoke with me and the waiter were from the same minority group.

"You wouldn't know anything about it," the man told me, but I'd been watching my blotching husband; I hadn't been paying attention.

"Well," I said defensively, "I can certainly imagine what it must have been like."

"Imagine!" the man shouted. He tugged the waiter's sleeve for support. "This was the real thing. No amount of *imagining* could ever make you feel it like we did. We had to live with it every day!" The waiter guessed he should agree.

Another woman, sitting next to Brennbar, suddenly said, "That's no different from what women have always had to face — what we still have to face today."

"Yes," I said quickly, turning on the man. "For example, you're bullying me right now."

"Look, there's no persecution like religious persecution," the man said, yanking the waiter's arm for emphasis.

"You might ask a black," I said.

"Or any woman," said the woman next to Brennbar. "You talk as if you had a monopoly on discrimination."

"You're all full of shit," said Brennbar, slowly uncoiling his lounging tongue. The others stopped talking and looked at my husband as if he were a burn hole developing in a costly rug.

"Darling," I said, "we're talking about minority groups."

"As if that counts me out?" Brennbar asked. He made me disappear in a roil of cigar smoke. But the woman next to him seemed to feel provoked by this; she responded recklessly.

"I don't see that you're black," she said, "or a woman or a Jew. You're not even Irish or Italian or something like that, are you? I mean — *Brennbar* — what's that? German?"

"*Oui,*" said the waiter. "That's German, I know it."

And the man whose pleasure had been to abuse me said, "Oh, that's a fine minority group." The others — but not I — laughed. I was familiar with my husband's signals for the control he gradually lost on polite conversation; blowing cigar smoke in my face was a fairly advanced phase.

"My husband is from the Midwest," I said cautiously.

"Oh, you poor man," said the woman next to Brennbar. Her hand lay with facetious sympathy on Brennbar's shoulder.

"How appalling: the Midwest," someone far down the table muttered.

And the man who held the waiter's sleeve with the importance he might lavish on a mine detector said, "Now, there's a minority group!" Laughter embraced the table while I observed my husband's journey through one more lost control he held on polite conversation: the stiff smile accompanied by the studied tossing off of his third cognac and the over-steady pouring of his fourth. I'd forgotten that he bought the bottle.

I was so full I felt I'd temporarily lost my cleavage, but I said, "I'd like dessert. Would anyone else have anything else?" I asked, watching the studied tossing off of my husband's fourth cognac and the fantastically deliberate pouring of his fifth.

The waiter remembered his job; he fled to fetch the menu. And the man who had sought in the waiter an ethnic kinship boldly faced Brennbar and said with unctuous condescension, "I was merely trying to establish that religious discrimination — at least historically — is of a more subtle and pervasive kind than those forms of discrimination we have all jumped on the bandwagon about lately, with our cries of racist, sexist —"

Brennbar belched: a sharp shot like a brass bed-post ball flung at random into the kitchenware. I was familiar with this phase, too; I knew now that the dessert would come too late and that my husband scarcely needed to pause before he would launch forth.

Brennbar began: "The first form of discrimination

I encountered while growing up is so subtle and pervasive that even to this day no group has been able to organize to protest it, no politician has dared mention it, no civil-liberty case has been taken to the courts. In no major, nor in any minor, city is there even a suitable ghetto where these sufferers can support one another. Discrimination against them is so total that they even discriminate against one another; they are ashamed to be what they are, they are ashamed of it when they're alone — and all the more ashamed to be seen together."

"Listen," said the woman next to Brennbar, "if you're talking about homosexuality, what you're saying is no longer the case —"

"I'm talking about pimples," Brennbar said. "Acne," he added, with a meaningful and hurting glance about the table. "Zits," Brennbar said. The others, those who dared, stared into my husband's deeply cratered face as if they were peeking into a disaster ward in a foreign hospital. Alongside that terrible evidence, the fact that we were ordering dessert *after* brandy and cigars was of little consequence. "You all knew people with pimples," Brennbar accused them. "And pimples disgusted you, didn't they?" The diners all looked away from him, but their memory of his pockmarks must have been severe. Those indentations, those pits, appeared to have been made by stones. My God, he was lovely.

Nearby, but coming no nearer, the waiter hovered and held back the dessert menus from this queer party as if he feared the menus could be consumed by our silence.

"Do you think it was easy to go into a drugstore?" Brennbar asked. "A whole cosmetic counter devoted to reminding you, the saleslady grinning at your zits and saying loudly, 'What can I do for you?' As if she didn't know. Even your own parents were ashamed of you! Subtle indications that your pillowcase was not washed with the rest of the laundry, and at breakfast your mother would say to you, 'Dear, you know, don't you, that the *blue* washcloth is yours?' Then watch your sister's face pale; she excuses herself from the table and rushes to rewash. Talk about myths involved with discrimination! God, you'd think pimples were more communicative than clap! Some kid after gym class asks if someone has a comb; you offer him yours, you see his mind melt — praying for an alternative, imagining his precious scalp alive with your zits. It was a common fable: If you saw a pimple, you assumed dirt. People who produce pus never wash.

"I swear on my sister's sweet ass," Brennbar said (he has no sister), "I washed my entire body three times a day. One day I washed my face eleven times. Every morning I went to the mirror to read the news. Like a body count in a war. Maybe the acne plaster killed two overnight, but four more have arrived. You learn to expect the greatest humiliation at the worst time: The morning of the night you achieved that blind date, there's a new one pulling your lips askew. Then one day, out of misguided pity or a vast and unfathomable cruelty, those few people who pass for your friends secure you a date with *another* pimple freak! Mortified, you both wait for it to end. Did they expect we would exchange remedies or count our permanent scars?

"Zitism!" Brennbar yelled. "That's what it is, zitism! And you're *zitists,* all of you, I'm sure of it," he muttered. "You couldn't begin to understand how awful . . ." His cigar was out; apparently shaken, he fumbled to relight it.

"No," said the man next to me. "I mean, yes . . . I can understand how terrible that must have been for you, really."

"It's nothing like your problem," Brennbar said morosely.

"No, well, yes — I mean, really, it *is* sort of what I mean," the man groped. "I can truly imagine how awful —"

"*Imagine?*" I said, my face alert, my mouth turning toward my best smile. "But what about what you said to me? You can't possibly *feel* it like he did. He had to *live* with it every day." I smiled at my husband. "Those were real pimples," I told my former attacker. "They're not to be imagined." Then I leaned across the table and touched Brennbar's hand affectionately. "Nice work, darling," I said. "You got him."

"Thanks," said Brennbar, totally relaxed. His cigar was relit; he passed the rim of his brandy snifter under his nose like a flower.

The woman next to Brennbar was unsure. She touched him gently, but urgently, and said to him, "Oh, I see, you were kidding — sort of. Weren't you?" Brennbar consumed her in cigar smoke before she could read his eyes; I can always read his eyes.

"Well, not kidding, exactly — were you, darling?" I said. "I think it was a metaphor," I told the others, and they looked at Brennbar with all the more suspicion. "It was a metaphor for growing up with intelligence in a stupid world. It meant that intelligence is so peculiar — so rare — that those of us with any real brains are constantly being discriminated against by the masses of stupidity around us." The entire table looked more pleased. Brennbar smoked; he could be an infuriating man.

"Of course," I went on, "people with intelligence really constitute one of the smallest minority groups. They have to endure the wallowing sheep-mindedness and flagrant idiocy of what's forever being *popular*. Popularity is probably the greatest insult to an intelligent person. Hence," I said, with a gesture to Brennbar, who was resembling a still life, "acne is a perfect metaphor for the feeling of being unpopular, which every intelligent person must suffer. Intelligence is unpopular, of course. Nobody likes an intelligent person. Intelligent people are not to be trusted. We suspect that their intelligence hides a kind of perversity. It's a little like thinking that people with pimples are unclean."

"Well," began the man next to me — he was warming up to the conversation, which he must have felt was returning to more comfortable ground. "Of course, the notion of the intellectual constituting a kind of ethnic group — this is hardly new. America is predominantly anti-intellectual. Look at television. Professor types are all batty eccentrics with the sort of temperaments of grandmothers. All idealists are fanatics or saints, young Hitlers or young Christs. Children who read books wear glasses and secretly wish they could play baseball as well as the other kids. We prefer an armpit evaluation of a man. And we like his mind to be possessed by the kind of stubborn loyalty we admire in dogs. But I must say, Brennbar, to suggest that pimples are analogous to intellect —"

"Not intellect," I said. "Intelligence. There are as many stupid intellectuals as there are stupid baseball players. Intelligence simply means the perception of what is going on." But Brennbar was cloaked in an enigma of cigar smoke and even the woman next to him could not see through to his point of view.

The man who had momentarily experienced the illusion of returning to more comfortable ground said, "I would dispute with you, Mrs. Brennbar, that there are as many stupid intellectuals as there are stupid baseball players."

Brennbar released a warning belch: a long, tunneling, and muffled signal like a trash can thrown down an elevator shaft while you are far away, in a shower on the 31st floor ("Who's there?" you'd call out to your empty apartment).

"Dessert?" said the waiter, distributing menus. He must have thought Brennbar had asked for one.

"I'll have the *pommes normandes en belle vue,*" said the faraway man who had found the Midwest appalling. His wife wanted the *pouding alsacien,* a cold dessert.

"I'd like the *charlotte Malakoff aux fraises,*" said the woman next to Brennbar.

I said I'd have the *mousseline au chocolat.*

"*Shit,*" said Brennbar. Whatever he'd meant as a metaphor, his ravaged face was no invention; we could all see that.

"I was just trying to help you, darling," I said, in a shocking new tone.

"Smart bitch," Brennbar said.

The man for whom comfortable ground was now a hazardous free fall away sat in this uneasy atmosphere of warring minority feelings and wished for more intelligence than he had. "I'll have the *clafoutis aux pruneaux,*" he said sheepishly.

"You would," said Brennbar. "That's just what I figured you for."

"I got him right, too, darling," I said.

"Did you guess *her?*" Brennbar asked me, indicating the woman next to him.

"Oh, she was easy," I said. "I got everyone."

"I was wrong on yours," Brennbar told me. He seemed troubled. "I was sure you'd try to split the savarin with someone."

"Brennbar doesn't eat dessert," I explained to the others. "It's bad for his complexion."

Brennbar sat more or less still, like a contained lava flow. I knew that in a very short time we would go home. I wanted, terribly, to be alone with him.

Brennbar's Rant (1973)

AUTHOR'S NOTES

This angry little story was much more fun to write than it is to read. It was originally a part of my third novel, *The 158-Pound Marriage* (1974), wherein the story served as an example of the writing of one of the characters, Edith Winter; it also served as an example of how Edith "fictionalized" her husband, because Brennbar was meant to be identifiable to the reader (of the novel) as an exaggeration of Edith's husband, Severin Winter. Such a heightened degree of playfulness became exasperating to me; it seemed too much a story within a story for its own good — I cut it from the novel.

But before then, an argument ensued — I forget with whom — about whether or not I could write a convincing short story from the point of view of a woman. (The argument must have been with a woman, now that I think of it.) Anyway, I set out to demonstrate that this story could have been written by a woman — namely, Edith Winter — and to prove the point I submitted "Brennbar's Rant" to *Playboy*. The story was not presented to *Playboy* as a story by John Irving; it was submitted as a story by Edith Winter — an unknown writer, who would remain unknown (except to readers of *The 158-Pound Marriage*).

A problem arose when *Playboy* accepted the story; they were very interested in who Edith Winter was — and had she written anything else? Peter Matson, my agent at the time, had warned me that this might happen, and that *Playboy* might not look upon being fooled with good humor. The confession was made: *I* was the author of "the zitism story," as it was called; if there were hard feelings, they weren't lingering. *Playboy* published "Brennbar's Rant" — in their December 1974 issue — as a story by John Irving. Edith Winter was thus denied the only opportunity she was given to publish her own work; I had created Brennbar and his rant for *her* — in the end, I felt I had robbed her of something.

When I saw the illustration that accompanied "Brennbar's Rant" in *Playboy,* I sincerely wished that Edith Winter had been the author of the story — the illustration was so utterly tasteless and disgusting. A woman's breast with a thumb and index finger pinching her nipple, only it is *not* a nipple but a pimple — pus and all. "Gross!" said my son Colin; he was nine at the time. For a while, the picture made me want to disown the story, which was foolish because the story was not to blame.

Today I can point to "Brennbar's Rant" as my opinion of political correctness — before there *was* any political correctness so-called. I can also point to it as an example of my opinion of popularity before I was popular, for in the story Edith Winter says, "Popularity is probably the greatest insult to an intelligent person." Edith was wrong. Popularity is only an insult to those people who presume they are more intelligent than the person who is popular. But "Brennbar's Rant" was written in 1973; I didn't know much about popularity then.

THE PENSION
GRILLPARZER

My father worked for the Austrian Tourist Bureau. It was my mother's idea that our family travel with him when he went on the road as a Tourist Bureau spy. My mother and brother and I would accompany him on his secretive missions to uncover the discourtesy, the dust, the badly cooked food, the shortcuts taken by Austria's restaurants and hotels and pensions. We were instructed to create difficulties whenever we could, never to order exactly what was on the menu, to imitate a foreigner's odd requests — the hours we would like to have our baths, the need for aspirin and directions to the zoo. We were instructed to be civilized but troublesome; and when the visit was over, we reported to my father in the car.

My mother would say, "The hairdresser is always closed in the morning. But they make suitable recommendations outside. I guess it's all right, provided they don't claim to have a hairdresser actually *in* the hotel."

"Well, they *do* claim it," my father would say. He'd note this in a giant pad.

I was always the driver. I said, "The car is parked off the street, but someone put fourteen kilometers on the gauge between the time we handed it over to the doorman and picked it up at the hotel garage."

"That is a matter to report directly to the management," my father said, jotting it down.

"The toilet leaked," I said.

"I couldn't open the door to the W.C.," said my brother, Robo.

"Robo," Mother said, "you always have trouble with doors."

"Was that supposed to be Class C?" I asked.

"I'm afraid not," Father said. "It is still listed as Class B." We drove for a short while in silence; our most serious judgment concerned changing a hotel's or a pension's rating. We did not suggest reclassification frivolously.

"I think this calls for a letter to the management," Mother suggested. "Not too nice a letter, but not a really rough one. Just state the facts."

"Yes, I rather liked him," Father said. He always made a point of getting to meet the managers.

"Don't forget the business of them driving our car," I said. "That's really unforgivable."

"And the eggs were bad," said Robo; he was not yet 10 and his judgments were not considered seriously.

We became a far harsher team of evaluators when my grandfather died and we inherited Grandmother — my mother's mother, who thereafter accompanied us on our travels. A regal dame, Johanna was accustomed to Class A travel, and my father's duties more frequently called for investigations of Class B and Class C lodgings. They were the places, the B and C hotels (and the pensions), that most interested the tourists. At restaurants we did a little better. People who couldn't afford the classy places to sleep were still interested in the best places to eat.

"I shall not have dubious food tested on me," Johanna told us. "This strange employment may give you all glee about having free vacations, but I can see there is a terrible price paid: the anxiety of not knowing what sort of quarters you'll have for the night. Americans may find it charming that we still have rooms without private baths and toilets, but I am an old woman and I'm not charmed by walking down a public corridor in search of cleanliness and my relievement. Anxiety is only half of it. Actual diseases are possible — and not only from food. If the bed is questionable, I promise I shan't put my head down. And the children are young and impressionable; you should think of the clientele in some of these lodgings and seriously ask yourselves about the influences." My mother and father nodded; they said nothing. "Slow down!" Grandmother said sharply to me. "You're just a young boy who likes to show off." I slowed down. "Vienna," Grandmother sighed. "In Vienna I always stayed at the Ambassador."

"Johanna, the Ambassador is not under investigation," Father said.

"I should think not," Johanna said. "I suppose we're not even headed toward a Class A place?"

"Well, it's a B trip," my father admitted. "For the most part."

"I trust," Grandmother said, "that you mean there is one A place en route?"

"No," Father admitted. "There is one C place."

"It's okay," Robo said. "There are fights in Class C."

"I should imagine so," Johanna said.

"It's a Class C pension, very small," Father said, as if the size of the place forgave it.

"And they're applying for a B," said Mother.

"But there have been some complaints," I added.

"I'm sure there have," Johanna said.

"And animals," I added. My mother gave me a look.

"Animals?" said Johanna.

"Animals," I admitted.

"A *suspicion* of animals," my mother corrected me.

"Yes, be fair," Father said.

"Oh, wonderful!" Grandmother said. "A suspicion of animals. Their hair on the rugs? Their terrible waste in the corners! Did you know that my asthma reacts, severely, to any room in which there has recently been a cat?"

"The complaint was not about cats," I said. My mother elbowed me sharply.

"Dogs?" Johanna said. "Rabid dogs! Biting you on the way to the bathroom."

"No," I said. "Not dogs."

"Bears!" Robo cried.

But my mother said, "We don't know for sure about the bear, Robo."

"This isn't serious," Johanna said.

"Of course it's not serious!" Father said. "How could there be bears in a pension?"

"There was a letter saying so," I said. "Of course, the Tourist Bureau assumed it was a crank complaint. But then there was another sighting — and a second letter claiming there had been a bear."

My father used the rearview mirror to scowl at me, but I thought that if we were all supposed to be in on the investigation it would be wise to have Grandmother on her toes.

"It's probably not a real bear," Robo said, with obvious disappointment.

"A man in a bear suit!" Johanna cried. "What unheard-of perversion is *that*? A *beast* of a man sneaking about in disguise! Up to what? It's a man in a bear suit, I know it is," she said. "I want to go to that one *first!* If there's going to be a Class C experience on this trip, let's get it over with as soon as possible."

"But we haven't got reservations for tonight," Mother said.

"Yes, we might as well give them a chance to be at their best," Father said. Although he never revealed to his victims that he worked for the Tourist Bureau, Father believed that reservations were simply a decent way of allowing the personnel to be as prepared as they could be.

"I'm sure we don't need to make a reservation in a place frequented by men who disguise themselves as animals," Johanna said. "I'm sure there is *always* a vacancy there. I'm sure the guests are regularly dying in their beds — of fright, or else of whatever unspeakable injury the madman in the foul bear suit does to them."

"It's probably a *real* bear," Robo said, hopefully — for in the turn the conversation was taking, Robo certainly saw that a real bear would be preferable to Grandmother's imagined ghoul. Robo had no fear, I think, of a real bear.

I drove us as inconspicuously as possible to the dark, dwarfed corner of Planken and Seilergasse. We were looking for the Class C pension that wanted to be a B.

"No place to park," I said to Father, who was already making note of that in his pad.

I double-parked and we sat in the car and peered up at the Pension Grillparzer; it rose only four slender stories between a pastry shop and a Tabak Trafik.

"See?" Father said. "No bears."

"No *men,* I hope," said Grandmother.

"They come at night," Robo said, looking cautiously up and down the street.

We went inside to meet the manager, a Herr Theobald, who instantly put Johanna on her guard.

"Three generations traveling together!" he cried. "Like the old days," he added, especially to Grandmother, "before all these divorces and the young people wanting apartments by themselves. This is a *family* pension! I just wish you had made a reservation — so I could put you more closely together."

"We're not accustomed to sleeping in the same room," Grandmother told him.

"Of course not!" Theobald cried. "I just meant that I wished your *rooms* could be closer together." This worried Grandmother, clearly.

"How far apart must we be put?" she asked.

"Well, I've only two rooms left," he said. "And only one of them is large enough for the two boys to share with their parents."

"And my room is how far from theirs?" Johanna asked coolly.

"You're right across from the W.C.!" Theobald told her, as if this were a plus.

But as we were shown to our rooms, Grandmother staying with Father — contemptuously to the rear of our procession — I heard her mutter, "This is not how I conceived of my retirement. Across the hall from a W.C., listening to all the visitors."

"Not one of these rooms is the same," Theobald told us. "The furniture is all from my family." We could believe it. The one large room Robo and I were to share with my parents was a hall-sized museum of knickknacks, every dresser with a different style of knob. On the other hand, the sink had brass faucets and the headboard of the bed was carved. I could see my father balancing things up for future notation in the giant pad.

"You may do that later," Johanna informed him. "Where do *I* stay?"

As a family, we dutifully followed Theobald and my grandmother down the long, twining hall, my father counting the paces to the W.C. The hall rug was thin, the color of a shadow. Along the walls were old photographs of speed-skating teams — on their feet the strange blades curled up at the tips like court jesters' shoes or the runners of ancient sleds.

Robo, running far ahead, announced his discovery of the W.C.

Grandmother's room was full of china, polished wood, and the hint of mold. The drapes were damp. The bed had an unsettling ridge at its center, like fur risen on a dog's spine — it was almost as if a very slender body lay stretched beneath the bedspread.

Grandmother said nothing, and when Theobald reeled out of the room like a wounded man who's been told he'll live, Grandmother asked my father, "On what basis can the Pension Grillparzer hope to get a B?"

"Quite decidedly C," Father said.

"Born C and will die C," I said.

"I would say, myself," Grandmother told us, "that it was E or F."

In the dim tearoom a man without a tie sang a Hungarian song. "It does not mean he's Hungarian," Father reassured Johanna, but she was skeptical.

"I'd say the odds are not in his favor," she suggested. She would not have tea or coffee. Robo ate a little cake, which he claimed to like. My mother and I smoked a cigarette; she was trying to quit and I was trying to start. Therefore, we shared a cigarette between us — in fact, we'd promised never to smoke a whole one alone.

"He's a great guest," Herr Theobald whispered to my father; he indicated the singer. "He knows songs from all over."

"From Hungary, at least," Grandmother said, but she smiled.

A small man, clean-shaven but with that permanent gun-blue shadow of a beard on his lean face, spoke to my grandmother. He wore a clean white shirt (but yellow from age and laundering), suit pants, and an unmatching jacket.

"Pardon me?" said Grandmother.

"I said that I tell dreams," the man informed her.

"You *tell* dreams," Grandmother said. "Meaning, you *have* them?"

"Have them and tell them," he said mysteriously. The singer stopped singing.

"Any dream you want to know," said the singer, "he can tell it."

"I'm quite sure I don't want to know any," Grandmother said. She viewed with displeasure the ascot of dark hair bursting out at the open throat of the singer's shirt. She would not regard the man who "told" dreams at all.

"I can see you are a lady," the dream man told Grandmother. "You don't respond to just every dream that comes along."

"Certainly not," said Grandmother. She shot my father one of her how-could-you-have-let-this-happen-to-me? looks.

"But I know one," said the dream man; he shut his eyes. The singer slipped a chair forward and we

suddenly realized he was sitting very close to us.
Robo, though he was much too old for it, sat in Father's lap. "In a great castle," the dream man began,
"a woman lay beside her husband. She was wide
awake, suddenly, in the middle of the night. She
woke up without the slightest idea of what had
awakened her, and she felt as alert as if she'd been
up for hours. It was also clear to her, without a look,
a word, or a touch, that her husband was wide
awake too — and just as suddenly."

"I hope this is suitable for the child to hear, ha
ha," Herr Theobald said, but no one even looked at
him. My grandmother folded her hands in her lap
and stared at them — her knees together, her heels
tucked under her straight-backed chair. My mother
held my father's hand.

I sat next to the dream man, whose jacket
smelled like a zoo. He said, "The woman and her
husband lay awake listening for sounds in the castle,
which they were only renting and did not know inti-
mately. They listened for sounds in the courtyard,
which they never bothered to lock. The village people always took walks by the castle; the village children were allowed to swing on the great courtyard
door. What had woken them?"

"Bears?" said Robo, but Father touched his finger-
tips to Robo's mouth.

"They heard horses," said the dream man. Old
Johanna, her eyes shut, her head inclined toward her
lap, seemed to shudder in her stiff chair. "They heard
the breathing and stamping of horses who were trying to keep still," the dream man said. "The husband
reached out and touched his wife. 'Horses?' he said.
The woman got out of bed and went to the courtyard
window. She would swear to this day that the court-

yard was full of soldiers on horseback — but *what* soldiers they were! They wore *armor!* The visors on their helmets were closed and their murmuring voices were as tinny and difficult to hear as voices on a fading radio station. Their armor clanked as their horses shifted restlessly under them.

"There was an old dry bowl of a former fountain, there in the castle's courtyard, but the woman saw that the fountain was flowing; the water lapped over the worn curb and the horses were drinking it. The knights were wary, they would not dismount; they looked up at the castle's dark windows, as if they knew they were uninvited at this watering trough — this rest station on their way somewhere.

"In the moonlight the woman saw their big shields glint. She crept back to bed and lay rigidly against her husband.

"'What is it?' he asked her.

"'Horses,' she told him.

"'I thought so,' he said. 'They'll eat the flowers.'

"'Who built this castle?' she asked him. It was a very old castle, they both knew that.

"'Charlemagne,' he told her; he was going back to sleep.

"But the woman lay awake, listening to the water, which now seemed to be running all through the castle, gurgling in every drain, as if the old fountain were drawing water from every available source. And there were the distorted voices of the whispering knights — *Charlemagne's* soldiers speaking their dead language! To this woman, the soldiers' voices were as morbid as the eighth century and the people called Franks. The horses kept drinking.

"The woman lay awake a long time, waiting for

the soldiers to leave; she had no fear of actual attack from them — she was sure they were on a journey and had only stopped to rest at a place they had once known. But for as long as the water ran she felt that she mustn't disturb the castle's stillness or its darkness. When she fell asleep, she thought Charlemagne's men were still there.

"In the morning her husband asked her, 'Did you hear water running, too?' Yes, she had, of course. But the fountain was dry, and out the window they could see that the flowers weren't eaten — and everyone knows horses eat flowers.

"'Look,' said her husband; he went into the courtyard with her. 'There are *no* hoofprints, there are no droppings. We must have *dreamed* we heard horses.' She did not tell him that there were soldiers, too; or that, in her opinion, it was unlikely that two people would dream the same dream. She did not remind him that he was a heavy smoker who never smelled the soup simmering; the aroma of horses in the fresh air was too subtle for him.

"She saw the soldiers, or dreamed them, twice more while they stayed there, but her husband never again woke up with her. It was always sudden. Once she woke with the taste of metal on her tongue as if she'd touched some old, sour iron to her mouth — a sword, a chest plate, chain mail, a thigh guard. They were out there again, in colder weather. From the water in the fountain a dense fog shrouded them; the horses were snowy with frost. And there were not so many of them the next time — as if the winter or their skirmishes were reducing their numbers. The last time the horses looked gaunt to her, and the men looked more like unoccupied suits of armor balanced delicately in the saddles. The horses wore long masks of ice on their muzzles. Their breathing (or the men's breathing) was congested.

"Her husband," said the dream man, "would die of a respiratory infection. But the woman did not know it when she dreamed this dream."

My grandmother looked up from her lap and slapped the dream man's beard-gray face. Robo stiffened in my father's lap; my mother caught her mother's hand. The singer shoved back his chair and jumped to his feet, frightened, or ready to fight someone, but the dream man simply bowed to Grandmother and left the gloomy tearoom. It was as if he'd made a contract with Johanna that was vital but gave neither of them any joy. My father wrote something in the giant pad.

"Well, wasn't *that* some story?" said Herr Theobald. "Ha ha." He rumpled Robo's hair — something Robo always hated.

"Herr Theobald," my mother said, still holding Johanna's hand, *"my father died of a respiratory infection."*

"Oh, dear," said Herr Theobald. "I'm sorry, *meine Frau,"* he told Grandmother, but old Johanna would not speak to him.

We took Grandmother out to eat in a Class A restaurant, but she hardly touched her food. "That person was a gypsy," she told us, "a satanic being, and a Hungarian."

"Please, Mother," my mother said. "He couldn't have known about Father."

"He knew more than you know," Grandmother snapped.

"The schnitzel is excellent," Father said, writing in the pad. "The Gumpoldskirchner is just right with it."

"The Kalbsnieren are fine," I said.

"The eggs are okay," said Robo.

Grandmother said nothing until we returned to the Pension Grillparzer, where we noticed that the door to the W.C. was hung a foot or more off the floor, so that it resembled the bottom half of an American toilet-stall door or a saloon door in the Western movies. "I'm certainly glad I used the W.C. at the restaurant," Grandmother said. "How revolting! I shall try to pass the night without exposing myself where every passerby can peer at my ankles!"

In our family room Father said, "Didn't Johanna live in a castle? Once upon a time, I thought she and Grandpa rented some castle."

"Yes, it was before I was born," Mother said. "They rented Schloss Katzelsdorf. I saw the photographs."

"Well, *that's* why the Hungarian's dream upset her," Father said.

"Someone is riding a bike in the hall," Robo said. "I saw a wheel go by — under our door."

"Robo, go to sleep," Mother said.

"It went 'squeak squeak,'" Robo said.

"Goodnight, boys," said Father.

"If you can talk, we can talk," I said.

"Then talk to each other," Father said. "I'm talking to your mother."

"I want to go to sleep," Mother said. "I wish no one would talk."

We tried. Perhaps we slept. Then Robo whispered to me that he had to use the W.C.

"You know where it is," I said.

Robo went out the door, leaving it slightly open; I heard him walk down the corridor, brushing his hand along the wall. He was back very quickly.

"There's someone *in* the W.C.," he said.

"Wait for them to finish," I said.

"The light wasn't on," Robo said, "but I could still see under the door. Someone is in there, in the dark."

"I prefer the dark myself," I said.

But Robo insisted on telling me exactly what he'd seen. He said that under the door was a pair of *hands*.

"Hands?" I said.

"Yes, where the feet should have been," Robo said; he claimed that there was a hand on either side of the toilet — instead of a foot.

"Get out of here, Robo!" I said.

"Please come see," he begged. I went down the hall with him but there was no one in the W.C. "They've gone," he said.

"Walked off on their hands, no doubt," I said. "Go pee. I'll wait for you."

He went into the W.C. and peed sadly in the dark. When we were almost back to our room together, a small dark man with the same kind of skin and clothes as the dream man who had angered Grandmother passed us in the hall. He winked at us, and smiled; I had to notice that he was walking on his hands.

"You see?" Robo whispered to me. We went into our room and shut the door.

"What is it?" Mother asked.

"A man walking on his hands," I said.

"A man *peeing* on his hands," Robo said.

"Class C," Father murmured in his sleep; Father often dreamed that he was making notes in the giant pad.

"We'll talk about it in the morning," Mother said.

"He was probably just an acrobat who was showing off for you, because you're a kid," I told Robo.

"How did he know I was a kid when he was in the W.C.?" Robo asked me.

"Go to *sleep,*" Mother whispered.

Then we heard Grandmother scream down the hall.

Mother put on her pretty green dressing gown; Father put on his bathrobe and glasses. I pulled on a pair of pants, over my pajamas. Robo was in the hall first. We saw the light coming from under the W.C. door. Grandmother was screaming rhythmically in there.

"Here we are!" I called to her.

"Mother, what is it?" my mother asked.

We gathered in the broad slot of light. We could see Grandmother's mauve slippers and her porcelain-white ankles under the door. She stopped screaming. "I heard whispers when I was in my bed," she said.

"It was Robo and me," I told her.

"Then, when everyone seemed to have gone, I came into the W.C.," Johanna said. "I left the light *off.* I was *very* quiet," she told us. "Then I saw and heard the wheel."

"The *wheel?*" Father asked.

"A wheel went by the door a few times," Grandmother said. "It rolled by and came back and rolled by again."

Father made his fingers roll like wheels alongside his head; he made a face at Mother. "Somebody needs a new set of wheels," he whispered, but Mother looked crossly at him.

"I turned on the light," Grandmother said, "and the wheel went away."

"I told you there was a bike in the hall," said Robo.

"Shut up, Robo," Father said.

"No, it was not a bicycle," Grandmother said. "There was only one wheel."

Father was making his hands go crazy beside his head. "She's got a wheel or two *missing,*" he hissed at my mother, but she cuffed him and knocked his glasses askew on his face.

"Then someone came and looked *under* the door," Grandmother said, "and *that* is when I screamed."

"Someone?" said Father.

"I saw his hands, a man's hands — there was hair on his knuckles," Grandmother said. "His hands were on the rug right outside the door. He must have been looking *up* at me."

"No, Grandmother," I said. "I think he was just standing out here on his hands."

"Don't be fresh," my mother said.

"But we saw a man walking on his hands," Robo said.

"You did *not,*" Father said.

"We *did,*" I said.

"We're going to wake everyone up," Mother cautioned us.

The toilet flushed and Grandmother shuffled out the door with only a little of her former dignity intact. She was wearing a gown over a gown over a gown; her neck was very long and her face was creamed white. Grandmother looked like a troubled goose. "He was evil and vile," she said to us. "He knew terrible magic."

"The man who looked at you?" Mother asked.

"That man who told my *dream,*" Grandmother said. Now a tear made its way through her furrows of face cream. "That was *my* dream," she said, "and he told everyone. It is unspeakable that he even *knew* it," she hissed to us. "*My* dream — of Charlemagne's horses and soldiers — I am the only one who should know it. I had that dream before you were born," she told Mother. "And that vile, evil magic man told my dream as if it were *news*.

"I never even told your father all there was to that dream. I was never sure that it *was* a dream. And now there are men on their hands, and their knuckles are hairy, and there are magic wheels. I want the boys to sleep with *me*."

So that was how Robo and I came to share the large family room, far away from the W.C., with Grandmother, who lay on my mother's and father's pillows with her creamed face shining like the face of a wet ghost. Robo lay awake watching her. I do not think Johanna slept very well; I imagine she was dreaming her dream of death again — reliving the last winter of Charlemagne's cold soldiers with their strange metal clothes covered with frost and their armor frozen shut.

When it was obvious that I had to go to the W.C., Robo's round, bright eyes followed me to the door.

There was someone in the W.C. There was no light shining from under the door, but there was a unicycle parked against the wall outside. Its rider sat in the dark W.C.; the toilet was flushing over and over again — like a child, the unicyclist was not giving the tank time to refill.

I went closer to the gap under the W.C. door, but the occupant was not standing on his or her hands. I saw what were clearly feet, in almost the expected position, but the feet did not touch the floor; their soles tilted up to me — dark, bruise-colored pads. They were *huge* feet attached to short, furry shins.

They were a *bear's* feet, only there were no claws. A bear's claws are not retractable, like a cat's; if a bear had claws, you would see them. Here, then, was an impostor in a bear suit, or a declawed bear. A domestic bear, perhaps. At least — by its presence in the W.C. — a *housebroken* bear. For by its smell I could tell it was no man in a bear suit; it was all bear. It was real bear.

I backed into the door of Grandmother's former room, behind which my father lurked, waiting for further disturbances. He snapped open the door and I fell inside, frightening us both. Mother sat up in bed and pulled the feather quilt over her head. "Got him!" Father cried, dropping down on me. The floor trembled; the bear's unicycle slipped against the wall and fell into the door of the W.C., out of which the bear suddenly shambled, stumbling over its unicycle and lunging for its balance. Worriedly, it stared across the hall, through the open door, at Father sitting on my chest. It picked up the unicycle in its front paws. "*Grauf?*" said the bear. Father slammed the door.

Down the hall we heard a woman call, "Where are you, Duna?"

"*Harf!*" the bear said.

Father and I heard the woman come closer. She said, "Oh, Duna, practicing again? Always practicing! But it's better in the daytime." The bear said nothing. Father opened the door.

"Don't let anyone else in," Mother said, still under the featherbed.

In the hall a pretty, aging woman stood beside the bear, who now balanced in place on its unicycle, one huge paw on the woman's shoulder. She wore a vivid red turban and a long wrap-around dress that resembled a curtain. Perched on her high bosom was a necklace strung with bear claws; her earrings touched the shoulder of her curtain-dress and her other, bare shoulder where my father and I stared at her fetching mole. "Good evening," she said to Father. "I'm sorry if we've disturbed you. Duna is forbidden to practice at night — but he loves his work."

The bear muttered, pedaling away from the woman. The bear had very good balance but he was careless; he brushed against the walls of the hall and touched the photographs of the speed-skating teams with his paws. The woman, bowing away from Father, went after the bear calling, "Duna, Duna," and straightening the photographs as she followed him down the hall.

"*Duna* is the Hungarian word for the Danube," Father told me. "That bear is named after our beloved *Donau.*" Sometimes it seemed to surprise my family that the Hungarians could love a river, too.

"Is the bear a *real* bear?" Mother asked — still under the featherbed — but I left Father to explain it all to her. I knew that in the morning Herr Theobald would have much to explain, and I would hear everything reviewed at that time.

I went across the hall to the W.C. My task there was hurried by the bear's lingering odor, and by my suspicion of bear hair on everything; it was only my suspicion, though, for the bear had left everything quite tidy — or at least neat for a bear.

"I saw the bear," I whispered to Robo, back in our room, but Robo had crept into Grandmother's bed and had fallen asleep beside her. Old Johanna was awake, however.

"I saw fewer and fewer soldiers," she said. "The last time they came there were only nine of them. Everyone looked so hungry; they must have eaten the extra horses. It was so cold. Of course I wanted to help them! But we weren't alive at the same time; how could I help them if I wasn't even born? Of course I knew they would die! But it took such a long time.

"The last time they came, the fountain was frozen. They used their swords and their long pikes to break the ice into chunks. They built a fire and melted the ice in a pot. They took bones from their saddlebags — bones of all kinds — and threw them in the soup. It must have been a very thin broth because the bones had long ago been gnawed clean. I don't know what bones they were. Rabbits, I suppose, and maybe a deer or a wild boar. Maybe the extra horses. I do not choose to think," said Grandmother, "that they were the bones of the missing soldiers."

"Go to sleep, Grandmother," I said.

"Don't worry about the bear," she said.

In the breakfast room of the Pension Grillparzer we confronted Herr Theobald with the menagerie of his other guests who had disrupted our evening. I knew that (as never before) my father was planning to reveal himself as a Tourist Bureau spy.

"Men walking about on their hands," said Father.

"Men looking under the door of the W.C.," said Grandmother.

"*That* man," I said, and pointed to the small, sulking fellow at the corner table, seated for breakfast with his cohorts — the dream man and the Hungarian singer.

"He does it for a living," Herr Theobald told us, and as if to demonstrate that this was so, the man who stood on his hands began to stand on his hands.

"Make him stop that," Father said. "We know he can do it."

"But did you know that he can't do it any other way?" the dream man asked suddenly. "Did you know that his legs were useless? He has no shin-bones. It is *wonderful* that he can walk on his hands! Otherwise, he wouldn't walk at all." The man, although it was clearly hard to do while standing on his hands, nodded his head.

"Please sit down," Mother said.

"It is perfectly all right to be crippled," Grandmother said, boldly. "But you are evil," she told the dream man. "You know things you have no right to know. He knew my *dream,*" she told Herr Theobald, as if she were reporting a theft from her room.

"He is a *little* evil, I know," Theobald admitted. "But not usually! And he behaves better and better. He can't help what he knows."

"I was just trying to straighten you out," the dream man told Grandmother. "I thought it would do you good. Your husband has been dead quite a while, after all, and it's about time you stopped making so much of that dream. You're not the only person who's had such a dream."

"Stop it," Grandmother said.

"Well, you ought to know," said the dream man.

"No, be quiet, please," Herr Theobald told him.

"I am from the Tourist Bureau," Father announced, probably because he couldn't think of anything else to say.

"Oh my God!" Herr Theobald said.

"It's not Theobald's fault," said the singer. "It's *our* fault. He's nice to put up with us, though it costs him his reputation."

"They married my sister," Theobald told us. "They are *family,* you see. What can I do?"

"'They' married your sister?" Mother said.

"Well, she married *me* first," said the dream man.

"And then she heard *me* sing!" the singer said.

"She's never been married to the *other* one," Theobald said, and everyone looked apologetically toward the man who could only walk on his hands.

Theobald said, "They were once a circus act, but politics got them in trouble."

"We were the best in Hungary," said the singer. "You ever hear of the Circus Szolnok?"

"No, I'm afraid not," Father said, seriously.

"We played in Miskolc, in Szeged, in Debrecen," said the dream man.

"*Twice* in Szeged," the singer said.

"We would have made it to Budapest if it hadn't been for the Russians," said the man who walked on his hands.

"Yes, it was the Russians who removed his shin-bones!" said the dream man.

"Tell the truth," the singer said. "He was *born* without shinbones. But it's true that we couldn't get along with the Russians."

"They tried to jail the bear," said the dream man.

"Tell the truth," Theobald said.

"We rescued his sister from them," said the man who walked on his hands.

"So of course I must put them up," said Herr Theobald, "and they work as hard as they can. But who's interested in their act in this country? It's a Hungarian thing. There's no *tradition* of bears on unicycles here," Theobald told us. "And the damn dreams mean nothing to us Viennese."

"Tell the truth," said the dream man. "It is because I have told the wrong dreams. We worked a nightclub on the Kärntnerstrasse, but then we got banned."

"You should never have told *that* dream," the singer said gravely.

"Well, it was your wife's responsibility, too!" the dream man said.

"She was *your* wife, then," the singer said.

"Please stop it," Theobald begged.

"We get to do the balls for children's diseases," the dream man said. "And some of the state hospitals — especially at Christmas."

"If you would only do more with the bear," Herr Theobald advised them.

"Speak to your sister about that," said the singer. "It's *her* bear — she's trained him, she's let him get lazy and sloppy and full of bad habits."

"He is the only one of you who never makes fun of me," said the man who could only walk on his hands.

"I would like to leave all this," Grandmother said. "This is, for me, an awful experience."

"Please, dear lady," Herr Theobald said, "we only wanted to show you that we meant no offense. These are hard times. I need the B rating to attract more tourists, and I can't — in my heart — throw out the Circus Szolnok."

"*In his heart,* my ass!" said the dream man. "He's afraid of his sister. He wouldn't dream of throwing us out."

"If he dreamed it, you would know it!" cried the man on his hands.

"I am afraid of the *bear,*" Herr Theobald said. "It does everything she tells it to do."

"Say 'he,' not 'it,'" said the man on his hands. "He

is a fine bear, and he never hurt anybody. He has no claws, you know perfectly well — and very few teeth, either."

"The poor thing has a terribly hard time eating," Herr Theobald admitted. "He is quite old, and he's messy."

Over my father's shoulder, I saw him write in the giant pad: "A depressed bear and an unemployed circus. This family is centered on the sister."

At that moment, out on the sidewalk we could see her tending to the bear. It was early morning and the street was not especially busy. By law, of course, she had the bear on a leash, but it was a token control. In her startling red turban the woman walked up and down the sidewalk, following the lazy movements of the bear on his unicycle. The animal pedaled easily from parking meter to parking meter, sometimes leaning a paw on the meter as he turned. He was very talented on the unicycle, you could tell, but you could also tell that the unicycle was a dead end for him. You could see that the bear felt he could go no further with unicycling.

"She should bring him off the street now," Herr Theobald fretted. "The people in the pastry shop next door complain to me," he told us. "They say the bear drives their customers away."

"That bear makes the customers *come!*" said the man on his hands.

"It makes some people come, it turns some away," said the dream man. He was suddenly somber, as if his profundity had depressed him.

But we had been so taken up with the antics of the Circus Szolnok that we had neglected old Johanna. When my mother saw that Grandmother was quietly crying, she told me to bring the car around.

"It's been too much for her," my father whispered to Theobald. The Circus Szolnok looked ashamed of themselves.

Outside on the sidewalk the bear pedaled up to me and handed me the keys; the car was parked at the curb. "Not everyone likes to be given the keys in that fashion," Herr Theobald told his sister.

"Oh, I thought he'd rather like it," she said, rumpling my hair. She was as appealing as a barmaid, which is to say that she was more appealing at night; in the daylight I could see that she was older than her brother, and older than her husbands, too — and in time, I imagined, she would cease being lover and sister to them, respectively, and become a mother to them all. She was already a mother to the bear.

"Come over here," she said to him. He pedaled listlessly in place on his unicycle, holding on to a parking meter for support. He licked the little glass face of the meter. She tugged his leash. He stared at her. She tugged again. Insolently, the bear began to pedal — first one way, then the next. It was as if he took interest, seeing that he had an audience. He began to show off.

"Don't try anything," the sister said to him, but the bear pedaled faster and faster, going forward, going backward, angling sharply and veering among the parking meters; the sister had to let go of the leash. "Duna, stop it!" she cried, but the bear was out of control. He let the wheel roll too close to the curb and the unicycle pitched him hard into the fender of a parked car. He sat on the sidewalk with the unicycle beside him; you could tell that he hadn't injured himself, but he looked very embarrassed and nobody laughed. "Oh, Duna," the sister said, scoldingly, but she went over and crouched beside him at the curb. "Duna, Duna," she reproved him, gently. He shook his big head; he would not look at her. There was some saliva strung on the fur near his mouth and she wiped this away with her hand. He pushed her hand away with his paw.

"Come back again!" cried Herr Theobald, miserably, as we got into our car.

Mother sat in the car with her eyes closed and her fingers massaging her temples; this way she seemed to hear nothing we said. She claimed it was her only defense against traveling with such a contentious family.

I did not want to report on the usual business concerning the care of the car, but I saw that Father was trying to maintain order and calm; he had the giant pad spread on his lap as if we'd just completed a routine investigation. "What does the gauge tell us?" he asked.

"Someone put thirty-five kilometers on it," I said.

"That terrible bear has been in here," Grandmother said. "There are hairs from the beast on the back seat, and I can *smell* him."

"I don't smell anything," Father said.

"And the perfume of that gypsy in the turban," Grandmother said. "It is hovering near the ceiling of the car." Father and I sniffed. Mother continued to massage her temples.

On the floor by the brake and clutch pedals I saw several of the mint-green toothpicks that the Hungarian singer was in the habit of wearing like a scar at the corner of his mouth. I didn't mention them. It was enough to imagine them all — out on the town, in our car. The singing driver, the man on his hands beside him — waving out the window with his feet. And in back, separating the dream man from his former wife — his great head brushing the uphol-stered roof, his mauling paws relaxed in his large lap — the old bear slouched like a benign drunk.

"Those poor people," Mother said, her eyes still closed.

"Liars and criminals," Grandmother said. "Mystics and refugees and broken-down animals."

"They were trying hard," Father said, "but they weren't coming up with the prizes."

"Better off in a zoo," said Grandmother.

"I had a good time," Robo said.

"It's hard to break out of Class C," I said.

"They have fallen past Z," said old Johanna. "They have disappeared from the human alphabet."

"I think this calls for a letter," Mother said.

But Father raised his hand — as if he were going to bless us — and we were quiet. He was writing in the giant pad and wished to be undisturbed. His face was stern. I knew that Grandmother felt confident of his verdict. Mother knew it was useless to argue. Robo was already bored. I steered us off through the tiny streets; I took Spiegelgasse to Lobkowitzplatz. Spiegelgasse is so narrow that you can see the reflec-tion of your own car in the windows of the shops you pass, and I felt our movement through Vienna was superimposed (like that) — like a trick with a movie camera, as if we made a fairy-tale journey through a toy city.

When Grandmother was asleep in the car, Mother said, "I don't suppose that in this case a change in the classification will matter very much, one way or another."

"No," Father said, "not much at all." He was right

about that, though it would be years until I saw the Pension Grillparzer again.

When Grandmother died, rather suddenly and in her sleep, Mother announced that she was tired of traveling. The real reason, however, was that she began to find herself plagued by Grandmother's dream. "The horses are so thin," she told me once. "I mean, I always knew they would be thin, but not *this* thin. And the soldiers — I knew they were miserable," she said, "but not *that* miserable."

Father resigned from the Tourist Bureau and found a job with a local detective agency specializing in hotels and department stores. It was a satisfactory job for him, though he refused to work during the Christmas season — when, he said, some people ought to be allowed to steal a little.

My parents seemed to me to relax as they got older, and I really felt they were fairly happy near the end. I know that the strength of Grandmother's dream was dimmed by the *real* world, and specifically by what happened to Robo. He went to a private school and was well liked there, but he was killed by a homemade bomb in his first year at the university. He was not even "political." In his last letter to my parents he wrote: "The self-seriousness of the radical factions among the students is much overrated. And the food is execrable." Then Robo went to his history class, and his classroom was blown apart.

It was after my parents died that I gave up smoking and took up traveling again. I took my second wife back to the Pension Grillparzer. With my first wife, I never got as far as Vienna.

The Grillparzer had not kept Father's B rating very long, and it had fallen from the ratings alto-

gether by the time I returned to it. Herr Theobald's
sister was in charge of the place. Gone was her tart
appeal and in its place was the sexless cynicism of
some maiden aunts. She was shapeless and her hair
was dyed a sort of bronze, so that her head resembled one of those copper scouring pads that you
use on a pot. She did not remember me and was suspicious of my questions. Because I appeared to
know so much about her past associates, she probably knew I was with the police.

The Hungarian singer had gone away — another
woman thrilled by his voice. The dream man had
been *taken* away — to an institution. His own dreams
had turned to nightmares and he'd awakened the
pension each night with his horrifying howls. His removal from the seedy premises, said Herr Theobald's
sister, was almost simultaneous with the loss of the
Grillparzer's B rating.

Herr Theobald was dead. He had dropped down
clutching his heart in the hall, where he ventured
one night to investigate what he thought was a
prowler. It was only Duna, the malcontent bear, who
was dressed in the dream man's pinstriped suit. Why
Theobald's sister had dressed the bear in this fashion
was not explained to me, but the shock of the sullen
animal unicycling in the lunatic's left-behind clothes
had been enough to scare Herr Theobald to death.

The man who could only walk on his hands had
also fallen into the gravest trouble. His wristwatch
snagged on a tine of an escalator, and he was suddenly unable to hop off; his necktie, which he rarely
wore because it dragged on the ground when he
walked on his hands, was drawn under the step-off
grate at the end of the escalator — where he was
strangled. Behind him a line of people formed —

marching in place by taking one step back and allowing the escalator to carry them forward, then taking another step back. It was quite a while before
anyone got up the nerve to step over him. The world
has many unintentionally cruel mechanisms that are
not designed for people who walk on their hands.

After that, Theobald's sister told me, the Pension
Grillparzer went from Class C to much worse. As the
burden of management fell more heavily on her, she
had less time for Duna; the bear grew senile and
indecent in his habits. Once he bullied a mailman
down a marble staircase at such a ferocious pace that
the man fell and broke his hip; the attack was reported and an old city ordinance forbidding unre-
strained animals in places open to the public was
enforced. Duna was outlawed at the Pension Grillparzer.

For a while, Theobald's sister kept the bear in a
cage in the courtyard of the building, but he was
taunted by dogs and children, and food (and worse)
was dropped into his cage from the apartments that
faced the courtyard. He grew unbearlike and devi-
ous — only pretending to sleep — and he ate most
of someone's cat. Then he was poisoned twice and
became afraid to eat anything in this perilous envi-
ronment. There was no alternative but to donate him
to the Schönbrunn Zoo, but there was even some
doubt as to his acceptability. He was toothless and
ill, perhaps contagious, and his long history of having been treated as a human being did not prepare
him for the gentler routine of zoo life.

His outdoor sleeping quarters in the courtyard of
the Grillparzer had inflamed his rheumatism, and
even his one talent, unicycling, was irretrievable.
When he first tried it in the zoo, he fell. Someone

laughed. Once anyone laughed at something Duna did, Theobald's sister explained, Duna would never do that thing again. He became, at last, a kind of charity case at Schönbrunn, where he died a short two months after he'd taken up his new lodgings. In the opinion of Theobald's sister, Duna died of mortification — the result of a rash that spread over his great chest, which then had to be shaved. A shaved bear, one zoo official said, is embarrassed to death.

In the cold courtyard of the building I looked in the bear's empty cage. The birds hadn't left a fruit seed, but in a corner of his cage was a looming mound of the bear's ossified droppings — as void of life, and even odor, as the corpses captured by the holocaust at Pompeii. I couldn't help thinking of Robo; of the bear, there were more remains.

In the car I was further depressed to notice that not one kilometer had been added to the gauge, not one kilometer had been driven in secret. There was no one around to take liberties anymore.

"When we're a safe distance away from your precious Pension Grillparzer," my second wife said to me, "I'd like you to tell me why you brought me to such a shabby place."

"It's a long story," I admitted.

I was thinking I had noticed a curious lack of either enthusiasm or bitterness in the account of the world by Theobald's sister. There was in her story the flatness one associates with a storyteller who is accepting of unhappy endings, as if her life and her companions had never been exotic to *her* — as if they had always been staging a ludicrous and doomed effort at reclassification.

The Pension Grillparzer (1976)

AUTHOR'S NOTES

Readers of *The World According to Garp* may remember that "The Pension Grillparzer" is T. S. Garp's first short story, and the first evidence in the novel of Garp's abilities as a young writer. Indeed, he is a *very* young writer when he is supposed to have written "Grillparzer" — he is only 19. The late Henry Robbins, who was a dear friend and the editor of *The World According to Garp,* told me that the story was much too good for a 19-year-old to have written it.

I argued that I wanted to make a point about Garp, which is a point I have made about many American writers: the first thing they write is the best thing they *ever* write — in Garp's case, it was all downhill after "Grillparzer." But Henry insisted that I had made "Grillparzer" seem too easy to write; it was Henry's suggestion that, for the credibility of the novel, I break up the story — that I have Garp begin it and get stuck in it and put it aside. Garp takes up the story and finishes it only after an interval of several months; the death of a friend, a Viennese prostitute, is the real-life episode that informs the young author about the end of his story.

I agreed with Henry, and so "The Pension Grillparzer" was divided; readers who read it in the novel read it in two parts. I knew Henry was right, but I hated breaking up the story, which was originally published, two years before *The World According to Garp,* in *Antaeus* (Winter 1976); it won a Pushcart Prize — the Best of the Small Presses — but I suspect that most readers saw it first in *Garp,* in its divided form. That is why I wanted to publish it here — for the first time, for many readers, *whole;* of one piece.

In the middle of the story, when Garp gets "stuck" and stops writing, Garp ponders the following: "But what did they mean? That dream and those desperate entertainers, and what would happen to them all — everything had to connect. What sort of explanation would be natural? What sort of ending might make them all part of the same world?"

What made "The Pension Grillparzer" special to me (it is my favorite among my short stories) was both the grandmother's dream and the epilogue — everything *does* "connect." The "ludicrous and doomed effort at reclassification" is a foreshadow of the "terminal cases" theme of the novel, which has its own epilogue — I like epilogues, as anyone who's read my novels knows. The younger brother blown up in a history class, the innkeeper frightened to death by the bear "unicycling in the lunatic's left-behind clothes" — the bear himself is "embarrassed to death" — and especially the man who could only walk on his hands, strangled by his necktie on an escalator . . . these calamities foreshadow some of the violent ends that my characters will meet, not only in *Garp* but in later novels; these are the unlikely disasters that many book reviewers have called my penchant for the bizarre.

But, according to Henry Robbins — and I believed him; I believe him to this day — the *most* bizarre element in *The World According to Garp* is that a 19-year-old could have written "The Pension Grillparzer." Not one book reviewer ever made mention of that.

At the time *I* wrote "Grillparzer," I had already written three-and-a-half novels; I was 34. And I already knew I was a novelist, not a short-story writer; yet I never worked as hard on a short story, before or since, because I wanted the readers of *The World According to Garp* to know that T. S. Garp was a good writer.

OTHER
PEOPLE'S DREAMS

Fred had no recollection of having had a dream life until his wife left him. Then he remembered some vague nightmares from his childhood, and some specific, lustful dreams from what seemed to him to be the absurdly short period of time between his arrival at puberty and his marrying Gail (he had married young). The 10 dreamless years he had been married were wounds too tender for him to probe them very deeply, but he knew that in that time Gail had dreamed like a demon — one adventure after another — and he'd woken each morning feeling baffled and dull, searching her alert, nervous face for evidence of her nighttime secrets. She never told him her dreams, only that she had them — and that she found it very peculiar that he didn't dream. "Either you *do* dream, Fred," Gail told him, "and your dreams are so sick that you prefer to forget them, or you're really dead. People who don't dream at all are quite dead."

In the last few years of their marriage, Fred found neither theory so farfetched.

After Gail left, he felt "quite dead." Even his girl-friend, who had been Gail's "last straw," couldn't re-vive him. He thought that everything that had happened to his marriage had been his own fault: Gail had appeared to be happy and faithful — until he'd created some mess and she'd been forced to pay him back. Finally, after he had repeated himself too many times, she had given up on him. "Old fall-in-love Fred," she called him. He seemed to fall in love with someone almost once a year. Gail said: "I could possibly tolerate it, Fred, if you just went off and got laid, but why do you have to get so stupidly involved?"

He didn't know. After Gail's leaving, his girl-friend appeared so foolish, sexless and foul to him that he couldn't imagine what had inspired his last, alarming affair. Gail had abused him so much for this one that he was actually relieved when Gail was gone, but he missed the child — they had just one child in 10 years, a nine-year-old boy named Nigel. They'd both felt their own names were so ordinary that they had stuck their poor son with this label. Nigel now lay in a considerable portion of Fred's fat heart like an arrested case of cancer. Fred could bear not seeing the boy (in fact, they hadn't gotten along together since Nigel was five), but he could not stand the thought of the boy's hating him, and he was sure Nigel hated him — or, in time, would learn to. Gail had learned to.

Sometimes Fred thought that, if he'd only had dreams of his own, he wouldn't have had to act out his terrible love affairs with someone almost once a year.

For weeks after the settlement he couldn't sleep in the bed they'd shared for 10 years. Gail settled for cash and Nigel. Fred kept the house. He slept on the couch, bothered by restless nights of blurry discomfort — too disjointed for dreams. He thrashed on the couch, his groaning disturbed the dog (he had settled for the dog, too), and his mouth in the morning was the mouth of a hangover — though he hadn't been drinking. One night he imagined he was throwing up in a car; the passenger in the car was Mrs. Beal, and she was beating him with her purse while he retched and spilled over the steering wheel. "Get us home! Get us home!" Mrs. Beal cried at him. Fred didn't know then, of course, that he was having *Mr.* Beal's dream. Mr. Beal had passed out on Fred and Gail's couch many times; he had no doubt had that terrible dream there and had left it behind for the next troubled sleeper.

Fred simply gave up on the couch and sought the slim, hard bed in Nigel's room — a child's captain's bed, with little drawers built under it for underwear and six-guns. The couch had given Fred a backache, but he was not ready to resume his life in the bed he'd shared with Gail.

The first night he slept in Nigel's bed he understood what strange ability he suddenly possessed — or what a strange ability had suddenly possessed him. He had a nine-year-old's dream — Nigel's dream. It was not frightening to Fred, but Fred knew it must have been pure terror for Nigel. In a field Fred-as-Nigel was trapped by a large snake. The snake was immediately comic to Fred-as-Fred, because it was finned like a serpent and breathed fire. The snake struck repeatedly at Fred-as-Nigel's chest; he was so stunned he couldn't scream. Far across the field Fred saw Fred the way Nigel would have seen him. "Dad!" Fred-as-Nigel whispered. But the real Fred was standing over a smoldering fire pit; they had just had a barbecue, apparently. Fred was pissing into the pit — a strong steam of urine rising around him — and he didn't hear his son crying.

In the morning Fred decided that the dreams of nine-year-olds were obvious and trite. He had no fear of further dreams when he sought his own bed that night; at least, while he slept with Gail, he had never had a dream in that bed — and although Gail

had been a steady dreamer, Fred hadn't had any of
her dreams in that bed before. But sleeping alone is
different from sleeping with someone else.

He crept into the cold bed in the room reft of the
curtains Gail had sewn. Of course he had one of
Gail's dreams. He was looking in a floor-length mirror, but he was seeing Gail. She was naked, and for
only a second he thought he was having a dream of
his own — possibly missing her, an erotic memory, a
desirous agonizing for her to return. But the Gail in
the mirror was not a Gail he had ever seen. She was
old, ugly, and seeing her nakedness was like seeing
a laceration you wished someone would quickly
close. She was sobbing, her hands soaring beside her
like gulls — holding up this and that garment, each
more of a violation to her color and her features than
the last. The clothes piled up at her feet and she finally sagged down on them, hiding her face from
herself; in the mirror, the bumped vertebrae along
her backbone looked to him (to her) like some back-
alley staircase they had once discovered on their
honeymoon in Austria. In an onion-domed village,
this alley was the only dirty, suspicious path they had
found. And the staircase, which crooked out of sight,
had struck them both as ominous; it was the only
way out of the alley, unless they retraced their steps,
and Gail had suddenly said, "Let's go back." He immediately agreed. But before they turned away, an
old woman reeled around the topmost part of the
staircase and, appearing to lose her balance, fell
heavily down the stairs. She'd been carrying some
things: carrots, a bag of gnarled potatoes and a live
goose whose paddle-feet were hobbled together.
The woman struck her face when she fell and lay
with her eyes open and her black dress bunched

above her knees. The carrots spread like a bouquet on her flat, still chest. The potatoes were every-where. And the goose, still hobbled, gabbled and struggled to fly. Fred, without once touching the woman, went straight to the goose, although — ex-cepting dogs and cats — he had never touched a live animal before. He tried to untie the leather thong that bound the goose's feet together, but he was clumsy and the goose hissed at him and pecked him fiercely, painfully, on the cheek. He dropped the bird and ran after Gail, who was running out of the alley the way they had come.

Now in the mirror Gail had gone to sleep on the pile of her unloved clothes on the floor. That was the way Fred had found her the night he came home from his first infidelity.

He woke up from her dream in the bed alone. He had understood, before, that she had hated him for his infidelity, but this was the first time he real-ized that his infidelity had made her hate herself.

Was there no place in his own house he could sleep without someone else's dream? Where was it pos-sible to develop a dream of his own? There was another couch, in the TV room, but the dog — an old male Labrador — usually slept there. "Bear?" he called. "Here, Bear." Nigel had named the dog "Bear." But then Fred remembered how often he had seen Bear in the fits of his own dreams — woofing in his sleep, his hackles raised, his webbed feet running in place, his pink hard-on slapping his belly — and he thought that surely he had not sunk so low as to submit to dreams of rabbit-chasing, fighting the neighborhood Weimaraner, humping the Beals' sad bloodhound bitch. Of course, baby-sitters had slept on that couch, and might he not expect some savory dream of *theirs?* Was it worth risking one of Bear's dreams for some sweet impression of that lacy little Janey Hobbs?

Pondering dog hair and recalling many unattractive baby-sitters, Fred fell asleep in a chair — a dreamless chair; he was lucky. He was learning that his newfound miracle-ability was a gift that was as harrowing as it was exciting. It's frequently true that we have offered to us much of the insecurity of sleeping with strangers, and little of the pleasure.

When his father died, he spent a week with his mother. To Fred's horror, she slept on the couch and offered him the master bedroom with its vastly historical bed. Fred could sympathize with his mother's reluctance to sleep there, but the bed and its potential for epic dreaming terrified him. His parents had always lived in this house, had always — since he could remember — slept on that bed. Both his mother and father had been dancers — slim, graceful people even in their retirement. Fred could remember their morning exercises, slow and yogalike movements on the sun-room rug, often to Mozart. Fred viewed their old bed with dread. What embarrassing dreams, and *whose,* would enmesh him there?

He could tell, with some relief, that it was his mother's dream. Like most people, Fred sought rules in the chaos, and he thought he had found one: impossible to dream a dead person's dream. At least his mother was alive. But Fred had expected some elderly sentiment for his father, some fond remembrance, which he imagined old people had; he was not prepared for the lustiness of his mother's dream. He saw his father gamboling in the shower, soapy in the underarms and soapy and erect below. This was not an especially young dream, either; his father was already old, the hair white on his chest, his breasts distended in that old man's way — like the pouches appearing around a young girl's nipples. Fred dreamed his mother's hot, wet affection for the goatishness he'd never seen in his father. Appalled at their inventive, agile, even acrobatic lovemaking, Fred woke with a sense of his own dull sexuality, his clumsy straightforwardness. It was Fred's first sex dream as a woman; he felt so stupid to be learning now — a man in his thirties, and from his *mother* — precisely how women liked to be touched. He had dreamed how his mother came. How she quite cheerfully *worked* at it.

Too embarrassed to look in her eyes in the morning, Fred felt ashamed that he had not bothered to imagine this of her — that he'd assumed too *little* of her, and too little of Gail. Fred was still condescending enough, in the way a son is to his mother, to assume that if his mother's appetite was so rich, his wife's would surely have been richer. That this was perhaps not the case didn't occur to him.

He was sadly aware that his mother could not make herself do the morning exercises alone, and in the week he stayed with her — an unlikely comfort he felt himself to be — she seemed to be growing stiffer, less athletic, even gaining weight. He wanted to offer to accompany her in the exercises; to insist that she continue her good physical habits, but he had seen her *other* physical habits and his inferiority had left him speechless.

He was also bewildered to find that his instincts as a voyeur were actually stronger than his instincts as a proper son. Though he knew he would suffer his mother's erotic memories each night, he would not abandon the bed for what he thought to be the dreamless floor. Had he slept there he would have encountered at least one of his father's dreams from the occasional nights that his father had slept on the floor. He would have disproven his easy theory that dead persons' dreams don't transfer to the living. His mother's dreams were simply stronger than his father's, so her dreams dominated the bed. Fred could, for example, have discovered his father's real feelings for his Aunt Blanche on the floor. But we are not known for our ability to follow through on our unearned discoveries. We are top-of-the-water adventurers, who limit our opinions of the icebergs to what we can see.

Fred was learning something about dreams, but there was more that he was missing. Why, for instance, did he usually dream *historical* dreams? — that is, dreams which are really memories, or exaggerated memories of real events in our past, or secondhand dreams. There are other kinds of dreams — dreams of things that haven't happened. Fred did not know much about those. He didn't even consider that the dreams he was having *could* be his own — that they were simply as close to him as he dared to approach.

He returned to his divorced home, no longer intrepid. He was a man who'd glimpsed in himself a wound of terminal vulnerability. There are many unintentionally cruel talents that the world, indiscriminately, hands out to us. Whether we can use these gifts we never asked for is not the world's concern.

Other People's Dreams (1976)

AUTHOR'S NOTES

Here is another short story that spent a number of years in my bottommost drawer; every few months, I would take it out and revise it — then I would put it away again. After six years of this abuse, the story — what was left of it — was anthologized in a collection called *Last Night's Stranger: One Night Stands & Other Staples of Modern Life,* edited by Pat Rotter (A & W Publishers, New York, 1982). "Other People's Dreams" ended up in good company — also in that collection were stories by Raymond Carver, Hilma Wolitzer, Richard Ford, Gail Godwin, Richard Selzer, Don Hendrie, Jr., John L'Heureux, David Huddle, Joyce Carol Oates and Robert Coover — but the story, for such a *little* thing, drove me crazy.

I went through a series of first sentences, all of which eventually became the end lines of paragraphs deeper in the story. These false beginnings were all statements of one sort or another. "Sleeping alone is different from sleeping with someone else" was the *first* first sentence. It was replaced, for a short while, by "It's frequently true that we have offered to us much of the insecurity of sleeping with strangers, and little of the pleasure." (These statements were so self-evident that they seemed more tolerable when buried in the story.) Another was "We are not known for our ability to follow through on our unearned dis-coveries." (For a while, "Unearned Discoveries" was the title of the story.) And my last effort to begin the story became, after six years, the end of the story instead. "There are many unintentionally cruel talents that the world, indiscriminately, hands out to us. Whether we can use these gifts we never asked for is not the world's concern." (These sentences had earlier been *cut* from "The Pension Grillparzer," where they were companions to the line about the death of the man who could only walk on his hands, which I kept: "The world has many unintentionally cruel mechanisms that are not designed for people who walk on their hands.")

And I see now that my "terminal" theme, which extended throughout the writing of *The World According to Garp*, is repeated here. "He was a man who'd glimpsed in himself a wound of terminal vulnerability." It's funny how this jumps out at me now — it didn't then. In addition to terminal patients and terminal cases, and even terminal *trees*, here's a poor guy whose vulnerability is terminal, too. (I don't know where all of this doomsaying came from.)

WEARY
KINGDOM

Minna Barrett, 55, looks precisely as old as she is, and her figure suggests nothing of what she might have looked like "in her time." One would only assume that always she looked this way, slightly oblong, gently rounded, not puritanical but almost asexual. A pleasant old maid since grammar school, neat and silent; a not overly stern face, a not overly harsh mouth, but a total composure, which now, at 55, reflects the history of her many indifferences and the conservative going of her own way.

Minna has her own room in a dormitory of Fairchild Junior College for Young Women, where she is the matron of the dormitory's small dining hall, in charge of the small kitchen crew, responsible for the appropriate dress of the girls at mealtime. Minna's room has a private entrance and a private bath, is shaded in the mornings by the elms of the campus, and is several blocks from Boston Common — not too far for her to walk on a nice day. This room is remarkably uncluttered, remarkable because it's a very small room, which shows very little of the nine years she has lived there. Not that there is, or should be, a great deal to show; it is only as permanent a residence as any other place Minna has lived since she left home. This room has a television and Minna stays up at night, watching the movies. She never watches the regular programs; she reads until the news at 11:00. She likes biographies, prefers these to autobiographies, because someone's account of his own life embarrasses her in a way she doesn't understand. She is partial to the biographies of women, although she does read Ian Fleming. Once at a party for the alumnae and trustees of the school, a lady in a soft lavender suit, who wanted, she said, to meet *all* of the school's personnel, found out about Minna's interest in biographies. The lavender lady recommended a book by Gertrude Stein, which Minna bought and never finished. It wasn't anything Minna would have called a biography, but she wasn't offended by it. She just felt that nothing ever happened.

So Minna reads until 11:00, then watches the news and a movie. The kitchen crew comes early in the morning, but Minna doesn't have to be in the dining hall until the girls come in. After breakfast she takes a cup of coffee to her own room, then maybe naps until lunch. Her afternoons, too, are quiet. Some of the girls in the dormitory will visit her at 11:00, to watch the evening news — there is an entrance to Minna's room from the dormitory corridor. The girls probably come to see the television more than they come to see Minna, although they are very considerate of her and Minna is amused at the varying stages of their undress at this hour. Once they were interested in how long Minna's hair would be if she let it down. She obliged them, unwinding, unfurling the long gray hair — somewhat stiff, but falling to her hips. The girls were impressed with how thick and healthy it was; one of the girls, with hair almost that long, suggested to Minna that she wear it in a braid. The next evening the girls brought a deep orange ribbon and they braided Minna's hair. Minna was meekly pleased, but she said that she never could wear it that way. She still might be tempted, the girls were so impressed, but it is too much to think of changing her hair from the tightly wrapped bun it has been all these years.

After the girls leave, after the movie, Minna sits in her bed, thinking of her retirement. The farm where she grew up, in South Byfield, comes back to her mind. If she thinks of it with a certain nostalgia she is not aware of this; she thinks only how much more restful her work at the school is, how much easier than on the farm. Her younger brother lives there now, and in a few years she'll return, to live with her brother's family, taking her tidy nest egg with her, and relinquishing herself and her savings to the care of her brother. It was only last Christmas, when she was visiting his family, that they asked her when she would come to stay for good. By the time she feels it is right for her to come, in another year or so, not *all* of her brother's children will be grown-up, and there will be things for her to do. Certainly no one would think of Minna as an imposition.

She thinks of South Byfield, what past and what future — after the news, after the movie — and she feels, now, no resentment toward this present time. She has no memories of a painful loss or separation, or failure. There were friends in South Byfield, whom she simply saw married or who just remained there after she quietly moved the 30 miles to Boston; her mother and father died, almost shyly, but there is nothing that she misses with particular pain. She doesn't think of herself as very anxious to retire, although she does look ahead to being a part of her brother's healthy family. She wouldn't say that she has a lot of friends in Boston, but friends for Minna always have been the pleasant and familiar people connected with the regular episodes of her life; they

never have been emotional dependents. Now, for example, there is Flynn, the cook, who is Irish with a
large family in South Boston, who complains to
Minna of Boston housing, Boston traffic, Boston cor-
ruption, Boston this-and-that. Minna knows little of
this but she listens attentively to him; in his swearing
Flynn reminds her of her father. Minna doesn't swear
herself, but she doesn't find Flynn's swearing unpleasant. He has a way of coaxing things that makes
her feel as if his swearing really *works*. The daily
battles with the coffee urn are invariably won by
Flynn, who after long and dark curses, heavy jostles
and violent threats of dismantling the whole thing,
emerges the victor; for Minna, Flynn's animated ob-
scenities seem constructive, the way her father would
shout the tractor into starting, during the winter
months. Minna thinks Flynn is nice.

Also, there is Mrs. Elwood, a widow, with deeper
lines on her face than Minna has — lines which
move like rubber bands when Mrs. Elwood talks, as
if her chin were hinged to these lines. Mrs. Elwood is
the housemother of the dormitory, and she speaks
with a British accent; it is well known that Mrs. Elwood is a Bostonian, but she spent one summer in
England, after her graduation from college. Apparently, she had a whale of a time there. Minna tells
Mrs. Elwood whenever there's a movie with Alec
Guinness on the late show, and Mrs. Elwood comes,
discreetly after the news, after her girls have gone
back to their rooms. It often takes a good half of the
movie for Mrs. Elwood to remember if she's seen this
one before.

"I must have seen them all, Minna," Mrs. Elwood
says.

"I always miss the ones at Christmastime," Minna

replies. "At my brother's we usually play cards or have folks in."

"Oh, Minna," Mrs. Elwood says, "you really should go out more."

And, too, there is Angelo Gianni. Angelo is pale and slight, a bewildered-looking man, or boy, gray eyes that are merely a deeper shade of the color of his face, and there is nothing about him, outside of his name, to suggest that he's Italian. If his name were Cuthbert, or Cadwallader, there would be nothing in his appearance to suggest that. If he were a Devereaux or a Hunt-Jones you would see nothing of that in his awkward, embarrassed body — anticipating, with awe, the most minor crisis, and reacting dumbstruck every time. Angelo could be 20 or 30; he lives in the basement of the dormitory, next to his janitor's closet. Angelo empties ashtrays, washes dishes, sets and cleans tables, sweeps, does things like that wherever he is needed, and does other, more complicated things when he is asked, and when the problem has been thoroughly explained to him, more than once. He is exceptionally gentle, and he behaves toward Minna with a curious combination of the deepest respect — at times, calling her "Miss Minna" — and the odd, shy, flirtatious gestures of true affection. Minna likes Angelo, she is tender and cheerful with him as she is with her brother's children, and she is aware of even *worrying* about him. Angelo, she feels, stands on precarious ground, and at every moment of his simple, delicate life — unguarded, she thinks — he is prone to the cruelest of injuries. The injuries go unnamed, yet Minna can picture a hoard of sufferings lying in wait for Angelo, who lives fragilely, artlessly, in his isolated world of kindness and faith. Minna seeks to protect Angelo, seeks to instruct him, although these sufferings she envisions for him are quite nebulous to her; she can think of no great injury she has received, no great threatening and destructive force which ever has loomed over her. Yet, for Angelo she fears this, and she tells him her instructive stories, inevitably ending in a proverb (one of those proverbs she cuts from the daily newspaper and sticks with a small piece of Scotch tape to the thick, black pages of her photograph album, which contains only two photographs — one brownish print of her parents, stonily posed, and one color shot of her brother's children). Minna's stories are her own, stripped of any prelude, stripped of time and place, even names of characters, and certainly stripped of any emotional involvement of her own that might have existed at the time, might linger still — *might,* if Minna ever remembered anything in that way, or if anything could affect her, personally, in that way. The proverbs range from "A little knowledge is a dangerous thing!" to a whole assembly of mottoes urging compromise. The danger of trusting *too* much, of believing *too* much. Angelo nods to her advice; a frequent, awesome seriousness seems to fix his eyes, suspend his mouth, until Minna is bothered so much by Angelo's painful concentration that she tells him, as a footnote, not to take anything that *any*one says too seriously. This only further puzzles Angelo, and seeing what effect she has had, Minna changes the subject to something lighter.

"Why, the other day," she says, "some of the girls tried to get me to wear my hair in a braid, a long braid."

"I'll bet you looked nice," Angelo tells her.

"Oh, you know, Angelo, I just didn't see the good in changing my hair from what it's been so long."

"You should do what you think best, Miss Minna," Angelo says, and Minna is helpless to break the penetrating and dangerous kindness which Angelo bears to everyone, bringing them the burden of his exposed heart, to do with as they may. Well, Minna thinks, it's time they were both back to work.

Minna has no complaints about her work. She has asked for another woman to help her, another matron for the dining hall so that when Minna has her day off, on Mondays, the girls and the kitchen crew won't be alone. No one, apparently, regards this request as very important. Mrs. Elwood thought it would be a fine idea; she said she'd speak to the Director of Housing. Then later, when Minna asked her about it, Mrs. Elwood said that she thought it might be better if Minna spoke to the Director, or to someone, herself. Minna wrote to the Director, weeks ago; she has heard nothing. It's not really important, she thinks, and so there's nothing to complain about. It would just be nice to have another woman, an older woman, of course, and someone who's had some experience with young girls. There's even an extra room in the dormitory for her, if the college could find a woman like that, who'd like a room of her own — a free room, after all, and all the protection a woman living alone could ask for. It would be nice to have someone like that, but Minna doesn't push it. She is content to wait.

The first, bored ducks were roaming about as Minna, on her day off, walked through Boston Common. She shawled and unshawled as she walked, warm and then shivering, regarding the optimists in their short-sleeved shirts, their chilly seersucker. Several worldly mallards strutted with the awkward and stunned dignity of someone who'd been conspicu- ously insulted at a large, unfamiliar party. Shopping, summery mothers with winter-bundled children, stag- gering in the short blasts of cold wind, paused to find something to feed the ducks. The children leaned out too far, got wet feet, were scolded, hurried and dragged along, looking over their shoulders at the floating pieces of bread and the indifferent ducks. The ducks would get better about this as the spring wore on, but now, in the early stages of their hope- less revolution for privacy, they refused to eat if they were watched. Old men in year-round overcoats, clutching papers and knobby loaves of bread, hurled heavy chunks to the ducks — the men looked cau- tiously about, to see if anyone noticed that the pieces were too big (intended to hit and sink the ducks).

Minna was coolly aware of their feeble arms and their bad aim. She didn't stay long, but turned out of the Common to Boylston Street. She window- shopped at Shreve's, warming herself in the elegance of crystal and silver, thinking what would be the loveliest piece for her brother's table. Schraft's was around the corner and she ate a small lunch there. Outside of Schraft's she pondered what to do next; it was two o'clock and the weather was typically, inde- cisively March. Then Minna saw a girl come out of Shreve's; the girl smiled in Minna's direction — a denim skirt came above her knees, sandals, a green crew-neck sweater, obviously some boy's. The sweater hung low on her hips, the cuffs were rolled, and the stretched knobs on the sleeves, which would have been the boy's elbows, swung like goiters under the girl's slender wrists. She called, "Hi,

Minna!" and Minna recognized her as one of the girls who came to watch the news in her room. Not remembering her name, names always bothered her, Minna called the girl "Dear." Dear was going to Cambridge, taking the MTA, wanted to know if Minna would like to come and browse the shops. They went together, Minna greatly pleased at this; she noticed how differently people watched her on the subway — did they think she was this girl's grandmother, or, even, her mother? The smiles were for having such a pretty companion, and Minna felt as if she was being congratulated. In Cambridge they stopped at an extraordinary little delicatessen, where Minna bought several cans of exotic food, the labels in some foreign language, sealed with precious-looking stamps. It was like receiving some gift package from an imaginary uncle, a world traveler, adventurer sort. In a dusty little shop of orange crates and awnings, a shop with a lot of dulled and dented pewter, Minna bought a silver hors d'oeuvre fork, with which, the girl called "Dear" told her, she could comfortably eat the exotic foods. The girl was very kind to Minna, so kind that Minna felt she must not be well liked by the other girls. At four o'clock the day turned ragged and cold once more, and the two of them went to a foreign movie in Brattle Square. They had to sit quite close to the front because Minna had difficulty reading the subtitles. Minna was embarrassed that the girl should see this film, but later the girl spoke so knowingly and seriously about it that Minna was somewhat eased. They had a nice meal after the movie — dark beer, sauerkraut and stuffed peppers, in a German restaurant that the girl knew well. The girl told Minna that they wouldn't have served her the beer if Minna hadn't been with her. It was well after dark when they returned to the dormitory, and Minna told the girl what a lovely time she'd had. With her little bag of funny foods and the hors d'oeuvre fork, and feeling pleasantly tired, Minna went to her room. Although it was only nine o'clock she felt she could go to bed right away, but on her desk where she gently set her bag, she saw a curious beige folder with a note attached. The note was from Mrs. Elwood.

> Dear Minna, I dropped this in your room this afternoon. The Director of Housing called me this morning to say that he'd found you a helper, another matron for the dining hall, and *with* experience. The Director said he was sending her over here. Since you were out I showed her around, got her settled in her room — it's a bit of a shame that she has to share the bathroom with the girls on that floor, but she did seem quite pleased with everything. She's most attractive — Angelo seems rather taken with her — and I told her that you'd take care of her in the morning. If you want to go and meet her tonight, she said she was tired — she'll be in her room.

So, Minna thought, they really got someone. She couldn't imagine what might be in the folder, and opening it, delicately, she saw it was a duplicate of the woman's job application. She felt a little uncertain about looking at this, it appeared to be such a private thing, but her eye caught the little bag of worldly foods and this, somehow, gave her confidence to read the application. Celeste was her name and she was 41. She'd done a "lot of waiting-on table," had been a counselor at a summer camp for

girls, and she was from Heron's Neck, Maine —
where her brother-in-law now operated an inn for
summer tourists. She had also worked there. The inn
had been owned by her parents. It sounds very nice,
Minna thought, and she forgot how tired she had
been. She suddenly became organized — arranging,
proudly, the little cans of the curious food on the
overhanging shelf of her desk. Then she checked the
TV bulletin to see if there was an Alec Guinness
movie on the Late Show. Mrs. Elwood would like to
know, and the new woman might be lonely. Indeed,
on this most surprising day, there was an Alec Guinness movie. Minna opened the door to the dormitory
corridor and walked humming to Celeste's room. She
thought, what a wonderful day it's been. She only
wished she knew that Dear Girl's name, but she
could ask Mrs. Elwood about that.

Minna rapped lightly on Celeste's door and
heard, or thought she heard, a murmured "Come in."
She opened the door, hesitating on the threshold because the room was dark — all dark, except for the
wobbly-necked desk lamp, which pointed its feeble
light to the cushion of the desk chair. The room, like
most end rooms in dormitories, was neither square
nor rectangular. Any symmetry appeared as an accident; there were *five* corners where the ceiling
sloped almost to the floor, and several alcoves in juxtaposition to the corners. In one of those low-
ceilinged alcoves was the bed, a cot really, and
Minna saw that some attempt had been made to conceal the bed from the rest of the room. A heavy crimson blanket was draped from the molding and hung
in such a way as to wall off the bed in the alcove.
Minna saw the blanket flap and she guessed there
was a window open over the bed. The whole room

was somewhat windy in the early-evening cool, yet
the room smelled of a heavy, animal musk, rich as
coffee, and reminded Minna — oddly, she thought —
of one late evening last summer when her brother
had been in Boston and had taken her to a show.
They were riding back on the subway, alone in the
car, when a massive woman in a gaudy, flowered
dress came in and sat just a few seats away. The big
woman had stepped in from the steamy rain, the
damp underground, and suddenly the car was filled
with her rich scents — she smelled of a hot summer
day in a dirt-floor cellar, closed all winter with
its jams and pickled beans. Minna whispered, "Celeste?" — heard another murmur from behind the
crimson blanket, was aware of the odor again, somehow arousing and malign. Minna gently pulled back
a corner of the blanket; the faint light from the desk
lamp dully illuminated the long, large body of Celeste in a weird sleep. The pillow rested under
her shoulder blades, tipping her head back and
stretching a long, graceful neck — graceful, despite a
sinewy muscled look, visible in the swollen cords
which even in the poor light Minna could trace to the
high, arched collarbones and chest. Her breasts were
rigid, full and not sagging, not fallen to her armpits.
Minna saw, only with this observation of the breasts,
that Celeste was naked. Her hips were hugely broad;
flat dents lay inside her pelvis, neatly symmetrical;
and despite a certain heaviness to every part of her
body — a forceful, peasant weight to her ankles, a
rounded smoothness in her thighs — the length of
Celeste's waist, the incredible length of her legs,
made her appear almost slender. Minna spoke to her
again, louder this time, and then, as soon as she
heard her own voice, wished she hadn't said any-

thing — thinking, how awful it would be if the poor woman woke up and saw *me* here. Yet Minna didn't leave. This terrible body — terrible, in its intimate potential for strength and motion — fixed Minna to the bedside. Now Celeste began to move slightly, first her hands. The broad, flat fingers curled, her hands cupped, as if to hold some tiny, wounded animal. Then her hands turned palms down on the bed and her fingers picked at the folds and wrinkles in the sheet. Minna wanted to reach out and calm the hands, fearing they would wake Celeste, but her own hands, her whole body, felt frozen. Celeste turned on one elbow, arched her back, and the hands fell with a soft plop on her wide, flat stomach. Slowly and lightly at first, then with more weight and force, pressing with the heels of her hands, Celeste rubbed her stomach. The hands moved into the flat hollows of her pelvis, rolled the loose, puppylike skin; the hands pulled down on the hips, pulled away from the waist, turned under the thighs — up, beneath the buttocks, up, to the small of the back. Celeste lifted herself, arched her back again, higher; her great neck cords thickened, empurpled by this exertion, and her mouth — slack, only a moment ago — curled up at the corners to a senseless grin. Celeste opened her eyes, blinked, saw nothing (Minna saw nothing but whites), and then Celeste's eyes closed. Her whole body now softly relaxed, appeared to sink deeply into the bed, and into a truer sleep; the long, still hands rested lightly inside her thighs. Minna backed out of the alcove, noticed the desk lamp, turned it off. Then she left, careful not to let the door bang behind her.

Back in her room, the bright cans of happy food smiled at Minna from her desk. Minna sat and looked at them. She felt strangely exhausted, and it would have been so nice for Mrs. Elwood and Celeste to join her for the movie — dining, exquisitely, out of the exotic cans. But then, there wouldn't have been enough hors d'oeuvre forks to go around. Even if Mrs. Elwood came alone there wouldn't be a fork for her — and, Minna thought, I don't have a can opener. She had to tell Mrs. Elwood about the movie, too, but she felt again the strange exhaustion, just sitting where she was. Celeste, Minna thought, certainly *looked* a lot younger than 41. Of course the light had been poor, and in sleep the crow's-feet always are softened and smoothed. Had she *really* been asleep? It hadn't looked, to Minna, *quite* like a dream. And how black her hair was! Perhaps it was dyed. Poor thing, she must have been very tired, or upset. Still, Minna couldn't escape the embarrassment of it! It was a little like reading one of the autobiographies. (Embarrassment, for Minna, was a general feeling she experienced often for others, almost never for herself; there didn't seem to be different *kinds* of embarrassment, and the degree to which Minna felt embarrassed could be measured only by how long the feeling lasted.)

Well, there were all these things to be done and she'd better get at them. First, Mrs. Elwood and the movie. Another fork and a can opener. She would ask Mrs. Elwood about that Dear Girl, and find out her name. But Mrs. Elwood would surely ask Minna about Celeste, had Minna gone to meet her? — and *what* would she say? Why, yes, she'd gone to meet her, but the poor woman was asleep. Then Celeste would know she'd been there; and the desk lamp — Minna shouldn't have turned it off. She should have left everything as it was. Minna thought, for one wild moment, that she could go back to Celeste's room and turn on the lamp. Then she thought, What nonsense! Celeste had been asleep — not aware, in her sleep, of anything Minna might have seen. Except, of course, that she was naked, and she would certainly know she'd been naked. Well, what of it? Celeste wouldn't care about that. And Minna suddenly realized that she was thinking she already *knew* Celeste; she couldn't get that idea out of her mind. It seemed that she *did* know her, and how silly that was. Knowing someone, for Minna, was a matter of long, slow familiarity. Why that girl, for instance, with whom she'd spent such a delightful afternoon — Minna didn't *know* her at all.

Again, cheerily, the cans on Minna's desk hailed her. But there came, too, the curious exhaustion. If she didn't tell Mrs. Elwood about the movie she could go to bed right now; of course, there would have to be a note on the door to tell the girls, NO NEWS TONIGHT. But the thought of bed seemed not quite what her exhaustion asked of her; in fact, going to bed was out of the question. Mrs. Elwood enjoyed the Alec Guinness movies so much. Minna thought, How could I think of such a thing? She looked at the cans again, and there was something about the foreignness of the little colored labels that repelled her. Then someone knocked on the door, two raps, and Minna was startled — as if, it struck her, she'd been caught doing something wrong.

"Minna? Minna, are you in?" It was Mrs. Elwood. Minna opened the door, too slowly, too cautiously, and she saw Mrs. Elwood's puzzled face.

"My word, Minna, were you in bed?"

"Oh, no!" Minna cried.

Mrs. Elwood came in and said, "Lord, how dark it

is in here!" and Minna noticed that she hadn't turned on the overheads. Only her desk lamp was on — a single, unsteady shaft of light, which illuminated the gaudy foods.

"Oh, what are these?" Mrs. Elwood asked, moving warily to the desk.

"I had the nicest afternoon," Minna said. "I met one of the girls downtown and we went to Cambridge together, shopping, and we saw a movie and ate in a German place. I only got back a moment ago. Or, maybe, twenty minutes."

"I'd say it was more like twenty minutes," Mrs. Elwood said. "I saw you both come in."

"Oh, then you saw her. What *is* her name?"

"You spent the afternoon with her and you don't know her name?"

"I should have known it, really. She watches television. I just would have felt foolish to ask."

"Lord, Minna!" Mrs. Elwood said. "The girl is Molly Cabot, and she seems to spend more time shopping and moviegoing than she does in her classes."

"Oh, she was so nice to me," Minna said. "I didn't think about her classes, she was such a sweet girl. I *did* think she was lonely. But she's not in any trouble, is she?"

"Well, trouble," Mrs. Elwood repeated, turning one of the strange cans in her hand, scrutinizing the label and setting the can back in the row with a disapproving scowl. "I should say she's in trouble if she doesn't start going to her classes."

"Oh, I'm so sorry," Minna said. "She was so nice. I had a lovely day."

"Well," Mrs. Elwood said toughly, "perhaps she'll pull herself together."

Minna nodded, feeling sad, wishing she could help. Mrs. Elwood was still looking at the cans, and Minna hoped that she wouldn't notice the extravagant hors d'oeuvre fork.

"What's *in* these things?" Mrs. Elwood asked, holding another can in her lumpy palm.

"They're delicacies from other countries. Molly said they were very good."

"I wouldn't buy anything to *eat* if I didn't know what it was," Mrs. Elwood said. "Lord, they might be *unclean!* They might be from *Korea,* or somewhere."

"Oh, I just thought they were pretty," Minna said, and the familiar exhaustion seemed to numb her whole body and her speech. "It was a pleasant way to spend the afternoon," she mumbled, and there was something bitter which came into her voice and surprised her, surprised Mrs. Elwood, too, and brought an unsettling quiet to the small room.

"I think you're very tired," Mrs. Elwood said. "Let me put a note up for the girls, and you go to bed." The authority of Mrs. Elwood's voice seemed to fill Minna's exhaustion, so perfectly, and it made unnecessary any protest. Minna didn't even mention the Alec Guinness movie.

But her sleep was bothered by vague phantoms, in conspiracy, it seemed, with the occasional scratching in the dormitory corridor — presumably the girls who came to see the news and shuffled, puzzled, around the note on the door. Once Minna was sure that Celeste was in the room, still awesomely naked and huge, surrounded by grotesque dwarfs. Once Minna woke, felt the warm weight of her tired hands against her sides, and felt repelled by her own touch. She lay back again, her arms outstretched to the sides of her bed, her fingers curled beneath the mattress as if she were manacled to a rack. If Minna had eaten one of the strange foods, which she had not, she would have attributed her nightmares to this. But as it was inexplicable, her troubled sleep struck her as somewhat of an enigma.

If Minna had any recurrent flickers of embarrassment, any lasting reservations regarding Celeste, nothing of the kind was at all apparent. If she was envious of Celeste's easy vibrancy — her immediate intimacy with the girls, with gruff Flynn, especially with Angelo — she wasn't conscious of such an envy. In fact, it was not until several weeks after the first, awful night that Minna recalled how Mrs. Elwood had not even *asked* her if she'd gone to meet Celeste. Also, Minna had occasion to see more of Molly Cabot; she felt obligated to see more of her, to mother her, in some small, inoffensive way. But Minna's sense of duty took none of the former pleasures away from Molly's company. Minna enjoyed the shy, secretive closeness of her times with Molly. As she saw more of Molly, she saw less of Angelo — not that she stopped worrying about him. Angelo, as Mrs. Elwood had said, was "rather taken with" Celeste. He brought her flowers — expensive, gaudy and tasteless flowers, which he couldn't have stolen in the Common but would have had to buy. And Celeste received other, less open admiration. On Saturdays the girls were allowed to bring their weekend dates to the dining hall for lunch, and Celeste certainly was noticed. The looks which the boys gave her were seldom casual; they were the penetrating weighted looks which Celeste, when her head was turned, received from Flynn — darkly and stealthily watching her from behind various pots and counters. Minna, if she thought anything of this, thought it rather unbecoming of Flynn, and simply rude of the boys. If she worried about Angelo's adoration, she thought of it as nothing more than another example of Angelo's tragic exposure of himself. Celeste, certainly, offered no threat to Angelo. Angelo, as before, simply was a threat to himself.

Minna was perfectly at ease with Celeste. In two months Celeste had made herself at home; she was jolly, a little raucous, always pleasant. The girls were obviously impressed with (or envious of) what Molly called "her Modigliani allure," and Flynn appeared to get great pleasure from his dark observations. Mrs. Elwood thought Celeste was charming, even if a bit bold. Minna liked her.

In June, with only a few weeks of regular classes remaining, Celeste bought an old car — a dented relic of Boston traffic. Once she drove Minna and Molly Cabot to Cambridge, for an afternoon's shopping. The car smelled of suntan oil and cigarettes and, Minna noticed, of the curious heavy scent, coffee-rich, the musk of sheeted furniture in unattended summer homes. Celeste drove like a man, one arm out the window, forceful wrenches on the wheel, fond of shifting from third to second, fond of competing with taxis. The car labored and knocked with sudden acceleration; Celeste explained that the carburetor was dirty or ill-adjusted. Minna and Molly nodded their bewildered respect. Celeste took her days off at Revere Beach; she became deeply tanned but complained about the "pee-like" condition of the water. It was an eager and active time of year.

And June brought a certain impatience to the girls, an irritable quality to Flynn, who always was great at sweating but seemed to suffer most acutely from this in Boston's early and long summers. Minna had grown quite used to the heat; it didn't seem to bother her much, and she noticed that she rarely sweated anymore. Angelo, of course, was forever pale and dry, a completely aseasonal face and body. Celeste looked damply hot.

June was an almost-over time of year, when the girls were brighter and more often in handsome company, when the weekend dining hall was something like a restless, overly chaperoned party. In a while, there would be different girls in the dormitory for the summer session, and summer sessions were so different anyway, lighter, breezier — and from the kitchen's point of view, people ate less. Now there was a distinctly light-handed way about things. Angelo, during the presentation of one horrendous bouquet to Celeste, asked her to see a movie with him. Their heads struggled on either side of the flowers, Angelo peering for an answer, Celeste amused, both at the size of the bouquet and at Angelo's question.

"What movie is it, Angelo?" Her wide, strong mouth; her rich, good teeth.

"Oh, some movie. We'll have to find one close. I don't have a car."

"Then sometime let's go in mine," Celeste said. And then, looking at the ridiculous bouquet, "Where on earth shall we put this? — by the window, out of Flynn's way? I like flowers in a window."

And Angelo scurried to arrange the windowsill. Flynn's following eyes, from somewhere out of the steam, found Celeste's long back and strong legs — her broad, taut buttocks laboring under the weight of lilies and anonymous greens, lilac branches and unopened buds.

There were very few girls who came to see the

news on this Friday night, the last Friday of the school year, the last weekend before the final exams. Presumably the girls were studying, and those who weren't had chosen to go out and *really* not study (rather than compromise with the news). It had rained that afternoon, a rain you could smell, steaming off the sidewalks and leaving the streets nearly dry — only a few tepid puddles remained, and the evening air resembled the damp stuffiness of a laundromat. The heat was of that sensuous, gluttonous kind that people in Boston imagine is like the swamp-surrounded porches of a Southern estate, complete with a woman lolling nude in a hammock. Minna felt pleasantly tired; she sat by the window, looking out to the circular driveway in front of the dormitory. It was a private gravel driveway with a high curb, and from the window it appeared to be carved, or etched, through the rows of elms and the green, green lawn. Minna saw Celeste, arms akimbo, sitting with her back against a tree. Her legs were extended straight in front of her so that her ankles stuck out over the curb of the driveway. It would have been an entirely unbecoming posture for almost any woman, but somehow Celeste lent to it a kind of magnificence in repose; a figure in semirecline that seemed not exactly sluggish but rather wantonly indisposed to any motion. She was somewhat arrogantly dressed: a sleeveless, high-necked jersey, untucked and fallen outside one of those wraparound skirts — the kind that always had a slit somewhere.

The girls stayed after the news to hear the weather report, and to see the dapper little man in the weather station at Logan Airport tediously interpret his complex map. The girls' plans for the weekend obviously hinged on the good weather, and they were all there, Minna still at the window, Celeste still at the tree, when a motorcycle, the gas tank painted fire-engine red, neatly cornered the right-angled entrance to the driveway, leaned cautiously into the gravel circle, and stopped (sliding just a little) in front of the dormitory. The motorcyclist was a young man, very tanned and very blond, with a remarkably babyish face. His shoulders were almost pointed and his head seemed too small for the rest of him; long, thin arms and legs, snugly fitted in a beige summer suit, which sported a wild silk handkerchief in the breast pocket. He wore no tie, just a white shirt open at the throat. His passenger was Molly Cabot. Molly skipped lightly away from the cycle and the curb, then waited for the driver to step off his machine, which he did quite stiffly and slowly. He walked with Molly into the front lobby of the dormitory, walking in the manner of a stoically injured athlete. Minna turned, to see how the weather was progressing, and saw that all the girls were surrounding her at the window.

One of the girls said, "So she *did* get a date with him!"

"We'll never hear the end of this," another girl added.

Everyone sat or stooped rather gravely about the window, waiting for the cyclist to reappear. He wasn't long inside, and when he came out he looked all around him and fiddled with several small parts of his motorcycle. His gestures seemed hurried and not really intended to fix anything; they were the gestures of one who was conscious of being watched. He rose up on the seat and came down heavily on the kick starter; the report which followed the first sucking sound was startling to those in the window. It even caught the attention of Celeste, who straightened up from her repose against the tree and sat a little farther out on the curb. The motorcycle moved around the driveway in Celeste's direction, and when it was a few feet past her the brake light flickered, the rear wheel slid gently sideways toward the curb, and the cyclist brought his right foot to the ground as the machine stopped. He then straightened up off the seat and walked the motorcycle backward to where Celeste sat. One of the girls moved away from the window and shut off the television; then she came quickly back to her position in the huddle. No one could hear what the boy was saying because he kept the engine running. Celeste didn't seem to be saying anything. She just smiled, engaged in looks of practiced scrutiny of the motorcycle and the boy. Then she got up, moved in front of the cycle, moved her hand once or twice in front of the headlamp, touched one of the instrument dials mounted on the handlebars, and stood back from the boy and his machine — giving what appeared from the window to be one last appraisal of everything that met her eyes. At that moment, or so it seemed to the window watchers, Molly Cabot knocked once on the door of Minna's room, entered and said, "Wow!" Everyone stood up and tried to be doing something; one girl made an awkward move to the television, but Molly came directly to the window and looked out to the driveway, asking, "Has he gone?" She was in time to see Celeste offer her hand to the cyclist and deftly swing herself up behind him — it was a move executed with surprising agility for her long weight. The skirt was a slight problem; she had to twist it so that the slit was directly behind her. Then she gripped the seat and the driver with her strong legs, rolled her long arms completely around him — her head was a full two inches higher than his, her back and her shoulders seemed broader, stronger than his. The cyclist shifted all his weight to his left leg, held the motorcycle up with some difficulty, and with his right foot shifted the machine into gear. They pulled away slowly, weaving slightly to the end of the driveway; then, once free of the gravel, and with a minimum of fishtailing from the rear wheel, the cycle lurched into the traffic on the broad street. From the window they were able to follow the sound through the first three gears; then the machine and its riders either stayed in that gear or were lost to the window watchers and listeners in the random blaring of horns and the other sounds of traffic in the night.

"That bastard," Molly Cabot said, coolly, analytically — and, from the faces of the other girls, expectedly.

"Maybe he's just taken her for a ride around the block," someone said, not too convincingly, not even too hopefully.

"Sure," Molly said, and she turned from the window and walked directly out of the room.

All the girls went back to the window. They sat for another 20 minutes, just looking into the night, and finally Minna said, "It's surely time for the movie. Will anyone stay and see it with me?" It was suddenly a night when something extraordinary was called for, Minna thought, and so she considered the extravagance of asking all of them to stay for the movie. If Mrs. Elwood came, as she might, she would not be pleased about it; she would speak to Minna about it — after the girls were gone.

"Why not?" someone said.

The movie, as if things weren't cruel enough, was an old musical. The girls commented harshly on each scene and song. During the commercials the girls went and sat by the window, and whenever there was a likely roar in the street they ran over, regardless of what new horror in song the movie then explored. When the movie was over, the girls were unwilling to leave (some of them had rooms that didn't face the driveway), and they appeared bitterly resolved to a nightlong vigil. Minna asked politely, shyly, if she might go to bed, and the girls straggled into the corridor, aimlessly bitching. They didn't seem angry at Celeste, or angry because they felt badly for Molly; on the contrary, it struck Minna that they were almost glad about it, and certainly excited. Their anger came from a feeling that they had been deeply cheated out of witnessing the climax to the show. They'll be up all night, Minna thought. How awful.

But Minna waited up herself. She occasionally dozed at the window, waking every time with a start — ashamed at the thought that someone might see her there, watching. It was after 3:00 when she went to bed, and she didn't sleep well. She was too tired to get up at every sound, but listened intently to them all. Finally she woke to a sound which was unmistakably the motorcycle, or at least *some* motorcycle. It was stopped at the beginning of the driveway, she could tell, still out on the street, the engine still running. It growled warily out there, making funny, laboring sounds. Then she heard it pull away, heard it pass through three gears again, and lost it as all of them had lost it before, many blocks or even miles away. She listened for the driveway itself now, for the little crunching sounds it made while supporting feet. She heard the little pops and snaps of the stones, the grating sound of feet and stones on the cement steps. She heard the screen door open, the main door open (she had thought, horribly, intriguingly, that it might have been locked), and then she heard, sometime later, the door at the end of the corridor. It was light in her room and she saw that it was nearly five o'clock. Angelo and Flynn would be in the kitchen soon, perhaps they were already there. Then she heard other doors open along the corridor, and the hurried bare feet of the girls padding from room to room. She heard whispering and then she fell asleep.

Saturday morning it rained. A fine, inadequate kind of summer rain that did nothing but fog the windows and leave tiny beads of sweat on everyone's upper lip. It might just as well have been sunny and dazzling for all the difference it made on the temperature, and on Flynn's disposition. Flynn remarked, shortly before lunch, that there hadn't been so few people to breakfast since the flu epidemic in December. It always irritated him to prepare a lot of food and have no one there to eat it. Also, he was bothered by the luncheon menu, angry that they were still serving soup when it was so damn hot (and no one did anything but spill it anyway). Despite the weather, there were a lot of boys and parents in the dining hall. Minna always thought this odd, that everyone spent a year talking about the final exams, and that the weekend before the exams was invariably most festive.

Minna watched Celeste rather carefully that morning, wishing she could say something, although she couldn't think of what on earth she even wanted to say. It hadn't, of course, been wrong of Celeste, but Minna had to confess that Celeste just hadn't *looked* very nice. It was only sad because everyone had to *see* it, had to be hurt or angry because of it. And there wasn't much you could say about that. A peculiar uneasiness passed over Minna — some warm remembrance of a pervasive scent, fecund and coffee-rich, which quickly evanesced.

There was lunch to get ready. Most of the girls had filled the dining hall before the soup was served on every table. Angelo looked sadly at the drooping flowers on the many windowsills, and received angry commands from Flynn that he finish serving the soup. Celeste worked steadily, carrying trays of potato salad, tureens of soup; every time she returned to the kitchen from the dining hall she took one luxurious pull on her cigarette, left dangling over the counter during her exits. Minna neatly arranged the lettuce in pretty patterns around the rim of the salad trays, being careful to hide the wilted and brown parts under the potatoes.

Celeste was taking what had to be the last drag on her cigarette when Molly Cabot swung open the aluminum door to the kitchen; she stepped inside, biting her lips, and allowed the door to swing closed behind her. Angelo, with a handful of flowers, turned to see who'd come in. Flynn stared indifferently. And Minna felt a tremendous weight on her diaphragm, pushing in or pushing out — it was hard to tell where the force was coming from. Molly Cabot, unsteady and small, stepped a little forward and away from the door. She squinted painfully at Celeste, in what might have been an attempt to intimidate the long, calm woman.

"You bitch, you whore!" Molly shouted. A voice as shrill and delicate as a coffee spoon striking a saucer. "You *really* dirty whore!"

And Celeste just looked, smiling gently — an inquiring, still puzzled face, which invited Molly to please continue.

Molly gained a certain composure, a practiced restraint of the kind suggested in Beginning Speech Class, and said, "I will not stoop so low as to compete on *your* level!" It was not haughty, it was still the spoon on the saucer.

Minna said, "Molly, dear. Don't." And Molly, without taking her eyes from Celeste, stepped gingerly backward, feeling for the door with her hand, and when her weight rested against the door she leaned back and swung with it — revolved out of the kitchen. The door swung back, bringing no new horrors in its path, swung twice before it squeaked and closed. Minna looked apologetically at Celeste. "Celeste, dear," she began, but Celeste turned to her with the same penetrating calm, the same inquiring face she had turned to Molly.

"It's all right, Minna," she said, soothingly, as if she spoke to a child.

Minna shook her head and looked away; it seemed she would cry at any second. Flynn banged some pans against the aluminum shelves. "Christ!" he hollered. "What's going on?"

There was a long moment when no one spoke, and then there was Angelo; with a curiously studied fury that never could have been his own, but something mimicked from countless bad movies and college plays, he stepped awkwardly to the middle of the kitchen, throwing himself off balance as he flung his wilted flowers to the floor. "Who does she think she is?" he demanded. "Who does she think she's talking to? Who *is* she?"

"She's just a girl who thinks I stole her boy," Celeste said. "We went out for a ride last night, after he brought her back here."

"But she can't say that!" Angelo cried, and Minna saw that his consistently pale face was deeply flushed.

"I got a daughter her age," Flynn said. "I'd wash her damn mouth out with soap if she ever pulled any of that stuff."

"Oh, that's really good, Flynn," Celeste snapped, "that's really good, coming from you! Why don't you just shut up?"

But Angelo, they should have known, had at last encountered the dark, illogical fate which any one of them might have envisioned for him. He made some quick, secretive movement with his hands and walked to the aluminum door — like one who'd seen a specter of his potential self beckon and bid him follow. He was gone before anyone could say anything, even before anyone could move, leaving the kitchen in ghoulish silence.

Then Flynn said, "He took the lye soap out of the sink. He took it with him!" Celeste moved more quickly than Flynn and Minna; she moved in front of them, out through the swinging door.

The dining hall was very crowded, but very quiet. The occasional tinkle of ice cubes in the tea, the nervous creakings of chairs. Mrs. Elwood sat at the head table, surrounded by well-dressed parents and children with napkins tucked into their collars. Minna looked helplessly at Mrs. Elwood, whose chin was twitching in random little spasms. Angelo stood in the aisle between two rows of tables at the far end of the dining hall, the yellow-green bar of lye soap in his right hand — held as if it were extremely heavy or dangerous, held like a shot put or a grenade.

Molly Cabot peered into her soup, prodigiously counting the noodles or rice. Angelo leaned across the table until his nose was almost in her hair.

"You got to apologize to Miss Celeste. Girl," he said softly, "you got to get up and do it right now."

Molly didn't look up from her soup. She said, "No, Angelo." And then, very quietly, she added, "You go back to the kitchen. Right now."

Angelo put his hand on the edge of Molly's soup dish, palm up, and he let the bar of lye soap slide into her soup.

"Right now," Angelo softly commanded. "You apologize or I'll wash your mouth out good."

Molly pushed her chair back from the table and began to stand up, but Angelo caught her by the shoulders, pulled her across the table to him, and began to force her head down, down to the soup dish. The girl sitting next to Molly screamed — one shrill and aimless scream — and Angelo got his hand on the back of Molly's neck and shoved her face into the soup. He dunked her swiftly, just once, and then he caught her by one shoulder and pulled her to him, his right hand groping for the soap. There was a boy sitting across the aisle from Molly's table. He jumped up and shouted, "Hey!" But Celeste was the first to get to Angelo; she seized him around the waist and picked him off the floor, loosened his grip on Molly, and then tried to shift him over her hip, tried to carry him down the aisle to the kitchen. But Angelo wriggled free of her; he wriggled into hairy Flynn. Flynn grabbed Angelo in a bear hug and everyone heard Angelo grunt. Flynn just turned and walked Angelo toward the kitchen, bending the thin body to a sharp curve at the spine; Celeste ran in front of them, got to the door first and held it open.

Angelo kicked and clawed, snapping his head around to try and see where Molly had gone. "You whore!" Angelo screamed, his breath pinched out of him in thin soprano. And then they passed through the great door — Angelo peering madly over the shoulders of Flynn, Celeste hurrying after them, the door swinging heavily closed.

Minna caught one glimpse of Molly Cabot, leaving the dining hall with a napkin over her face, her blouse spattered with soup and clinging to her bird-like chest. Her scalded, offended, demure breasts seemed to point the way of her determined exit. Then Mrs. Elwood took Minna by the arm and whispered, confidingly, "I must know what this is about. Whatever possessed him? He must leave at once. At once!"

In the kitchen Angelo sat in grand disorder on the floor, leaning against an aluminum cabinet. Flynn roughly dabbed at Angelo's mouth with a wet towel; Angelo was bleeding from his mouth, and he slumped, bespattered with soup, bleeding slowly down his chin. He moaned a high, complaining moan — the whine of an abandoned dog — and his eyes were closed.

"What did you do to him?" Celeste asked Flynn.

"He must have bit his tongue," Flynn mumbled.

"I did, I did," Angelo said, his voice muted by the towel which Flynn squeezed against his mouth.

"Christ, what a stupid wop," Flynn grumbled.

Celeste took the towel from Flynn and shoved him away from Angelo. "Let me do that," she said. "You'll rub his whole face off."

"I should have hit her," Angelo blurted. "I should have just hit her a good one."

"Christ, listen to him!" Flynn shouted.

"Shut up, Flynn," Celeste said.

And Minna, silent all this time, moused in a corner of the kitchen. She said, "He'll have to leave. Mrs. Elwood said he'll have to leave at once."

"Christ, what'll he do?" Flynn asked. "Where in hell can he go?"

"Don't worry about me," Angelo said. He blinked his eyes and smiled at Celeste. She knelt in front of him, made him open his mouth so that she could see his tongue; she had a clean handkerchief in the pocket of her dress and she gently touched his tongue with it, gently closed his mouth, took his hand and made him hold the wet towel to his lips. Angelo shut his eyes again, leaned forward, his head falling on Celeste's shoulder. Celeste settled back on her ankles, wrapped one great arm around Angelo, and slowly rocked him, forward and backward, until he made himself into a little ball on her breast — his curious moan began again, only now it was more like someone making up a song.

"I'll lock the door," Flynn said, "so's no one can come in."

Minna watched, a dull ache in her throat, the prelude to great weeping and sorrow; and arising with the ache was a coldness in her hands and feet. This was hate — oddly enough, she thought — hate for Angelo's possessor, for Celeste, his captor, who now held him as if he were a wild, trapped rabbit. She calmed him, she would tame him; Angelo, dutifully, was her pet and her child, her charge — possessed by this vast, sensuous body, which now and forever would be his magnificent, unachievable goal. And he wouldn't even be aware of what it was that held him to her.

"Angelo," Celeste said softly, "my brother-in-law has an inn in Maine. It's very nice there, on the ocean, and there would be work for you — a free place to stay. In the winter it's quiet, just clean snow to be shoveled and things to be fixed. In the summer the tourists come to swim and sail; there's boats and beaches, and you'd like my family."

"No," Minna said. "It's too far. How could he get there?"

"I'll take him myself," Celeste told her. "I'll drive him there tonight. I'd only miss one day, just tomorrow."

"He's never been out of Boston," Minna said. "He wouldn't like it."

"Of course he'd like it!" Flynn shouted. "It'll be perfect."

"Celeste?" Angelo asked. "Will you be there?"

"On weekends, in the summer," she said. "And all my vacations."

"What's it called?" Angelo asked her. He sat up, back against the counter cabinet, and he touched her hair with his hand. His wondering, adoring eyes passed over her thick, black hair, her strong-boned face and wide mouth.

"It's called Heron's Neck," Celeste told him. "Everybody's very friendly. You'd get to know them all, right away."

"I'll bet you'd like it just fine, Angelo," Flynn said.

"We'll go tonight," Celeste prompted. "We'll go as soon as we put your things in my car."

"You can't do it," Minna said. "You can't take him there."

"She'll only miss one day!" Flynn shouted. "Christ, Minna, what's one day?"

Minna passed her hand over her face, the pow-
der wet and clotted at the corners of her eyes. She
looked at Celeste.

"You can't have the day off," Minna told her. "It's
a busy time of year."

"Christ!" Flynn hollered. "Speak to Mrs. Elwood
about it!"

"I'm in charge of this kitchen!" Minna cried. "I
saw to getting her hired, and I'll see to this." Flynn
evaded Minna's eyes. It was very quiet in the kitchen.

"What if I just left with Angelo tonight?" Celeste
asked.

"Then you just leave for good," Minna said.

"Put Angelo on a bus!" Flynn bellowed.

"I don't want to go there alone!" Angelo cried. "I
don't know anybody," he added meekly.

It was quiet again, and this time Flynn evaded
Celeste's eyes. Celeste looked down at her knees,
then she touched Angelo's damp head.

"I'll take you right now," Celeste told him slowly.

"We'll be there together," Angelo said, rapidly
nodding his head. "You can show me around."

"It'll be nicer that way," Celeste told him. "We'll
just do that."

"I should say good-bye to Mrs. Elwood," Angelo
said.

"Why don't we just send her a postcard when we
get there?" Celeste suggested.

"Yeah," Angelo said. "And we can send one to
Flynn and to Minna. What kind of postcard do you
want, Flynn?"

"Maybe one of the water and cliffs," he answered
gently.

"Cliffs, huh?" Angelo asked Celeste.

"Sure," she said.

"What kind do you want, Minna?" Angelo asked, but she had turned away from them. She was stooping to pick up the flowers from the floor.

"Anything you'd like to send," she told him.

"Then let's get ready," Celeste said.

"Do you want to go out the other door?" Flynn asked. "To get some air." He opened the door which led to the campus yard. It had stopped raining. The grass was shiny and smelled very lush.

When they were gone, when Flynn had shut the door behind them, Minna said, "Well, it's going to be busy with just the two of us, but I guess we'll get on."

"Sure we'll get on," Flynn told her. Then he added, "I think that was a pretty stinking thing to do."

"I *am* sorry, Flynn," she said — a thin, breaking voice — and then she saw the tureens of soup, the trays of potato salad. God, she thought, have they been waiting out there all this time? But when she peeked into the dining hall, gingerly leaning on the door, she saw that everyone was gone. Mrs. Elwood must have shooed them all away.

"There's no one out there," she told Flynn.

"Just look at all this food," he said.

Before the news, before the movie. Minna sits in her room, waiting for it to be finally dark. A soft, gray light falls over the driveway and over the elms, and Minna listens for sounds from Celeste's room — she watches for Celeste's car in the driveway. They must have gone by now, she thinks. They probably loaded the car somewhere else; Celeste would think of that. It is dusky in Minna's room; the faint light of early evening touches what few bright articles are placed on Minna's desk and bedside table, on the chest of drawers and television, on the coffee table. Most striking are the uneaten, unopened cans of foreign food. The hors d'oeuvre fork throws a dull reflection of the evening light back to Minna at the window. Poor Molly, Minna thinks. How awful that she has to go on *being* here, in front of everyone. And suddenly she feels the same sympathy for herself. It is a more ephemeral pity, though, and she soon feels thankful that school is so nearly over.

The street lights go on, whole rows of them lining the campus, giving the same luster to the elms and lawn that Minna noticed a night ago — a watery landscape, with canal, missing only Celeste. Minna moves from the window, turns on her desk lamp, mechanically hunts for a book. Then she sits deeply in the plush of her leather chair. She just sits, listening for nothing now, not reading, not even thinking. The toys of her weary mind seem lost.

A moth catches her eye. It has come from somewhere, somewhere safe, come to flutter wildly about the single light in the room. What on earth can it be that lures a moth out of the safety of darkness and into the peril of light? Its wings flap excitedly, it beats against the hot bulb of the lamp — it surely must scorch itself. Clumsily, carelessly, it bangs into things in an aimless frenzy. Minna thinks for a moment of getting up and turning off the light, but she doesn't feel like sitting in the dark — she doesn't feel like finding a newspaper to swat the moth. She sits, it grows darker, the buzz of the moth becomes soothing and pleasant. Minna dozes peacefully, briefly.

She wakes, startled, and thinks she is not awake — only dreaming. Then she sees the persistent moth and she knows she is really awake. It is completely dark outside now and she hears the familiar, restless growl of a motorcycle. She gets up from her chair and from the window she sees it, the same one, fire-engine red. The cycle waits at the beginning of the driveway. Minna thinks, If he is coming for Molly he'll come into the dormitory. The cyclist glances around him, turns the throttle up and down, looks at his watch, jounces lightly on the seat. He has come for Celeste, Minna knows, and she watches him, aware that other windows around her are open, other eyes watching him. No one comes out of the dormitory; Minna hears whispers pass from window screen to window screen, like a bird looking for a place to get in or out. The motorcyclist turns the throttle up again, holds the throttle there a moment, then lets the engine fall to its wary idle. Nothing happens, the cyclist jounces more heavily on the seat, looks again at his watch. Minna wonders, Do the girls know that Celeste is gone? Of course, the girls know everything; some of them probably knew that the motorcyclist would be back tonight — and not for Molly. But the cyclist is impatient now — sensing, perhaps, that Celeste isn't coming. Minna wishes she could see his face, but it is too dark. Only the pale blond hair flashes at her window, the lustrous red gas tank of the motorcycle shimmers like water; and then the throttle turns up again, the rear wheel skids sideways in the gravel, squeaks on the street. The whispering window screens are now silent, listening for the first three gears. Each gear seems to reach a little further than the night before.

Now Minna is alone with the moth. She wonders whether the girls will come for the news, wonders what time it is. And if the girls come, will Molly come with them? Oh, Minna hopes not, at least not tonight. The moth soothes her again, she dozes or half-dozes to the drone. She has a final, alarming thought before she falls to a deeper sleep. What will she ever say to Mrs. Elwood? But the moth manages to calm even this. The happy, smudge-mouthed faces of her brother's children flood Minna's tiny room, and Angelo is somewhere among them. The motorcycle comes by once more, stops, snarls, goes madly on, ushered away to its dark journey by the titters at the window screens. But Minna doesn't hear it this time. She sleeps — lulled by the whirring, furry music of the moth.

Weary Kingdom (1967)

AUTHOR'S NOTES

For me to publish "Weary Kingdom" in this collection requires either a little courage or a lot of sentimentality, or both. On many levels the story seems amateurish to me, and there is ample evidence of writing habits that I now deplore — lengthy passages in the present tense, which both begin and end the story; clumsy and inconsistent punctuation; overlong paragraphs, which were intended to convey the claustrophobic quality of Minna's mind but which mainly convey to me . . . uh, well, an intense feeling of overall claustrophobia. Furthermore, that Celeste complains about the "pee-like" condition of the water at Revere Beach is embarrassing. Molly Cabot might think of water as "pee-like"; for a woman like Celeste, the correct word is "piss." But what makes me wince most about "Weary Kingdom" is that Minna Barrett is *only* 55 — she sounds and thinks like someone who is at least 115! Of course I was only 25 when I wrote this story — I was still a student at the Iowa Writers' Workshop — and, at the time, I thought 55 was *old*. (Now that I'm only a couple of years away from my 55th birthday, 55 strikes me as entirely too youthful an age for such a dullness of body and mind as Minna's.)

I spent a year revising the story; at the same time I was finishing my first novel, *Setting Free the Bears* (1969). "Weary Kingdom" was published before the novel — in *The Boston Review* (Spring–Summer 1968) — and what endears it to me today, despite the many indications of its amateurism, is that it was from this story that I gained a little confidence concerning how to create a *minor* character in the third-person voice, which is an absolutely necessary ability for a writer of any novel of substance and length. Even in a first-person novel, there must be minor characters introduced *by* the narrator; essentially, these are also characters created in a third-person voice.

And minor characters are all the more essential to any story that entails plot; they are the often-hapless figures who move the story in unexpected ways — often because they are blind to the course of action the main character is following. Minna Barrett is simply a precursor to the lineup of supporting characters in *The World According to Garp;* to the lesser members of the Berry family (or the rapist, Chipper Dove) in *The Hotel New Hampshire;* to Wally Worthington (or the superstitious stationmaster at St. Cloud's) in *The Cider House Rules;* to Hester (or Major Rawls or the Reverend Lewis Merrill) in *A Prayer for Owen Meany;* to Martin Mills (or Inspector Dhar or Nancy) in *A Son of the Circus.* They are *major*-minor characters, all, and to get inside their points of view is fundamental to storytelling.

With Minna Barrett, I can see that I was just learning how, albeit clumsily.

 ALMOST IN IOWA

The driver relied on travel as a form of reflection, but the Volvo had never been out of Vermont. Usually, the driver was a sensible traveler; he kept his oil up and his windshield clean and he carried his own tire gauge in his left breast pocket next to a ball-point pen. The pen was for making entries in the Grand Trip List, such things as gas mileage, toll fees and riding time.

The Volvo appreciated this carefulness of the driver; Route 9 across Vermont, Brattleboro to Bennington, was a trip without fear. When the first signs for the New York state line appeared, the driver said, "It's all right." The Volvo believed him.

It was a dusty tomato-red two-door sedan, 1969, with all-black Semperit radial tires, standard four-speed transmission, four cylinders, two carburetors and 45,238 miles of experience without a radio. It was the driver's feeling that a radio would be distracting to them both.

They had started out at midnight from Vermont. "Dawn in Pennsylvania!" the driver told the worried Volvo.

In Troy, New York, the driver used steady downshifting and a caressing voice to reassure the Volvo that all this would soon pass. "Not much more of this," he said. The Volvo took him at his word. Sometimes it is necessary to indulge illusions.

At the nearly abandoned entrance to the New York State Thruway, West, an innocent Volkswagen exhibited indecision concerning which lane to use.

The driver eased up close behind the Volkswagen and allowed the Volvo's horn to blare; the Volkswagen, near panic, swerved right; the Volvo opened up on the left, passed, cut in with aggression, flashed taillights.

The Volvo felt better.

The New York State Thruway is hours and hours long; the driver knew that monotony is a dangerous thing. He therefore left the Thruway at Syracuse and made an extended detour to Ithaca, driving a loop around Lake Cayuga and meeting up with the Thruway again near Rochester. The countryside bore a comforting resemblance to Vermont. The smell of apples was in the air; maple leaves were falling in front of the headlights. Only once was there an encounter with a shocking, night-lit sign which seemed to undermine the Volvo's confidence. LIVE BAIT! the sign said. The driver had troublesome visions with that one himself, but he knew it could be infectious to express his imagination too vividly. "Just little worms and things," he said to the Volvo, who purred along. But there lurked in the driver's mind the possibility of *other* kinds of "live bait" — a kind of reverse-working bait, which rather than luring the fish to nibble would scare them out of the water. Throw in some of this special bait and retrieve the terrified, gasping fish from where they'd land on shore. Or perhaps LIVE BAIT! was the name of a nightclub.

It was actually with relief that the driver returned to the Thruway. Not every excursion from the main road leads one back. But the driver just patted the dashboard and said, "Pretty soon we'll be in Buffalo."

A kind of light was in the sky — a phase seen

only by duck hunters and marathon lovers. The driver had seen little of that light.

Lake Erie lay as still and gray as a dead ocean; the cars on the Pennsylvania Interstate were just those few early risers who commute to Ohio. "Don't let Cleveland get you down," the driver warned.

The Volvo looked superbly fit — tires cool, gas mileage at 22.3 per gallon, oil full up, battery water ample and undisturbed. The only indication that the whole fearsome night had been journeyed was the weird wingmash and blur of bug stains which blotched the windshield and webbed the grille.

The gas-station attendant had to work his squeegee very hard. "Going a long way?" he asked the driver, but the driver just shrugged. I'm going all the way! he longed to shout, but the Volvo was right there.

You have to watch who you hurt with what you say. For example, the driver hadn't told anyone he was leaving.

They skirted the truck traffic around Cleveland before Cleveland could get them in its foul grasp; they left behind them the feeling that the morning rush hour was angry it just missed them. COLUMBUS, SOUTH, said a sign, but the driver snorted with scorn and sailed up the west ramp of the Ohio Turnpike.

"Crabs in ice water to you, Columbus," he said.

When you've come through a night of well-controlled tension and you're underway in the morning with that feeling of a headstart advantage on the rest of the world, even Ohio seems possible — even Toledo appears to be just a short sprint away.

"Lunch in Toledo!" the driver announced, with

daring. The Volvo gave a slight shudder at 75, skipped to 80 and found that fabled "second wind"; the sun was behind them and they both relished the Volvo's squat shadow fleeing in front of them. They felt they could follow that vision to Indiana.

Early-morning goals are among the illusions we must indulge if we're going to get anywhere at all.

There is more to Ohio than you think; there are more exits to Sandusky than seem reasonable. At one of the many and anonymous rest pavilions off the turnpike, the Volvo had a severe fit of pre-ignition and the driver had to choke off the car's lunging coughs by executing a sharp stallout with the clutch. This irritated them both. And when he made the mileage calculations on the new full tank, the driver was hasty and thoughtless enough to blurt out the disappointing performance. "Fourteen and six tenths miles a gallon!" Then he quickly tried to make the Volvo know that this wasn't offered as criticism. "It was that last gas," he said. "They gave you some bad gas."

But the Volvo was slow and wheezing to start; it idled low and stalled pulling away from the pumps, and the driver thought it was best to say, "Oil's full up, not burning a drop." This was a lie; the Volvo was down half a quart — not enough to add, but below the mark. For a sickening moment, past one more countless exit for Sandusky, the driver wondered if the Volvo *knew*. For distance, trust is essential. Can a car feel its oil level falling?

"Lunch in Toledo" hulked in the driver's mind like a taunt; lapsed hunger informed him that lunchtime could have been dawdled away at any of 14 exits which pretended to lead to Sandusky. God, what *was* Sandusky?

The Volvo, though quenched and wiped, had gone without a proper rest since breakfast in Buffalo. The driver decided to let his own lunch pass. "I'm not hungry," he said cheerfully, but he felt the weight of his second lie. The driver knew that some sacrifices are tokens. If you're in a thing together, a fair share of the suffering must be a top priority. The area referred to as "Toledo" was silently passed in the afternoon like an unmentionable anticlimax. And as for the matter of a falling oil level, the driver knew he was down half a quart of his own. Oh, Ohio.

Fort Wayne, Elkhart, Gary, and Michigan City — *ah, Indiana!* A different state, not planted with cement. "Green as Vermont," the driver whispered. *Vermont!* A magic word. "Of course, flatter," he added, then feared he might have said too much.

A drenching, cleansing thunderstorm broke over the Volvo in Lagrange; gas mileage at Goshen read 20.2, a figure the driver chanted to the Volvo like a litany — past Ligonier, past Nappanee. Boring their way into the heartland, the driver sensed the coming on of an unprecedented "third wind."

Cows appeared to like Indiana. But what was a "Hoosier"?

Shall we have supper in South Bend? A punt's distance from Notre Dame. Nonsense! Gas mileage 23.5! Push on!

Even the motels were appealing; swimming pools winked alongside them. Have a good night's sleep! Indiana seemed to sing.

"Not yet," the driver said. He had seen the signs for Chicago. To wake up in the morning with Chicago already passed by, successfully avoided, outmaneuvered — what a headstart *that* would be!

At the Illinois line, he figured the time, the distance to Chicago, the coincidence of his arrival with the rush hour, etc. The Volvo's case of pre-ignition was gone; it shut off calmly; it appeared to have mastered the famous "kiss start." After the uplift of Indiana, how bad could Illinois be?

"We will be bypassing Chicago at six-thirty P.M.," the driver said. "The worst of the rush hour will be over. We'll drive an hour away from Chicago, downstate Illinois — just to get out in the country again — and we'll definitely stop by eight. A wash for you, a swim for me! Mississippi catfish poached in white wine, an Illinois banana boat, a pint of STP, a cognac in the Red Satin Bar, let some air escape from your tires, in bed by ten, cross the Mississippi at first light, breakfast in Iowa, sausage from homegrown hogs, Nebraska by noon, corn fritters for lunch . . ."

He talked the Volvo into it. They drove into what the license plates call the "Land of Lincoln."

"Good-bye, Indiana! Thank you, Indiana!" the driver sang from the old tune: "I Wish I Was a Hoosier," by M. Lampert. We will often do anything to pretend that nothing is on our minds.

Smog bleared the sky ahead, the sun was not down but it was screened. The highway changed from clear tar to cement slabs with little cracks every second saying, "*Thunk ker-thunk, thunk ker-thunk* . . ." Awful, endless, identical suburbs of outdoor barbecue pits were smoldering.

Nearing the first Chicago interchange, the driver stopped for fresh gas, a look at that falling oil, a pressure check on the tires — just to be sure. The traffic was getting thicker. A transistor radio hung round the gas-station attendant's neck announced that the water temperature in Lake Michigan was 72 degrees.

"*Ick!*" the driver said. Then he saw that the clock on the gas pump did not agree with his watch. He had crossed a time zone, somewhere — maybe in that fantasy called Indiana. He was coming into Chicago an hour earlier than he thought: dead-center, rush-hour traffic hurtled past him. Around him now were the kinds of motels where swimming pools were filled with soot. He imagined the cows who could have woken him with their gentle bells, back in good old Indiana. He had been 18½ hours on the road — with only a breakfast in Buffalo to remember.

"One bad mistake every eighteen and a half hours isn't so bad," he told the Volvo. For optimists, a necessary comeback. And a remarkable bit of repression to think of this mistake as the first.

"Hello, Illinois. Hello to you, half of Chicago."

The Volvo drank a quart of oil like that first cocktail the driver was dreaming of.

If the driver thought Sandusky was guilty of gross excess, it would be gross excess itself to represent the range of his feelings for Joliet.

Two hours of lane-changing inched him less than 30 miles southwest of Chicago and placed him at the crossroads for the travelers heading west — even to Omaha — and south to St. Louis, Memphis and New Orleans. Not to mention errant fools laboring north to Chicago, Milwaukee and Green Bay — and rarer travelers still, seeking Sandusky and the shimmering East.

Joliet, Illinois, was where Chicago parked its trucks at night. Joliet was where people who mistook

the Wisconsin interchange for the Missouri interchange discovered their mistake and gave up.

The four four-lane highways that converged on
Joliet like mating spiders had spawned two Howard
Johnson Motor Lodges, three Holiday Inns and two
Great Western Motels. All had indoor swimming
pools, air conditioning and color TV. The color TV
was an absurd attempt at idealism: to bring color to
Joliet, Illinois, an area which was predominantly gray.

At 8:30 P.M. the driver resigned from the open
road.

"I'm sorry," he said to the Volvo. There was no
car wash at the Holiday Inn. What would have been
the point? And it's doubtful that the Volvo heard him,
or could have been consoled; the Volvo was suffering from a bout of pre-ignition that lurched and
shook the madly clutching driver so badly that he
lost all patience.

"Damn car," he muttered, at an awkward
silence — a reprieve in the Volvo's fit. Well, the damage was done. The Volvo just sat there, *pinging* with
heat, tires hot and hard, carburetors in hopeless disagreement, plugs caked with carbon, oil filter no
doubt choked as tightly closed as a sphincter muscle.

"I'm sorry," the driver said. "I didn't mean it. We'll
get off to a fresh start in the morning."

In the ghastly green-lit lobby, arranged with
turtle aquariums and potted palms, the driver encountered about 1100 registering travelers, all in a
shell-shocked state resembling his own, all telling
their children and wives and cars: "I'm sorry, we'll
get off to a fresh start in the morning . . ."

But disbelief was everywhere. When good faith
has been violated, we have our work cut out for us.

*   *   *

The driver knew when good faith had been violated. He sat on the industrial double bed in Holiday Inn Room 879 and placed a collect phone call to his wife in Vermont.

"Hello, it's me," he said.

"Where have you *been?*" she cried. "God, everyone's been looking."

"I'm sorry," he told her.

"I looked all around that awful party for you," she said. "I was sure you had gone off somewhere with Helen Cranitz."

"Oh, no."

"Well, I finally *humiliated* myself by actually finding her . . . she was with Ed Poines."

"Oh, no."

"And when I saw you'd taken the car I got so worried about what you'd been drinking . . ."

"I was sober."

"Well, Derek Marshall had to drive me home and he *wasn't.*"

"I'm sorry."

"Well, nothing *happened!*"

"I'm sorry. . . ."

"*Sorry!*" she screamed. "Where are you? I needed the car to take Carey to the dentist. I called the police."

"Oh, no."

"Well, I thought you might be in a ditch somewhere off the road."

"The car's fine."

"The *car!*" she wailed. "Where are you? For God's sake . . ."

"I'm in Joliet, Illinois."

"I've had more than enough of your terrible humor. . . ."

"We screwed up at Chicago or I'd be in Iowa."

"Who's we?"

"Just me."

"You said we."

"I'm sorry. ... ."

"I just want to know if you're coming home tonight."

"It's unlikely I could get there," the driver said.

"Well, I've got Derek Marshall on my hands again, you can thank yourself for that. He took Carey to the dentist for me."

"Oh, no."

"He's been a perfect gentleman, of course, but I really had to ask him by. He's worried about you, too, you know."

"Like hell . . ."

"You're in no position to talk like that to me. When are you coming back?"

The thought of "coming back" had not occurred to the driver and he was slow to respond.

"I want to know where you are, *really,*" his wife said.

"Joliet, Illinois."

She hung up.

The longer distances take teamwork. The driver had his work cut out for him, for sure.

Bobbing in the indoor pool, the driver was struck with a certain bilious sensation and the resemblance the pool bore to the turtle aquariums in the Holiday Inn lobby. I don't want to be here, he thought.

In the Grape Arbor Restaurant the driver pondered the dizzying menu, then ordered the chef's crab salad. It came. Lake Michigan should be suspected as a possible, ominous source.

In the Tahiti Bar he was served cognac.

The local Joliet TV station reported the highway fatalities of the day: a grim body count — the vision of the carbon-covered carnage sending travelers away from the bar and to bed early, for a night of troubled sleep. Perhaps this was the purpose of the program.

Before he went to bed himself, the driver said goodnight to his Volvo. He felt its tires, he felt the black grit in the oil, he sought the degree of damage in a pockmark on the windshield.

"That one must have stung."

Derek Marshall! That one stung, too.

The driver remembered what has been referred to as "that awful party." He told his wife he was going to the bathroom; cars were parked all over the lawn and he went to the bathroom there. Little Carey was staying at a friend's house; there was no baby-sitter to see the driver slip home for his toothbrush.

A dress of his wife's, a favorite one of his, hung on the back of the bathroom door. He nuzzled it; he grew fainthearted at its silky feel; his tire gauge snagged on the zipper as he tried to pull away from it. "Good-bye," he told the dress, firmly.

For a rash moment he considered taking all her clothes with him! But it was midnight — time for turning to pumpkin — and he sought the Volvo.

His wife was a dusty tomato-red . . . no. She was a blonde, seven years married with one child and without a radio. A radio was distracting to them both. No. His wife took a size-10 dress, wore out three pairs of size-7 sandals between spring and fall, used a 36B bra and averaged 23.4 miles per gallon . . . *no!* She was a small dark person with strong fingers and intense sea-blue eyes like airmail envelopes; she had the habit of putting her head back like a wrestler about to bridge or a patient preparing for mouth-to-mouth resuscitation whenever she made love. . . . oh, yes. She had a svelte, not a voluptuous, body and she liked things that clung to her, hugged her, hung around her . . . clothes, children, big dogs and men. She was tall with long thighs and a loping walk, a great mouth, a 38D. . . .

Then the driver's sinuses finally revolted against the nightlong endurance test forced upon them by the air conditioning; he sneezed violently and woke himself up. He put his thoughts for his wife and all other women in a large, empty part of his mind which resembled the Volvo's roomy, unpacked trunk. He took a forceful shower and thought that today was the day he would see the Mississippi.

People actually learn very little about themselves; it's as if they really appreciate the continuous act of making themselves vulnerable.

The driver planned to leave without breakfast. You'd have thought he'd be used to ups and downs, but the early morning sight of the violence done to the Volvo was a shock even to this veteran of the ways of the road. The Volvo had been vandalized. It sat at the curb by the driver's motel room like a wife he'd locked out of the house in the drunken night — she was waiting there to hit him hard with his guilt in the daylight.

"Oh, my God, what have they done to you . . . ?"

They had pried off the four hubcaps and left the cluster of tire nuts exposed, the tires naked. They had stolen the side-view mirror from the driver's side. Someone had tried to unscrew the whole mounting for the piece, but the screwdriver had been

either too big or too small for the screws; the work
had left the screwheads maimed and useless; the
thief had left the mounting in place and simply
wrenched the mirror until it had snapped free at the
ball joint. The ruptured joint looked to the driver like
the raw and ragged socket of a man whose arm had
been torn off.

They had tried to violate the Volvo's interior with
repeated digging and levering at the side-vent windows, but the Volvo had held. They had ripped the
rubber water seal from under the window on the driver's side but they had not been able to spring the
lock. They had tried to break one window: a small
run of cracks, like a spider web blown against the
glass, traced a pattern on the passenger's side. They
had tried to get into the gas tank — to siphon gas, to
add sand, to insert a match — but although they had
mashed the tank-top lock, they had been unable to
penetrate there. They had cranked under the hood,
but the hood had held. Several teeth of the grille
were pushed in, and one tooth had been bent out-
ward until it had broken; it stuck out in front
of the Volvo as if the car were carrying some crude
bayonet.

As a last gesture, the frustrated car rapists, the
wretched band of Joliet punks — or were they other
motel guests, irritated by the foreign license plate, in
disagreement with Vermont? . . . whoever, as a finally
cruel and needless way of leaving, *someone* had
taken an instrument (the corkscrew blade on a
camper's knife?) and gouged a four-letter word into
the lush red of the Volvo's hood. Indeed, deeper than
the paint, it was a groove into the steel itself. SUCK
was the word.

"Suck?" the driver cried out. He covered the

wound with his hand. "Bastards!" he screamed. "Swine, filthy creeps!" he roared. The wing of the motel he was facing must have slept 200 travelers; there was a ground-floor barracks and a second-floor barracks with a balcony. "Cowards, car-humpers!" the driver bellowed. "Who did it?" he demanded. Several doors along the balcony opened. Frightened, wakened men stood peering down at him — women chattering behind them: "Who is it? What's happening?"

"Suck!" the driver yelled. "Suck!"

"It's six o'clock in the morning, fella," someone mumbled from a ground-floor door, then quickly stepped back inside and closed the door behind him.

Genuine madness is not to be tampered with. If the driver had been drunk or simply boorish, those disturbed sleepers would have mangled him. But he was insane — they could all see — and there's nothing to do about that.

"What's going on, Fred?"

"Some guy losing his mind. Go back to sleep."

Oh, Joliet, Illinois, you are worse than the purgatory I first took you for!

The driver touched the oily ball joint where his trim mirror used to be. "You're going to be all right," he said. "Good as new, don't worry."

SUCK! That foul word dug into his hood was so *public* it seemed to expose *him* — the rude, leering ugliness of it shamed him. He saw Derek Marshall approaching his wife. "Hi! Need a ride home?"

"All right," the driver told the Volvo, thickly. "All right, that's enough. I'll take you home."

The gentleness of the driver was now impressive. It is incredible to find occasional discretion in human beings; some of the people on the second-floor balcony were actually closing their doors. The driver's hand hid the SUCK carved into his hood; he was crying. He had come all this way to leave his wife and all he had done was hurt his car.

But no one can make it as far as Joliet, Illinois, and not be tempted to see the Mississippi River — the main street of the Midwest, and the necessary crossing to the real Outwest. No, you haven't really been West until you've crossed the Mississippi; you can never say you've "been out there" until you've touched down in Iowa. If you have seen Iowa, you have seen the beginning.

The driver *knew* this; he begged the Volvo to indulge him just a look. "We'll turn right around. I promise. I just want to see it," he said. "The Mississippi. And Iowa . . ." where he might have gone.

Sullenly, the Volvo carried him through Illinois: Starved Rock State Park, Wenona, Mendota, Henry, Kewanee, Geneseo, Rock Island and Moline. There was a rest plaza before the great bridge which spanned the Mississippi — the bridge which carried you into Iowa. Ah, Davenport, West Liberty and Lake MacBride!

But he would not see them, not now. He stood by the Volvo and watched the tea-colored, wide water of the Mississippi roll by; for someone who's seen the Atlantic Ocean, rivers aren't so special. But *beyond* the river . . . there was *Iowa* . . . and it looked really *different* from Illinois! He saw corn tassels going on forever, like an army of fresh young cheerleaders waving their feathers. Out there, too, big hogs grew; he knew that; he imagined them — he had to — because there wasn't actually a herd of pigs browsing on the other side of the Mississippi.

"Someday . . ." the driver said, half in fear that this was true and half wishfully. The compromised Volvo sat there waiting for him; its bashed grille and the word SUCK pointed east.

"Okay, okay," the driver said.

Be thankful for what dim orientation you have. Listen: the driver *could* have gotten lost; in the muddle of his east-west decision, he could have headed north — in the southbound lane!

Missouri State Police Report # 459: "A red Volvo sedan, heading north in the southbound lane, appeared to have a poor sense of direction. The cement mixer who hit him was absolutely clear about its right-of-way in the passing lane. When the debris was sorted, a phone number was found. When his wife was called, another man answered. He said his name was Derek Marshall and that he'd give the news to the guy's wife as soon as she woke up."

We should know: it can always be worse.

Certainly, real trouble lay ahead. There was the complexity of the Sandusky exits to navigate, and the driver felt less than fresh. Ohio lay out there, waiting for him like years of a marriage he hadn't yet lived. But there was also the Volvo to think of; the Volvo seemed destined to never get over Vermont. And there would be delicate dealings to come with Derek Marshall; that seemed sure. We often need to lose sight of our priorities in order to see them.

He had seen the Mississippi and the lush, fertile flatland beyond. Who could say what sweet, dark mysteries Iowa might have revealed to him? Not to mention Nebraska. Or *Wyoming!* The driver's throat ached. And he had overlooked that he once more had to pass through Joliet, Illinois.

Going home is hard. But what's to be said for staying away?

In La Salle, Illinois, the driver had the Volvo checked over. The windshield wipers had to be replaced (he hadn't even noticed they were stolen), a temporary side-view mirror was mounted and some soothing antirust primer was painted into the gash which said SUCK. The Volvo's oil was full up, but the driver discovered that the vandals had tried to jam little pebbles in all the air valves — hoping to deflate his tires as he drove. The gas-station attendant had to break the tank-top lock the rest of the way in order to give the Volvo some gas. Mileage 23.1 per gallon — the Volvo was a tiger in the face of hardship.

"I'll get you a paint job at home," the driver told the Volvo, grimly. "Just try to hang on."

There was, after all, Indiana to look forward to. Some things, we're told, are even better "the second time around." His marriage struck him as an unfinished war between Ohio and Indiana — a fragile balance of firepower, punctuated with occasional treaties. To bring Iowa into the picture would cause a drastic tilt. Or: some rivers are better not crossed? The national average is less than 25,000 miles on one set of tires, and many fall off much sooner. He had 46,251 miles on the Volvo — his first set of tires.

No, despite that enchanting, retreating portrait of the Iowa future, you cannot drive with your eyes on the rear-view mirror. And, yes, at this phase of the journey, the driver was determined to head back East. But dignity is difficult to maintain. Stamina requires constant upkeep. Repetition is boring. And you pay for grace.

Almost in Iowa (1973)

AUTHOR'S NOTES

I loathe the subject of divorce — my own especially. When people start telling me their divorce stories, I feel stricken with the same combination of pending illness and apprehension that I feel when encountering "turbulence" on an airplane and the pilot asks us all to put on our seatbelts; I want to get off the plane. I do not tell stories about my divorce, nor have I ever written about it — nor would I. I feel most strongly that writers who have children, and who have been divorced, *should not* write about their divorces; to do so is a form of child abuse. I even detest watching movies about people who are divorcing; personally, I think that pornography is less offensive — it's less personal.

With this in mind, I haven't much to say about "Almost in Iowa," except that it is a story about divorce — or at least about a pending divorce — and therefore I hate it. My first choice was not to include it in this collection, but my publishers persuaded me that *other* people might like it. I yielded to their opinion, because I would never claim to have the slightest degree of objectivity on this subject. "Almost in Iowa" isn't about *my* divorce, anyway. I was first married in 1964 and divorced in 1982 — almost 10 years after I wrote this story. (I met my second wife in 1986 and was remarried in 1987.)

"Almost in Iowa" was first published in *Esquire*

(November 1973). I suppose I once thought that the story was awfully clever; rereading it now, I am struck by a quality of loathsome cuteness — not a very remarkable observation, because I have long associated *Esquire* with writing that is loathsomely cute or smart-ass (or both).

The story also reminds me of a student's story I once made fun of — that previously mentioned story about eating from the point of view of a fork. In this case, the car is a better character — meaning a more developed character — than the driver. A man who would leave his wife at a party in Vermont, and not call her to tell her where he was until he got to Illinois, is a shallow sort of lout; in "Almost in Iowa," my sympathies reside entirely with the Volvo.

HOMAGE

THE KING OF THE NOVEL

1. Why I Like Charles Dickens; Why Some People Don't

Great Expectations is the first novel I read that made me wish I had written it; it is the novel that made me want to be a novelist — specifically, to move a reader as I was moved then. I believe that *Great Expectations* has the most wonderful and most perfectly worked-out plot for a novel in the English language; at the same time, it never deviates from its intention to move you to laughter and to tears. But there is more than one thing about this novel that some people don't like — and there is one thing in particular that they don't like about Dickens in general. Here is the thing highest on the list that they don't like: the intention of a novel by Charles Dickens is to move you emotionally, not intellectually; and it is by emotional means that Dickens intends to influence you socially. Dickens is not an analyst; his writing is not analytical — although it can be didactic. His genius is descriptive; he can describe a thing so vividly — and so influentially — that no one can look at that thing in the same way again.

You cannot encounter the prisons in Dickens's novels and ever again feel completely self-righteous about prisoners being where they belong; you cannot encounter a lawyer of Mr. Jaggers's terrifying ambiguity and ever again put yourself willingly in a lawyer's hands — Jaggers, although only a minor character in *Great Expectations,* may be our literature's greatest indictment of living by abstract rules.

Dickens has even provided me with a lasting vision of a critic; he is Bentley Drummle, "the next heir but one to a baronetcy," and "so sulky a fellow that he even took up a book as if its writer had done him an injury."

Although his personal experiences with social evil had been brief and youthful, they never ceased to haunt Dickens — the humiliation of his father in the debtors' prison at Marshalsea; his own three months' labor (at age 11) in a blacking warehouse at Hungerford Stairs, pasting labels on bottles; and because of his father's money problems, the family's several moves — especially, when Charles was nine, to meaner accommodations in Chatham, and shortly thereafter, away from the Chatham of his childhood. "I thought that life was sloppier than I expected to find it," he wrote. Yet his imagination was never impoverished; in *David Copperfield,* he wrote (remembering his life as a reader in his attic room at St. Mary's Place, Chatham), "I have been Tom Jones (a child's Tom Jones, a harmless creature)." He had been Don Quixote, too — and all the even less likely heroes of the Victorian fairy tales of his time. As Harry Stone has written: "It is hard to know which came first, Dickens's interest in fairy tales or his conditioning by them." Dickens's fine biographer, Edgar Johnson, describes the sources of the author's imagination similarly, claiming further that Dickens had devised "a new literary form, a kind of fairy tale that is at once humorous, heroic, and realistic."

The Chatham of Dickens's childhood is sharply recalled in *Great Expectations* — in the churchyard graves he could see from his attic room, and in the black convict hulk, "like a wicked Noah's ark," which he saw looming offshore on the boating trips he took up the Medway to the Thames; that is where he saw his first convicts, too. So much of the landscape of *Great Expectations* is Chatham's landscape: the foggy marshes, the river mist; and his real-life model for the Blue Boar was there in nearby Rochester, and Uncle Pumblechook's house was there — and Satis House, where Miss Havisham lives. On walks with his father, from Gravesend to Rochester, they would pause in Kent and view the mansion atop a two-mile slope called Gad's Hill; his father told him that if he was very hardworking, he might get to live there one day. Given his family's Chatham circumstances, this must have been hard for young Charles to believe, but he did get to live there one day — for the last 12 years of his life; he wrote *Great Expectations* there, and he died there. For readers who find Dickens's imagination farfetched, they should look at his life.

His was an imagination fueled by personal unhappiness and the zeal of a social reformer. Like many successful people, he made good use of disappointments — responding to them with energy, with near-frenzied activity, rather than needing to recover from them. At 15, he left school; at 17, he was a law reporter; at 19, a parliamentary reporter. At 20, he was a witness to the unemployment, starvation, and cholera of the winter of 1831–32, and his first literary success, at 21, was made gloomy by the heartbreak of his first love. She was a banker's daughter, whose family shunned Dickens; years later, she returned to him in her embarrassing maturity — she was plump and tiresome, then, and he shunned her. But when he first met her, her rejection made him work all the harder; Dickens never moped.

He had what Edgar Johnson calls a "boundless confidence in the power of the will." One of his earliest reviews (by his future father-in-law; imagine that!) was absolutely right about the talents of the young author. "A close observer of character and manners," George Hogarth wrote about the 24-year-old Dickens, "with a strong sense of the ridiculous and a graphic faculty of placing in the most whimsical and amusing lights the follies and absurdities of human nature. He has the power, too, of producing tears as well as laughter. His pictures of the vices and wretchedness which abound in this vast city are sufficient to strike the heart of the most careless and insensitive reader."

Indeed, Dickens's young star so outshone that of Robert Seymour, the *Pickwick Papers*'s first illustrator, that Seymour blew his brains out with a muzzle-loader. By 1837 Dickens was already famous for Mr. Pickwick. He was only 25. He even took command of his hapless parents; having twice bailed his father out of debtors' prison, Dickens moved his parents forcibly from London to Exeter — an attempt to prevent his feckless father from running up an unpayable tab in his famous son's name.

Dickens's watchdog behavior regarding the social ills of his time could best be described, politically, as reform liberalism; yet he was not to be pinned down. His stance for the abolition of the death penalty, for example, was based on his belief that the death penalty did nothing to deter crime — not out of sentiment for any malefactor. For Dickens, "the major evil" — as Johnson describes it — "was the psychological effect of the horrible drama of hanging before a brutalized and gloating mob." He was tireless in his support of reform homes for women, and of countless services and charities for the poor; by the time of *Dombey and Son* (1846–48), he had a firmly developed ethic regarding the human greed evident in the world of competitive business — and a strongly expressed moral outrage at the indifference shown to the welfare of the downtrodden; he had begun to see, past *Oliver Twist* (1837–39), that vice and cruelty were not randomly bestowed on individuals at birth but were the creations of society. And well before the time of *Bleak House* (1852–53), he had tenacious hold of the knowledge that "it is better to suffer a great wrong than to have recourse to the much greater wrong of the law."

He was 30 when he had his first fling at editing "a great liberal newspaper," dedicated to the "Principles of Progress and Improvement, of Education, Civil and Religious Liberty, and Equal Legislation"; he lasted only 17 days. With *Household Words,* he did much better; the magazine was as successful as many of his novels, full of what he called "social wonders, good and evil." Among the first to admire the writing of George Eliot, he was also among the first to guess her sex. "I have observed what seem to me to be such womanly touches," he wrote to her, "that the assurance on the title-page is insufficient to satisfy me, even now. If they originated with no woman, I believe that no man ever before had the art of making himself, mentally, so like a woman, since the world began." Of course, she was charmed — and she confessed to him.

He was so industrious that (despite his generosity) even the work of his own friends failed to impress him. "There is a horrid respectability about the most of the best of them," he wrote, " — a little, finite, systematic routine in them, strangely expressive to me of the state of England herself." Yet he was

ever the champion of the *un*championed — as in Mr.
Sleary's heartfelt and lisped plea for the circus artists
in *Hard Times*. "Don't be croth with uth poor
vagabondth. People must be amuthed. They can't be
alwayth a learning, nor yet can they be alwayth a
working, they ain't made for it. You *mutht* have uth,
Thquire. Do the withe thing and the kind thing, too,
and make the betht of uth; not the wortht!" It is this
quality in Dickens that has been blessed by Irving
Howe, who writes that "in [his] strongest novels, en-
tertainer and moralist come to seem shadows of one
another — finally two voices out of the same mouth."

Dickens's gift is how spontaneously he can render a situation both sympathetic and hilarious — and
charged with his fierce indignation, with what Johnson calls his "furious exposure of social evils." Yet
Dickens's greatest risk taking, as a writer, has little to
do with his social morality. What he is most unafraid
of is sentimentality — of anger, of passion, of emotionally and psychologically revealing himself; he is
not self-protective; he is never careful. In the present,
postmodernist praise of the *craft* of writing — of the
subtle, of the exquisite — we may have refined the
very heart out of the novel. Dickens would have had
more fun with today's literary elitists and minimalists
than he had with Mr. Pumblechook and Mrs. Jellyby.
He was the king of the novel in the same century that
produced the models of the form.

Dickens wrote great comedy — high and low —
and he wrote great melodrama. At the conclusion of
the first stage of Pip's expectations, Dickens writes:
"Heaven knows we need never be ashamed of our
tears, for they are rain upon the blinding dust
of earth, overlying our hard hearts." But we *are*
ashamed of our tears. We live at a time when critical

taste tells us that to be softhearted is akin to doltish-ness; we're so influenced by the junk on television that even in reacting against it we overreact — we conclude that *any* attempt to move an audience to laughter or to tears is shameless, is either sitcom or soap opera or both.

Edgar Johnson is correct in observing that "though much has been said about Victorian re-straint, emotionally it is we who are restrained, not they. Large bodies of modern readers, especially those called 'sophisticated,' distrust any uncurbed yielding to emotion. Above all when the emotion is noble, heroic, or tender, they wince in skeptical sus-picion or distaste. A heartfelt expression of sentiment seems to them exaggerated, hypocritical, or embar-rassing." And Johnson offers a reason for this. "There are explanations, of course, for our peculiar fear of sentiment as sentimental. With the enormous growth of popular fiction, vulgar imitators have cheapened the methods they learned from great writers and coarsened their delineation of emotion. Dickens's very powers marked him out as a model for such emulation."

To the modern reader, too often when a writer risks being sentimental the writer is already guilty. But as a writer it is cowardly to so fear sentimentality that one avoids it altogether. It is typical — and for-givable — among student writers to avoid being mush-minded by simply refusing to write about people, or by refusing to subject characters to emo-tional extremes. Dickens took sentimental risks with abandon. "His weapons were those of caricature and burlesque," Johnson writes, "of melodrama and unre-strained sentiment."

And here's another wonderful thing about him:

his writing is never vain — I mean that he never sought to be original. He never pretended to be an explorer, discovering neglected evils. Nor was he so vain as to imagine that his love or his use of the language was particularly special; he could write very prettily when he wanted to but he never had so little to say that he thought the object of writing was pretty language; he did not care about being original in that way either. The broadest novelists never cared for that kind of original language — Dickens, Hardy, Tolstoy, Hawthorne, Melville . . . their so-called style is every style; they use all styles. To such novelists, originality with language is mere fashion; it will pass. The larger, plainer things — the things they are preoccupied with, their obsessions — these will last: the story, the characters, the laughter and the tears.

Yet writers who are considered masters of style have also marveled at Dickens's technical brilliance, while recognizing it as instinctual — as nothing anyone ever learned, or could be taught. G. K. Chesterton's *Charles Dickens: A Critical Study* is both an appreciative and a precise view of Dickens's techniques; Chesterton also offers a marvelous defense of Dickens's characters. "Though his characters often were caricatures, they were not such caricatures as was supposed by those who had never met such characters," Chesterton writes. "And the critics had never met the characters; because the critics did not live the common life of the English people; and Dickens did. England was a much more amusing and horrible place than it appeared to the sort of man who wrote reviews."

It is worth noting that both Johnson and Chesterton stress Dickens's fondness for the *common;* Dickens's critics stress his eccentricity. "There can be no question of the importance of Dickens as a human event in history," Chesterton writes, ". . . a naked flame of mere genius, breaking out in a man without culture, without tradition, without help from historic religions and philosophies or from the great foreign schools; and revealing a light that never was on sea or land, if only the long fantastic shadows that it threw from common things."

Vladimir Nabokov has pointed out that Dickens didn't write every sentence as if his reputation depended on it. "When Dickens has some information to impart to his reader through conversation or meditation, the imagery is generally not conspicuous," Nabokov writes. Dickens knew how to keep a reader reading; he trusted his descriptive powers — as much as he trusted his ability to make his readers feel emotionally connected to his characters. Very simply, narrative momentum and emotional interest in the characters are what make a novel more compellingly readable on page 300 than it is on page 30. "The bursts of vivid imagery are spaced" is how Nabokov puts it.

But didn't he exaggerate everything? his critics ask.

"When people say that Dickens exaggerates," George Santayana writes, "it seems to me that they have no eyes and no ears. They probably have only *notions* of what things and people are; they accept them conventionally, at their diplomatic value." And to those who contend that no one was ever so sentimental, or that there was no one ever *like* Wemmick or Jaggers or Bentley Drummle, Santayana says: "The polite world is lying; there *are* such people; we are such people ourselves in our true moments." Santayana also defends Dickens's stylistic excesses: "This faculty, which renders him a consummate comedian, is just what alienated him from a later generation in which people of taste were aesthetes and virtuous people were higher snobs; they wanted a mincing art, and he gave them copious improvisation, they wanted analysis and development, and he gave them absolute comedy."

No wonder that — both because of and in spite of his popularity — Dickens was frequently misunderstood, and often mocked. In his first visit to America he was relentless in his attack on America's practice of ignoring international copyright; he also detested slavery, and said so, and he found loathsome and crude the American habit of *spitting* — according to Dickens, practically everywhere! For his criticism he was rewarded by our critics, who called him a "flash reporter" and "that famous penny-a-liner"; his mind was described as "coarse, vulgar, impudent, and superficial"; he was called "narrow-minded" and "conceited," and among all visitors, ever, to "this original and remarkable country," he was regarded as "the most flimsy — the most childish — the most trashy — the most contemptible. . . ."

So, of course, Dickens had enemies; they could not touch his splendid instincts, or match his robust life. Before beginning *Great Expectations,* he said, "I must make the most I can out of the book — I think a good name?" Good, indeed, and a title many writers wish were free for them to use, a title many wonderful novels could have had: *The Great Gatsby, To the Lighthouse, The Mayor of Casterbridge, The Sun Also Rises, Anna Karenina, Moby Dick* — all great expectations, of course.

2. A Prisoner of Marriage; the "One Happiness I Have Missed in Life . . ."

But what about the plot? his critics ask. Aren't his plots unlikely?

Oh, boy; are they ever "unlikely"! I wonder how many people who call a plot "unlikely" ever realize that they do not like any plot at all. The nature of plot *is* unlikely. And if you've been reading a great many contemporary novels, you're probably unused to encountering much in the way of plot there; should you encounter one now, you'd be sure to find it unlikely. Yet when the British sailed off to their little war with Argentina in 1982, they used the luxury liner, the *Queen Elizabeth II,* as a troop transport. And what became the highest military priority of the Argentinean forces, who were quite overpowered in this war? To sink that luxury liner, the *Queen Elizabeth II,* of course — to salvage, at the very least, what people call a "moral victory." Imagine that! But we accept far more unlikely events in the news than we accept in fiction. Fiction is, and has to be, better made than the news; plots, even the most unlikely ones, are better made than real life, too.

Let us look at Charles Dickens's marriage for a moment; the story of his marriage, were we to encounter it in any novel, would seem highly unlikely to us. When Dickens married Catherine Hogarth, Catherine's younger sister Mary, who was only 16, moved in with them; Mary adored her sister's husband, and she was an ever-cheerful presence in their house — perhaps seeming all the more good-natured and even-tempered alongside Catherine's periods of sullen withdrawal. How much easier it is to be a visitor than to be a spouse; and to make matters worse,

Mary died at 17, thus perfectly enshrining herself in Dickens's memory — and becoming, in the later years of his marriage to Kate (Catherine was called Kate), an even more impossible idol, against whom poor Kate could never compete. Mary was a vision of perfection as girlish innocence, of course, and she would appear and reappear in Dickens's novels — she is Little Nell in *The Old Curiosity Shop,* she is Agnes in *David Copperfield,* she is Little Dorrit. Surely her goodness finds its way into Biddy in *Great Expectations,* too, although Biddy's capabilities for criticizing Pip come from stronger stuff than anything Dickens would have had the occasion to encounter in Mary Hogarth.

In his first visit to America, while Dickens made few references to the strains that Kate felt while traveling (her anxieties for the children back in England, especially), he did observe the profound lack of interest in America that was expressed by Kate's maid. Kate herself, he documented — in the course of getting on and off boats and coaches and trains — had fallen 743 times. Although this was surely an exaggeration, Mrs. Dickens did compile an impressive record of clumsiness; Johnson suggests that she suffered from a nervous disorder, for her lack of physical control was remarkable. Dickens once cast her in one of his amateur theatrical company's performances — it was a small part in which Kate spoke a total of only 30 lines; yet she managed to fall through a trapdoor on stage and so severely sprained her ankle that she had to be replaced. It seems an extreme step to take to gain Dickens's attention; but Kate surely suffered their marriage in her own way as acutely as her husband did in his.

When Dickens's 23-year-old marriage to Kate

was foundering, who would be living with them but another of Kate's younger sisters? Dickens found Georgina "the most admirable and affectionate of girls"; and such was her loyalty to him that after Dickens and Kate separated, Georgina remained with Dickens. She might have been in love with him, and quite more to him than a help with the children (Kate bore Dickens 10 children), but there is nothing to suggest that their relationship was sexual — although, at the time, they were subject to gossip about that.

At the time of his separation from Kate, Dickens was probably in love with an 18-year-old actress in his amateur theatrical company — her name was Ellen Ternan. When Kate discovered a bracelet that Dickens had intended as a present for Ellen (he was in the habit of giving little gifts to his favorite performers), Kate accused him of having already consummated a relationship with Ellen — a relationship that, in all likelihood, was not consummated until some years after Dickens and Kate had separated. (Dickens's relationship with Ellen Ternan must have been nearly as guilt ridden and unhappy as his marriage.) At the time of the separation, Kate's mother spread the rumor that Dickens had already taken Ellen Ternan as his mistress. Dickens published a statement under the headline "PERSONAL" on the front page of his own, very popular magazine (*Household Words*) that such "misrepresentations" of his character were "most grossly false." Dickens's self-righteousness in his own defense invited controversy; every detail of his marriage and separation was published in *The New York Tribune* and in all the English newspapers. Imagine that!

It was 1858. Within three years, Dickens would

change the name of *Household Words* to *All the Year Round* and continue his exhausting habit of serializing his novels for his magazine; he would begin the great numbers of fervent public readings that would undermine his health (he would give more than 400 readings before his death in 1870); and he would complete both *A Tale of Two Cities* and *Great Expectations*. "I am incapable of rest," he told his best and oldest friend, John Forster. "I am quite confident I should rust, break, and die, if I spared myself. Much better to die, doing."

As for love: he would lament that a true love was the "one happiness I have missed in life, and the one friend and companion I never made." More than a little of that melancholic conviction would haunt Pip's quest of Estella's love (and profoundly influence Dickens's first version of the ending of *Great Expectations*). And the slowness and the coldness with which the teenaged Ellen Ternan responded to the famous author in his late forties would cause Dickens to know more than a little of what Pip's longing for Estella was.

His marriage to Kate had, in his view, been a prison; but in taking leave of it, he had encountered a most public scandal and humiliation, and a reluctant mistress — the relationship with Ellen Ternan would never be joyously celebrated. The lovelessness of his marriage would linger with him — just as the dust of the debtors' prison would pursue Mr. Dorrit, just as the cold mists of the marshes would follow young Pip to London, just as the "taint" of Newgate would hang over Pip when he so hopefully meets Estella's coach.

Pip is another of Dickens's orphans, but he is never so pure as Oliver Twist and never so nice as

David Copperfield. He is not only a young man with unrealistic expectations; he is a young brat who adopts the superior manners of a gentleman (an un-earned position) while detesting his lowly origins and feeling ashamed in the company of men of a higher social class than his. Pip is a snob. "It is a most miserable thing to feel ashamed of home," he admits; yet as he sets out to London to enjoy his unknown benefactor's provisions, Pip heaps "a gallon of con-descension upon everybody in the village."

It must have been a time of self-doubt for Dick-ens — at least, he suffered some reevaluation of his self-esteem. He had kept his workdays in the black-ing warehouse a secret from his own children. Al-though his origins were not so lowly as young Pip's, Dickens must have thought them low enough. He would never forget how deeply his spirits sank when he was pasting labels on the bottles at Hungerford Stairs.

And was he feeling guilty, too, and considering some of his own ventures to have only the airs of a gentleman (without real substance) about them? Surely the patrician goals to which young Pip aspires are held in some contempt in *Great Expectations:* the mysterious and elaborate provisions that enable Pip to "live smooth," to "be above work." At the end — as often at the end with Dickens — there is a soften-ing of the heart; the work ethic, that bastion of the middle class, is graciously given some respect. "We were not in a grand way of business," Pip says of his job, "but we had a good name, and worked for our profits, and did very well." This is an example of what Chesterton means: that "Dickens did not write what the people wanted. Dickens wanted what the people wanted." This is an important distinction, especially when regarding Dickens's popularity; the man did not write *for* an audience so much as he expressed an audience's hunger — he made astonishingly vivid what an audience feared, what it dreamed of, what it wanted.

In our time, it is often necessary to defend a writer's popularity; from time to time, in literary fashion, it is considered bad taste to be popular — if a writer is popular, how can he be any good? And it is frequently the role of lesser wits to demean the accomplishments of writers with more sizable audiences, and reputations, than their own. Oscar Wilde, for example, was a teenager when Dickens died; regarding Dickens's sentimentality, Wilde remarked that "it would take a heart of steel not to laugh at the death of Little Nell." It was also Wilde who said that Flaubert's conversation was on a level with the conversation of a pork butcher; but Flaubert was not in the conversation business — which, in time, may prove to be Wilde's most lasting contribution to our literature. Compared to Dickens or Flaubert, Wilde's *writing* is on a level with pork butchery. Chesterton, who was born four years after Dickens's death and who occupied a literary period wherein popularity (for a writer) was suspect, dismissed the *charges* against Dickens's popularity very bluntly. History would have to pay attention to Dickens, Chesterton said — because, quite simply, "the man led a mob."

Dickens was abundant and magnificent with description, with the atmosphere surrounding everything — and with the tactile, with every detail that was terrifying or viscerally *felt*. Those were among his strengths as a writer; and if there were weaknesses, too, they are more easily spotted in his endings than in his be-

ginnings or middles. In the end, like a good Christian, he wants to forgive. Enemies shake hands (or
even marry!); every orphan finds a family. Miss Havisham, who is a truly terrible woman, cries out to Pip,
whom she has manipulated and deceived, "Who am
I, for God's sake, that I should be kind?" Yet when
she begs his forgiveness, he forgives her. Magwitch,
regardless of how he "lived rough," is permitted to
die with a smile on his lips, secure in the knowledge
that his lost daughter is alive. Talk about *unlikely!*
Pip's horrible sister finally dies, thus allowing the
dear Joe to marry a truly good woman. And, in the
revised ending, Pip's unrequited love is rectified; he
sees "no shadow of another parting" from Estella.
This is mechanical matchmaking; it is not realistic; it
is overly tidy — as if the neatness of the *form* of the
novel requires that all the characters be brought together. This may seem, to our cynical expectations,
unduly hopeful.

The hopefulness that makes everyone love *A
Christmas Carol* draws fire when Dickens employs it
in *Great Expectations;* when Christmas is over, Dickens's hopefulness strikes many as mere wishful
thinking. Dickens's original ending to *Great Expectations,* that Pip and his impossible love, Estella,
should stay apart, is thought by most modern critics
to be the proper (and certainly the modern) conclusion — from which Dickens eventually shied away;
for such a change of heart and mind he is accused of
selling out. After an early manhood of shallow goals,
Pip is meant finally to see the falseness of his
values — and of Estella — and he emerges a sadder
though a wiser fellow. Many readers have expressed
the belief that Dickens stretches credulity too far
when he leads us to suppose, in his revised ending,

that Estella and Pip could be happy ever after; or that anyone can. Of his new ending — where Pip and Estella are reconciled — Dickens himself remarked to a friend: "I have put in a very pretty piece of writing, and I have no doubt that the story will be more acceptable through the alteration." That Estella would make Pip — or anyone — a rotten wife is not the point. "Don't be afraid of my being a blessing to him," she slyly tells Pip, who is bemoaning her choice of a first husband. The point is, Estella and Pip are linked; fatalistically, they belong to each other — happily or unhappily.

Although the suggestion that Dickens revise the original ending came from his friend Bulwer-Lytton, who wished the book to close on a happier note, Edgar Johnson wisely points out that "the changed ending reflected a desperate hope that Dickens could not banish from within his own heart." That hope is not a last-minute alteration, tacked on, but simply the culmination of a hope that abides throughout the novel: that Estella might change. After all, Pip changes (he is the first major character in a Dickens novel who changes realistically, albeit slowly). The book isn't called *Great Expectations* for nothing. It is not, I think, meant to be an entirely bitter title — although I can undermine my own argument by reminding myself that we first hear that Pip is "a young fellow of great expectations" from the ominous and cynical Mr. Jaggers, that veteran hard-liner who will, quite rightfully, warn Pip to "take nothing on its looks; take everything on evidence. There's no better rule." But that was never Dickens's rule. Mr. Gradgrind, from *Hard Times,* believed in nothing and possessed nothing but the facts; yet it is Mr. Sleary's advice that Dickens heeds, to "do the withe thing and the kind thing too." It is both the kind and the "withe" thing that Pip and Estella end up together.

In fact, it is the first ending that is out of character — for Dickens and for the novel. Pip, upon meeting Estella (after two years of hearing only rumors of her), remarks with a pinched heart: "I was very glad afterwards to have had the interview, for in her face and in her voice, and in her touch, she gave me the assurance that suffering had been stronger than Miss Havisham's teaching, and had given her a heart to understand what my heart used to be." Although that tone — superior and self-pitying — is more modern than Dickens's romantic revision, I fail to see how we or our literature would be better off for it. There is a contemporary detachment in it, even a smugness. Remember this about Charles Dickens: he was active and exuberant when he was happy; he was twice as busy when he was unhappy. In the first ending, Pip is moping; Dickens never moped.

The revised ending reads: "I took her hand in mine, and we went out of the ruined place; and as the morning mists had risen long ago when I first left the forge, so the evening mists were rising now, and in all the broad expanse of tranquil light they showed to me, I saw no shadow of another parting from her." A very pretty piece of writing, as Dickens noted, and eternally open — still ambiguous (Pip's hopes have been dashed before) but far more the mirror of the quality of trust in the novel as a whole. It is that hopeful ending that sings with all the rich contradiction we should love Dickens for; it both underlines and undermines everything before it. Pip is basically good, basically gullible; he starts out being human, he learns by error — and by becoming ashamed of himself — and he keeps on being

human. That touching illogic seems not only generous but true.

"I loved her simply because I found her irresistible,"
Pip says miserably; and of falling in love in general,
he observes, "How could I, a poor dazed village lad,
avoid that wonderful inconsistency into which the
best and wisest of men fall every day?" And what
does Miss Havisham have to tell us about love? "I'll
tell you what real love is," she says. "It is blind devo-
tion, unquestioning self-humiliation, utter submis-
sion, trust and belief against yourself and against the
whole world, giving up your whole heart and soul to
the smiter — as I did!"

In her jilted fury, Miss Havisham wears her wedding dress the rest of her life and, by her own admission, replaces Estella's heart with ice — to make
Estella all the more capable of destroying the men in
her life as savagely as Miss Havisham was destroyed.
Miss Havisham is one of the greatest witches in the
history of fairy tales, because she actually *is* what she
first seems. She appears more wicked and cruel to
Pip when he meets her than that runaway convict
who has accosted Pip as a child on the marshes;
later, she greedily enjoys Pip's misunderstanding
(that she is not the witch he first thought her to be,
but an eccentric fairy godmother). She knows he is
mistaken, yet she encourages him; her evil is com-
plicitous. In the end, of course, she turns out to be
the witch she always was. This is real magic, real
fairy-tale stuff, but the eccentricity of Miss Havisham,
to many of Dickens's critics, makes her one of his
least believable characters.

It might surprise his critics to know that Miss
Havisham did not spring wholly from his imagina-

tion. In his youth, he would often see a madwoman on Oxford Street, about whom he wrote an essay for his magazine, *Household Words*. He called the essay "Where We Stopped Growing," in which he described "the White Woman . . . dressed entirely in white. . . . With white boots, we know she picks her way through the winter dirt. She is a conceited old creature, cold and formal in manner, and evidently went simpering mad on personal grounds alone — no doubt because a wealthy Quaker wouldn't marry her. This is her bridal dress. She is always . . . on her way to church to marry the false Quaker. We observe in her mincing step and fishy eye that she intends to lead him a sharp life. We stopped growing when we got at the conclusion that the Quaker had had a happy escape of the White Woman." This was written several years before *Great Expectations*. Three years before that he had published in a monthly supplement to *Household Words* (called *Household Narrative*) a true-life account of a woman who sets herself on fire with a lit Christmas tree; she is saved from death, but severely burned, when a young man throws her to the floor and wraps her up in a rug — Miss Havisham's burning, and Pip's rescue of her, almost exactly.

Dickens was not so much a fanciful and whimsical inventor of unlikely characters and situations as he was a relentlessly keen witness of the real-life victims of his time. He sought out the sufferers, the people seemingly singled out by Fate or rendered helpless by their society — not those people complacently escaping the disasters of their time but the people who stood in the face of or on the edge of those disasters. The accusations against him that he was a sensationalist are the accusations of conventionally secure and smug people — certain that the mainstream of life is both safe and right, and therefore the only life that's true.

"The key of the great characters of Dickens," Chesterton writes, "is that they are all great fools. There is the same difference between a great fool and a small fool as there is between a great poet and a small poet. The great fool is a being who is above wisdom and not below it." A chief and riveting characteristic of "the great fool" is, of course, his capacity for destruction — for self-destruction, too, but for all kinds of havoc making. Look at Shakespeare: think of Lear, Hamlet, Othello — they were *all* "great fools," of course.

And there is one course that the great fools of literature often seem to follow without hesitation; they are trapped by their own lies, and/or by their vulnerability to the lies of others. In a story with a great fool in it, there's almost inevitably a great lie. Of course, the most important dishonesty in *Great Expectations* is Miss Havisham's; hers is a lie of omission. And Pip lies to his sister and Joe about his first visit to Miss Havisham's; he tells them that Miss Havisham keeps "a black velvet coach" in her house, and that they all pretended to ride on this stationary coach while four "immense" dogs "fought for veal-cutlets out of a silver basket." Little can Pip know that his lie is less extraordinary than what will prove to be the truth of Miss Havisham's life in Satis House, and the connections with her life that Pip will encounter in the so-called outside world.

The convict Magwitch, who threatens young Pip's life in the book's opening pages, will turn out to have a more noble heart than our young hero has. "A man who had been soaked in water, and smothered in mud and lamed by stones, and cut by flints, and stung by nettles, and torn by briars; who limped, and shivered, and glared, and growled" — a man whom Pip sees disappearing on the marshes in the vicinity of "a gibbet, with some chains hanging to it which had once held a pirate . . . as if he were the pirate come to life, and come down, and [was] going back to hook himself up again" — that this same man will later be a model of honor is part of the great mischief, the pure fun, of the plot of *Great Expectations.* Plot is entertainment to Dickens, it is pure pleasure giving to an audience — enhanced by the fact that most of his novels were serialized; great and surprising coincidences were among the gifts he gave to his serial readers. A critic who scoffs at the chance meetings and other highly circumstantial developments in a Dickens narrative must have a most underdeveloped sense of enjoyment.

Unashamedly, Dickens wrote *to* his readers. He chides them, he seduces them, he shocks them; he gives them slapstick and sermons. It was his aim, Johnson says, "not to turn the stomach but to move the heart." But it is my strong suspicion that in a contemporary world, where hearts are far more hardened, Dickens would have been motivated to turn the stomach, too — as the one means remaining for reaching those hardened hearts. He was shameless in that aim; he cajoled his audiences; he gave them great pleasure so that they would also keep their eyes open and not look away from his visions of the grotesque, from his nearly constant moral outrage.

In *Great Expectations,* maybe he felt he had given Pip and Estella — and his readers — enough pain. Why not give Pip and Estella to each other at the end? Charles Dickens would never find that "one happiness I have missed in life, and the one friend and companion I never made." But to Pip he would give that pleasure; he would give Pip his Estella.

3. "No Help or Pity in All the Glittering Multitude"; in "the Ruined Garden"

But what about the *plot?* his critics keep asking. How can you believe it?

Very simply: just accept as a fact that everyone of any emotional importance to you is related to everyone else of any emotional importance to you; these relationships need not extend to blood, of course, but the people who change your life emotionally — all those people, from different places, from different times, spanning many wholly unrelated coincidences — are nonetheless "related." We associate people with each other for emotional not for factual reasons — people who've never met each other, who don't know each other exist; people, even, who have forgotten us. In a novel by Charles Dickens, such people really *are* related — sometimes, even, by blood; almost always by circumstances, by coincidences; and most of all by plot. Look at what a force Miss Havisham is: anyone of any importance to Pip turns out to have (or have had) some kind of relationship with her!

Miss Havisham is so willfully deceptive, so deliberately evil. She is far worse than a vicious old woman made nasty and peculiar by her own hysterical egotism (although she is that, too); she is actively engaged in *seducing* Pip — she consciously intends for Estella to torment him. If you are so unimaginative that you believe such people don't exist, you must at least acknowledge that we (most of us) are as capable as Pip of allowing ourselves to be seduced. Pip is warned; Estella herself warns him. The story is not so much about Miss Havisham's absolute evil as it is about Pip's expectations overriding his common sense. Pip wants to be a gentleman; he wants Estella — and his ambitions guide him more forcefully than his perceptions. Isn't this a failing we can recognize within ourselves?

Do not quarrel with Dickens for his excesses. The weaknesses in *Great Expectations* are few, and they are weaknesses of underdoing — not overdoing. The rather quickly assumed friendship, almost instant, between Pip and Herbert is never really developed or very strongly felt; we are supposed to take Herbert's absolute goodness for granted (it is never very engagingly demonstrated) — and that Herbert's nickname for Pip is "Handel" drives me crazy! I find Herbert's goodness much harder to take than Miss Havisham's evil. And Dickens's love for amateur theatrical performers overreaches his ability to make Mr. Wopsle and that poor fool's ambitions interesting. Chapters 30 and 31 are boring; perhaps they were hastily written, or else they represent a lapse in Dickens's own interest. For whatever reason, they are surely *not* examples of his notorious *over*-writing; everything that he overdid he at least did with boundless energy.

Johnson writes that "Dickens liked and disliked people; he was never merely indifferent. He loved and laughed and derided and despised and hated; he never patronized or sniffed." Witness Orlick: he is as dangerous as a mistreated dog; there is little sympathy for the social circumstances underlying Orlick's

villainy; he's a bad one, plain and simple — he
means to kill. Witness Joe: proud, honest, hardworking, uncomplaining, and manifesting endless goodwill despite the clamorous lack of appreciation
surrounding him; he's a good one, plain and simple —
he means no one any harm. Despite his strong sense
of social responsibility and his perceptions of society's conditioning, Dickens also believed in good
and evil — he believed there were truly good
people, and truly bad ones. He loved every genuine
virtue, and every kindness; he detested the many
forms of cruelty, and he heaped every imaginable
scorn upon hypocrisy and selfishness. He was incapable of indifference.

He prefers Wemmick to Jaggers; but toward Jaggers he shows less loathing than fear. Jaggers is too
dangerous to despise. When I was a teenager, I
thought that Jaggers was always washing his hands
and digging with his penknife under his fingernails
because of how morally reprehensible (how morally
filthy-dirty) his clients were; it was a case of the
lawyer trying to rid his body of the contamination
contracted by his proximity to the criminal element. I
think now that this is only partially why Jaggers can
never be entirely clean; I am far more certain that the
filth Jaggers accumulates in his work is dirt from the
work of the law itself — it is his *own* profession's
crud that clings to him. This is why Wemmick is more
human than Jaggers; it strikes Pip that Wemmick
walks "among the prisoners much as a gardener
might walk among his plants" — yet Wemmick is capable of having his "Walworth sentiments"; when
he's at home with his "aged parent," Wemmick is a
sweetheart. The contamination is more permanently
with Jaggers; his home is nearly as businesslike as his

office, and the presence of his housekeeper, Molly —
who is surely a murderess, spared the gallows *not*
because she was innocent but because Jaggers got
her off — casts the prison aura of Newgate over Jaggers's dinner table.

Of course, there are things to learn from Jaggers:
the attention he pays to that dull villain Drummle
helps to open Pip's eyes to the unjust ways of the
world — the world's standard of values is based on
money and class, and on the assured success of brute
aggressiveness. Through his hatred of Drummle, Pip
also learns a little about himself — "our worst weaknesses and meannesses are usually committed for the
sake of the people whom we most despise," he observes. We might characterize Pip's progress in the
novel as the autobiography of a slow learner. He
thinks he has grasped who Pumblechook is right
from the start; but the *degree* of Pumblechook's
hypocrisy, his fawning, his dishonesty, and his false
loyalty — based on one's station in life and revised,
instantly, upon one's turn of fortune — is a continuing surprise and an education. Pumblechook is a
strong minor character, a good man to hate.
Missing — from our contemporary literature — is
both the ability to praise as Dickens could praise
(without reservation), and to hate as he could hate
(completely). Is it our timorousness, or that the soci-
ologist's and psychologist's more complicated view
of villainy has removed from our literature not only
absolute villains but absolute heroes?

Dickens had a unique affection for his characters,
even for most of his villains. "The bores in his books
are brighter than the wits in other books," Chesterton
observes. "Two primary dispositions of Dickens, to
make the flesh creep and to make the sides ache,

were . . . twins of his spirit," Chesterton writes. Indeed, it was Dickens's love of the theatrical that made each of his characters — in his view — a *performer*. Because they were all actors, and therefore they were all important, all of Dickens's characters behave dramatically; heroes and villains alike are given memorable qualities.

Magwitch is my hero, and what is most exciting and visceral in the story of *Great Expectations* concerns this convict who risks his life to see how his creation has turned out. How like Dickens that Magwitch is spared the real answer: his creation has not turned out very well. And what a story Magwitch's story is! It is Magwitch who enlivens the book's dramatic beginning: an escaped convict, he frightens a small boy into providing food for his stomach and a file for his leg iron. And by returning to London, a hunted man, Magwitch not only contributes to the book's dramatic conclusion; he as effectively destroys Pip's expectations as he has created them. It is also Magwitch who provides us with the missing link in the story of Miss Havisham's jilting — he is our means for knowing who Estella is.

In "the ruined garden" of Satis House, the rank weeds pollute a beauty that might have been; the rotting wedding cake is overrun with spiders and mice. Pip can never rid himself (or Estella, by association) of that prison "taint." The connection with crime that young Pip so inexplicably feels at key times in his courtship of Estella is, of course, foreshadowing the revelation that Pip is more associated with the convict Abel Magwitch than he knows. There is little humor remaining in Pip upon the discovery of his true circumstances. Even as a maltreated child, Pip is capable of exhibiting humor (at least, in remembrance): he recalls he was "regaled with the scaly tips of the drumsticks of the fowls, and with those obscure corners of pork of which the pig, when living, had had the least reason to be vain." But there is sparse wit in Dickens's language after Pip discovers who his benefactor is. The language itself grows thinner as the plot begins to race.

Both in the lushness of his language, when Dickens means to be lush, and in how spare he can be when he simply wants you to follow the story, he is ever conscious of his readers. It was relatively late in his life that he began to give public readings, yet his language was consistently written to be read aloud — the use of repetition, of refrains; the rich, descriptive lists that accompany a newly introduced character or place; the abundance of punctuation. Dickens overpunctuates; he makes long and potentially difficult sentences slower but easier to read — as if his punctuation is a form of stage direction, when reading aloud; or as if he is aware that many of his readers were reading his novels in serial form and needed nearly constant reminding. He is overly clear. He is a master of that device for making short sentences seem long, and long sentences readable — the semicolon! Dickens never wants a reader to be lost; but, at the same time, he never wants a reader to *skim*. It is rather hard going to skim Dickens; you will miss too much to make sense of anything. He made every sentence easy to read because he wanted you to read every sentence.

Imagine missing this parenthetical aside about marriage: "I may here remark that I suppose myself to be better acquainted than any living authority with the ridgy effect of a wedding-ring passing unsympathetically over the human countenance." Of course, young Pip is referring to having his face scrubbed by his sister, but for the careful reader this is a reference to the general discomfort of marriage. And who cannot imagine that Dickens's own exhaustion and humiliation in the blacking warehouse informed Pip's sensitivity to his dull labors in the blacksmith's shop? "In the little world in which children have their existence . . . there is nothing so finely perceived and so finely felt as injustice." For "injustice" was always Dickens's subject — and his broadest anger toward it is directed at injustice to children. It is both the sensitivity of a child and the vulnerability of an author in late middle age (with the conviction that most of his happiness is behind him, and that most of his loneliness is ahead of him) that enhance young Pip's view of the marshes at night. "I looked at the stars, and considered how awful it would be for a man to turn his face up to them as he froze to death, and see no help or pity in all the glittering multitude."

Images of such brilliance are as enchanting in *Great Expectations* as its great characters and its humbling story. Dickens was a witness of a world moving at a great pace toward more powerful and less human institutions; he saw the outcasts of society's greed and hurry. "In a passion of glorious violence," Edgar Johnson writes, "he defended the golden mean." He believed that in order to defend the dignity of man it was necessary to uphold and cherish the individual.

When Dickens first finished *Great Expectations,* he was already running out of time; he was already exhausted. He would write only one more novel (*Our Mutual Friend,* 1864–65); *The Mystery of Edwin Drood* was never completed. He worked a full day on that last book the day he was stricken. Here is the final sentence he wrote: "The cold stone tombs of centuries ago grow warm; and flecks of brightness dart into the sternest marble corners of the building, fluttering like wings." Later, he tried a few letters; in one of them, Johnson tells us, he quoted Friar Laurence's warning to Romeo: "These violent delights have violent ends." Perhaps this was a premonition; in his novels, he exhibited a great fondness for premonitions.

Charles Dickens died of a paralytic stroke on a warm June evening in 1870; at his death, his eyes were closed but a tear was observed on his right cheek; he was 58. He lay in an open grave in Westminster Abbey for three days — there were so many thousands of mourners who came to pay their respects to the former child laborer whose toil had once seemed so menial in the blacking warehouse at Hungerford Stairs.

The King of the Novel (1979)

AUTHOR'S NOTES

Portions of this Introduction to *Great Expectations* were first published in *The New York Times Book Review* of November 25, 1979, in an essay titled "In Defense of Sentimentality." That essay was much revised before making its first appearance as an Introduction to the Dickens novel in a Bantam Classic edition (1986); in that edition, both the original and the revised ending of *Great Expectations* were printed. My Introduction has since been published in several foreign-language translations of *Great Expectations;* it remains my favorite of what little nonfiction I have written.

My affection for Dickens is undiminished. I remember that I was outraged upon my first reading of Evelyn Waugh's *A Handful of Dust* to discover that Waugh had condemned Tony Last to the Amazon, where he is saved from death by a crazed illiterate who forces poor Tony to read Dickens aloud to him (we presume, forever). Waugh is making the claim that reading Dickens aloud, forever, would be a fate worse than death. Upon rereading both Dickens and Waugh, it strikes me that a *worse* fate would be to read *Waugh* aloud forever.

My fondness for Dickens extends to an eccentricity I have not duplicated in the case of any other writer I admire — namely, I have left one Dickens novel unread. I am saving *Our Mutual Friend* for a rainy day, as they say; it is the last novel Dickens completed, and I have long imagined that it is the last novel I want to read. Of course this is madness: I am thinking of a 19th-century deathbed scene, where I am given proper warning that the end is near, and thus I am permitted to surround myself with friends and family — and I'll have just enough time remaining to read *Our Mutual Friend*. Violence and the unforeseen accident are the late 20th-century equivalents of the deathbed scene; even my doctor friends discourage me from thinking that I will necessarily be allowed to pick the time to read *Our Mutual Friend*. The conventional wisdom says I'd better read it now.

I am saving it, nevertheless. My friend and editor Harvey Ginsberg has given me the original monthly parts of the first edition of *Our Mutual Friend* (London: Chapman & Hall, 1864–65), although I doubt that the pages could survive being turned, except carefully — more carefully, I fear, than I usually turn the pages of a Dickens novel. I have other editions in my library — just to be prepared, both in my Vermont house and in the Toronto apartment — and so *Our Mutual Friend* is waiting for me to read it. In whatever terms, a sufficiently bad day will come — maybe it won't be as dramatic a bad day as a deathbed scene — and I will turn to Mr. Dickens, the first writer I read who made me want to be a writer.

An INTRODUCTION TO *A CHRISTMAS CAROL*

"I wear the chains I forged in life."

— Marley's Ghost

In January of 1990, I was living with the Great Royal Circus in Junagadh, Gujarat, in the northwest of India. The TV and VCR were almost as common in the troupe tents of the performers and their families as they are where I more frequently live — in Vermont and Toronto. That January, the popular Hindu epic the *Mahabharata* was continuing its Sunday-morning journey of 93 televised episodes, each an hour long; at that pace, the story wouldn't end (at the gates of heaven) until the coming summer. A record number of robberies had occurred during the broadcasts because the thieves knew that a great majority of Indians would be glued to their television sets.

That Sunday, in the troupe tent of the Great Royal's ringmaster and lion tamer, Mr. Pratap Singh, the TV was faithfully encircled; the only members of the circus not watching the *Mahabharata* were a half-dozen elephants and two dozen lions and tigers, in addition to a dozen horses and as many chimpanzees, and uncounted cockatoos and parrots — and dozens of dogs. But of the 150 *human* members of the Great Royal Circus, including almost a dozen dwarfs, everyone was enjoying the epic.

The rest of the week, the videocassette players in the troupe tents treated the acrobats and wild-animal trainers to various wonders and excesses of the Hindi cinema. Nowadays, the Great Royal rarely travels outside the states of Maharashtra and Gujarat; the movies that are hits in Bombay are similarly successful with the circus performers. But that Sunday, after the conclusion of the weekly episode of the *Mahabharata,* I wandered away from the television set and into the family kitchen of the ringmaster's troupe tent. Sumi, the lion tamer's wife, made me a cup of tea. From the VCR, I heard a surprisingly familiar burst of dialogue — in English. I couldn't see the TV screen, but I knew that the speaker was none other than that most literary of ghosts, Jacob Marley — the dead business partner of the infamous Ebenezer Scrooge. It was that part when Marley's Ghost is rejecting Scrooge's compliment: "But you were always a good man of business, Jacob." Marley's Ghost cries out, "Business! Mankind was my business. The common welfare was my business; charity, mercy, forbearance, and benevolence, were, all, my business. The dealings of my trade were but a drop of water in the comprehensive ocean of my business!" (It's a stirring speech, followed by the rattling of the ghost's chains.)

I repaired to the television set in the Singh family's troupe tent to watch the video of *A Christmas Carol;* it was the Alastair Sim version. There — in Junagadh, at an Indian circus — the child acrobats were seated on the rugs that covered the tent's dirt floor; they were illiterate Hindu children but they were riveted to the story, which was as fascinating to them as it remains to our children. If the principal point of *A Christmas Carol* is that Scrooge reforms — that he learns "how to keep Christmas well" — these child acrobats had never kept Christmas at all; moreover, they would never keep it. Also, they spoke and understood little English, yet they knew and loved the tale.

One of them — a 12-year-old contortionist, a girl named Laxmi who was also skilled as a tightrope walker — saw me looking at the TV. Since I was the foreigner among them, I suppose Laxmi thought I needed to be told something about *A Christmas Carol;* she mistook my astonishment at what I was seeing and where I was seeing it — she assumed I was ignorant of the characters and the narrative.

"Scrooge," she said, identifying old Ebenezer for me. "A ghost," Laxmi said, indicating the shade of the late Jacob Marley. "More coming," she added.

"*A Christmas Carol,*" I replied. This didn't impress Laxmi; Christmas wasn't her subject.

It was then that the ringmaster and lion tamer, who was also the chief trainer of the child performers, spoke to me. Pratap Singh was not a man who kept Christmas either. "The children's favorite ghost story," Pratap explained. I remember thinking that Charles Dickens would have been pleased.

A Christmas Carol was originally subtitled "Ghost Story of Christmas"; the accent on the ghostly (*not* the Christmasy) elements of the tale was further emphasized in Dickens's Preface to the 1843 edition. "I have endeavoured in this Ghostly little book, to raise the Ghost of an Idea, which shall not put my readers out of humour with themselves, with each other, with the season, or with me."

If that doesn't alert his readers sufficiently, Dickens titles the first stave of his *Carol* "Marley's Ghost," *and* the author states no fewer than four times in the first four paragraphs that Marley is dead. "Marley was dead: to begin with" — the first sentence of the first paragraph. "Old Marley was as dead as a door-nail" — the last sentence of the first paragraph. "You will therefore permit me to repeat, emphatically, that Marley was as dead as a door-nail" — the last sentence of the second paragraph. And, finally: "There is no doubt that Marley was dead. This must be distinctly understood, or nothing wonderful can come of the story I am going to relate" — the second and third sentences of the fourth paragraph.

I think we get the idea. An editor of today's less-is-more school of fiction would doubtless have found this repetitious, but Dickens never suffered a minimalist's sensibilities; in Dickens's prose, the refrain is as common as the semicolon.

Also common is Dickens's penchant for the juxtaposition of extremes. (In his own words: "It is a fair, even-handed, noble adjustment of things, that while there is infection in disease and sorrow, there is nothing in the world so irresistibly contagious as laughter and good-humour.") Scrooge's nephew is the old curmudgeon's opposite, a true celebrant of Christmas — "the only time I know of," the nephew says, "when men and women seem by one consent to open their shut-up hearts freely, and to think of people below them as if they really were fellow-passengers to the grave, and not another race of creatures bound on other journeys."

But Ebenezer Scrooge *is* from "another race of creatures." From the beginning, Scrooge's cantankerous character is unsparing with his cynicism; his miserliness — more so, his utter shunning of humanity — makes him seem a fair match for any ghost. "The cold within him froze his old features," as Dickens describes him. "He carried his own low temperature always about with him; he iced his office in the dog-days; and didn't thaw it one degree at Christmas." Even beggars don't dare to approach him. "Even the blindmen's dogs" give Scrooge a wide berth. "It was the very thing he liked. To edge his way along the crowded paths of life, warning all human sympathy to keep its distance" — Ebenezer Scrooge is the original Bah-humbug man. "If I could work my will," Scrooge declares, "every idiot who goes about with 'Merry Christmas,' on his lips, should be boiled with his own pudding, and buried with a stake of holly through his heart."

Old Ebenezer may strike us as a mere caricature of anti-Christmas scorn; yet, to Dickens, Scrooge's greed was both realistic and detestable. Dickens hated the political economists of his time — namely, their rationalizing that ruthlessness was justified for the sake of gain; that wealth and industrial power were the "natural" objectives of 19th-century society; that if Scrooge's poor clerk, Bob Cratchit, is unable to support his large family on his small wages, Bob should have had a smaller family. Today, the discrepancy between Scrooge's tyrannical authority and Bob Cratchit's meekness might be dismissed as Dickensian exaggeration, but Dickens stood squarely on Bob Cratchit's side. Modern critics have been skeptical of Dickens's flagrantly sentimental choice: to emotionally railroad the reader's sympathy for Bob Cratchit, Dickens saddles poor Bob with a crippled child — Tiny Tim. Dickens's answer to skeptics, like Scrooge, is to terrify them with ghosts.

Scrooge is such a pillar of skepticism he at first resists believing in Marley's Ghost. ("You may be an undigested bit of beef, a blot of mustard, a crumb of cheese, a fragment of an underdone potato. There's more of gravy than of grave about you, whatever you are!") Yet Scrooge is converted; beyond the seasonal lessons of Christian charity, *A Christmas Carol* teaches us that a man — even a man as hard as Ebenezer Scrooge — can change. What is heartening about the change in Scrooge is that he learns to love his fellowman; in the politically correct language of our insipid times, Scrooge learns to be *more caring*. But, typical of Dickens, Scrooge has undergone a deeper transformation: that he is persuaded to believe in ghosts means that Scrooge has been miraculously returned to his childhood, and to a child's powers of imagination and make-believe.

Dickens's celebration of ghosts, and of Christmas, is but a small part of the author's abiding faith in the innocence and magic of children; Dickens believed that his own imagination — in fact, his overall well-being — depended on the contact he kept with his childhood. Furthermore, his popularity with his fellow Victorians, which is reflected by the ongoing interest of young readers today, is rooted in Dickens's remarkable ability for rendering *realistically* what many adults condescendingly call "fantasy."

Additionally, it was Dickens's "fullness of heart" that caused Thackeray to praise *A Christmas Carol* to the skies. "Who can listen to objections regarding such a book as this?" Thackeray wrote. "It seems to be a national benefit, and to every man or woman who reads it a personal kindness." Even the dour Thomas Carlyle was so moved by *A Christmas Carol* that he was (in the words of his wife) "seized with a perfect *convulsion* of hospitality"; apparently, this was quite contrary to the Scots philosopher's nature. Remember: as Chesterton once wrote of Dickens, "The man led a mob." Part of the reason is that relationship which Dickens forces his readers to maintain with children.

As for the ghosts — "You will be haunted by Three Spirits," Marley's Ghost warns Scrooge — they have become emblematic of *our* Christmases, too. The first of these phantoms is the easiest to bear. "It was a strange figure — like a child: yet not so like a child as like an old man, viewed through some supernatural medium, which gave him the appearance of having receded from the view, and being diminished to a child's proportions."

Shortly thereafter, the spirit introduces himself: "I am the Ghost of Christmas Past."

"Long past?" Scrooge asks.

"No. Your past," the ghost answers — a chilling reply.

It is from the Ghost of Christmas Present that Scrooge is confronted by his own words; his own insensitivity is thrown back at him and leaves him "overcome with penitence and grief." This happens because Scrooge asks the spirit if Tiny Tim will live. "I see a vacant seat in the poor chimney-corner," replies the ghost, in a ghostly fashion, "and a crutch without an owner, carefully preserved." When Scrooge protests, the spirit quotes Scrooge verbatim: "If he be like to die, he had better do it, and decrease the surplus population."

As for the last visitor, that silent but most terrifying phantom, the Ghost of Christmas Yet to Come appears before Scrooge "draped and hooded, coming, like a mist along the ground, towards him." This ghost is taking no prisoners; this spirit shows Scrooge his own corpse. "He lay in the dark empty house, with not a man, a woman, or a child, to say that he was kind to me in this or that, and for the memory of one kind word I will be kind to him. A cat was tearing at the door, and there was a sound of gnawing rats beneath the hearth-stone. What *they* wanted in the room of death, and why they were so restless and disturbed, Scrooge did not dare to think."

This is a Christmas story, yes; yet it is first and foremost a cautionary tale. *We* are that corpse whose face is covered with a veil; we dare not take the veil away, for fear we shall see ourselves lying there. ("Oh cold, cold, rigid, dreadful Death, set up thine altar here, and dress it with such terrors as thou hast at thy command: for this is thy dominion!") This is a Christmas story, yes; as such, it has a happy ending. But, as Marley's Ghost tells Scrooge, the tale is truly a warning. We had best improve our capacity for human sympathy — or else! We must love one another or die unloved.

Most of us have seen so many renditions of *A Christmas Carol* that we imagine we know the story, but how long has it been since we've actually *read* it? Each Christmas we are assaulted with a new *Carol;* indeed, we're fortunate if all we see is the delightful Alastair Sim. One year, we suffer through some treacle in a Western setting: Scrooge is a grizzled cattle baron, tediously unkind to his cows. Another year, poor Tiny Tim hobbles about in the Bronx or in Brooklyn: old Ebenezer is an unrepentant slum landlord. In a few years, I'll be old enough to play the role of Scrooge in one of those countless amateur theatrical events that commemorate (and ruin) *A Christmas Carol* every season. We should spare ourselves these syrupy enactments and reread the original — or read it for the first time, as the case may be.

It may surprise us to learn that there is not one scene of Scrooge *interacting* with Tiny Tim, although that is a cherished moment in many made-for-television versions; it is also surprising that, in the epilogue, Dickens anticipates his own detractors. Of Scrooge, the author writes: "Some people laughed to see the alteration in him, but he let them laugh, and little heeded them; for he was wise enough to know that nothing ever happened on this globe, for good, at which some people did not have their fill of laughter in the outset; and knowing that such as these would be blind anyway, he thought it quite as well that they should wrinkle up their eyes in grins, as have the malady in less attractive forms. His own heart laughed: and that was quite enough for him.

"He had no further intercourse with Spirits," the author adds in the final paragraph.

Ironically, the success of *A Christmas Carol* prompted greed of such a shameless nature that only Ebenezer Scrooge (*before* his conversion) could have been pleased. It was not the first time that Dickens was plagiarized. Previously there had been published *The Posthumous Notes of the Pickwickian Club,* and *Nicholas Nickleberry* — and even *Oliver Twiss.* But the imitations of *A Christmas Carol* were more offensive, more bold; in a weekly called *Parley's Illuminated Library* there appeared a plagiarism of *A Christmas Carol* — together with the outrageous claim that it was "reoriginated from the original by Charles Dickens." Dickens attempted to stop publication, but the pirate publishers argued that when they had "reoriginated" *The Old Curiosity Shop* and *Barnaby Rudge,* Dickens hadn't objected. Furthermore, the pirates argued, they had actually "improved" *A*

Christmas Carol; among their additions to the original was a song for Tiny Tim!

The legal efforts that Dickens made were not rewarded; in fact, his court costs of 700 pounds were a bitter blow to him. In *A Christmas Carol,* he had written of greed and redemption, but the law had treated him as if he "were the robber instead of the robbed." Only his readers would treat him faithfully.

To his readers, Charles Dickens called himself "Their faithful Friend and Servant." In his Preface to the 1843 edition of *A Christmas Carol,* Dickens bestowed a generous benediction; he confessed his hopes for his "Ghostly little book" *and* for his readers — "May it haunt their houses pleasantly." In truth, even in the troupe tent of an Indian circus — not to mention here and now, 150 years after the *Carol* was written — Dickens's "Ghost Story of Christmas" continues to haunt us pleasantly.

The most famous child cripple in fiction is still wringing hearts. "His active little crutch was heard upon the floor," Dickens writes. Indeed, we can hear Tiny Tim's crutch tapping today.

An Introduction to *A Christmas Carol* (1993)

AUTHOR'S NOTES

A few fragments of this Introduction to *A Christmas Carol* first appeared in the same essay ("In Defense of Sentimentality") that *The New York Times Book Review* published on November 25, 1979, but that essay is more clearly identifiable as the origin of my Introduction to *Great Expectations* than it is recognizable as the origin of *this* Introduction. It is mystifying to me, however, to see how many readers reserve Dickens — and hopefulness in general — for Christmas. Indeed, what we applaud in Dickens — his kindness, his generosity, his belief in our dignity — is also what we condemn him for (under another name) in the off-Christmas season. (The other name is sentimentality.) The same Dickens of *A Christmas Carol* can be found in Dickens's other work; yet today *A Christmas Carol* is loved around the world — while much of Dickens's "other work" is not nearly as widely read.

My Introduction to the *Carol,* not quite in its present form, was published on December 24, 1993, in *The Globe and Mail,* under the title "Their Faithful Friend and Servant"; it was also published, in the form you find it here, as "An Introduction to *A Christmas Carol*" in a Modern Library edition (1995).

More than a century and a half ago, Charles Dickens gave his first public reading of *A Christmas*

Carol; it was just two days after Christmas — 2,000 people gave the author their rapt attention, and frequent applause. The reading took three hours, though in later years Dickens would prune *A Christmas Carol* to a two-hour performance; he liked it well enough that first time, however, to repeat the same reading three days later — this time to an audience of 2,500, almost exclusively composed of working people, for whom he requested that the auditorium be reserved. He always thought they were his best audience.

"They lost nothing, misinterpreted nothing, followed everything closely, laughed and cried," Dickens said, "and [they] animated me to that extent that I felt as if we were all bodily going up into the clouds together." He makes me wish I could have been there.

It was at the author's insistence that the price of *A Christmas Carol* was kept as low as five shillings — so that it might reach a wider audience. Dickens needn't have worried.

GÜNTER GRASS: KING OF THE TOY MERCHANTS

There is still a youthful restlessness to the work of Günter Grass — an impatience, a total absence of complacency, a shock of unexpected energy that must be gratifying to those German writers who, in 1958, awarded Grass the prize of the Group 47 for his first novel, *The Tin Drum*. In the more than 20 years since its publication, *Die Blechtrommel,* as it is called in German, has not been surpassed; it is the greatest novel by a living author. More than 14 books later, Grass himself has not surpassed *The Tin Drum,* but — more importantly — he hasn't limited himself by trying. He has allowed himself the imaginative range of an international wanderer, while at the same time, at 54, he has remained as recognizably German as he was at 31 — he was only 31 when he wrote *The Tin Drum*.

One reason Grass remains forever young is that he exercises no discernible restraint on the mischief of his imagination or on the practical, down-to-earth morality of his politics. Günter Grass is a writer whose political activism has included writing almost a hundred election speeches for Willy Brandt (in 1969), and whose recent fictional undertakings have included a dense, short, but crammed-full historical novel — *The Meeting at Telgte* — set at the end of the Thirty Years' War (1647), and a huge, discursive novel — *The Flounder* — that begins in the Stone Age and arrives in the present at a most contemporary "Women's Tribunal," where a talking fish is on trial for male chauvinism.

Fortunately for the pleasure of his readers, Grass

has not acquired a single gesture of literary detachment or intellectual pompousness. He remains
engaged — at once dead serious and a tireless prank-
ster. He is our literature's most genuine eccentric.
Writers as unique as Gabriel García Márquez and as
derivative as Jerzy Kosinski are under the shadow of
what Grass does better than anyone else: against the
authoritative landscape of history, he creates characters so wholly larger than life, yet vivid, that they
confront the authority of history with a larger authority — Grass's relentless imagination. He does not dis-
tort history; he outimagines it.

Perhaps, one day, he'll slow down and write an
introduction to his work — either to something new
(if he feels old enough), or (if he feels patient
enough to offer us some hindsight) to something old:
possibly to a new edition of *The Tin Drum,* or to one
of the less popular, more difficult works, *Local
Anaesthetic, From the Diary of a Snail,* or *Dog Years.*
(The last is an expansive odyssey of a novel set
in wartime and postwar Germany; it suffered popu-
larly — and wrongly — by being ill-compared to *The
Tin Drum.*) But until such a time, when Grass is will-
ing to check his astonishing forward progress with
the necessary calm required of reflection, we have
no better *general* introduction to the methods of his
genius than *Headbirths.*

Written in late 1979, shortly after Grass returned
from China (from a trip with the film director of *The
Tin Drum,* Volker Schlöndorff), *Headbirths* is first a
political speculation — set just before the 1980 German elections, when Helmut Schmidt of the Social
Democrats (Grass's party) defeated the Christian Democrat and Bavarian Prime Minister, Franz Josef
Strauss. It is also the creative musings for a film Grass

never made (with Schlöndorff) about a fictional German couple who travel to Asia to investigate how that part of the world is living, carrying with them the loaded political and personal problem of world population growth and their own ambivalent feelings about having a child. The premise of this slim, innocent-appearing book is what Grass calls a "speculative reversal."

"What if," he writes, "from this day on, the world had to face up to the existence of 950 million Germans, whereas the Chinese nation numbered barely 80 million, that is, the present population of the two Germanys."

As Grass mischievously asks, "Could the world bear it?"

The title of the book, and the would-be film — *Headbirths* — refers to the god Zeus, "from whose head the goddess Athene was born: a paradox that has impregnated male minds to this day." The subtitle, *The Germans Are Dying Out,* originates from Franz Josef Strauss — a fear-inspiring notion meant to provoke the anxiety, among Germans, that other, less-restrained nations are outreproducing them and will overtake them.

"And since fear in Germany," Grass writes, "has always had a high rate of increment and multiplies more quickly than do the Chinese, it has provided fear-mongering politicians with a program." Thus, right-wing election tactics and a trip to China provide Grass with an insight to a moral and political global concern: world population growth, world starvation, and the complicated, personal dignity that is called for in a conscientious contemporary couple's decision to have or not to have a child. With the accessibility of a diary or a journal — an accessibility rare to the writer's more recent work — Grass constructs a fictional couple and imagines *their* trip to Asia (on the eve of the German elections in which they are seriously, and liberally, involved).

Within this deceptively plain narrative, Grass uncovers insoluble, irreducible complexity; he writes at his baroque best. "A couple straight out of a contemporary picture book," he calls his invented family — he, named Harm; she, Dörte. "They keep a cat and still have no child." (They met at a sit-in against the Vietnam War.) They're serious; their political consciousness is keen. She belongs to the Free Democrats; he lectures about the Third World at Social Democratic meetings. Regarding China — their Asian adventure — they are schoolteachers traveling for their education; they care about being informed, and about being right. This problem about having a child or not having one — it nags at them, personally and politically. "The child is always present. Whether they are shopping at Itzehoe's Holstein Shopping Center or standing on the Elbe dike at Brokdorf, bedded on their double mattress or looking for a new secondhand car: the child always joins in the conversation, makes eyes at baby clothes, wants to crawl on the Elbe beach, longs at ovulation time for the sprinkling that fructifies, and demands auto doors with childproof locks. But they never get beyond the what-if or supposing-that stage, and Harm's mother (as surrogate child) is alternately moved to their apartment and shipped to an old-people's home, until some forenoon shock derails their single-tracked dialogue."

Like so many motifs in Grass's work, the couple's dilemma is repeated, is used as a refrain, is compounded; sometimes it is converted into elegy, sometimes it is mocked. That he is writing a book as instructions for a film provides Grass with the opportunity to *visualize* the couple's indecision. He accomplishes this with characteristic irony and compassion. "This time Dörte's laugh is really a bit too loud. And just as spontaneously, she can take the contrary view. 'But I want a child, I want a child! I want to be pregnant, fat, round, cow-eyed. And go moo. Do you hear? Moo! And this time, my dear Harm, father of my planned child, we're not calling it off after two months. So help me. As soon as we're airborne . . . I'm going off the pill!'

"The director's instructions are roughly: Both laugh. But because the camera is still on them, they do more than laugh. They grab hold of each other, roughhouse, peel each other's jeans off, 'fuck,' as Harm says, 'screw,' as Dörte says, each other on the dike among the cows and sheep, under the open sky. A few guards at the still-future construction site of the Brokdorf nuclear power plant may be watching them, no one else. Then two low-flying pursuit planes. ('Shit on NATO!' Dörte moans.) In the distance, ships on the Elbe at high tide.

"A note on one of the slips I took with me to Asia and then home again says, 'Shortly before landing in Bombay or Bangkok — breakfast has been cleared away — Dörte takes the pill.' Harm, who only seems to be asleep, sees her and accepts it with fatalism."

And, intricately woven through this would-be screenplay, Grass reveals his actual Asian travels with Schlöndorff. "In every city we stopped in I read simple chapters from *The Flounder:* how Amanda Woyke introduced the potato into Prussia." In every great novelist's mind, everything *is* related to everything else; the history of *food,* Grass notes, "is timely in present-day Asian regions." It takes a cook, which Grass is reputed to be — and a good one — to give food the honorable role of subplot, which a German liver sausage is given here. A "plot-fostering sausage," it is rightly called. Harm and Dörte are stuck with a kilo of it to take with them to Asia, a typically German gift intended for some obscure relative of a friend of a friend, supposed to be living in Java and pining away, of course, for liver sausage from the Fatherland.

And so our German tourists, despite their serious-mindedness, carry a sausage with them, a sausage that never finds its customer. In countless hot hotel rooms, deprived of refrigeration, the sausage sits, grows green and dubious, gets packed up and travels again. Finally, this world-traveling sausage returns to Germany — in somewhat the same state as the accompanying couple, a little the worse for wear, and symbolically undelivered: Dörte and Harm, at the book's end, *still* don't know whether or not to have a child. "Even in China," Grass chastises them, *they* wouldn't know "whether or not to bring a child into the world." (It's not an easy question.)

As with the characters in his other books, Grass makes fun of Harm and Dörte without ever removing his sympathy from them. As with his masterful handling of the subplot of the liver sausage, he demonstrates — even in this little book — his scrupulousness of detail, which is the truest indication of a writer's conscience. On a "wide sandy beach . . . a stranded turtle becomes a photograph"; in a village of 5,000 inhabitants, 3,000 are children ("worm-ridden, visibly ill, marked by eye diseases. They

don't beg, they don't laugh or play; they're just quietly too many").

Of his travels, Grass writes that he "loyally wrote
'writer' on the profession line of [his] immigration
card. A profession with a long tradition, if the word
was really in the beginning. A fine, dangerous, pre-
sumptuous, dubious profession that invites meta-
phoric epithets. An East German apparatchik, a
Chinese Red Guard, or Goebbels in his day might
have said what Franz Josef Strauss, leaving his Latin
on the shelf, said a year ago in German. Writers, he
said, were 'rats and blowflies.'"

Of himself and Schlöndorff, Grass remarks:
"What did we drink to? Since our glasses were often
refilled, we drank to contradictions, to the repeatedly
contested truth, naturally to the health of the people
(whoever they may be), and to the white, still-
spotless paper that clamors to be spotted with words.
And we drank to ourselves, the rats and blowflies."

He calls himself "childlike like most writers."
Probably this is why the mischief lives in him still. He
is serious enough to know what any truly serious
person knows: that the confidence for enduring mischief can come from only the greatest seriousness. In
The Flounder he writes, "Fairy tales only stop for a
time, or they start up again after the end. The truth is
told, in a different way each time." And at one point
in *Headbirths,* he keeps Dörte and Harm "circling
over Bombay without permission to land, because I
forgot to inject something that's in my notes and
should have been considered before takeoff: the
future."

As for the future, Grass is wisely cautious about
ours. He even speculates that the Germans *may* be

dying out. "And is it not possible that German culture (and with it literature) will come to be prized as an indivisible but manifold unity only after and because the Germans have become extinct?" Although he is *fun* to read, Grass is never so insecure as to be *polite*.

(In praising the work of Céline, Kurt Vonnegut has written: "He was in the worst possible taste . . . he did not seem to understand that aristocratic restraints and sensibilities, whether inherited or learned, accounted for much of the splendor of literature . . . he discovered a higher and more awful order of literary truth by ignoring the crippled vocabularies of ladies and gentlemen and by using, instead, the more comprehensive language of shrewd and tormented guttersnipes. Every writer is in his debt . . . no honest writer . . . will ever want to be polite again.")

Grass also knows how to be harsh. Of his character Dörte: "Now that she wants a child — 'This time my mind is made up!' — she has been tiptoeing on religious pathways. With Balinese women she offers up little flower-patterned bowls of rice in temples under holy trees, in each of which a white, fertility-bestowing woman is said to dwell." On the other hand, she stops sleeping with Harm ("'I haven't got to that stage yet'").

Of the limitations of the movie art: "The cave breathes what a film cannot communicate: stink."

Of Dörte and Harm's whole generation, which is my generation, the student-protest generation: "They have found themselves knee-deep in prosperity-determined consumption and pleasureless sex, but the student protest phase left sufficient imprint to keep the words and concepts of their early years available to them as an alternative, as something they can relapse into wherever they may be sitting or lying."

Of us all: "Our complexities and neuroses are mass-produced articles."

He writes (in 1979): "There's no shortage of great Führer figures; a bigoted preacher in Washington and an ailing philistine in Moscow let others decide what they then proclaim to the world as their decision. Of course we still have (as trademarks of salvation) good old capitalism and good old communism; but thanks to their tried and true enmity, they are becoming more and more alike . . . two evil old men whom we have to love, because the love they offer us refuses to be snubbed.

"And so we grope our disconsolate way into the next century. In school essays and first novels, gloom vies with gloom."

But the gloom that Grass perceives is always underlined with wit, and elevated by it: "My proposal to my Eastern neighbor-dictator would be that the two states should exchange their systems every 10 years. Thus, in a spirit of compensatory justice, the Democratic Republic would have an opportunity to relax under capitalism, while the Federal Republic could drain off cholesterol under communism."

Grass asks, "How will Sisyphus react to Orwell's decade?"

To Orwell he writes: "No, dear George, it won't be quite so bad, or it'll be bad in an entirely different way, and in some respects even a little worse."

Of Sisyphus he asks: "What is my stone? The toil of piling words on words? The book that follows book that follows book? . . . Or love, with all its epileptic fits?" (The writer's stone, he says, is a "good traveling companion.")

Headbirths also provides us with some terse, shorthand insights into Grass's earlier work: "It was a mistake to imagine that *Cat and Mouse* would abreact my schoolboy sorrows. I never run out of teachers. I can't let them be: Fräulein Spollenhauer tries to educate Oskar; in *Dog Years,* Brunies sucks his cough drops; in *Local Anaesthetic,* Teacher Starusch suffers from headaches; in *The Diary of a Snail,* Hermann Ott remains a teacher even when holed up in a cellar; even the Flounder turns out to be a pedagogue; and now these two teachers from Holstein . . ." his Dörte and Harm, who take up teaching, Grass admits, "with the best intentions." What prevents him from letting his teachers be, he writes, is "that my growing children bring school into the house day after day: the generation-spanning fedupness, the to-do over grades, the search, straying now to the right and now to the left, for meaning, the fug that stinks up every cheerful breath of air!"

For such a small book, this is such a rich one. "In our country everything is geared to growth," Grass writes. "We're never satisfied. For us enough is never enough. We always want more. If it's on paper, we convert it into reality. Even in our dreams we're productive. We do everything that's feasible. And to our minds everything thinkable is feasible."

And of that truly German question — its divided East and West parts — he says, "Only literature (with its inner lining: history, myths, guilt, and other residues) arches over the two states that have so sulkily cut themselves off from each other." It is what Grass provides us with every time he writes: "Only literature." His gift for storytelling is so instinctually shrewd, so completely natural. If it's true, as he says, that he never runs out of teachers, he never stops *being* a teacher either. In *The Flounder* — which is, he writes, "told while pounding acorns, plucking geese, peeling potatoes" — he doesn't resist indulging his irritation with the world of fools on whom fiction is largely wasted. "A good deal has been written about storytelling. People want to hear the truth. But when the truth is told, they say, 'Anyway, it's all made up.' Or, with a laugh, 'What that man won't think up next!'"

Scherbaum, the favorite student in *Local Anaesthetic,* tries to reach the conscience of Berliners by setting fire to his beloved dachshund. He observes, with a sad truthfulness, that human beings are more apt to notice the suffering of animals, and be moved, than they are likely to care for the suffering of fellow humans. It's possible that, in the character of Scherbaum, Grass was thinking of the radical Rudi Dutschke, whom Grass calls (in *Headbirths*) a "revolutionary out of a German picture book." (Following an epileptic fit, Dutschke drowned in a bathtub.)

"What makes me sad?" Grass asks. "How he was carried away by his wishes. How his ideals escaped him at a gallop. How his visions degenerated into paperbacks."

At the time of his death, Dutschke was 39 — my age (as of this writing). "Seldom has a generation exhausted itself so quickly," Grass writes. "Either they crack up or they stop taking risks." How true: we *are* a generation lacking in staying power.

Headbirths is not the literary jewel that Grass's second novel, *Cat and Mouse,* is. That gem is as fine a short novel as *The Tin Drum* is a triumphant major undertaking. And *Cat and Mouse* remains the best book with which a new reader might introduce himself to Grass, the *novelist.* But in all of Grass's work (and abundant, even, in this fictional, nonfictional, would-be movie of a book) one finds that flowering honesty that V. S. Pritchett calls fundamental to the Russian novelists of the 19th century ("the call to bare the breast and state one's absolute convictions"). Turgenev, Pritchett reminds us, believed that "art must not be burdened with all kinds of aims," that "without art men might not wish to live on earth," and that "art will always live man's real life with him." Grass celebrates this *Russian* conviction with everything he writes.

In 1920, seven years before Grass was born, Joseph Conrad wrote in his Introduction to *The Secret Agent* (published 12 years earlier): "I have always had a propensity to justify my action. Not to defend. To justify. Not to insist that I was right but simply to explain that there was no perverse intention, no secret scorn for the natural sensibilities of mankind at the bottom of my impulses."

Like Conrad, Grass freely indulges in such a "propensity to justify" his action — *and* his work. It was unnecessary, however, for Conrad to conclude his Introduction as he did, claiming that he *never* "intended to commit a gratuitous outrage on the feelings of mankind." Of course he didn't! Gratuitousness is a charge fashionably aimed at good writers by squeamish and second-rate critics.

Writers today need to be thicker-skinned than Conrad, somehow more immune to such moralistic posing in intellectual garb — though of course we aren't. "We all bear wounds," as Thomas Mann has noted. "Praise is a soothing if not necessarily healing balm for them. Nevertheless," Mann wrote, "if I may judge by my own experience, our receptivity for praise stands in no relationship to our vulnerability to mean disdain and spiteful abuse. No matter how stupid such abuse is, no matter how plainly impelled by private rancors, as an expression of hostility it occupies us far more deeply and lastingly than the opposite. Which is very foolish, since enemies are, of course, the necessary concomitant of any robust life, the very proof of its strength."

Like Mann's, Grass's literary self-confidence is always present. He seems somehow born knowing that *any* violence done in the course of a novel's discovery of the truth is *never* gratuitous. In *The Tin Drum,* when the Nazis force the Jewish toy merchant, Sigismund Markus, to kill himself, little Oskar Matzerath knows he has seen his last tin drum. For poor Herr Markus, for himself — for a Germany forever guilty for its Jews — little Oskar mourns: "There was once a toy merchant, his name was Markus, and he took all the toys in the world away with him out of this world."

For readers who found *The Flounder* and *The Meeting at Telgte* too inaccessible, *Headbirths* will seem warmer, more personable and approachable. For the hard core of Grass's fans — those of us who have tolerated (indeed, loved) each of his excesses — *Headbirths* has the clear voice and familiar consciousness of a letter from an old friend. And to those nonreaders, if there still are any — to those moviegoers who know of him only through Volker Schlöndorff's admirable rendition of *The Tin Drum* — this little book would be a mild, wise, mischievous starting place: a view of Grass, the good artist, taking notes, setting his shop in order.

Some readers find that the diary form offers access to a fiction writer's mind by exposing components rarely made available in the fiction (more often, concealed). Personally, I'd still recommend that one's initial experience with Grass be *Cat and Mouse,* but *Headbirths* is broadly entertaining enough to satisfy the most strenuous and demanding of Grass's faithful readers, and it is accessible enough to be inviting to the beginner. In whatever category of reader you see yourself, you can't be called well read today if you haven't read him. Günter Grass is simply the most powerful and versatile writer alive.

Günter Grass: King of the Toy Merchants (1982)

AUTHOR'S NOTES

"Günter Grass: King of the Toy Merchants" was originally published in *Saturday Review* (March 1982). Ten years later, I introduced Grass to an audience at the Poetry Center of the 92nd Street Y in New York City; the occasion was a public reading from *The Call of the Toad* — Grass read in German, and I followed with the English translation. Some of my notes (from that spoken introduction) make a worthwhile follow-up to my essay of 13 years ago.

That night in New York, I said it was important for us to realize that Günter Grass has a longstanding reputation of telling Germans what they don't want to hear. Understandably, there are many Germans who do not find Mr. Grass to be a *friendly* writer. When Grass made very serious fun of the Germany of the Third Reich (in *The Tin Drum*), many Germans laughed with him. When Grass makes very serious fun of the Germany of *today,* fewer Germans are laughing.

I know this firsthand. I was on a silly TV show with Mr. Grass at the Frankfurt Book Fair in the beginning of October 1990. On October 3rd, when the two Germanys became one, I was lying in my bed in my hotel room in Frankfurt, watching television. (I didn't know that — precisely one year later — my son Everett would be born on the first anniversary of this historic day.) In Bonn and in Berlin, the Germans were singing the publicly approved stanza of the anthem — the official hymn of the Federal Republic: "*Einigkeit und Recht und Freiheit für das deutsche Vaterland*." I asked my wife to turn off the TV; I was afraid I would soon be singing in my sleep — it was already after midnight. Almost an hour later, in the dark, I woke up hearing another stanza, those different but familiar words (to the same melody).

"I thought you turned off the TV," I said to Janet.

"I *did*," Janet said. But the television had not turned itself back on. In the streets of Frankfurt, even under our hotel window, some conservative louts and general shitheads were singing "*Deutschland, Deutschland über alles*."

In the morning I went to a bookstore where I was supposed to autograph some books. The bookseller was embarrassed by the swastika that someone had painted on his window with a can of spray paint. "This means nothing," the bookseller told me. "They are merely vandals."

But how could a swastika in Germany mean exactly nothing?

On the silly TV show at the book fair, there had been three writers: Mr. Grass, myself, and the Russian poet, Yevtushenko. Mr. Yevtushenko was the oddest-looking of the three of us, because he wore an orange leather suit and American cowboy boots of a similar color; I remember that what he said was odd, too. Yevtushenko said he thought that the reunification of Germany was a good idea because it clearly made so many people happy. But Günter Grass wasn't happy about it, and what was even odder than Mr. Yevtushenko's remark was how no one in the television audience really wanted to hear

what Mr. Grass was unhappy about. They already
knew.

Grass had already said that if Germany unified
too quickly — without certain careful stages (in prep-
aration for the devastating changes) — there would
be rioting against foreigners, and renewed right-wing
extremism; and Grass asked, wisely, what could possibly alleviate the anticipated bitterness of the greatly
disadvantaged new citizens from the East ... about
17 million of them. In essence, he was saying SLOW
DOWN!

Frankly, this was the point of view I'd expected
Grass to have, and I agreed with him. Quite the
opposite of trivializing the past, Mr. Grass has
always said that it is impossible to maximize the
Holocaust — that too much could never be made of
it. And as for his predictions regarding a reunified
Germany, he has been largely right; to be right about
such horrors as now befall the new Germany does
not make Mr. Grass any happier. Nor are Grass's critics in Germany altogether happy with him. On a recent cover of *Der Spiegel* (August 21, 1995), there is
a photograph of Marcel Reich-Ranicki — a senile ty-
rant, but a celebrated critic — ripping Grass's newest
novel in half; actually, Reich-Ranicki appears to have
butted the book in half with his bald head. One
would think that Germans would be sensitive to such
a symbolic display of publicly and literally destroying
a book. (Is ripping a novel in half a politically correct
substitute for book-burning?) Grass, at least, *was*
sensitive to the image: he withdrew a recent interview with *Der Spiegel* from publication.

The concept of a celebrated critic is an oxy-
moron to me; nevertheless, I feel I must explain to
my fellow Americans that German literary culture is

quite different from our own. Our literary culture is small and contained; our writers are of no political influence in our society. One happy result of the relative unimportance of writers in the U.S. is that literary critics are of even *less* importance to us. (Try to imagine *any* critic on the cover of *Time* or *Newsweek!*) But writers *are* important in German society, and they are of political influence, too; the perversion is that a critic of Reich-Ranicki's shrill and pompous sort can — if only temporarily — achieve a stature in Germany almost equal to Günter Grass's stature there.

Would Woody Allen be on the cover of *People* magazine, and be on *60 Minutes,* if what Woody wanted to tell us was why he disapproved of speedy reunification of Germany? Woody Allen is this country's most original filmmaker; I would be very interested to hear his views on German reunification — and on a host of subjects related to his *work* — but the only subject that has made Mr. Allen such widespread cover-story material in *our* culture is the melodrama of his legal battles with Mia Farrow.

We must remember that what writers *say* — I mean, not only in their work — is of much more sizable interest in Europe than it is here. And what Günter Grass says in Germany is of the utmost interest to Germans. Furthermore, it is not just Germany that Mr. Grass has been critical of. In 1982, following a trip to Nicaragua, Grass said he felt ashamed that the United States was an ally of his country. He asked this provocative question: "How impoverished must a country be before it is *not* a threat to the U.S. government?"

This was first published in *Die Zeit* and later reprinted in Grass's collected essays *On Writing and*

Politics, which include his essay called "What Shall We Tell Our Children?" In it, Grass cites the guilt of the Protestant and Catholic churches for what happened to the Jews.

"In Danzig," Grass writes, "the bishops of both churches looked on, or stood indifferently aside, when in November of 1938 the synagogues in Langfuhr and Zoppot were set on fire and the shrunken Jewish community was terrorized by *SA Sturm 96.* At that time I was 11 years old and both a Hitler Youth and a practicing Catholic. In the Langfuhr Church of the Sacred Heart, which was 10 minutes' walk from the Langfuhr Synagogue, I never, up to the beginning of the war, heard a single prayer on behalf of the persecuted Jews, but I joined in babbling a good many prayers for the victory of the German armies and the health of . . . Adolf Hitler. Individual Christians and Christian groups shared the utmost bravery in resisting Nazism, but the cowardice of the Catholic and Protestant churches in Germany made them tacit accomplices.

"No television series says a word about that. The many-faceted moral bankruptcy of the Christian West would not lend itself to gripping, shattering, horror-inspiring action. What shall we tell our children? Take a good look at the hypocrites. Distrust their gentle smiles. Fear their blessing."

Günter Grass, both in his fiction and in his courageous, often unpopular politics, has done exactly this: he has consistently spoken out against the "many-faceted moral bankruptcy of the Christian West." He has not limited his speaking out to the repression of the West *and* the East, nor to the insidious fear-mongering of the right wing; he has also bashed the irresponsibility of the New Left. It is not surprising that he's made many enemies among those literati who are merely fashionable; among polemicists; among the politically cynical and the politically impatient. Predictably, Grass's critics have complained that his novels have become deliberately terrifying and apocalyptic. No kidding — and no wonder. He has never been a writer who seeks to be liked. As a novelist, he is a wide-ranging moral authority; he's not supposed to be polite. In fact, he's often at his best when he's a little *im*polite.

That was what my former landlady in Vienna said about him. This was 1962, when I was a student at the University of Vienna. I was carrying around the German edition of *Die Blechtrommel,* pretending my German was good enough so that I could read Grass in the original. I knew the book was terrific, but unfortunately I couldn't read it without a dictionary — or without one or two Austrian students sitting beside me. Nevertheless, I carried the book around with me; it was a great way to meet girls. And one day my landlady saw me carrying the book around and she asked me what was taking me so long — or was I reading *Die Blechtrommel* twice?

Well, I was surprised that a woman of my landlady's generation was also reading Günter Grass — in those days, I thought of Grass as exclusively student property — and so I asked her what *she* thought of Grass, and (proper Viennese that she was) she said only: "*Er ist ein bisschen unhöflich.*" ("He is a little impolite.")

In his 21st book, *The Call of the Toad,* Mr. Grass is even a little impolite about such a revered subject as death — especially concerning where we want to be buried. If Grass once described a writer's gradual progress as "the diary of a snail," now the writer has swallowed a toad; it is this creature (the toad within him) that compels him to speak. Günter Grass's toads have a way of speaking to us even after they've been flattened in the road.

The Call of the Toad is an exquisite novel, both political and a love story. It is as bitterly comic and ironic a short novel as Mr. Grass's *Cat and Mouse;* it is as moving and touching a love story as García Márquez's *Love in the Time of Cholera,* but it doesn't drift as far into fantasy as that novel — as wonderful as that novel is, *The Call of the Toad* is better. Indeed, as in the very best of his novels, Mr. Grass is Dickensian — in the sense that he combines darkly comic satire with the most earthly love, the most positively domestic affection.

In his excellent review of *The Call of the Toad* (on the front page of *The New York Times Book Review*), John Bayley observes that Grass's "fellow Germans may be inclined to say that he is becoming all too obviously a merely humorous and lightweight novelist, but they will be wrong." I agree: many of Mr. Grass's fellow Germans and critics have *already* been wrong about him.

Just as Günter Grass is capable of outimagining history, he will outlast his critics — just as snails make their own progress, and toads go on crossing the road.

In 1962, I was proceeding at less than a snail's pace through *Die Blechtrommel;* it was embarrassing, because I could handle my professors at the University of Vienna — I could fake it, in German, well enough to pass my courses — but I couldn't read German as complex as the German of Günter Grass. Finally, a friend from the States saved me: he sent me the English translation of *The Tin Drum,* and from that moment I knew that all I ever wanted to do was to be like Oskar Matzerath; was to be funny and to be angry; was to *stay* funny and to *stay* angry.

Then one night — this was easily more than 10 years ago — Günter and I had dinner in New York; as we were saying good-bye, I thought that he looked a little worried. Grass often looks worried, but what he said surprised me because I realized that he was worried about *me*. He said: "You don't seem quite as angry as you used to be." This was a good warning; I've never forgotten it.

After leaving Günter in Frankfurt, the day after reunification, I traveled to several other German cities. I was on a book tour. I was reading largely to university students — in Bonn, in Kiel, in Munich, in Stuttgart. About a hundred times, students asked me if I had given Owen Meany the same initials as Oskar Matzerath as a gesture of homage to Günter Grass — a kind of tipping the hat — and I said Yes, Yes, Yes (of course, of course, of course) about a hundred times. But I had also been quoted in the press as agreeing with Grass about the problems of reunifying Germany too quickly; everywhere I went, although the audiences at my readings were generally friendly, there was always at least one *un*friendly question from the audience — it always concerned the matter of my agreeing with Grass.

It was Grass they were angry with. As for me, they thought I was just some fool foreigner who was going along with what Grass had said. All I did was repeat what he had said, *and* repeat that Günter Grass had always made good sense to me. But this answer was unsatisfying to the students; they had already embraced the future — they did not want to be reminded of the past.

To them, there was comfort in a mob, for a mob can drown out any single voice. It is inevitable that we writers take no comfort from a mob. A mob always wants to go too fast. Our method is moving slowly and speaking at length, like snails and toads.

That was the end of my book tour in Germany, about one week after reunification.

That night in New York, when I introduced Günter Grass to an appreciative audience at the 92nd Street Y, I concluded my introduction by stating my opinion that Grass is "one of the truly great writers of the 20th century." It sounded monumental in German — even in my German. *"Hier ist meiner Meinung nach einer der wirklich Grossen der Weltliteratur des 20. Jahrhunderts — Günter Grass."*

And now, as I write, comes a letter from Günter in Berlin. We will be together at the Frankfurt Book Fair again; the German translation of *A Son of the Circus* (in German, *Zirkuskind*) will be published in the fall of '95, at the same time as a new novel by Grass — *Ein weites Feld*. A literal translation: *A Wide Field*. A novel of epic proportions.

Grass suggests that Janet and Everett and I visit him and his wife, Ute, in their house in Behlendorf in September, before the madness of the book fair. My German publisher is planning some readings for me in several German theaters — in Kiel, in Hamburg, in Munich, in Berlin (in addition to Frankfurt). It shouldn't be difficult for me to get away from Hamburg on my first weekend in Germany — I can take the train to Lübeck, and then a taxi, or I can drive directly to Behlendorf from Hamburg in about an hour.

In his letter, Günter says that he hopes my shoulder surgery has been successful; he is facing some surgery on his nose, he adds — he came down with a virus infection immediately upon completing the manuscript of his new novel. (This has happened to almost every writer I know: the body lets down after the end of a big book.)

In his letter, there are some directions to his house in Behlendorf; the house is described as "*weissgetüncht*," which I think means "white-tinted" — probably "whitewashed." (Grass's English is much better than my German, yet he always writes to me in German. I write to him in English.)

I'm looking forward to seeing him — this time especially, because I have a story to tell him. It's a true story — about meeting Thomas Mann's daughter on an airplane.

I was taking an Air France flight from Toronto to Paris. Everett and Janet were seated across the aisle from me; my seat companion was an elderly woman with a disturbingly deep cough. She had a refined German accent and a face of patrician detachment, of unending wisdom and constraint; with hindsight, this should have been all that was necessary in order for me to recognize her father in her, but I was mis-led by the only name that was printed on her board-ing pass, which she repeatedly turned face-up and face-down, like a playing card, on the armrest be-tween us. The name on her boarding pass was Borgese — she was a German who'd married an Ital-ian, I supposed.

I liked her very much, but not her cough. I drank a beer, she sipped a Scotch. She was so eloquent, but concise. I began to wish I were better dressed. I think she said her first husband was Czech; the Ital-ian was her second — by the brevity of her account-ing for them, I presumed she'd outlived them both.

Of her children and grandchildren she spoke at length; on this trip, she told me, she would be visiting her daughter in Milan. But she had some business in France to attend to first, she said.

And what business was she in? I asked her. Oceans, she replied. She was on her way to a conference on oceans — she was invited to conferences on oceans all over the world. Europe, Mexico, India, the Caribbean — after all, oceans are everywhere. Was she a marine biologist? An environmentalist? An expert on fishing or fish? It was with some impatience that she dismissed my crude attempts to categorize her. Her field was "everything to do with oceans," she said.

I ordered the fish. She told the flight attendant that she was a vegetarian; she would choose the vegetables she wanted when she could *see* them, she said. This sounded so sensible; I felt like a cannibal for eating the fish — her business was probably *protecting* the oceans from the likes of me.

Since our flight had left for Paris from Toronto, she assumed I was a Canadian. No, I was an American, I confessed. She had lived in the United States, she told me; she'd not liked it. She was a professor at Dalhousie University in Halifax now; I imagined that Nova Scotia was a wise choice for someone who loved oceans — the warm current of the Gulf Stream flowing near the cold land.

I had a glass of red wine with my fish; I can't help it — I despise white wine. She continued to sip her one Scotch with her judicious selection of vegetables. As she talked, her elegance made me feel more and more oafish. I was en route to France to promote the French translation of *A Son of the Circus;* self-engendered publicity for my own novel

struck me as exceedingly crass in comparison to her
field — she promoted *oceans*. (The title in French,
Un enfant de la balle, sounded slightly less crass, but
I was unsure of how to pronounce it.)

It reluctantly emerged that I was a novelist; she
hadn't heard of me, or read any of my novels.
Frankly, I felt relieved. Novels can't compare to
oceans — not even long novels. Furthermore, I had
the feeling that, when she'd been a girl in Germany,
even the bankers in her family were more cultured
and better educated than what traipsed among us as
literary types today — myself included.

Oh, her father had been a novelist, she said —
she didn't offer his name. Meanwhile, I had swallowed some red wine the wrong way; my eyes were
watering. She even *ate* exquisitely. I felt I might as
well throw down my knife and fork, and dig in with
both hands. Finally, she had a second Scotch; she
drank so little I'd begun to feel like a drunk, too.

Suddenly there was spontaneous agreement between us: I believe the topic of conversation concerned how few good books had *not* been belittled
by the movies that had been made from them . . .
well, who *wouldn't* spontaneously agree with that?
And then a coughing fit overcame her. It was too terrible a seizure to ignore, but there was nothing I
could do — she coughed and coughed. It was a
cough worthy of the daughter of the man who gave
us Hans Castorp and *The Magic Mountain,* and all
the rest; it was a cough that sounded ready for the
sanatorium. But it was only after she quieted her
cough, and dismissed it with an utter lack of
concern — she said she'd had the flu — that I suddenly saw, in her noble profile, that haunted face of
her father.

Elisabeth Mann Borgese was her name, the last
surviving child of Thomas Mann. She must have
made the move to Princeton and to Los Angeles —
and then to Zürich, where he died. I regret that I
didn't ask her. Instead, we talked about the film of
Death in Venice. Visconti's idea to make Gustave
Aschenbach a composer instead of a writer — Visconti made him Mahler — was not at all bad for a
film, she declared. But the obviousness of the sexual
attraction that Aschenbach feels for Tadzio, the beautiful boy, was nothing her father had intended —
"purely Italian" was what I think Ms. Mann Borgese
said of such obviousness. (Maybe *I* said that.)

Elisabeth Mann Borgese would go on to say that
she experimented with dogs — cheerfully comparing
their intelligence to that of her grandchildren. While
she loved her grandchildren, and they were doubtless very smart, her dogs were far more educable,
she said. One dog could play the piano, another
could type — with their noses. At first I doubted this:
dogs' noses seem too sensitive for piano playing and
typing. If she'd said, with their *paws* . . . well, possibly. I felt guilty for thinking that there was some element of her father's fiction-writing capacities in her.

I felt far worse for imagining that whatever was
making her cough was terminal. It was all because of
the way she'd dismissed her cough by saying that
she'd had the flu — implying that she was over it. I
became worried about her; only later did I realize
that I could not escape thinking of her as someone I
had met in one of her father's novels.

There is that air of dismissal about the first sentence of *The Magic Mountain,* too. It is one of my
favorite beginnings. "An unassuming young man
was traveling, in midsummer, from his native city of

Hamburg to Davos-Platz in the Canton of the Grisons, on a three weeks' visit." Poor Hans Castorp! From the first sentence, we know it's no "three weeks' visit" that this "unassuming young man" is taking — it is a trip to the end of his life.

Is it any wonder that I have the hardest time trying to separate Elisabeth Mann Borgese from her cough? Even looking at a biography of Thomas Mann, and at a picture of Elisabeth — she was a pretty little girl — I feel afraid for her, as I have so often felt afraid for the people in a Thomas Mann story. There's no logic to this. It would be impertinent of me to write to Ms. Mann Borgese and ask her if she is truly over the flu; yet I liked her so much — and I *loved* the story about her dogs. (I have since revised my first impression and convinced myself that one of them *does* type, and another plays the piano — with their noses.)

Of course, I *could* write to her, and politely inquire as to her health. She gave me her address, because I foolishly promised to send her one of my books — "foolishly," because who would dare send a novel to Thomas Mann's daughter? And which one of mine should I send? There's nothing about oceans in any of them, and only one of them has "water" in the title; I somehow think that *The Water-Method Man* would be the *worst* of my novels to send her — what fool would send a story about a man who delays having urinary-tract surgery to Thomas Mann's daughter? It's becoming a dilemma.

If this were fiction, only a story, I would call it "Elisabeth's Cough." Like Hans Castorp, Elisabeth would be depicted as having already entered that final sanatorium, which she would never leave. By the way that she ate, and sipped her Scotch, and by the way that she spoke about her dogs, and absolutely because of her cough, she has already become (in my mind) one of her father's exquisitely doomed characters.

But Elisabeth Mann Borgese is real. In reality, she probably *did* have the flu — and now she's long over it. That she physically resembles her father is only natural; and that her father's imagination has captured even my memory of my brief meeting with his daughter is not surprising — her father's imagination was vast.

It was 6:40 A.M. when our Air France flight arrived in Paris. Janet and I were a little slow leaving the cabin, what with having to wake up Everett and gather together his books and toys; I saw that the regal Ms. Mann Borgese had remained in her seat while the other passengers left the plane. It was only when I took Everett's hand and we left the cabin that I saw the attendant who was waiting for her, with the wheelchair. Fittingly, a Thomas Mann detail.

"Which book of mine would *you* send to Elisabeth Mann?" I asked my friend Harvey Loomis.

He said, "A short one." (This was deliberately unfair; Harvey knows that all my novels are long.)

I am considering *A Son of the Circus,* not only because it's the most recent of my novels but because Ms. Mann Borgese told me that she'd been to ocean conferences in India. Then again, India isn't for everyone — and *A Son of the Circus* is the longest of my books.

I am considering *The Cider House Rules* because isn't Maine a little like Nova Scotia? Also, it's a historical novel — and sort of scientific. Then again, obstetrics and gynecological surgery aren't for everyone either.

I am considering *A Prayer for Owen Meany* because the narrator ends up living in Canada because he hates the United States — and didn't Elisabeth say to me that she didn't like living in the U.S.? Then again, it's a religious novel — religion isn't for everyone either.

And I am considering *The World According to Garp* because of how much I've read about it — namely, that it is the *only* one of my novels that anyone actually *likes* (I see this in print all the time). Then again, I may be the only person who remembers that, at the time *Garp* was published, the reviews were very mixed; the reviews of *A Son of the Circus, The Cider House Rules,* and *A Prayer for Owen Meany* were better than the reviews of *Garp.* (Look who's talking about reviews!)

The matter is unresolved. The point is: I think that Günter Grass will like my story about meeting Thomas Mann's daughter on an airplane. And maybe Günter will have his own ideas about which of my books I should send to Elisabeth. Maybe this one.

Postscript: I decided that I couldn't make Elisabeth wait for this collection; it wouldn't be published for 10 months after my meeting her on the Air France flight to Paris. Having promised to send Ms. Mann Borgese a book in April '95, it would have been entirely too cavalier of me to deliver the goods in February '96; nor could I have permitted myself the informality of beginning an accompanying letter to Elisabeth with "Hi! Remember me?" (Or words to that effect.)

No; it simply wouldn't have been proper to make her wait — not that I presumed she was "waiting." By June, in fact, I feared that she had probably for-

gotten that she'd ever met me — or else she remembered me as the liar she'd met on the airplane, the
shabbily dressed man who drank red wine with fish
and who claimed to be a novelist (a likely story). Nor
could I bear to wait until September, until I would be
with Günter Grass, to tell him the story, which (more
than a month after the Air France flight) I still thought
of as a story called "Elisabeth's Cough." Instead, I
wrote to Günter in May: I told him the details of my
encounter with Elisabeth Mann Borgese; he replied
immediately, demanding to know which book I had
sent her. It further shamed me that Grass presumed I
had been enough of a gentleman to have *already*
sent Elisabeth a book.

And so I sent her *The Cider House Rules;* it was as
spontaneous a decision as any decision that takes two
months — I sent the novel off to Halifax in June, addressed to Professor Elisabeth Mann Borgese at the International Ocean Institute of Dalhousie University. I
happened to have a handsome leather-bound edition
of *The Cider House Rules* on hand; this lent to the
novel a certain elegance that it might otherwise have
lacked. Also — and this was truly spontaneous — I
thought that the atmosphere of the orphanage hospital
in St. Cloud's, Maine, owed its inspiration (in part) to
the atmosphere of no escape that I remembered so
powerfully from the sanatorium in *The Magic Mountain*. At least my accompanying letter to Elisabeth said
that this was the case; I may have added that I thought
The Cider House Rules was among the more "atmos-
pheric" of my novels — if one doesn't come away
from Thomas Mann with *atmosphere,* what does one
come away with? (Or words to that effect.)

Elisabeth graciously responded, at once. She
thanked me for my book and expressed her regret

that she had no book of her own to send me. ("The oceans do not leave me any time, and when they release me, I'll be too old to write anything.") Instead of a book, Elisabeth sent me a tape recording. On the audio cassette, there was her photograph: she was at the piano with four or five dogs — all English setters. I must confess that the one nosing the keyboard looked remarkably self-possessed. The pianist's name was Claudio; Elisabeth explained in her letter that what I would hear on the tape was her fingers playing the left hand and Claudio's nose playing the right.

Indeed, that is what I heard; I have heard it many times since that first time, when I played the tape in my car. I have played it for countless appreciative houseguests, and at almost every dinner party where the conversation (predictably) flags. Only my most musically inclined friends are quick to recognize the three pieces that Elisabeth and Claudio play: a minuet by Mozart, a Schumann (one of the pieces for children), and a Bartók (also for children). And none of my friends has been able to identify Claudio as an English setter; they generally offer the guess that Claudio is a somewhat gifted child.

It was Claudio's great-great-grandfather, Arlecchino, who was the typist. Elisabeth included some samples of the typist's masterful nosework — Arlecchino was called Arli, for short. And so it happened that Arli's great-great-grandson Claudio would learn to play the right-hand part of a minuet by Mozart, and pieces for children by Schumann and Bartók — with his nose — and that Claudio's piano teacher would be an oceanographer, who herself is a great novelist's daughter.

It is exactly as Günter Grass has written: "People

want to hear the truth. But when the truth is told, they say, 'Anyway, it's all made up.' Or, with a laugh, 'What that man won't think up next!'"

As for the story that I used to call "Elisabeth's Cough," I would now suggest a different title. Besides, Elisabeth assured me in her letter that she was completely recovered from the cough that conjured up the sanatorium in my mind. "Many years ago," she wrote, "a lot of young people thought they had TB, after reading *The Magic Mountain,* but don't worry about me: I don't have it. That cough was passing and harmless."

The matter of a suitable title for this story will doubtless be an ongoing subject of conversation between Günter Grass and me; naturally, I plan to take the tape recording of Claudio's nosework with me to Behlendorf in September. Grass is a much more symbolic writer than I am; he is a more subtle writer, too. I imagine him thinking that "The Right Hand" — in reference to the side of the keyboard that Claudio plays — would be both the symbolic choice and the most subtle title. But there's very little that's symbolic and even less that's subtle about me. From now on, whenever I tell the story of meeting Thomas Mann's daughter on an airplane, I am calling the whole adventure "Claudio's Nose."

As soon as I come to this conclusion, I hear again from Elisabeth. I had sent her the German edition of *Owen Meany* — she reported that she found the German translation excellent — and she responded with a book of her own. (Having first said she had no book of her own to send me, she is an author after all!) This one is called *Chairworm & Supershark,* a cautionary tale for children about the pollution of the oceans. I read it to Everett, who is disturbed by the part about the dead fish floating on a poisoned sea. From the author's biography, I learn that Elisabeth has written and edited a series of books on the oceans, and that she teaches Political Science at Dalhousie. I also learn that Elisabeth Mann Borgese was born in Munich in 1918, which makes her a year older than my mother.

But there is sad news in Elisabeth's most recent letter: Claudio has passed away. "There won't be another dog like Claudio," Elisabeth concludes. Now when I play the tape, it seems unsuitable for dinner-party entertainment; I like to listen to it alone.

The other night Everett heard the minuet by Mozart, and then the pieces for children by Schumann and Bartók. "What are you listening to, Daddy?" he asked me.

How do you answer a four-year-old? (Everett will turn four on the fifth anniversary of German reunification. We'll take him to Amsterdam, interrupting the German book tour between Hamburg and Berlin; Amsterdam is a pleasant city for Everett to enjoy his birthday in, and we'll thereby avoid the celebrations and/or demonstrations that will doubtless mark the anniversary of reunification in Germany.)

"What are you listening to, Daddy?" Everett repeated.

"'Claudio's Nose,'" I told him — trying out my new title.